Swansea Summer

ALSO BY CATRIN COLLIER

Historical
Hearts of Gold
One Blue Moon
A Silver Lining
All That Glitters
Such Sweet Sorrow
Past Remembering
Broken Rainbows
Spoils of War
Swansea Girls

Crime
(as Katherine John)
Without Trace
Six Foot Under
Murder of a Dead Man
By Any Other Name

Modern Fiction
(as Caro French)
The Farcreek Trilogy

Swansea Summer

CATRIN COLLIER

ORION

First published in Great Britain in 2002 by Orion,
an imprint of the Orion Publishing Group Ltd.

Copyright © 2002 Catrin Collier

The moral right of Catrin Collier to be identified as the author
of this work has been asserted in accordance with
the Copyright, Designs and Patents Act of 1988.

A CIP catalogue record for this book is available
from the British Library.

ISBNs 0 75283 234 4 (hardback) 0 75285 146 2 (trade paperback)

Printed in Great Britain by
Clays Ltd, St Ives plc

The Orion Publishing Group Ltd
Orion House
5 Upper Saint Martin's Lane
London, WC2H 9EA

Dedication

For Margaret, Ken, Sarah and James Williams – greatly missed exiles from Swansea who gave so much to the city while bringing fun, happiness and humour into so many lives.

Acknowledgements

I would like to express my gratitude to all those who helped with the writing and research of *Swansea Summer*.

Jill Forwood for her friendship, impeccably researched articles on Swansea's Past for the *South Wales Evening Post*, and her unstinting help whenever I asked for it.

Dr Marguerite Aitcheson for her assistance in researching private adoption in the 1950s and the horrendous effects back-street abortions had on women and young girls half a century ago.

The 'old guard' of Swansea Writers' Circle who took the time and trouble to guide a novice writer at the outset of her career, especially Irene 'Topsy' Evans, Peggy Carter and Geoff Hemmings.

My husband John, our children Ralph, Ross, Sophie and Nick and my parents, Glyn and Gerda Jones for their love and the time they gave me to write this book.

Margaret Bloomfield for her friendship and help in so many ways.

Everyone at Orion, especially Emma Noble, and my editor Yvette Goulden for her encouragement, constructive criticism and insight into the human condition.

My agent Ken Griffiths and his wife Marguerite for their friendship and making my life so much more interesting than I ever thought it could be.

No writer can exist without readers. I am truly privileged to have so many sympathetic and understanding people among mine. Thank you.

Catrin Collier, September 2001

Chapter 1

MARTIN STOOD IN the doorway of the bedroom he shared with his brother. Oblivious to his presence, Jack whistled a few bars of 'With This Ring' as he lifted a shirt from his side of the old-fashioned wardrobe. Folding it carefully so as not to crease the collar, he laid it on top of a pile of clothes inside a battered suitcase opened out on the double bed.

'You sound happy.'

Jack glanced up. 'That's because I am happy.'

'You finished packing?' Martin walked in and sat on the only chair in the room.

'Just about, except for what I'm wearing now and tomorrow.' Jack slammed the case shut. 'I thought you were plotting stag night bridegroom tortures in the kitchen with the others.'

'Adam's record is stuck in a groove. I couldn't listen to any more of his moans about the good drinking time you're wasting.'

'It's my stag night,' Jack said pointedly.

'Adam considers all booze-ups to be his nights.' Martin looked around. 'It's going to be odd having no one but myself to blame for the mess in here.'

'Seeing as I'll only be next door, I could come in and throw things around every once in a while.' Jack snapped the catches on the suitcase locks.

'Remind me to ask you for your key.' Martin picked up a smaller new case from beside the bed. 'I'll give you a hand to carry these next door.'

'This is the only one that's going.' Jack lifted the large suitcase from the bed. 'That' – he beamed as he took the small case from Martin and set it down in the corner – 'is for the honeymoon.'

'I feel I should say something.' Martin paused awkwardly. 'Give you some advice but . . .'

'The time for that was a few months ago and I wouldn't have listened.' Jack grinned.

'If that's supposed to make me feel better, it doesn't.' As the older brother, Martin had always felt responsible for Jack – and guilty that he hadn't managed to prevent him from making quite so many disastrous mistakes. 'It's just that . . . blast it, Jack, eighteen's no age to be getting married.'

'You thinking of me or Helen?'

'Neither of you have been anywhere, done anything . . .'

'Most people in this street think we've done too much.'

Refusing to see any humour in the situation, Martin frowned.

'It's all right, Marty, it really is.' Jack's smile broadened as he slapped him across the shoulders. 'You don't have to play the big brother any more. Little brother's grown up and couldn't give a damn what the neighbours say about him.'

'To hell with the neighbours – most of them,' Martin qualified. 'Doesn't it scare you? A wife and in a few months a baby. Your life mapped out for you. Marriage isn't just sleeping with a girl . . .'

'That you know about.' Jack raised his eyebrows.

'That's just the problem.' Martin fell serious. 'What do either of us know about family life, growing up the way we did? Dad drunk most of the time, using Mam, Katie and us as punchbags every time he came home from the pub . . .'

'It's over, Marty.' Jack wished his brother could forget their past, or at least stop talking about it. 'Let Mam rest in peace. If there's any justice in the afterlife she's in a very different place from Dad. As for him, I hope the torments of hell are as bad as the chapel minister used to paint them before we began to mitch off Sunday school.'

Martin clenched his fists so Jack wouldn't see his hands trembling, just as they had done whenever their father had turned his attention to them when they were small. 'You can't forgive him either.'

'No. But one good thing's come out of having a bastard for a father. After seeing what he did to Mam, and having to live with what he did to us, I'll top myself before I'll raise my hand to Helen or the baby – when it comes. This wedding can't come quick enough for me, Marty. I really am looking forward to being married.'

'Given Helen's looks, I can understand that,' Martin conceded. 'Although she does have a wild streak and one hell of a temper to go with her blonde hair and blue eyes.'

2

'Nothing I can't handle.' Jack's mouth curved at a memory he hadn't shared.

'And look where your handling's got you.'

'As you said, there's more to marriage than bed – although that's great. If you haven't already, I recommend you and Lily try it some time.' He sat on the bed. 'Look, I know a couple of months ago I would have laughed at the idea of getting married and having a kid but now it feels as though all I've ever wanted is a family of my own. With Helen's help I'll be able to give our son everything we never had. Trips to the beach, the park, the toyshops in town and on Sunday afternoons I'll teach him to swim, play football . . .'

'Fight, mitch off school, drink, smoke . . .' Martin interceded.

'I'll grant you I messed up,' Jack admitted. 'But I won't let him make the mistakes I did.'

'You're sure it's a boy?' Martin smiled for the first time since he'd entered the room.

'Absolutely and Helen agrees with me.'

'And if it's a girl?'

'We'll know the hospital switched him at birth.' Jack picked up his case. 'I'll take this round to the flat, then I'll be with you.'

'If you're any longer than five minutes Adam will haul you out,' Martin warned.

'Let him try. I've no intention of crawling through tomorrow with a hangover after a skinful tonight.' Jack winked broadly. 'I've made plans with Helen that require me to be one hundred and ten per cent on form.'

Despite his misgivings, Martin couldn't help laughing as Jack changed his tune from 'With This Ring' to 'The Magic Touch'.

Martin opened the wardrobe and spread his clothes out along the rail after Jack left. Neither of them had much in the way of possessions but with only his hairbrushes on the chest of drawers and mechanics' manuals on the shelf in the alcove next to the boarded-up fireplace, the room looked bare and empty.

'Jack all right?' Their old flatmate Brian Powell, who'd returned from London for the wedding, looked in on him.

'You know Jack.'

'He and Helen will be fine,' Brian insisted confidently.

'He seems to think so.'

'Big brother not convinced?' Brian took a packet of Players from his shirt pocket and offered Martin one.

'Someone has to worry about him.' Taking the cigarette, Martin pushed it between his lips and felt in his pockets for his matches.

'It's amazing the changes a month has made. The Jack I knew spent his evenings and weekends servicing his motorbike and testing brew strengths in pubs, not picking out colour schemes and decorating. And I overheard Lily telling Judy that all Helen can talk about is bed linen, saucepans and recipes.' Brian pulled his lighter from his shirt pocket and lit Martin's cigarette, then his own.

Martin closed the door of the wardrobe. 'I just can't believe that as of tomorrow my kid brother is going to be a married man.'

'With a cracking wife.'

'They're so young.'

'Lose the gloom, Marty. You sound more like forty than twenty-one.'

'They both have a temper.'

'So they'll throw a few pots and pans at one another.' Brian shrugged his shoulders.

'One or both of them could end up in hospital.'

'Before that honeymoon glow wears off, they'll have a baby to take care of and from what I've seen of nippers they'll be too exhausted to do anything except survive until the next sleepless night.' Taking the ashtray Martin handed him, Brian sat on the bed. 'And then it will be, "Uncle Martin, please take over, just for one night so we can get some sleep."'

'Me? I know nothing about babies.'

Amused by the panic-stricken expression on Martin's face, Brian adopted a look of mock gravity. 'Then it's high time you learned. Let's see, there's folding and changing nappies but that's best left until after it's born. Boys' are folded different from girls'; get it wrong and you could warp the poor mite for life.'

'You've got to be joking.'

'I assure you I'm not.' Leaning back, Brian blew a smoke ring at the ceiling. 'There's making up bottles, that can be really complicated, you have to check the mix and temperature of the milk is just right and that the nipper is fed at the right pace. Too fast and it will throw up – and always over your best suit, shirt and tie. Too slow and it will starve and yell its head off, but before that you ought to know how to hold a baby so it doesn't fall apart. The best winding techniques . . .'

'What's winding?' Martin looked sideways at Brian.

'As you'll find out, everything's connected to one end or the other.'

'And how come you know so much about babies?' Martin questioned suspiciously.

'I have twelve nieces and nephews.'

'You're kidding.' Despite having lived with Brian for several months, Martin had never quite been able to tell the difference between some of his more peculiar jokes and his attempts to impart serious advice.

'I wish. Would you like me to begin with the significance of nappy contents?'

'This is the living room. Like the bedroom and kitchen, we've had to make do with Dad's old furniture, but I've tried to give it a contemporary look.' Helen opened the door at the end of the passage in the basement of her father's house, switched on the light and stood back, watching Judy's face as she entered the room.

'It's gorgeous, Helen, and so big. The new window is huge. It must be light and airy in daytime.'

'It is. The builders lengthened this room when they extended the bedroom to make room for the bathroom. Dad said it didn't cost that much more to square off the back of the house but it's made a lot of difference in here.'

'Wherever did you get this material?' Judy fingered the black, white and red check heavy-duty linen decorated with yellow bows that covered the three-piece suite.

'The warehouse. Dad sold us a bale at cost and Lily helped me sew it up. She made the curtains too.' Helen smiled at Lily as she joined them.

'Clever Lily.'

'I had a good teacher in Auntie Norah.' Lily looked critically at the pleats she'd set on top of the curtains and wondered what her foster mother would have made of her efforts.

'You must miss her,' Judy sympathised. They fell silent, remembering the widow who'd brought Lily up and had been the friend and confidante of practically every woman in Carlton Terrace.

'Jack decorated this room too.' Helen ran her fingers over the red wallpaper that covered the boxing in on the fireplace that now housed a small gas fire. 'With Marty and their new flatmate Sam's help. Lily's

5

Uncle Roy kept an eye on them but they did well. Even Dad was surprised by the job they made of it. The building work cost a small fortune. Jack and I felt guilty enough without sticking Dad with the bill for painting and papering the place as well, but he'll get his money back in rent. Not that Jack and I intend to stay here for ever. As soon as we've saved enough for a deposit we're going to look for our own place.' Helen wiped a speck of dust from the Formica coffee table with her finger. Its striking black and white geometric design matched the shade on the standard lamp behind the sofa.

'More wedding presents?' Judy asked.

'From Martin and me,' Katie volunteered.

'We've had some lovely things.' Helen opened an old-fashioned china cabinet. 'Joe bought us this black and white contemporary dinner and tea set; we're keeping it for best and using a cheap one from the warehouse for every day. Lily's Uncle Roy gave us a stainless-steel cutlery set; Lily found some marvellous stainless-steel kitchen utensils. You have to see them to appreciate their shape. They're really unusual and . . . ' She saw Judy exchange an amused look with Lily. 'Sorry, I know I go on a bit but I can't wait to move in and start using everything.'

'You'll have to teach Jack how to use some things.' Katie switched the lamp on and the main light off so they could admire the effect. 'I don't think he'd recognise a duster or a dishcloth, let alone that carpet sweeper your aunt gave you.'

'This room is really smart.' Judy sat in one of the armchairs. 'Comfy too,' she added as she settled back against the cushions.

'We think so.' Helen sat on the sofa opposite her.

'I can't believe one of us is actually getting married. It seems so . . .'

'Grown up,' Lily finished for Judy. She looked at the others and they all laughed.

A thud echoed in from the garden. Helen peered through the window into the darkness and saw a suitcase in the middle of her father's onion bed. A few seconds later Jack landed beside it.

'Idiot! My father's always going on about the mess Jack's made of his vegetable plot by vaulting the wall instead of walking round. He'll kill him if he sees him.' Running into the passage, she opened the back door.

'Sorry,' Jack apologised sheepishly, as he retrieved his suitcase.

'You'll be sorrier still if my father sees you.'

'He has.' Jack waved cautiously to Helen's father who opened his kitchen window on the floor above.

'Thank God you two are getting married tomorrow,' John Griffiths shouted down. 'I don't think my garden will stand another day of your courtship.'

'Sorry, Mr Griffiths, I didn't think.' Drawing Helen towards the back door, Jack pulled her out of sight of the living room window and the ones on the floor above. 'Got a kiss for the bridegroom?' Without waiting for Helen to reply, he bent his head, kissing her slowly and thoroughly before caressing her breasts with his fingertips, evoking sensations they both knew from past experience could easily spiral out of control.

Reluctantly she pushed him away. 'Someone could come to the door.'

'You won't be able to say that tomorrow,' he whispered.

'I won't want to – tomorrow. Just think, twenty-four hours from now we'll be Mr and Mrs Clay and almost in London. In the middle of the theatres, shops . . .'

'Not too many expensive trips,' he warned. 'We need to save for the baby and our own house, remember.'

'Looking costs nothing,' she continued, undeterred. 'And there's the sights, Buckingham Palace, Westminster Abbey, Harrods . . .'

'All the sights I want to see will be in a hotel bedroom furnished with a large and hopefully comfortable double bed.' He nuzzled her neck.

'You've a one-track mind, Jack Clay.' She laughed, evading his touch.

'Only when you're around.'

As he twined his fingers gently in her hair and pulled her head to his again, Adam shouted from the other side of the wall.

'If you're not over here in sixty seconds, Jack, we're going down the Rose without you.'

Ignoring Adam, Jack kissed Helen again.

'The girls are here.' Helen broke free as voices drifted from the basement living room.

'Send them away. We'll have a quiet night in and christen that new mattress.'

'On your stag night?'

'I know exactly how I want to celebrate and it isn't getting drunk with the boys.' He slid his hands beneath her sweater.

7

'It's tradition.' She tried to push past him, but he cornered her against the wall.

'To hell with tradition.' His fingers slipped the hooks at the back of her brassiere.

'Just as it's tradition the bride spend the night before her wedding with her girlfriends.' She trembled as he succeeded in freeing her breasts and closed his hands round them.

'You want to?' His dark eyes glittered with a look she was becoming familiar with.

Just as she was about to say 'no' Judy's laughter rang out from the living room. 'They're already here. Please, Jack.' Twisting her hands behind her back, she struggled to refasten the hooks.

'Every married man I know complains his wife won't let him go down the pub. You're throwing me out before we're even married.'

'Stag nights are different.'

He rehooked her bra. 'I'll go, but only because I'll have you all to myself from two o'clock tomorrow.' Seeing dirt on his suitcase, he lifted it towards the light and brushed it down. 'Shall I leave this in the bedroom?'

'Please.' Helen felt suddenly and inexplicably shy as she followed him in through the back door and down the passage to the bedroom.

He dropped his case on the rug at the foot of the bed and looked around. 'You've put the eiderdown Brian and Judy gave us on the bed.'

'You like it?'

'Even I can see it goes great with the lamps and wallpaper.'

'I mentioned the colour scheme to Judy in one of my letters, but she sent a sample to Lily before buying it, just to be sure.' She glanced at his case. 'Do you want me to unpack for you?'

'There's only a couple of shirts, trousers and some underclothes. I can do it.'

'The boys are waiting.'

'I meant when we come back from honeymoon.'

'Everything will be creased by then, silly.' The thought of his clothes hanging next to hers in the wardrobe and his presence in the intimacy of the bedroom she had expended so much thought and time on brought the realisation just how close their lives would be from tomorrow on.

'Happy?' he questioned, concerned by the preoccupied expression on her face.

'I'll be happier tomorrow night.'

Gathering her in his arms, he tickled the soft skin at the base of her ear. 'Everything's going to be perfect. I'm going to take good care of you and' – he patted her stomach – 'little Jack.'

'I thought we'd settled on Dirk after Dirk Bogarde.'

'You settled on Dirk, I settled on Jack. We have another six and a half months to argue about it.'

'I didn't agree to that.'

'I only settled it with myself.' Hearing laughter, he glanced behind him to see Judy, Lily and his sister in the passage.

'The honeymoon's supposed to start after the wedding, Jack,' Judy reminded him tactlessly.

'What have you girls planned for tonight?'

'Babycham, sherry . . .' Helen began.

'Beauty treatments, girl talk – and peace from all men,' Judy added tartly.

Jack gave Helen a last hug before releasing her. 'Take it steady with the drink, love.'

'That's great advice coming from someone on their way to the Rose,' Judy retorted. 'I bet a penny to a pound none of you will be sober an hour from now.'

'You're on,' he agreed.

'How would we know?'

'You can check with Brian.'

'He'll be the first to get legless.'

Sensing an edge to Judy's voice, Jack turned back to Helen. 'Bye, sweetheart. See you tomorrow.'

'I'll be there.' As he kissed her again, Helen wished she had the courage to defy convention and do as he suggested, send the girls away and spend not only the evening but also the night with him.

'If you're giving out beauty advice, Judy, I'd be grateful for some,' Lily followed the other two up the stairs to the ground floor as Helen locked the basement.

'With your skin and hair, you don't need any. What's this?' Judy asked as Helen's brother, Joe, wheeled a trolley loaded with plates and bottles out of the dining room.

'Surprise for the bride.' He pushed it into the living room. 'Thought you girls might be peckish.' He said 'you girls' but Judy,

Helen and Katie noticed he only had eyes for Lily. They also noticed that she refused to meet his gaze.

'You made us sandwiches?' Helen asked suspiciously.

'Actually . . . no. I asked Mrs Jones to cut them, but I did buy the sausage rolls and pasties in the baker's and I picked up some extra Babychams and cocktail cherries in case you ran out.'

'This is a girls' night in, Joe,' Helen said ungraciously.

'Which is why I'm meeting Robin in ten minutes. We may even call in on my soon-to-be brother-in-law's bachelor party.'

'The two of you?' Helen was amazed. Joe and his friend Robin were final-year university students, 'stuck-up snobs' in the eyes of Jack and his friends who saw condescension and arrogance in every overture they made, in her opinion with some reason. Bolstered by mid-course examination successes and the publication of his poetry in local magazines, Joe's belief in his own social and intellectual superiority had grown to an irritating level.

'Why not? We can't study all the time and the finals are weeks away.' Checking his pocket to make sure he had his keys, he opened the front door. 'Enjoy your last night of freedom, sis.'

'Pints of best all round, a drink for yourself and one of your specials for the bridegroom.' Adam winked at the brassy middle-aged barmaid, as he thrust his hand in his pocket and pulled out a handful of change.

'Bit early to start on the shorts,' Brian cautioned, as he watched Lettie pour three measures of vodka into one of the beer mugs.

'Can't send a condemned man to the gallows sober.'

'After one of those, Jack won't be capable of standing upright,' Brian demurred.

'Jack can outdrink any of us.'

'Only if he sticks to beer. Here, I'll give you a hand.' Taking two of the glasses, Brian returned to the table that Jack, Martin and Sam had commandeered.

'Pint, Jack.' John Griffiths set a full glass in front of him.

'Cheers and thank you, Mr Griffiths. Why don't you join us?' Jack moved his chair to make room for John to sit at the table.

'I'm with a party in the lounge bar, but thank you for the invitation.'

'Maybe later?' Jack not only respected but had grown fond of John

Griffiths during the past few weeks. Instead of being outraged when he'd broken the news of Helen's pregnancy, John had welcomed him as a prospective son-in-law, conjuring solutions for all the practical problems like finding them somewhere to live and giving him a reasonably paid permanent job in his warehouse, so he'd be able to support Helen and the baby.

'If I can, Jack,' John replied. 'Enjoy your night.'

'His scars are even worse close up,' Sam whispered to Jack, as John limped away. 'How did he get them?'

'He was burned in a fire.'

'Recently?'

'When he was a kid.'

'It's made one hell of a mess of his face and hand.'

'His leg too,' Jack revealed, 'that's why he's lame.'

'I'd hate to have people staring at me wherever I went,' Sam murmured, seeing a few heads turn as John left the room.

'Since I've got to know him, I don't even notice Mr Griffiths's scars any more.'

'You call your father-in-law Mr Griffiths?' Brian set the pints he was holding in front of Brian and Sam.

'I thought it best to keep it formal lest the others in the warehouse think I was taking advantage,' Jack explained.

'How's that going?'

'After the last couple of weeks I'm not sure he did me any favours. At least I could skive off from the building site for the odd half-hour without feeling guilty.'

'But now he's finding out what work is really like.' Martin sipped his pint.

'And in another' – Adam glanced at the clock, as he set a tray holding three pints on the table – 'sixteen hours, give or take a few minutes, he'll find out what married life is like. All bliss, home cooking and romps between the sheets, as women would have us believe, or the shouting matches, burned messes and "Not tonight, I've a headache" that every shackled man makes it out to be.' Placing the spiked glass in front of Jack, he lifted his own pint and toasted, 'To Jack and Helen. Make the most of tonight, Jack, it may be the last time you've a life and loose change to call your own.'

'Jealous, Adam?' Jack suspected Adam was still smarting from his sister Katie's rejection.

'Jack and Helen,' Brian interrupted smoothly, touching his glass to Jack's.

To Adam's annoyance, he realised Jack had left the pint he'd bought him on the tray and was drinking another. 'Come on, get it down you.' He pushed the spiked drink towards him.

'It's only eight o'clock,' Martin warned.

'And that leaves just two and a half hours of drinking time.' As Adam returned the tray to the bar, Jack switched the spiked pint with Adam's.

'I was about to tip you off.' Brian moved his chair so Adam couldn't see what Jack was doing.

'I saw Lifebuoy Lettie pour in the vodka.'

'This is a new one; sensible Jack.'

'Too sensible to get pissed the night before my wedding. Anyone want to take bets on how many pints Adam will go after that one? My money's on two.'

'I thought the cutlery set was from you as well as Mr Williams, Mrs Hunt.' Helen took the beautifully wrapped box Judy's mother handed her.

'We're not married yet.' Joy Hunt smiled self-consciously.

'But soon, Mam,' Judy reminded her.

'July most probably.'

'And I'm going to be bridesmaid . . . '

'That's July, Judy. Helen's big day is tomorrow and we should concentrate on that.'

'Oh, Mrs Hunt, you shouldn't have. It's wonderful and so thoughtful. How did you know we didn't have one?' Helen opened the box and lifted out a camera.

'Your father happened to mention that you were borrowing his for your honeymoon. And with' – Joy faltered as she realised she'd been about to mention the baby – 'you just starting out on married life, there'll be a lot more occasions when you'll be wanting mementoes, so I thought it might be useful.'

'It will be, I promise you.' Helen hugged her.

'There are four films in the box so you don't have to go dashing off in the middle of your wedding tomorrow to buy one.'

'I've just been showing the girls my outfit.' Setting the camera down carefully on top of the cocktail cabinet, Helen lifted her costume from the sofa and peeled back the cotton dust cover.

12

'Isn't it beautiful.' Judy smoothed the textured silk as Helen held the full-skirted blue-and-white costume in front of her.

'Very. You're going to look stunning, Helen. I wish I could be there but you know how busy the salon is on Saturday and I dare not risk losing my regulars by letting them down.'

'I understand, Mrs Hunt. I'll save you a piece of the cake.'

'Auntie Norah used to say that if you put a piece of wedding cake under your pillow you'll dream of your future husband.' Lily took the costume from Helen.

'There's no point in you doing that, Mam, you know who he's going to be. Now Katie, Lily and I are different, so be sure to put at least three pieces in boxes strong enough to slip under pillows, Helen. Otherwise we'll make right messes of our beds.'

'You're welcome to stay and have a Babycham and some sandwiches with us, Mrs Hunt.'

Joy was touched by Helen's invitation but she also knew it had been given from politeness, not the heart. A middle-aged chaperone was the last thing Helen needed the night before her wedding. 'Thank you, but I'm meeting Roy in ten minutes. He has tickets for a concert.'

'See you later, Mam.' Judy turned back to Helen's outfit as Helen showed her mother out. 'I'm so envious.' Judy replaced the cover as Helen closed the door.

'It's hardly a white wedding dress but I put paid to my chances of wearing one of those.' Helen faced her friends. 'I'm not getting at your mother, Judy, but I'd rather you didn't pretend this is a normal wedding. Everyone in Carlton Terrace and half of Swansea knows my father would never have given his consent if it weren't for "my condition", as Mrs Jordan so coyly puts it. And, as Jack says, it's better to tell everyone I'm pregnant, so they can say whatever they want to our faces, instead of whispering it behind our backs.'

'But you do want to marry Jack?' Katie asked anxiously.

'I've never wanted anything more in my whole life. I just wish people would stop pretending I'm not having a baby when Jack and I are looking forward to his arrival.'

'Not just Jack and you.' Katie smiled. 'I can't wait to be Auntie Katie.'

'You're going to make a great one.'

'I've often wondered . . .' Judy began tentatively.

'What it's like to be an aunt?' Helen broke in. 'You'll soon find out because Jack and I intend to make you and Lily honorary ones.'

'Not that – but I'd love to be an aunt – I was thinking about what it's like to go all the way with a boy.'

'You and Brian are the sophisticated ones.' Helen took four glasses from her father's cocktail cabinet. 'Living in London . . .'

'In hostels where we aren't allowed visitors of the opposite sex in our rooms, only the common rooms which are cold, dreary and public.'

'You mean, you and Brian haven't . . .' Helen looked at her in surprise.

'We were able to get up to more when he lived with Martin and Jack. Then we could sneak into his bedroom for the odd half-hour, not that we did that much. Well – not as much as you and Jack,' Judy qualified. 'So, what is it like?'

'You don't really expect me to answer that.' Helen handed out the glasses and bottles of Babycham.

'Why not?'

'Because it's something private that you have to find out for yourself.'

'At least tell us if it hurt,' Judy pressed, 'and how you felt afterwards. And did Jack think any the less of you . . .'

'It's like nothing else that's ever happened to me,' Helen broke in hastily. More open than Lily and Katie, she had tended to discuss everything with her friends – but not this. It belonged to her and Jack and no one else.

'It must have been embarrassing to undress in front of Jack for the first time.' Lily blushed as they turned to her. 'I didn't mean to put it quite like that, but I've often wondered how any girl could . . .'

'You and Joe were practically engaged.' Judy passed her the bottle opener.

'We never got as far as undressing and not much beyond kissing,' Lily confessed.

'That doesn't surprise me after the lecture Joe gave me when he walked in on me and Jack.'

'He caught you?' Judy's eyes widened as she stared at Helen.

'Not actually. We were dressed – sort of – but Jack was holding my underclothes.'

Helen busied herself with the bottle opener and Babycham.

'Did Joe and Jack . . .'

'Joe didn't say a word to Jack but he said plenty to me. You should have heard him. He carried on worse than any maiden aunt. You were right to give him his ring back, Lily. I pity any girl daft enough to marry him. And as for it being embarrassing, it wasn't. Jack did most of the undressing and it seemed right at the time.'

'So?' Judy poured her Babycham and settled back in a chair.

'You're not going to give up, are you?' Helen asked.

'If I had been the first, I would have told you what it's like.'

'I don't know what it'll be like for you, only Jack and me, and it was magical – and personal.'

'Was it painful?'

'A bit, but like the undressing it didn't seem to matter.'

'And?'

'And I'm looking forward to married life. You want to know any more, talk to Brian,' Helen said firmly.

'In the common room.'

'You're staying until Sunday. Why don't you ask Brian to borrow Marty's bedroom?' Helen pushed the coffee table aside and wheeled the trolley Joe had brought in into its place.

'I'm not sure I want him to.'

'That's the difference between us, I wanted to.' Hoping to change the subject, Helen opened a carrier bag and pulled out a blue satin net and cream lace layered petticoat. 'What do you think of this?' As Judy took it from her, she glanced at Katie and realised she had been very quiet, but then Katie never had liked talking about sex. Not even when they were twelve and had first found out about it. She wondered if she'd embarrassed Katie by saying the little she had about herself and Jack. She wouldn't have minded a girl talking about Joe that way. At least it would prove he was human underneath the coating of self-righteous prig.

'It's gorgeous.' Judy turned back the layers.

'Matching bra and suspenders.' Helen lifted them out and held them up for inspection.

'They for you or Jack?' Judy queried artfully.

'My honeymoon present to both of us. They're part of a new range. Alice – she's the buyer in the warehouse – thought they'd be too fancy for most people in Swansea but I persuaded Dad to stock them and they've been so successful he, or rather Katie – who is the best secretary my father's ever had according to him – had to reorder.'

'They're stunning. Are they still in stock, Katie? I would love a set in green . . .'

'Sea-green, rose-pink, lemon and sky-blue,' Katie recited knowledgeably, 'and last time I looked, which was yesterday afternoon, we had a couple of sets left in each colour.'

'Katie and I splashed out after we saw Helen's and bought sets in pink.' Lily handed round plates and napkins.

'Then they're not too dear.'

'Depends what you mean by "dear",' Lily qualified. 'The bra's seven and six, the suspenders twelve and six but the petticoat was three pounds nineteen and eleven.'

'Ouch.'

'The lace is real and quality costs.' Helen folded the petticoat and bra back into the bag.

'That's just what the wardrobe mistress in work says.' Judy helped herself to a ham sandwich. 'She's always complaining about the cost of trimmings. She says she has to pay more for a yard of two-inch lace than thirty-six-inch-wide plain cotton.'

'How you can envy me when you work with famous people in London, Judy, I'll never know.' Helen wouldn't have switched places with Judy for all the money in Swansea but, bursting with happiness, she wanted her friends to feel just the way she did.

'The senior make-up and hair stylists work on the famous ones. I only get the people who come in for news interviews, or extras from the dramas.'

'But you'll get promoted.' Lily put a pasty and sausage roll on her plate.

'Possibly, when I'm a hundred and twenty and on the verge of retirement,' Judy said gloomily.

'Come on, Judy, it can't be that bad,' Helen admonished.

'I should never have gone up there.'

'But I thought you were having a great time. Your letters . . .'

'I could hardly write "Dear All in Carlton Terrace, London is a horrible, filthy city plagued by pea soup smogs you can't breathe in, the hostel food is worse than the pigswill that used to be left over from school dinners, the warden makes the wicked queen in *Snow White* look like a nice old granny and by the way, the job's not up to much either. It's bloody hard work – pardon my French – and boring. A junior make-up and hair stylist is at the beck and call of the entire department, gets the blame for every single thing that goes wrong and none of the thanks when it goes right. Love Judy. PS In case you haven't guessed, I'm homesick and miserable as sin."'

'But after work you have Brian,' Lily protested.

'We barely see enough of one another to ask, "How's it going?" I work late afternoons, evenings and every other weekend; he works shifts so we're lucky if we get together a couple of hours a week, and as I said earlier, there's nowhere we can go except the common rooms in the hostels, a café or, if they're open at that time of day, the pictures. And the rest of the time I'm so bloody lonely I could cry. Sorry, swearing's getting to be a bad habit. People I work with do it all the time.' Reaching into her pocket for a handkerchief, Judy dabbed her eyes. 'That's why I want to know what it's like, Helen. It might be different if I did have someone up there besides Brian but I don't, and I'm terrified he'll go off and find another girl. I thought that if I slept with him we might become closer and then he'd stop volunteering for overtime and spend more time with me.'

'It would be fantastic if you did come back.' Katie was almost in tears herself.

'That's the nicest thing anyone's said to me since I left Swansea and I had to come back to hear it.' Judy hugged Katie as she moved next to her on the sofa. 'I talked it over with my mother earlier. She said if I do come back, she'll open another salon and let me run it for her. I would have to answer to her, but she wouldn't be there day to day, so it would almost be like being my own boss. And there's you three. You've no idea how much I've missed you.' She hugged Katie again. 'And our talks and nights out together. In London I even go to the pictures by myself if Brian's not free on my night off. People there are too stuck up to give you the time of day. I thought before I went I'd make friends, but outside of Brian I hardly know a soul, certainly no one I can talk to beyond saying, "nice weather" or "it's raining again".'

'Does Brian want to come back too?' Helen demolished the pasty on her plate in two bites.

'I doubt it. All he can talk about is his new job and promotion prospects.'

'So what are you going to do?' Lily asked.

'Some hard thinking over the weekend.'

'So it's Brian and London or Swansea and your own salon.'

'You make it sound simple, Helen. But it's more complicated than that. There's my pride for one thing. I hate the thought of coming back here tagged with failure after barely a month.'

'Sounds more like common sense if you're that unhappy, unless you really love Brian and don't want to leave him.' Lily took the fresh bottle of Babycham Helen handed her.

'That's just it, I'm not sure whether I love him or not but I thought that if we made love . . .'

'He's trying to push you into it,' Helen broke in indignantly.

'No. To be honest he hasn't tried much beyond a quick kiss and fumble around my bra area since we lived here and I slapped his face for trying to take more liberties than I was prepared to give. That's another thing that's bothering me. If he loved me he'd want more. Wouldn't he?' Judy looked to Helen for confirmation.

'You just said you don't have anywhere private to go,' Lily pointed out.

'It wouldn't be easy to find a place but if he were serious he'd make an effort to look for one.'

'And what would you do if he did turn up on a date one night with a hotel key? Slap his face, or shout "goody" and run ahead of him up the stairs?' Helen questioned.

'I don't know because I've absolutely no idea what making love is like. Now if you told me . . .'

'You should never make love with a man until you are absolutely certain that you love him.'

They turned to Katie in amazement, the same thought in all their minds. Surely not! Not quiet, mousy Katie who had given gorgeous Adam Jordan the brush-off after only a couple of dates.

'At least, that's what I've always thought,' Katie qualified, her cheeks burning crimson.

Judy was the first to regain her composure. 'That's easy to say, but how do you know the difference between having a crush on someone and being really in love with them?'

'That's easy. Look at my brother and Helen.'

'We can't all fall in love with Jack,' Judy snapped irritably.

'I'd scratch the eyes out of any other girl who tried.' Helen threw a cushion at Judy.

'Careful, that nearly knocked over my drink.'

'I think that when making love seems like the right thing to do, which is what Helen said about her and Jack, it's the right time for it to happen,' Katie murmured.

'Some of the girls in the hostel said . . .'

'The ones who don't talk to you?' Helen teased.

'Some are better than others,' Judy continued irritably. 'They say

French letters aren't safe. That you can get pregnant even if you use them.'

'You're looking at proof.' Helen sipped her Babycham.

'You serious?' Judy dropped her plate on to a side table.

'To be honest, we didn't use them until it was too late, but then, everything worked out well for me.'

'Because you picked a boy who'd walk through fire for you. Given his present performance, I'm not sure Brian would cross the road for me.'

'If you're that unsure about him, why consider sleeping with him?' Helen asked.

'I told you.'

'I think it would be a big mistake to go to bed with Brian just because you're lonely and don't like London.'

'You're not even married yet, Helen, and you sound like "Mrs Marryatt advises" in *Woman's Weekly*.' Lily smiled.

'Can you imagine *Woman's Weekly* printing a problem like Judy's? How to curtsy and address your new mother-in-law and what colour bedsocks to wear on the honeymoon night maybe – but whether or not to undress in front of a man and actually make love before you have a wedding ring on your finger! Mrs Marryatt would curl up and die at the thought.'

'And what colour bedsocks are you wearing tomorrow night?' Judy asked curiously.

'Want to see?' Helen reached for another bag and pulled out a tiny white silk hat and veil. 'Wrong bag,' she muttered, among gales of laughter.

'No, don't put it away.' Brushing the crumbs from her hands, Judy took it from her. 'Have you thought about what hairstyle you're going to wear with this?'

'Down.'

'Up would be more sophisticated.'

'I'm wearing it down,' Helen said resolutely. 'Jack prefers it that way.'

Chapter 2

'I DON'T FEEL so good.'

'We've noticed.' Brian moved Adam's pint away from him as he slumped over the table.

'What are we going to do with him?' Sam shifted his chair away from Adam's.

'Take him home.' Martin finished the beer in his glass.

'And I win.' Jack held out his hand. 'Two bob from each of you, I said two pints, remember.' He watched the two-shilling pieces pile up in his palm. 'Right, next round's on me.'

'Bridegroom shouldn't pay on his stag night,' Martin demurred.

'I'm not.' Jack pocketed the money and went to the bar.

'You could charge Adam with drunk and disorderly, Sam.' Brian offered his cigarettes around, leaving one on the table in front of Jack's chair. 'Sergeant liked keen rookies when I worked out of Swansea.'

'Don't you lot ever forget you're coppers?' There was no malice in Martin's comment. After sharing rooms first with Brian, then Sam, he'd developed a grudging respect for their profession.

'He's too out of it to be disorderly.' Sam grimaced as Adam began to snore. Shifting Adam's head until he fell silent, he asked, 'What's it like in the Met, Brian?'

'Busier than here; in fact, most days it's a madhouse. Long hours, shift work, hardly any time to yourself but the boys are great and promotion prospects better than in Wales.'

'Then you like it.'

'I won't be coming back here, if that's what you're asking.'

'And Judy?' Martin ventured.

'She seems happy enough. Between the hours I work and the hours she works, we don't see one another as often as we'd like but you know what they say about absence.' Brian winked.

'Then it's still on between you two.'

'Most definitely. And what's this I hear from Judy about you and Lily?'

'I've taken her out a couple of times.' Martin's attempt to sound nonchalant didn't quite come off.

'A couple of times a week since we left according to Helen.'

'You only went to London a month ago.'

'A lot can happen in a month and you were always keen on her.'

'It's early days,' Martin mumbled, hoping to discourage further conversation about his relationship with Lily. Even after a month and twelve – not eight – dates, as Brian had hinted, not to mention all the times they had bumped into one another 'by accident' that he had engineered, he found it difficult to believe a girl like Lily could actually want to go out with an apprentice mechanic like him. It was simply too good to be true. Not normally superstitious, he was terrified if he tried to quantify his feelings for her it would somehow jinx his luck and she'd start walking – if not running – away from him.

'Pretty girl and she knows the way to a man's heart. She cooks like an angel.' Sam kissed the tips of his fingers in a parody of an Italian chef's blessing.

'She cooks for you two?' Brian turned to Sam.

'We've been invited to tea a couple of times.'

'By my sister as much as Lily,' Martin interposed swiftly. 'I'll give Jack a hand with the glasses.' He reached the bar in time to see his brother scowl as Joe Griffiths swept Jack's hand aside and ostentatiously handed the barmaid a pound note.

'I could stay,' Lily offered as Helen opened the front door.

'There's no need. There'll be bags of time in the morning. Not even I need more than a couple of hours to get ready.'

'I'll be over before nine to wash and set your hair.'

'Thanks, Judy, see you then.' Helen closed the door. She was finally alone to do what she'd been dying to do all evening: run down to the basement to unpack Jack's clothes and look over the flat one last time before she and Jack moved in.

As she hung Jack's shirts and trousers next to hers in the wardrobe, and folded his underclothes into the bottom two drawers in the chest she had reserved for his use, she noticed that, although finely repaired by Katie, most of his things were the worse for wear. It was just as well his birthday was coming up so she could replace some of his shirts, socks and underwear.

21

When she finished, she stowed Jack's case in the cupboard under the stairs, opened the doors and switched on all the lamps before viewing each room in turn.

First, the bedroom; its delicate blue and cream decor glowed softly and seductively in the subdued lighting. It didn't take much imagination to envisage the scenes that would be played out in the comfort of the double bed Jack couldn't wait to 'christen' – absolute luxury after the narrow confines of her father's old, overstuffed sofa. The bathroom beyond it with a bath Jack had hinted was big enough to accommodate both of them. The smart, contemporary living room where they'd sit every evening discussing Jack's day at work and hers with the baby, and listening to the radio. The well-equipped easy-to-clean kitchen where she'd prepare delicious meals that Jack would praise and there'd be other evenings when they would invite Lily, Katie, Martin and Sam in for supper. So many happy, perfect times to come – then she remembered in the coming months she'd be growing fatter and fatter.

Would Jack still love her then? He said he couldn't wait to see her grow big with their child but what if she became repulsive like Mrs Evans in Hanover Street who 'let herself go' when she was pregnant with her first and, now she was 'big in the way' with her fourth, rarely bothered to put in her false teeth and always wore her hair in curlers and her stockings rolled to her ankles because she was too stout to struggle into her corset?

Her teeth! Mrs Lannon had warned her that every baby cost a tooth. She tapped hers to make sure none were loose. They felt firm but . . .

'You down here, love?'

'Yes, Dad.' She switched off the lights and closed the doors.

'All alone?' John limped down the stairs.

'The girls have only just gone.'

'Last-minute check around?'

'No. Last-minute gloat.' Impulsively she kissed his cheek. 'You've done us proud.'

'You and Jack did all the hard work.'

'Only after the builders moved out. We could never have afforded to rent a place like this without your help. Would you like some tea?'

'Not on top of beer, love, but thanks for asking. You'll make Jack a thoughtful wife.'

'There's sandwiches in the fridge.'

'Now you're talking.'

Switching off the last light, she locked the door and followed her father up the stairs and into the kitchen. It was immaculate. Ever the practical one, Lily had insisted on washing the plates and glasses, and packing the leftover food into greaseproof paper before stowing it in the fridge.

'Cheese or ham sandwiches, or pasties and sausage rolls.'

'Ham sandwiches please, love.'

Helen laid the sandwiches on a plate, found the mustard, set out a place setting and retreated to the window seat that overlooked the back gardens. A sliver of new moon shone down from a clear starlit sky. 'Marry on a new and waxing moon, never a waning one.' Where had she heard that? It sounded like something Lily's Auntie Norah would have said. It would have been awful if she'd remembered that and seen an old moon. Drawing her knees to her chin, she curled herself into a ball.

'No second thoughts?' John asked.

'None.' She smiled.

'If you're marrying Jack just because of the baby . . .'

'The baby's a bonus, Dad, or should I say Grandad.'

'Now that is going to take some getting used to.'

'I am unbelievably lucky and I know it. I have Jack and the baby, and you for a father. Unlike poor Judy; she was saying tonight how much she misses Swansea and hates London.'

'She hasn't been there long.' John sat at the table and helped himself to a couple of sandwiches.

'Long enough to be miserable.'

'You can't make the whole world happy, love, so why don't you just settle for Jack and, speaking of which, as you're getting married tomorrow, isn't it high time you were in bed?'

'I'm too excited to sleep.'

'Tomorrow will be here soon enough.'

'It can't come soon enough for me.' Leaving the seat, she picked up the sandwiches he hadn't eaten.

'I'll clear up, love.'

'You sure, Dad?'

'I'm sure.' He watched her as she went to the door. 'Going for another last look round downstairs?'

'I just want to make sure everything's tidy for when we come back,' she smiled self-consciously.

* * *

'Adam's heavier than he looks,' Brian grumbled, as he and Sam manoeuvred his comatose body down the outside basement steps.

'If I do any permanent damage to myself, I'll know who to blame,' Sam gasped, as Jack unlocked the front door.

'Complaints, nothing but complaints.' Jack switched on the light. Walking through the kitchen to the passage, he opened the connecting door to the upstairs.

'Where you off to, Jack?' Martin asked suspiciously, as Brian dumped Adam in an easy chair and rubbed his aching arms.

'To borrow a couple of things from Katie.'

'At this time of night?'

'She won't be in bed.'

'What's he up to?' Brian picked up the kettle, filled it and set it on the stove to boil.

'I have no idea.' Martin studied Adam. 'If we take him home in this state, his mother will never let him hear the end of it. Either of you any idea how to bring him round?'

'Black coffee's the only remedy I know.' Sam opened the door to their food cupboard.

'The only way we'd be able to get it down him is lie him on the floor and pour it into his mouth, and he'd choke. What do your lot do with the drunks you pick up off the streets?'

'Throw them in a freezing cell and leave them until they come round.' Brian reached for the cups. 'You want tea or coffee?'

'Tea and cheese sandwiches.' Sam looked towards the corner as he lifted out the bread bin. The basement was serviced by an outside toilet and the kitchen did double service as a bathroom. Martin had covered the massive Victorian bath that almost spanned the length of one wall with an old door and a plastic cloth so it would be less obtrusive except when it was actually in use. 'We could fill that with cold water and drop him in.'

'He'd die of shock or pneumonia or both.' Brian warmed the teapot and reached for the tea caddy. 'Get what you wanted?'

'Yes.' Jack placed a large bottle of scent and a cheap lipstick on the table.

'What are you going to do with these?' Martin opened the lipstick and pushed up the bright-red stick with his thumb.

'Take revenge.' Unscrewing the top from the scent, Jack sniffed the bottle. 'Katie wasn't joking when she said this was strong.'

'I can smell it from here.' Brian spooned tea leaves into the pot.

'Put the top on, it's killing the cheese.' Sam threw a tea towel on top of the cheese dish as if to protect it.

Jack leaned over Adam and emptied the scent bottle over his shirt. 'What . . .'

'I told you, I'm taking revenge.' Jack grinned at Martin as Adam began to mutter in his sleep.

'More like gas us.' Brian wrenched open the skylight above the door.

'What has Adam done to deserve that?' Sam asked.

'Tried to get me drunk.'

'He didn't succeed.'

'Not for want of trying.' Jack picked out an orange from the fruit bowl on the table. Taking the lipstick from Martin, he drew a cupid's bow of a mouth on the side of the orange. After making a few slight adjustments with his fingernail he pressed it on to Adam's scent sodden shirt.

'Anyone watching us would think Adam's the bridegroom.' Brian poured out the tea.

'He'll murder you when he comes round.' Martin couldn't help laughing. The lipstick 'kiss' was perfect.

'There's no real damage done, Katie said it'll wash out.'

'Did you tell her why you wanted the scent and lipstick?' Martin asked.

'Yes.'

'And she still gave them to you?'

'After I told her Adam tried to get me drunk.'

Brian, Sam and Martin watched as Jack applied two more 'kisses' to Adam's shirt-front, one to his cheek and another to the centre of his forehead.

'If one of you holds up his shirt and vest, I'll put a few on his chest.' Jack redrew the 'lips' on the orange as he stood back to admire his handiwork.

'And when he wakes?' Brian sugared the teas.

'We'll tell him he got off with . . .' Jack thought for a few moments. 'Lifebuoy Lettie.'

'The barmaid!' Brian exclaimed. 'He'll never believe that. She's fifty if she's a day.'

'Why do you call her Lifebuoy Lettie?' Sam unclipped Adam's braces and rolled up his shirt and vest.

'Because she needs Lifebuoy soap. Have you ever stood close to

25

her? Silly question, you wouldn't be asking if you had.' Jack planted a neat circle of 'kisses' round Adam's right nipple.

'That's enough, Jack,' Martin protested as Jack began to repeat the pattern above Adam's navel.

'Just one more.' Opening Adam's belt, Jack unbuttoned his trousers and planted a final 'kiss' on the fly of his underpants.

'If we couldn't take him home before, we certainly can't take him now.' Brian sat at the table as Jack refastened Adam's flies.

'He's not sleeping in my room,' Sam pre-empted firmly.

'You can't expect me to drag him up to the attic with me,' Brian remonstrated.

'Put the two easy chairs together,' Jack suggested.

'He'll never sleep on those.' Martin joined Brian at the table.

'He's sleeping on one now.' Jack washed the lipstick from the orange and returned it to the bowl. 'I'll nip round to his mother's, tell her we're having a bit of a party and he's spending the night here.'

'I'll go.' Sam tucked Adam's vest and shirt back into his trousers and clipped on his braces. 'It'll be better coming from a policeman. Besides, she'll smell a rat if she sees you. You're way too sober for a bridegroom the night before his wedding.'

'I wish you'd left the scent until we'd gone to bed.' Brian sniffed.

'Sorry, I didn't realise it would linger.' Jack screwed the top back on the empty bottle.

'What it's called, "Evening in Sewage"?'

Jack read the label. 'French Chic.'

'Now I know what not to buy a girl.' Brian sliced the cheese.

'Thanks to Adam. Poetic justice, really, seeing as how he gave it to Katie.'

'I'm sorry, I . . .' Helen rushed out of her bedroom, across the landing and dived into the bathroom, slamming the door behind her. Judy dropped the hairbrush she was holding and looked quizzically at Lily and Katie as they heard the toilet seat bang.

'Morning sickness,' Katie diagnosed, having seen her mother suffer similar symptoms during three pregnancies, which had all ended in miscarriages after her father's beatings.

'Can we do anything to help?'

'Not much.' Picking up a bottle of cologne from Helen's dressing table, Katie sprinkled a few drops on to a handkerchief. 'Helen told Jack she's been having a bad time with it.'

'That settles it.' Judy dropped her handbag on Helen's bed. 'I'm never getting married and having children. I can't stand being sick.'

'It doesn't last for ever.' Katie handed Lily the handkerchief and ran downstairs.

Lily went to the bathroom, knocked on the door and opened it. White-faced, her forehead damp with perspiration, Helen was sitting on the floor, leaning against the bath.

'Katie put some cologne on your handkerchief.'

'Thanks.' Helen clamped it over her nose as Lily laid her hand on her forehead.

'We could send for the doctor.'

'For morning sickness?'

Turning on the cold tap, Lily took a flannel from the bath rack, soaked it, wrung it out and laid it over Helen's temples.

'I'll be fine by twelve.'

'It stops by then?'

'Usually. You won't tell Dad, will you? He worries far too much about me as it is.'

'Perhaps Judy should come in here to set your hair.'

'I wouldn't have so far to go if she's prepared to run the risk of seeing me throw up.'

'After seeing the state some people being interviewed on television get themselves into before they face the camera, Judy can bear the sight of almost anything.' Judy walked in, dumped a bag of hair curlers in the sink and sat on the edge of the bath. 'No, don't move, Helen, you're the perfect height for me to set your hair.'

'Glad I'm the perfect something.'

Katie ran back up the stairs. 'Here, this used to help my mother.' She held out a glass of water and a piece of dry toast.

'Thanks for the water but I can't face the toast.'

A door opened on the landing and Joe, unshaved, unwashed, bare chested in loosely corded pyjama trousers, emerged from his bedroom. Retreating smartly when he saw the girls, he returned in his dressing gown, collar pulled high, the belt tied tightly round his waist. He gave all of them, but especially Lily, his most charming smile. 'I wasn't expecting to find a ladies' convention in my bathroom.'

'Push off, Joe,' Helen ordered.

'I can hardly believe that after eighteen years of fighting you for the bathroom, from tomorrow I'll be able to walk in here whenever I like.'

'That's tomorrow. We're not budging.'

'I see getting married has put you in an even better mood than usual, sis. Poor Jack, I hope he knows what he's getting himself into.'

Before Helen had time to think of a suitable rejoinder, she had to throw up the toilet seat again.

'It's only just after nine, so you've bags of time,' Lily murmured sympathetically, as she held Helen's head.

'Is she really ill?'

Judy gave Joe an acid smile. 'No, she's just play-acting.'

'Perhaps I should telephone the doctor.'

'It's only morning sickness,' Helen protested, between bouts of nausea. 'I wish men had the babies.'

'If they did, the human race would have died out years ago and we wouldn't be here to discuss it.' Judy pulled a brush and comb from her pocket.

'I'll be downstairs if you want me to telephone or anything. Excuse me, Lily.' Joe brushed against her as he stepped in and retrieved his shaving gear and toilet bag from a shelf above her head.

'Stop flirting with Lily and get out of here.' Helen slumped back against the bath.

'I'm going.' Joe closed the door behind him.

'My hair . . .'

'Just thank your lucky stars I washed it as soon as I got here. Now if you can stop being sick long enough for me to put the rollers in, we'll get you to the Register Office on time. And with perfect hair,' Judy assured her.

'Is Helen all right?' John asked Joe as he walked down the stairs.

'Not really, but the girls are looking after her. As they've commandeered our bathroom, I thought I'd borrow the one in the basement.'

'Leave it clean and tidy.'

'Don't I always?'

'No.'

As Joe closed the door on the stairs that led down to the basement, the doorbell rang. Expecting the florist with the buttonholes, John opened it and started at the sight of his estranged wife, Esme, dressed for the occasion in a pale-grey, velvet-silk costume he recognised as Dior, with a matching hat and contrasting lilac leather handbag, gloves and shoes.

'Aren't you going to invite me in, John?'

'Have you come to see Helen?' he questioned warily. Esme had taken the news of Helen's pregnancy badly and even if she intended to extend the olive branch, he couldn't see Helen taking it, not after some of the things Esme had said about Jack Clay, the term he'd served in Borstal and his and Helen's morals.

'I think I should go to the wedding.'

'You "think", Esme?'

'Helen *is* my daughter and a mother's place is with her daughter on the most important day of her life.'

John gazed at Esme dispassionately for a moment and wondered how he could ever have imagined himself in love with her. Yet they'd been married – had a daughter together –

'May I come in, John?'

He suddenly realised he'd been staring at her. 'It's not up to me, Esme. I'll have to ask Helen what she wants.'

'If you'd let me see her . . .'

'She's not well.'

'All the more reason for me to come in, so I can look after her.'

'The girls are with her. I'm not sure she wants anyone else.'

Swallowing her pride, Esme forced herself to remain pleasant. 'At least give her the choice.'

'When she's dressed, I'll tell her you're here.'

'And in the meantime I stay on the doorstep.'

John fought his initial instinct to tell Esme to wait elsewhere. His solicitor had warned him that if he were alone with her for any length of time and it became public knowledge, the court might see it as cohabitation with a view to reconciliation and a reason to deny the divorce he desperately wanted. So desperately, he had swallowed his pride, sacrificed his reputation and met a prostitute in a hotel bedroom so she could help him and a paid photographer to fake the 'evidence' Esme needed to bring a petition against him for adultery. But the house was full of Helen's friends – and Helen was Esme's daughter as much as his . . .

'You can wait in the living room.' He stepped back, finally allowing her to enter the house. 'But I'd appreciate it if you'd stay there until I've had a chance to warn Joe as well as Helen that you're here.'

'Thank you.' Relieved, Esme allowed herself a small smile of triumph as she walked over the threshold. The first part of her plan had worked. She was actually in the house. All she had to do now was win Helen over to convince John she was sincere in wanting a reconciliation, and after the wedding arrange a quiet talk with him, put her proposition and persuade him to see the advantages for him if he went along with the decisions she'd made – for both of them.

That shouldn't be too difficult; most men came round to her way of thinking after she'd exercised her charm on them. It hadn't worked on John the last time she had tried, but that was understandable. She'd made the mistake of taking him for granted when they'd lived together. An hour alone, a few reminders of the more pleasurable aspects of married life and he'd drop his antagonism towards her. She was staking her future on it.

'The ring . . .'

Martin held up the box he'd put beside his plate.

'I should . . .'

'Sit down and eat your breakfast.' Brian pushed Jack back on to his chair and returned to the stove where he was preparing a fry-up for himself, the Clays, Sam – and Adam – if he ever emerged from the outside toilet where he'd been camped for the last half-hour. He lifted the lid on the frying pan and sniffed theatrically. 'This black pudding smells heavenly. I've spent the last month dreaming about this. London food tastes like wet cardboard. Looks like it too, especially in the hostel.' Chopping tomatoes and mushrooms, he added them to the pan.

'Hair of the dog.' Sam walked in from his room carrying an open bottle of beer.

'How can you even think about it at this time in the morning?' Wrinkling his nose in disgust, Jack reached for the teapot.

'Bridegroom's nervous.'

'Anyone would think he's going to the guillotine not the Register Office.' Brian cracked half a dozen eggs into a bowl.

'From what I know about women he might be.' Ashen-faced, hands shaking, Adam walked in from the passage.

'You don't look too good.' Martin handed him a towel as he washed his hands at the sink.

'I think some joker spiked my beer last night.'

'No. Really!' Jack exclaimed.

'And covered me with scent and lipstick.'

'Ah, that would be Lifebuoy Lettie.' Jack lifted a plate of bread

Brian had cut from the dresser and began buttering the slices as if he were being paid piecework rates to finish the task.

'Lifebuoy Lettie – she stinks – she's ancient ' Adam's face went from grey to puce.

'You didn't seem to think so last night.' Jack stared intently at the butter he was softening by scraping.

'Once she gave you the nod, there was no keeping you away from her.' Brian added pepper, salt, milk and butter to the eggs.

'It wasn't a pretty sight,' Sam elaborated. 'I've never seen a man maul a woman around so much, or in so many' – he paused as if he were searching for the right word – 'private places in public before. I was just about to arrest the pair of you for indecency when stop tap was called and she took you down the cellar.'

'You let me go!'

'It wasn't a question of "letting you". There was no keeping you away from her.'

'What did I do with her in the cellar?'

'How should we know? We're not Peeping Toms.' Jack turned a straight face to Adam.

'You must have known I was out of my skull.'

'You turned vicious when we suggested it,' Sam complained.

'You should have taken me home.'

'Vicious is an understatement. Ferocious might be a better word. Today's my big day, I wanted to stay in one piece.' Jack offered Adam a slice of bread and butter.

'It was love at first sight – well, perhaps not first, you had seen her before.' Brian tipped the eggs into a saucepan.

'Lust after many sights.' Sam held out his bottle of beer. 'It's warm and flat but wet. Want a swig?'

Stomach heaving, Adam brushed aside the bread and butter and beer, and rushed to the front door.

'Be back in time for the wedding.' Brian closed the door after him.

'Bring the milk in, Brian,' Sam asked.

'What did your last slave die of?'

'The beating I gave him for being mouthy.' Sam reached for the teapot.

Brian returned a few moments later with the milk. 'Helen's mother is sitting in her father's front room.'

'Don't you think we've had enough leg-pulling for one wedding?'

'I'm serious, Marty.' He looked at Jack. 'Judy told me what Mrs

31

Griffiths called you and Helen when you told her you were getting married. You're more forgiving than me, mate. If my future mother-in-law had said half the things about me that Mrs Griffiths said about you, there'd be no way I'd allow her to come to my wedding.'

'We didn't invite her.'

'Perhaps she wants to make amends,' Martin suggested.

'More likely she's turned up to say a whole lot more.' Jack's mouth settled in a grim line.

'You want me to go next door?'

'To do what?' Jack asked his brother.

'You're right. It's Helen's family's problem.'

'Only until twelve o'clock,' Jack muttered darkly.

'It's my day and I don't want her at the Register Office or wedding breakfast and that's an end to it.'

John had taken Helen into the kitchen to tell her that Esme was in the living room, so she deliberately raised her voice in the hope her mother would hear.

'She is your mother, Helen,' John reminded her mildly, feeling he ought to say something in his estranged wife's defence, lest Esme accuse him, yet again, of driving a wedge between her and the children, although she'd expressed no desire to have either of them move out to her mother's house with her when she left.

'All she's ever done is belittle me and try to make me look stupid.'

'If I have, I am sorry for it, Helen.' Esme pushed open the kitchen door but was careful to remain in the hall. 'I heard you arguing with your father,' she explained. 'The last thing I intended to do was to upset you on your wedding day.'

'Then why did you come here?' Helen demanded.

'To bring you these.' Esme removed two envelopes from her handbag. Inching round the door, she laid them on the Formica kitchen table. 'They are cards from your grandmother and me. We want to wish you well in your new life.'

'I don't believe you.'

'I am sorry, Helen, the last time I saw you I said some things I shouldn't have. The only explanation I can offer is that I was shocked and worried for you. You are my daughter. I don't expect you to forgive me but when you are a mother you may understand why I said what I did.'

'And where did you get that speech? Your last production in the

Little Theatre?' Helen turned her back on her mother and stared resolutely out of the window.

'Helen, darling . . .'

'You upset Jack.' Helen would have died rather than admit her mother had upset her more.

'For which I am trying to apologise.' Making an effort to ignore Helen's antagonism, Esme changed the subject. 'You really do look very lovely. That is a beautiful costume, it is so well cut and the blue matches your eyes. Your hair looks perfect . . .'

'You won't get round me by flattery.'

'I wasn't flattering you, simply speaking the truth. Please open the cards.'

Imagining how miserable he'd feel if the situation were reversed and Helen's anger was directed at him, John picked them up and handed them over.

'We thought cheques would be best. You can pay them into your bank account and buy whatever you want.'

Helen tossed them back on the table. 'I'll talk to Jack. He may not want to accept yours.'

'Helen, I really am very sorry if I hurt or upset you or Jack in any way. If it will help I'll apologise to him as well . . .'

'It's a quarter past eleven. Judy's waiting to pin on my hat.' Turning, Helen pushed past her mother and ran up the stairs.

'Please, Helen,' Esme called after her. 'May I come to your wedding?'

'There's no room for you in the cars,' Helen shouted from the landing.

'I could call a taxi.'

When Helen didn't answer, John went to the foot of the stairs. 'Your mother is waiting. What do you want me to tell her?'

'That she can do whatever she likes, as long as she doesn't expect me or Jack to talk to her.'

'Thank you, John, don't bother to call a taxi, I'll do it.' Esme went to the hall table.

'It's obvious Helen doesn't want you to come.'

'She'll change her mind,' Esme assured him glibly as she picked up the receiver.

'And if she doesn't?'

'I'll see her married, drink a toast to my daughter and her new husband, and leave.'

'Without making a scene.'

'It's other people who make the scenes.'

'Only because you push them, Esme.'

'It's Helen's wedding day.' She hesitated, as she looked him in the eye. 'Can't we at least pretend to be friends?'

'You're the actress.'

'You won't even meet me halfway,' she murmured seductively.

'Not any more.' He went to the top of the basement stairs. 'If you'll excuse me I have to warn Joe that you're coming to the wedding.'

'How is he? I haven't spoken to him in weeks.'

'You find that surprising?'

'Not when I consider he lives with you.' Hearing John's sharp intake of breath, Esme gave him a brittle smile. 'Sorry, that wasn't intended to sound the way it came out.'

'One more comment like that, Esme, and it's you who will be out. And for once I'll have no compunction about making a scene.'

'I promise I'll be the soul of tact and discretion.'

As John ran down the stairs, he was already regretting that he hadn't ordered her out of the house.

The ceremony in the Guildhall's Register Office was brief and devoid of the emotion Helen had come to associate with the few church weddings she had attended. It was also very much smaller. Martin was best man, Lily bridesmaid, and apart from Jack's and her friends there were only her parents and her mother's cousin, Dorothy Green, who had closed her hat shop in Sketty for an hour so she could attend the ceremony, and Lily's Uncle Roy, invited by Jack, because Roy had been more of a father to him than his own ever had.

Expecting to, but feeling no different than she had done when she had walked into the room with her father ten minutes before, Helen kissed Jack, her father, Martin, Lily, Judy, Katie and Auntie Dot, while studiously ignoring her mother. At a prompt from the Registrar, who had his eye on the clock and the next party, her father led the way outside.

Martin and Lily produced confetti, her father and Roy took a few photographs and she and Jack were showered with paper petals and shouted congratulations as they ran to the car Jack had booked to take them to the Mackworth Hotel where her father had reserved a private room for the wedding breakfast.

Helen stood back in amazement. 'A Rolls-Royce!'

Jack kissed her cheek. 'Nothing's too good for my bride.'

'It must have cost a fortune.'

'Martin knows a few people in the trade.'

'All the same, Jack . . .'

'Mrs Clay.' Jack squeezed her hand as he helped her into the car. 'Happy?' he asked, as they drove off.

'I thought I'd feel . . .'

'What?' he asked anxiously, hoping he hadn't done anything to disappoint her.

'Different. More married.'

He patted the inside pocket of his suit that held the certificate and kissed her ringed finger. 'What more proof do you need, Mrs Clay?'

She looked at him as though she were seeing him for the first time, slim, dark, impossibly handsome, with black curly hair and deep-brown eyes; as attractive as his brother Martin but with a sharper, more volatile edge. The first time he had asked her to dance he'd seemed dangerous, unpredictable, as befitted an ex-Borstal boy, but if there had ever been any danger outside her imagination, there was no evidence of it now. His eyes were calm, quiet and loving – so very, very loving.

'I love you, Mrs Clay.'

'And I love you, Mr Clay.'

'That's all right, then.'

'I'm sorry about my mother. I told her I didn't want her to come . . .'

He kissed the tips of her gloved fingers. 'We've done a good job of ignoring her so far, we'll just carry on.'

'I told her we would.'

He squeezed her fingers again. 'The train leaves at two.'

'The suitcases . . .'

'Martin and I dropped them off at the station. Have I told you that you look beautiful in that costume?'

'Twice, but you can tell me again.'

The car slowed to a halt outside the hotel, a porter stepped forward and opened the door. Jack offered her his arm. They were led upstairs to the function room where silver and porcelain gleamed on white damask tablecloths.

Helen barely had time to glance at the table decorations before the door opened behind them and Martin came in with Lily – and behind them her mother. Jack put his arm protectively round her waist. In an hour and a half they'd be on the train. If anyone could help her to forget her mother and the angry bitter things she had said it was Jack. And soon they'd be alone.

Smiling determinedly, she took the glass of champagne the waiter handed her and allowed Jack to lead her to the top table where her father, Lily and Martin were waiting.

Chapter 3

'. . . AND I KNOW Jack will do all he can to make Helen happy.' Martin waited for the ripple of applause to subside. 'Now, Ladies and Gentlemen, it is my pleasant duty to propose a second toast to a beautiful girl who has been an invaluable help to the bride – and the best man.' Martin smiled with relief as he finished his short speech. He raised his glass to Lily. 'Ladies and gentlemen, I give you the bridesmaid, Lily Sullivan.'

Joe shuffled to his feet and lifted his glass along with the other guests. His father had allowed Helen and Jack to opt for an informal seating arrangement that had resulted in Martin and Lily sitting next to one another, scuppering his hopes of commandeering Lily and persuading her to take back the engagement ring he had bought her.

He had brought it with him, along with plans to drive her in his father's car to Three Cliffs Bay after the reception, so he could formally propose a second time. After they'd reaffirmed their love for one another, he'd pictured himself slipping the solitaire on her finger, kissing her, and watching the sun set over the sea, before returning home and changing into evening clothes for the Saturday night dinner dance in the Langland Bay Hotel. The hotel had a few vacancies left – he had checked before leaving the house. He would have ordered champagne, a red rose for Lily . . .

Lily's laughter – light, silvery – shattered his daydream. Seeing her with Martin was like receiving a slap in the face. She couldn't have made it more obvious that she was enjoying the lout's company. The only break in their conversation had been when he had made his speech.

'I see Lily Sullivan has sunk her claws into Martin Clay now.' His mother crumbled the slice of wedding cake on her plate between her manicured, beringed fingers.

'They are bridesmaid and best man,' he reminded her pointedly.

'Then they aren't going out together?'

'If they are it's none of my business.' Joe took care to sound offhand, although it had hurt more than his pride when he had seen Martin bringing Lily home late one night shortly after she had broken off their engagement. He'd even risked rousing Helen's curiosity by asking her about their relationship. She'd told him it was just a casual date but the way Martin was looking at Lily now was anything but casual and he couldn't bear to see someone as special as Lily throw herself away on an uneducated boor like Martin Clay.

'Have you applied to schools for a teaching post, Joseph?'

'No,' he answered sharply. Too sharply, he realised, when Roy Williams, who was sitting on his mother's right, gave him a stern look. But then Roy didn't know how angry he was with Esme and not just because of his parents' impending divorce. Shortly after she'd left, he'd discovered John Griffiths wasn't his biological father and, as if that weren't enough, Esme had categorically refused to reveal the identity of the man who had fathered him.

'You'll be graduating in a couple of months. The best schools fill their vacancies quickly. If you don't apply soon . . .'

'I'm going to work for the BBC,' he said, cutting his mother short and rising from the table. Before the door swung shut behind him he heard Lily's laughter again. It sliced into him with a pain that was almost physical, stifling his breath and sending his heart pounding erratically against his ribcage.

Was she deliberately trying to hurt him? Did she want to make him suffer or . . . Or . . . That was it – it had to be. Why hadn't he realised before? It was obvious now he had thought of it. Lily was using Martin to make him jealous. She loved *him*. She had told him so many times when they were going out together that she loved *him* and only *him*. No man or woman could switch off the intense feelings they had for one another. Lily hadn't stopped loving him. She was simply trying to teach him a lesson. Well, two could play at that game . . .

No!

He'd wait – and patiently. He'd use the time to prove he was worthy of her. That he could take whatever punishment she chose to mete out stoically and uncomplainingly. He touched the ring in his pocket. It would eventually be back where it belonged, on her finger. In the meantime he would concentrate on his degree so he would be in a position to command the best possible salary that, together with the interest from his trust fund, would keep Lily in luxury, style and comfort, the elegance that the likes of Martin Clay could never aspire to – and which no girl in her right mind could possibly turn down.

'It wasn't easy for me to come here today,' Esme confessed to Roy, feeling the need to explain her presence.

'I shouldn't imagine it was,' he replied ambiguously.

'But a mother's place is with her daughter on the most important day of her life. Don't you agree?'

Roy nodded, although given John's and Joe's thinly veiled antagonism and Helen's refusal even to acknowledge her, he wondered why Esme had made the effort.

'Lily seems happy.' Esme leaned back as a waiter approached their table with a fresh bottle of wine. 'Is she going out with Martin Clay now?' she probed transparently.

'She and Martin have been friends since they were children,' Roy observed abruptly. He hadn't forgotten Esme's rage when she discovered that Joe had bought Lily an engagement ring.

'And Katie Clay looks happy with that policeman.'

'Sam Davies.' Roy looked across to the table Katie and Sam were sharing with Brian, Judy and a pale Adam Jordan. He smiled as Katie moved Brian's glass of wine closer to Sam so he could drop a plastic spider into it. 'Not that there's anything there either, Esme, they're just youngsters out for a good time.'

Esme frowned as Joseph returned. Instead of taking his seat opposite her and Roy as she'd expected, he pulled a spare chair between his father's and Helen's. As Helen made room for him, Esme glanced back to Katie's and Judy's table. The plastic spider was lying abandoned on the tablecloth and Brian, Sam and Adam were deep in conversation with Judy. Part of, yet separate from, the group, Katie sat with her elbows on the table, resting her chin on her hands and staring at Joseph with an expression of absolute love and devotion.

Incensed, Esme studied Katie until there was no doubt in her mind. The girl was clearly besotted; she had succeeded in extricating her son from one unfortunate entanglement, only to see him fall prey to another unsuitable girl. And with Jack moving into the house with Helen, it would give Katie an excuse to call at all hours of the day and night . . .

She turned back to Joseph. Apparently oblivious to Katie's loving look of adoration, he was engrossed in a discussion with John but that didn't mean he would remain immune to Katie's wiles. No matter how socially disastrous a relationship might be, few men – or in Joseph's case, boys – could resist the flattery and adulation of a young and, much as she hated to admit it, almost pretty girl.

Mousie, nondescript Katie Clay had blossomed. She had been a scrawny, runny-nosed, scruffy child in her hand-me-down clothes but since the death of her parents she had acquired a veneer of assurance and sophistication along with her salon-styled hair.

No doubt the secretarial job John had given her in the warehouse and the staff clothing discount helped. The fine wool russet costume she was wearing was the height of fashion without being showy, and the nipped waist and wide-shouldered cut of the jacket and voluminous folds of the skirt disguised her figure which, as far as she could tell from her wrists and ankles, was too skinny for beauty. The tan hat and matching veil brought out golden-brown highlights in her hair – strange that she had never noticed them before. Perhaps Katie'd had the highlights 'done'. Not that Joseph would notice if Katie's hair was dyed. Men only saw the effect, never the artifice. The problem was how to warn Joseph against Katie's intentions without infuriating him and driving him into not only ignoring her advice, but also Katie's arms.

Esme wasn't the only one watching Katie. John Griffiths had scarcely taken his eyes off her during the meal and realised that during the past few weeks she had transformed herself from the tongue-tied, insecure, badly dressed waif he had taken 'on trial' to replace his secretary. Smiling, confident, she looked happy and beautiful as she laughed and joked with Judy and the boys. He knew she had rejected Adam's advances but this was the first time he had seen her with her brothers' new flatmate.

Tall, with light-brown hair and grey eyes, Sam Davies was a good-looking young man, the perfect match for the new Katie and not only in looks. As a policeman he earned decent money and, according to Roy, had excellent career prospects. There was no denying they made a handsome couple. Just like Judy and Brian, Martin and Lily and – he glanced at Helen sitting beside him – his daughter and Jack. Not that this was the way he would have chosen to have her married, at eighteen and pregnant, but given the situation he'd seen little point in making another scene like the one Esme had engineered. He glanced across at his wife, noted the sour expression on her face and wondered if she enjoyed making him and her children miserable.

'We'll have to leave in ten minutes if we're going to catch the train, Helen.' Jack held out his hand to John as he rose from his chair. 'I can't begin to thank you for everything, Mr Griffiths. I only wish there was something I could do for you.'

'Just make Helen happy,' John answered gruffly, fighting the presentiment that the road lying before Jack and Helen was a rocky one as he shook his hand.

'If I don't, it won't be for lack of trying.'

John reached for his stick as he left his chair. 'I'll warn everyone you'll soon be off.'

'So they can throw more confetti.' Jack brushed a few paper petals from the top of Helen's hat.

'It's their way of making sure you won't be bored. It'll take you until London to pick it out of your hair.'

'Thank you, Daddy.'

As Helen gave him a hug that took his breath away, John realised she hadn't called him 'Daddy' since she was a small child. Without even a backward glance at her mother she left the room.

'You look every inch the perfect bride,' Judy reassured, as she secured Helen's hat with a pearl-headed pin.

'There's no straggly bits of hair?'

'Not a one.'

'The train won't wait, not even for a bride,' Martin shouted from the corridor.

'We know,' Judy called back.

Helen checked her reflection in the mirror. 'Thank you, Judy. All of you.' She hugged each of them in turn.

'Judy, Lily, hurry up.' Brian knocked on the door.

'The boys obviously don't know how to throw confetti without you,' Helen joked as Judy opened the door. Katie lingered, holding on to the door handle as if she couldn't decide whether to follow Judy and Lily, or stay with Helen.

'I've always wanted a sister.' Helen kissed her cheek.

'So have I.' Katie smiled.

'And isn't it great that we're already friends. We'll have to set aside one night a week for us to have a chat. Like every Friday or something.'

'And Jack?' Katie asked.

'We'll send him and Martin down the pub. It will be our sherry night.'

'I'd like that.' Katie opened her handbag and pulled out a packet of confetti. 'I'd better share this out.'

'Most of it goes over Jack, right?'

'I'll give it to Judy along with your instructions.'

'Our first sisterly secret.'

As Katie left, Helen picked up her gloves and handbag from the chair. The door opened again and she looked up to see her mother standing in the doorway.

'I hoped I'd catch you alone.'

'I'm on my way out.' Helen stood back, waiting for her mother to step aside.

'If there's anything you want to ask, or ever need advice . . .'

'You'd be the last person I'd go to,' Helen broke in resolutely.

'Helen . . .'

'I won't forget the things you said about Jack and me when we told you we were getting married.'

'I've apologised.'

'Saying sorry isn't enough.'

'You're going to need a mother in the coming months.'

'No more than I've needed one in the past and you were never around then. If you'll excuse me, the train won't wait.' Hoping her mother wouldn't notice she was shaking, Helen swept past and ran down the stairs. Esme went after her, but she hung back and watched from a distance as Jack helped Helen into the back of John's car, festooned with blue paper chains and a homemade *Just Married* sign.

Before climbing in, Helen embraced Lily, Katie and Judy with more warmth than she had ever shown towards her. The boys threw confetti again; then, to the rattle of tin cans that had been tied to the bumper, John drove up High Street towards the station.

'Take care of her.'

'I will, Mr Griffiths.' Jack shook his father-in-law's hand again. 'What's this?' He held up the bundle of notes John had pressed into it.

'Fun money. London's an expensive place. Don't go spending that on anything sensible. If you're tempted, give it to Helen. She knows how to waste it better than anyone.'

'I had hoped that could remain our secret, Dad.' Helen kissed her father's cheek. 'And thank you for a lovely wedding.'

'Enjoy yourselves.' He waved as Jack picked up their cases from Left Luggage and followed Helen on to the platform.

'Coach G.' Jack looked up and down the length of the train. 'There it is, straight ahead. You all right?'

'Now I'm away from my mother, brilliant.'

'Really?'

She beamed at him. 'The honeymoon starts here. Race you to our seats.'

'That's not fair, I'm carrying the cases.'

'And I'm carrying your son,' she shouted, not caring who was listening, 'but you don't hear me complaining.'

Esme returned to the private room to find it empty apart from a solitary waiter who was clearing plates and boxing leftover wedding cake. She collected her jacket and went to the Ladies Room to touch up her make-up and apply more scent. Confident she looked her best; she stood at a window that overlooked the street. A few minutes later John parked outside. She went downstairs to find him untying the tin cans.

'You saw them off.' The comment was superfluous but she felt the need to break the silence between them.

'As far as the gate to the platforms,' he replied tersely. 'Has everyone left?'

'They're in the lounge bar. I thought we could have a drink.'

'As soon as I've settled the bill I have to go to the warehouse.'

'Surely not on your daughter's wedding day.' She waited for him to answer and when he didn't, murmured, 'We don't have to stay here, John, we could . . .'

'I'm meeting new suppliers in half an hour.' Not wanting to remain with her a moment longer, John tossed the cans and *Just Married* sign into the boot of the car and limped as quickly as he could to the door, almost barging into Roy in the passageway outside the bar.

'Everyone seems to have adjourned downstairs, John.' Roy put his hand in his pocket. 'Can I buy you a drink?'

'Thanks, Roy, but not now. As soon as I've paid the bill I have to go into work.'

Roy looked from John to Esme who was watching every move John made. 'Tonight, then?'

'I'll be in the Rose. And thank you for coming.'

'My pleasure. Jack and Helen make a handsome couple. I hope they'll be very happy.'

'So do I,' John agreed fervently.

Roy tipped his hat. 'Esme.'

'Goodbye, Roy, and thank you.'

'Why did you thank Roy?' John asked after Roy had left, incensed that Esme had adopted the role of hostess after inviting herself to the wedding.

'Because he was kind and talked to me when everyone else ignored me.' She'd hoped to prick John's conscience but he remained unperturbed. 'We do have things to discuss . . .'

'We have nothing to discuss,' he interrupted, sensing a scene brewing and hoping to quash it. There was enough gossip in Swansea about their separation without Esme starting a quarrel in the doorway of the lounge bar of the Mackworth.

'The divorce . . .'

'I pay our solicitors handsomely to do the talking for both of us.'

'If we went over a few things it might lessen the bills,' she suggested in a sickly sweet voice.

'It's worth every penny to get things straight and watertight.'

'I don't want to be difficult . . .' She faltered as his mouth settled into a thin, hard line.

'Then don't.'

'You can't simply throw away twenty years of marriage, John.'

'What twenty years? We haven't lived as man and wife since Helen was born.'

Esme bit her lip; this wasn't going the way she'd intended at all. 'You know full well that was down to my health.'

'And now all of a sudden you've made a remarkable recovery.'

'What if I said I wanted to try again?' He'd reduced her to pleading and she hated him for it.

'I might have listened eighteen years ago, but not now, Esme.' Expecting her to walk out of the hotel, he stepped into the bar but she trailed behind him.

'How can you be so hard?'

'You were the one who walked out on me,' he reminded her.

'Only because you made it impossible for me to stay.'

As the area around the doorway was comparatively deserted, John crossed his arms, leaned against the wall and faced her head on. 'I rather think you did that when you began to spend your nights with other men,' he said quietly, hoping to embarrass her into leaving.

'The Little Theatre is very time-consuming, especially when you direct . . .'

'I'm not stupid, Esme.'

She eyed him coolly. 'No, you're not.'

'It will be easier if we see as little of one another as possible, given that we're about to become grandparents to the same child.'

'You mean it will be easier for you, John.'

'I can't say I'm enjoying this conversation.' He fell silent as a man and woman walked into the bar and glanced their way.

'And the children?'

'I've never stopped you from seeing them.'

'You don't exactly encourage them to contact me either,' she criticised.

'They're adults now, Esme, they make their own decisions.'

Katie looked up from the table where she was sitting with the others, saw John standing next to the door with Esme and assumed he was leaving. Making her apologies, she picked up her handbag and joined him. 'I'm ready to go to the warehouse whenever you are, Mr Griffiths. I only have to get my coat.'

'You're a good secretary but you're not indispensable, Katie.' Angered by Esme, John realised he'd sounded brusquer than he'd intended. 'I'll ask one of the supervisors to make notes during the meeting,' he added in a conciliatory tone. 'Go and enjoy yourself with the others.'

'I really don't mind.'

'Judy's only home for the weekend.'

Sensing she'd interrupted something, Katie looked from John to Esme. 'In that case, thank you, Mr Griffiths. I'll see you on Monday morning. Goodbye, Mrs Griffiths.' Turning, she rejoined the others.

Taking advantage of the interruption, John went to the door.

Laying her hand on his shoulder, Esme made one final, desperate attempt to put her plan into action. 'You're going, John. Just like that.'

'I told you I have to pay the bill; the manager's waiting. Shall I ask reception to call you a taxi?'

'I'll walk. I need to pick up a few things in Lewis's.' Dropping the veneer of politeness, she hissed, 'You really are an absolute bastard.'

'A moment ago you wanted to discuss reconciliation.'

'Only because a divorcee's position in this town is untenable. You have no idea what it has been like for me since I left Carlton Terrace. The only invitations I've received since I moved in with mother have been for charity coffee mornings and even at those, most of the women cut me dead. I've become a social pariah.'

'You have the Little Theatre.'

'I've been asked to resign from the committee.' Her hands shook as she pulled on her gloves. 'Once the women discovered we'd separated, they assumed I'd be after their husbands.'

'And you aren't.'

'That's cheap even for you.'

'Sorry, Esme,' he said wearily, 'but I can't help you. I never was a social animal.'

'I know, it's just that I thought if we could come to some arrangement . . .'

'The same arrangement we had for the last eighteen years where you go out with as many men as you choose, while I pay your bills and sit home at night with the children?'

If ever he'd needed evidence that she had never loved him, it was in her face at that moment. She didn't even attempt to conceal her contempt – or rage. 'You've seen to it that Helen has married beneath her. Don't think I'm going to do nothing while you let Katie Clay move in . . .'

'Katie,' he interrupted hoarsely, his mouth suddenly dry.

'You think I don't know what's going on?' She looked towards the table where Katie was sitting with Lily, Judy and the boys.

'She's my secretary and a damned good one.'

'But she intends to be a whole lot more.'

'You've an evil mind, Esme. I warn you, if you try to drag the name of an innocent girl through the mud, you'll be hearing from my solicitor.' Tired of her vicious tongue, her attempts to manipulate him, her contempt, but most of all her presence, he walked away.

Esme glanced around the bar as the door swung shut behind him. Katie, Lily and Judy were apparently engrossed in conversation with the boys. If they had overheard her argument with John they were tactfully ignoring it. There was no sign of Joseph. Feeling superfluous and unwanted, she pushed open the door of the hotel and walked out into the Saturday crowds thronging High Street.

* * *

'What do you want to see first in London?' Jack wrapped his arm round Helen's shoulders. They had the carriage to themselves but as they hadn't yet reached Cardiff to take on passengers from the capital, he intended to take full advantage of their privacy while he could.

'Harrods.' She snuggled close to him. 'You?'

'The Tower.'

'You're having me on.' She tried to read the expression on his face.

'I am not.'

'You're interested in history?'

'I am, especially the gory bits.' He linked his fingers with hers. 'A lot of people had their heads cut off in the Tower.'

'I think they've buried the bits by now.'

'In the Tower, or so I've read, and that means their ghosts could be walking around.'

'In daylight?'

'It's possible; ghosts have been seen at all hours of the day and night. Madame Tussaud's have a display of murderers. Martin went there on one of his leaves. He told me that they have a guillotine and an axe and execution block as well as mock-ups of prison cells.'

She shuddered. 'You go there, you go by yourself.'

'I didn't know you were squeamish.'

'And I didn't know you were a ghoul.'

Pulling the blind on the window to the corridor, he lifted her face to his with his fingertips and kissed her. 'There's a lot we don't know about one another. It's going to be fun finding out.'

'Someone could walk in,' she murmured, as his hand slid beneath her jacket.

He glanced at his watch. 'Another two and half hours before we get to London, I'm never going to hold out until then. You?'

'If we start our honeymoon in a railway carriage we'll get arrested.'

'Not necessarily.' He pulled her to her feet. Opening the blind, he looked up and down the corridor.

'What are you up to?'

Holding his finger to his lips, he slid back the door and led her to the end of the carriage. A man walked past them, turning his head to get a second look at Helen. Jack glared at him and he disappeared into a carriage. 'Quick.' Opening the door to the toilet, he pulled Helen in and locked it after them.

She looked into his eyes and they both burst out laughing. 'You'll get us thrown off the train,' she murmured as he slid her jacket over her arms and hung it on a hook on the back of the door.

'Not if we're quiet.' Undoing the buttons on her blouse, he pulled down her bra straps. 'God, you're beautiful.'

'I love you.' She slipped out of her skirt and hung it over her jacket.

'And I love you back, Mrs Clay. With every inch of my soul – and body.'

'Sea-green, sky-blue, rose-pink, lemon, whole sets and all in your size.' Katie gave the assistant a conspiratorial smile as she laid a bra, suspender belt and petticoat on the counter in front of Judy.

'It's an awful lot of money,' Judy murmured doubtfully.

'But they're quality and wash beautifully,' Lily said practically. 'And this is a lovely colour.'

'Sorry you bought the pink set now?' Judy asked.

'Not at all. I'm thinking of getting another in blue.'

'You're not serious.'

'Why not?' Lily looked around at the racks of frocks and blouses. 'I'm earning good money. It's time I splashed out on a few clothes, like a new dress for tonight.'

'Our afternoon and evening frocks are over there.' Katie indicated the back corner of the warehouse floor.

'"Our",' Judy teased.

'Our.' Katie repeated. 'I love working here and I'm proud of our stock.'

'I'll take the blue set, please.' Lily set them aside.

'I'll have them wrapped and ready for you to pick up at the cash desk, madam.' The assistant beamed at Katie as she folded them.

Judy hesitated, but only for a fraction of a second. 'And I'll take the green, please.'

'Miss Clay?' The assistant looked enquiringly at Katie.

'Maybe next week, Miss Evans.'

'Spoilsport,' Judy grumbled, as they walked over to the dresses. 'You brought us here; the least you can do is join us in our extravagances.'

'You haven't seen what I've bought since I started working here.'

'Katie has a fantastic wardrobe,' Lily complimented her. 'Why don't you dress for tonight in our house, Judy, then you can see it?'

'I'll call in for a few minutes but I have to go home. Brian's coming for tea.'

'And your mother'll be working.'

'It is just tea, Lily. Will you look at that rust and white polka dot. It's gorgeous and only forty-two shillings but I haven't any shoes that will match it.'

'Shoe department is behind you,' Katie advised.

'I won't have any money for rent if I carry on at this rate.'

'What do you think of this?' Lily held up a crimson shawl-collared cotton dress with a belted waist and wide skirt.

'Stunning, and the colour will look great on you. I wish I could wear red,' Judy answered wistfully.

'Don't tell me you still hate your hair.'

'Half the staff in the BBC call me "Ginger".'

'If you don't answer to it, they'll stop,' Lily counselled. 'Besides, your hair isn't ginger, it's . . .'

'Auburn.' Judy pulled a lock forward and examined it. 'I wish.'

Katie looked towards the glassed-in staircase that connected the floors of the warehouse and led to the offices. 'If you two are all right down here for a bit, I'll nip up and see Mr Griffiths.'

'I thought he gave you the day off.' Judy abandoned the polka dot in favour of a dark-green taffeta evening dress.

'He did, but he had an important meeting this afternoon and there may be notes to type up.'

'Surely they can wait until Monday.' Judy held the dress in front of her and considered the effect in a full-length mirror.

'Probably, but I'll just check.' Katie struggled to conceal her impatience. 'Anyway, by the look of things you two are going to be here for the next hour or two.'

'Where are the changing rooms?' Judy asked.

'Lily knows.' Katie headed for the staircase.

'Lock the door after me,' Jack whispered to Helen. 'Wait a couple of minutes, then leave.'

'It's going to take me at least fifteen minutes to dress and repair the damage to my make-up.' Throwing her arms round his neck, she stood on tiptoe and kissed him.

'Do that again and we'll be here until Paddington.'

'I can think of worse things.' She smiled brazenly as he caressed her naked body.

'And I can think of better.'

'For instance?'

'A comfortable double bed in a hotel room.' He rubbed his hands over her arms as she began to shiver. 'Did your Auntie Dot say anything about being able to eat meals in our room?'

'She just said it was owned by a friend of hers and a great place for a honeymoon. Seeing as how she's paying the first week's bill as a wedding present, I didn't like to ask any more, but' – she smiled mischievously as Jack gently disentangled himself from her and handed her the underclothes she'd stacked neatly on the shelf next to the sink '– I've a suspicion that if they do, we'll never get around to seeing any of the sights.'

'Depends on what you mean by sights.' He stroked her breast lightly with the back of his finger.

'You know what that does to me.' She shivered from more than cold.

'Yes.' He took her bra from her. 'And that's why I'll help you dress.'

'Tired?' She feigned innocence.

'Making sure you don't catch pneumonia. I want you fit and active.' He watched as she pulled on her panties, hooked her suspender belt and rolled her stockings over her legs. 'Pretty underwear,' he commented as she shook out her layered petticoat.

'I hoped you'd like it.'

'I do.' As soon as she had fastened her skirt and blouse, he opened the door and peeped out cautiously. 'See you in a few minutes.'

'I'm missing you already.'

'Katie, I told you not to come in.' John left his desk and walked into the outer office as she opened the door.

She dropped her gloves and handbag on to her desk. 'I'm here with Judy and Lily. They're buying up the warehouse.'

'That's good news for our cash flow.'

She glanced into her in-tray as she sat behind her desk. It was empty, just as she'd left it on Friday night. 'Did the meeting go well?'

'I think so. I've bought in some new lines of furniture; they'll be delivered next week but the paperwork can wait until Monday.' He sat on the edge of her desk. 'I'm glad you called. I want to talk to you.'

'And I want to talk to you.' She reached for his hand. 'I'm sorry if I interrupted something between you and Mrs Griffiths earlier . . .'

'Please, Katie.' He removed her hand and left the desk. Sitting in the visitor's chair, he tried to look anywhere but at her face, pale, concerned – and beautiful. 'Esme knows about us.'

'Knows . . .' She stared at him in bewilderment. 'How can she? We've been so careful . . .'

He hunched forward in his chair. 'Obviously not careful enough.'

'But it doesn't change anything between us. She would have had to know eventually . . .' She fell silent as she looked into his eyes. 'John . . .'

'Katie, you know I love you.'

'And I love you,' she broke in earnestly.

'You don't know Esme. How vicious she can be. She'll start gossip that will wreck your life.'

'I don't care. My life is nothing without you.'

'It isn't only us though, is it, love? There's Jack and Helen, Joe and Martin . . .'

'When you told Martin you wanted to marry me as soon as you were free, he understood and respected my choice, as I'm sure the others will, once they realise how much we mean to one another.'

'Martin didn't understand, Katie, he only said he would try. He was shocked, just as everyone else will be. Seeing Jack with Helen today – the way things should be for a girl of your age – made me realise how unfair I'm being in asking you to wait until my divorce is finalised.'

'Unfair? I don't understand.' Her eyes widened. 'Is the divorce going to take longer than you expected? Is that it, because if it is, I don't care how long we have to wait as long as we'll be together eventually.'

'Please, let me finish. I watched you with the others today. Helen and Jack, Brian and Judy, Martin and Lily, that's the way love should be. Between young people. I'm thirty-eight, crippled and soon to become a grandfather . . .'

'We've talked about that before, John. You know none of it matters, not to me.'

'But it does to me,' he said. 'You're eighteen. You should be going out with your friends, enjoying life, not waiting for a man more than twice your age to divorce his wife.'

'But I do go out with my friends. I'm going down the Pier with Lily and Judy tonight.'

'And young men will be chasing you.' He tried – and failed – to keep his voice light.

'No one will chase me because I won't let them, but I'll dance with some of the boys if they ask me. You know my nights out with Lily don't mean anything. But if you prefer me not to go . . .'

'I'm trying to tell you that you should go. And at the end of the evening you should walk home with one of those young boys, not come back alone thinking of an old fogey like me.'

'And if I want to come back alone, thinking of you?'

'It's not right, Katie. I feel as though I'm robbing you of your youth.'

'Don't you understand, I love *you*,' she stressed. 'You're everything to me . . .'

'And you to me.'

'How can you say you love me and talk like this? I want to be with you . . .'

'But you can't, not until the divorce is finalised and I'm free, and perhaps not even then. The gossips . . .'

'Let them tittle-tattle,' she said dismissively. 'My mother used to say they can't hurt you if you don't listen to them and she was right.'

John wondered what had made Esme suspicious. As Katie said, they had been careful. He also knew that her disregard of gossip was sincere. Her father's brutality towards his family had been a talking point in Swansea for years, and she had been taught from an early age to ignore what people said about her and her family, and she did just that. But he couldn't bear the thought of Esme saying things about the girl he loved more than any other person in the world; horrible, evil things that would blacken her character and cheapen a relationship that was everything to him. He could almost hear Esme whispering the words 'Gold-digging little tramp', 'Dirty old man' and he couldn't take that – not for himself, Joe, Helen – and especially Katie. He steeled himself.

'I won't have your name brought up in the divorce court. You've no idea how awful that would be.'

'I wouldn't care.'

'I want you to be free.'

'But I am free,' she insisted. 'Free to make up my own mind.'

'Not while we stay behind here a couple of evenings a week.'

Her voice dropped to a whisper. 'You don't want to make love to me any more.'

Concerned she'd read something in his eyes that he didn't want her to see, John left the chair and went to the window. An image came to mind of Katie and Sam, as they had been earlier, bending their heads so they almost touched, laughing together over the ridiculous plastic spider. He took a deep breath and forced himself to face her. 'I've been selfish but I can't go on feeling as though I'm stealing your youth. I want you to live your own life and grasp every opportunity that comes your way without having to think about me.'

'And if I don't agree?'

'This is the last time I'll see you — privately. I'm sorry if I've hurt you but I simply can't go on using you.'

'Is there anything I can say or do to change your mind?' She gazed intently at him.

'No.'

'Is this for ever' — even her voice trembled — 'or only until your divorce?'

'Who knows how you'll feel by then.'

'I know and nothing will have changed for me. I'll still love you.'

'We'll talk again then.'

'And in the meantime?'

'We'll see one another here.'

'But not like this.'

'Not alone like this, no, Katie. It wouldn't be fair on you.' He continued to face her. It would have been easier if she'd argued, ranted and raved, anything except stared at him through wounded, anguished eyes. 'But nothing will change here. I meant it when I said you're the best secretary I've ever had. We'll carry on working together. You will be here on Monday morning?' he asked, concerned by her silence.

'The girls will be waiting.'

'Katie . . .'

'I wish you'd change your mind.'

'I won't.'

She looked at him for a moment, then ran from the office.

Chapter 4

TEN MINUTES AFTER Katie left the office John walked out on to the staircase that connected the warehouse floors. He looked down and saw her standing outside the changing cubicles with Lily and Judy. Lily was wearing one of the dresses from the new spring range. Smiling, she flicked through the dresses Judy had chosen to try on as she chatted to Katie who had her back turned to him. He didn't need to see Katie's face to know she was miserable. He could sense the depth of her distress from the way her shoulders were hunched and it devastated him to know that he had caused it, but he had to free her so she would be safe from Esme's malicious tongue – and him. A beautiful young girl like her had no business being tied to an ugly cripple, twenty years older than her.

Katie believed she loved him but common sense told him it was only because he'd been the first man to show her kindness and he bitterly regretted allowing that kindness and her gratitude to lead to anything more. He should have remembered her vulnerability and the years between them. But there was no turning the clock back and undoing what had been done.

Katie might be unhappy now but she would soon forget him once she spent more time in the company of young, good-looking boys like Sam Davies. And Lily and Martin would see to it that she did. Better it should happen now, before she tied herself to him permanently. Because he wouldn't be able to bear seeing the same contempt for him on her face that Esme had shown him earlier. It was simply his bad luck that he had fallen as deeply in love with her as he had.

'I am not going in there.' Adam stood his ground on the pavement outside the White Rose.

'You'll disappoint your lady love.' Brian managed to keep a straight face, unlike Martin and Sam who both developed a sudden and avid interest in an office window across the road.

'I could thump the lot of you.'

'Why?' Brian asked innocently. 'We didn't tell you to make a pass at Lifebuoy Lettie.'

'You didn't stop me, either.'

'Come on, Adam, just one pint,' Martin coaxed, deciding the joke had gone far enough and the sooner they all sat down in a quiet corner of the pub, the sooner they could tell him the truth.

Turning on his heel, Adam strode up the road.

'Adam!' Martin shouted loud enough for everyone in Walter Road to hear, but Adam kept walking. 'We should go after him.'

'We won't manage a drink if we do,' Sam advised. 'It'll be stop tap in a quarter of an hour.'

'Let him stew until tonight, we'll tell him then.' Oiled by the four pints he had downed in the Mackworth, Brian beamed at them and the world in general.

'*We'll* tell him?' Martin queried.

'You two are chicken.'

'We have to live with him afterwards. You, on the other hand, are leaving for London tomorrow,' Sam opened the door of the pub.

'It'll cost you,' Brian cautioned.

'What?'

'A round of drinks.' Brian laid a hand on Sam's shoulder. 'And I'll have a packet of crisps as well. All this beer has given me a taste for the munchies.'

'You're very quiet, Katie,' Judy commented, as they walked home from the warehouse.

'Just tired,' Katie lied.

'Hard work, seeing a brother married.' Judy waved to Brian, Martin and Sam as they rounded the corner of Carlton Terrace.

'Someone's bought up half of Griffiths's warehouse.' Brian swayed as he noted the number of carrier bags emblazoned with the warehouse logo the girls were carrying.

'Shopping's more productive than propping up the bar of the Rose.' Judy had noticed the high spots of colour in Brian's cheeks and knew what they meant.

'We had a quick one after the wedding.'

'I'm surprised you had room for it after what you downed in the Mackworth.' She looked around. 'And you managed to lose Adam. Or is he collapsed in a drunken heap somewhere?'

'He didn't want join us,' Brian prevaricated.

'He looked like death warmed up at the reception. What did you do to him?' Judy persisted.

'Me, nothing.' Brian turned an innocent face to hers.

'Tea, everyone,' Martin offered, hoping to stave off a full-blown argument between Judy and Brian.

'Please,' Lily accepted. 'That way I'll be able to sneak up the basement stairs and avoid Mrs Lannon. Whenever I bring a bag in through the front door she thinks it's her duty to inspect the contents.'

'Your uncle's housekeeper is a dear old thing.' Sam pulled his keys from his trouser pocket.

'Not when you have to live with her.' Whichever part of the house Lily was in, even the basement the boys rented from her uncle, she suspected Mrs Lannon of crouching behind the door and eavesdropping on her conversations. Not only because the housekeeper was always hovering close by whenever she left a room, but also because the woman seemed to have an exhaustive knowledge of how she spent every minute of her free time.

'I can't stay.' Judy took a bag from Katie that she'd carried for her. 'I promised my mother I'd go through the clothes I left in my room when I went up to London.'

'Do it tomorrow,' Brian suggested.

'When? I'd like a lie-in and we're catching the two-thirty train. You'll be round for tea at five.'

'Not five minutes to.'

Accustomed to Brian's sense of humour, Judy didn't smile. 'Arrive when you like but you'll be on the doorstep until five.'

'You know how to keep a man in his place,' Sam quipped.

Ignoring Sam, Brian leaned forward and kissed Judy's cheek before following the others down the steps and into the basement. Martin had already set the kettle on to boil and Sam produced a box of biscuits. Lily stacked her bags in the passage ready to take them upstairs and Katie, who liked to make herself useful every time she visited her brothers, pulled out the mending basket.

'So, we all going to the Pier tonight?' Helping himself to a biscuit, Brian sat next to Lily.

'Where else?' she asked.

'Can I have a dance, or do you save them all for Martin now?'

Lily glanced at Martin, who averted his eyes. 'Martin and I are just friends, Brian.'

'So were Jack and Helen. It's weird to think they're married. I wonder who'll be next.'

'Not you and Judy if your arguments are anything to go by.' Sam retrieved the biscuit box from Brian and passed it round.

'That's all you know. The best marriages are the lively ones,' Brian pronounced decisively.

'I'd say fierce was a more suitable word than lively to describe Judy's attitude towards you.'

'That's because you don't understand women. They only insult men they are crazy about.' Brian looked at Katie. 'You're quiet.'

'It's been a long day.' She kept her head down as she concentrated on weaving strands of wool over the mushroom she'd placed under a hole in the heel of one of Martin's socks.

'But you are going to the Pier tonight.'

'I'm not sure.'

'Come on, Katie,' Lily cajoled. 'We can have a lie-in tomorrow. You can catch up on your sleep then.'

'Besides, I need someone to teach me to dance.' Sam stretched his long legs in Katie's direction and drummed his heels on the floor.

'I don't know how.'

'You can't fool me. I saw you jiving with Jack's friend from the building site last Saturday night. Say you'll come. Please, for me.' Sam bent his head, peering up at her with such a peculiar, pleading expression that Katie smiled despite the pain that gnawed inside her.

'I'll think about it,' she hedged.

'You'll feel more like going out after we've put our feet up for an hour.' Lily kicked off her new shoes and wriggled her toes. She hadn't realised how much they pinched until she'd taken them off.

'All I've done today is keep Jack calm, hand over a ring and make a speech, but I feel as though I've climbed Mount Everest twice over.' Martin poured the tea.

'Weddings take it out of you.'

'You sound as though you've had a dozen, Brian.'

'My family's pretty big. I've been to plenty and they're all the same after the bride and groom leave for the honeymoon. Flat.'

'Perhaps it's envy.' Lily blushed as Brian and Sam burst out laughing. 'I mean Jack and Helen going to London,' she amended hastily, as she realised how her comment could be misconstrued. 'Seeing the sights, going to theatres, eating in restaurants . . .'

'Lucky them, two whole weeks with nothing to do but have fun,' Brian moaned.

'You live in London.' Martin pulled up a chair and joined them at the table.

'I saw more sights on one weekend leave when I was doing National Service than in the month I've lived there.'

'And whose fault is that?' Martin asked.

'You try working shifts and see how much time it leaves you during normal opening hours. And even when I get an afternoon or evening off, Judy's usually working and it's no fun seeing sights by yourself.'

'She said she was fed up,' Lily concurred.

'She did?' The biscuit Brian had been dunking in his tea dissolved, bloating out on the surface like a mushroom.

Too late Lily remembered Judy's warning that she hadn't told Brian how she felt about living in London. 'It was only something she mentioned in passing.'

'Exactly what did she say?' Brian's voice was soft – ominously so.

'What you just said, that she works long hours and most afternoons and evenings.' The more Lily attempted to cover her embarrassment, the more she sensed she was arousing Brian's suspicions but the words kept tumbling out. 'That because she's the most junior person in the make-up department she gets the blame for everything that goes wrong and none of the praise . . .'

'She hasn't said a word to me,' Brian interrupted testily.

'Perhaps she didn't think it was important. You've only been there a month, hardly had time to settle in.'

'That makes sense,' Martin came to Lily's rescue.

'I suppose so.'

Something in Brian's tone told Lily he wasn't convinced. Looking for an excuse to leave, she finished her tea and carried her cup to the sink. 'I'd better hang my new clothes away before they crease.'

'Pick you up at half past seven.' Martin helped her gather her bags.

'I'll be ready.' Lily looked to Katie. 'You coming?'

'After I've finished the mending.'

'You don't have to do it today of all days,' Martin chided.

'I may as well. I've nothing better to do.'

Martin looked at Lily. They both knew something had upset Katie. But neither of them could think what.

* * *

Brian went up to the attic bedroom that Roy had generously insisted he occupy for the weekend because Sam had rented his old room in the basement. Taking a clean shirt, he washed and changed in the bathroom but no matter how he tried to concentrate on other things, he couldn't stop thinking about what Lily had said. The more he considered it, the more he realised Judy had been distant the last couple of times he'd taken her out in London. She had also been sharper with him since they had travelled down together on Friday night but he'd made allowances for her apparent hostility, putting her edginess down to the strain of returning home for the first time since moving away.

After giving his shoes a quick brush, he ran down the stairs, out through the front door and along the street to Judy's house. It was ten minutes to five, but she opened the door at his first knock.

'I'm early.'

'I'll forgive you.' She ushered him into the hall. 'Tea's ready.'

'And in the parlour.' He glanced round the door to see a white damask cloth on her mother's best rosewood table and two plates of sandwiches and one of cakes. 'To what do I owe the honour?'

'You are a guest.'

'I was hoping I was closer than that.' He walked into the room and saw a pile of estate-agents' brochures on one of the chairs.

'Excuse the mess.' Judy picked them up and was about to push them under a cushion when he took them from her.

He flicked through them – they all detailed commercial premises. 'Your mother is moving the salon?'

'Thinking of opening another one.'

'Business must be good.'

'It is,' she answered abruptly, retrieving the brochures. 'Sit down. I'll make the tea. And in case you're wondering, this isn't all we're having. I made a trifle specially last night.'

Unimpressed by the promise of trifle, he remained on his feet. 'Who's going to run the second business for her, Judy?'

Unable to meet his penetrating gaze, Judy picked up the teapot from the table. 'She'll oversee both salons.'

'There's no way one hairdresser can run two salons. Who is going to run the second business?' The question hung unanswered between them for an eternity before he broke the silence. 'You're coming back to Swansea, aren't you?'

'Nothing's been decided.' She replaced the teapot on the table and sank down on a chair.

'You appear to have discussed your plans with everyone except me.'

'Just because there are a few estate agents' brochures . . .'

'It's not just the brochures,' he interrupted angrily. 'Lily let slip that you weren't happy in London.'

'She had no right . . .'

'She didn't do it deliberately,' he countered, refusing to get sidetracked into an argument about Lily. 'She probably assumed that as I was your boyfriend you'd talked about it to me.' He looked at her hard for a full minute. 'For pity's sake, Judy, I thought we had something going for us. When I asked you to marry me and you refused because you needed more time, I agreed. Going to London was your idea not mine. It was me who followed you up there, not the other way round. And now I discover that you couldn't even bring yourself to tell me that you're miserable up there and making plans to come back!'

'I told you I don't like the job, I hardly ever see you . . .'

'There's a world of difference between saying you're unhappy at work and making full-blown plans to return to your mother's apron strings.'

'That's unfair.' Unable to meet his penetrating gaze, she stared down at the carpet.

'Is it?'

'I told you, nothing's been decided.'

'Of course not.' He hit the brochures in her hand. 'That's why your mother went to all the trouble of getting these.'

'She's only looking.'

'I've been a complete fool. I didn't even see what was under my nose. I asked if you were carrying bricks when I lifted your case on and off the train. It weighed ten times as much as mine and I still didn't get it. When you packed to come back this weekend, did you leave anything in your room in the hostel? Did you?' he repeated furiously, when she refused to look at him.

'My room in the hostel isn't secure,' she murmured in a small voice.

'So you're not returning with me tomorrow.'

'I told you, nothing's been decided.'

'Seems to me you've decided too damn much.'

'Where are you going?' she asked, alarmed as he opened the door to the porch.

'Back to London tomorrow.'

'Brian, please.' She slipped between him and the door, kicking it shut with the heel of her shoe. For the first time since he had taken the brochures from her, she looked him straight in the eye. 'We need to talk about this.'

'Too bloody right. I'd say a couple of weeks ago would have been a good time.' Lifting her by the shoulders, he moved her aside.

She laid a hand on his elbow, hoping to waylay him. 'I care for you.'

'Funny way you have of showing it.'

'But coming back here this weekend, seeing my mother and the girls, made me realise how much I miss them. It's different for you . . .'

'How?' he enquired frostily.

'You love your job. You've made friends in the Met. Outside of you I have no one and I hardly ever see you . . .' Incensed by her own weakness she fought back tears. She had always despised women who resorted to crying to gain sympathy.

'You should have told me.'

'I didn't want to spoil things for you. You seemed so happy, so full of work plans and talk of promotion . . .' As her tears finally fell, Brian handed her his handkerchief.

She blew her nose and looked up at him. 'Please, Brian . . .' Choking on her sobs, she buried her face in her hands.

Opening his arms he held her tight, pulling her head down on to his chest.

'I'm sorry,' she whispered. 'I should have talked to you about how I felt and now I've got mascara all over your shirt.'

'You can wash it.'

'I will,' she replied seriously, looking through the door to the tea table. 'I wanted this to be special, just the two of us. I thought we'd have time to talk this weekend but the train was so crowded we couldn't even sit together on the way down and since then you've spent all your time with Martin and the boys . . .'

'Just as you've spent yours with Lily and the girls.'

'That wasn't a criticism, just a statement of fact.'

'So now what?' His mind raced as he stood back and looked at her. He'd had many girlfriends but none had made him feel the way Judy did and he didn't even want to think about how much he'd miss her if she left London – and him – for good.

'I'll talk to my mother and go back with you tomorrow.'

'Don't go for my sake,' he snapped, allowing his damaged pride to show.

'Lily's right, I haven't given London a chance,' she conceded, in an attempt to diffuse his anger. 'A month's no time and perhaps if I made more of an effort I'd make friends. Then I wouldn't be so reliant on you.'

'And that would make a difference?'

'No couple can depend solely on one another for company. Not when they work the hours we do.' She looked up at him. 'I will try harder, Brian.'

'And if it doesn't work out?'

'You'll be the first to know if I do decide to come back.'

He gripped her hand. 'Promise.'

'I promise,' she reiterated solemnly. 'Shall we eat now?'

He hesitated for a fraction of a second. 'It would be a pity to waste all that food.'

'Then I'll make some tea.'

'Your auntie said you were on honeymoon, so I thought you'd like some privacy.' The manageress of the small hotel Dot had recommended led Jack and Helen up the stairs to the third floor. 'There's only two rooms on this floor and one bathroom, but no one has booked into the other room for the next two weeks and we're not expecting anyone. It's a small single, so it tends to be the last to go, and it is very early in the season. I hope you'll be comfortable.' She opened the door on a double bedroom furnished with two easy and two upright chairs, a table, dressing table, wardrobe, bedside cabinets and the largest double bed Jack had ever seen.

'It's lovely.' Helen looked around. 'Wine and fruit and flowers, are they for us?'

'The fruit and wine are from Mrs Green, the flowers are on the house.'

'Thank you.' Helen smiled.

'It's nice to have some young people around. Most of our guests are commercial travellers. Breakfast is from seven until nine. We don't do any other meals, but there are several restaurants in the area.

There's a very reasonable Italian on the corner that opens every lunchtime and from six to ten o'clock at night.'

'Thank you.' Jack dropped the suitcases in front of the wardrobe. 'You've been very kind.'

'If you want anything, extra soap, towels, just ring.'

'We will.'

'Enjoy your stay.' The housekeeper suppressed a smile as she closed the door on them. Jack waited until he heard her step on the stairs before sweeping Helen into his arms and pulling her down on the bed.

'Comfortable enough for you?' she asked.

'I'll tell you in five minutes.' He pulled off his tie and tossed his jacket on to one of the chairs.

'You're insatiable.'

'Yes.' He kissed her.

'What about food?' she asked as she came up for air.

'You hungry?'

'I will be afterwards.'

He glanced at his watch. 'Then let's hope that Italian place is as good as the manageress says it is.' He pulled his shirt over his head, slipped off his trousers and underpants, and climbed between the sheets.

Opening the suitcase she removed a long flowing white nylon negligee set. 'I won't be a minute.' When she came back he was sitting up in bed reading.

'Very nice.' He watched as she twirled around and slipped the negligee from her shoulders to reveal a white silk nightdress with plunging back and neckline.

'You brought a book on your honeymoon,' she complained. 'That's not very flattering.'

'It's a book the doctor recommended.' Closing it, he put it on the bedside table.

'You're ill.'

'I asked him about us, if we could hurt the baby, by making love.'

'He's too well protected.'

'You know?'

'I asked him when I went to get the results of the pregnancy test.' She picked up the book and thumbed through the pages. 'Jack this is . . .' Her voice tailed off as she flicked from one image to another.

'Well illustrated. The doctor said it was a sort of handbook on how married couples can make one another happy.'

Shocked, she closed the book and returned it to his bedside table. 'You already do that.'

He turned back the bedclothes. 'I'll do a whole lot more if you take that off and climb in here beside me.'

'Wow! Scarlet woman!' Brian exclaimed, coming up from the basement, as Lily walked down the stairs in her new frock.

'Thank you, kind sir.' When Lily had checked in her bedroom mirror earlier she could scarcely believe she was looking at herself. The crimson dress complemented her black hair, emphasised her slender waist and lent a glow to her cheeks and lips that made her feel positively glamorous for the first time in her life.

'Not a word for us.' Judy left the lounge and twirled in front of Brian in the brown satin polka dot dress she had finally settled on in the warehouse. With short, elasticised sleeves that could be pushed off the shoulder, it was the most daring evening frock she had ever owned.

'Me first. Note, clean shirt.' He flipped back his jacket and showed off a mascara-free shirt-front. 'And triple wow. Both you and Katie look stunning,' he told them sincerely, as Katie followed Judy in a short-sleeved, plain white cotton blouse and tightly belted, wide, pale-blue cotton skirt. Compared with Lily and Judy, she was 'dressed down' but somehow the plain clothes added attraction to her sweet features and enormous brown eyes. He caught himself giving her a second glance and quickly smiled at Judy lest she notice and get the wrong idea.

'Thank you.'

Katie spoke so quietly that Brian couldn't be sure he'd heard her. He looked enquiringly at Judy. She shook her head, warning him off, as the doorbell rang.

Lily opened the door.

Martin stood on the step in the new suit he had bought for the wedding wearing a clean white shirt and a blue tie she had given him. 'You look fantastic. That is a smashing dress.'

'That deserves a kiss.'

'Not in broad daylight.' Aware of Joe Griffiths watching them from his doorstep, Martin tried to avoid her.

'You're a prude.' Oblivious to Joe's presence, Lily grabbed the lapels of Martin's suit and planted a kiss on his cheek.

'Hello, Lily . . . Martin,' Joe called out in a deadpan tone.

Martin nodded a reply but to his annoyance Lily gave Joe a broad smile.

'Hello, Joe. Sorry, didn't see you there. It was a lovely wedding, wasn't it.'

'Considering it was Helen's, everything went relatively smoothly.' Joe locked his front door and went to his father's car, which was parked in front of the house.

'You coming in?' Lily asked Martin.

'Not if we're catching the eight-o'clock train.'

'I only have to get my coat and handbag.'

'Sam and Adam coming?' Brian offered Martin a cigarette as he walked into the porch.

'Sam's giving Adam a shout now.'

'He's recovered?' Judy asked.

'From what?' Martin enquired, puzzled by Judy's question.

'Whatever Brian fed him last night.'

'There were five of us last night and you have to blame me.' Brian helped Judy on with her coat.

'Only because I know what you're like.' Judy tempered her sharp words with a smile.

'Charming. My girl friend doesn't trust me.'

'If we're going to catch the eight-o'clock train, we ought to be going.' Katie lifted her coat from the stand and walked on ahead.

'What's up with Katie?' Martin whispered to Lily as she stopped to lock the door.

'I have no idea. She seemed fine this morning and all through the wedding. I tried to talk to her when we were getting ready, but you know Katie. It's impossible to get anything out of her unless she's ready to tell you.'

'I'll give it a go.'

'If I were you, I'd wait until she comes to you.'

'Knowing her, she'll just let whatever it is fester.' As they stopped at the corner and waited for Sam and Adam to catch up with them, Martin glanced at his sister who was standing silently next to Judy and Brian. Katie couldn't have chipped a word in edgewise between those two, even if she'd wanted to. But she showed no inclination to join him and Lily.

'You can't push people into talking when they don't want to, Marty,' Lily murmured.

'If I'd pushed Jack at times I might have stopped him from thieving and going to Borstal and, maybe, having to get married at eighteen.'

'You wouldn't have stopped him from seeing Helen,' she said lightly. 'Wild horses wouldn't have kept those two apart.'

'Perhaps not,' he granted, 'but if I'd given him a good talking-to when I came back from the army . . .'

'He wouldn't have listened. Not then. And you're forgetting Helen is every bit as wild as Jack and just as crazy about him as he is about her. Besides, all things considered it's turned out well. He's calmed down since you came back and that has to be down to you. And look where he is now, on honeymoon in London with a wife who adores him and a lovely home and a job with prospects to come back to.'

He offered her his arm, closing his hand round her gloved fingers as she hooked her hand into the crook of his elbow. 'You're brilliant at making people feel good about themselves.'

'You're so hard on yourself it only takes a couple of compliments – no, that's not the right word – home truths to make you realise you can't hold yourself responsible for the ills of the entire world.'

'You're quite something, Lily Sullivan.' He wondered, yet again, why she was with him, not someone with more education, money and better prospects, like Joe Griffiths.

'You two going to stand there spooning all night, or make a move towards the Mumbles train?' Adam demanded.

Martin looked up. While he and Lily had been talking, the others had walked on ahead and were standing on the corner of Verandah and Mansel Streets. 'We're with you.' Taking Lily's hand, he raced down to join them.

'You remember what happened the last time we went to the Pier Ballroom,' Robin Watkin Morgan reminded Joe, as they sat drinking beer with whisky chasers in the saloon bar of the Mermaid Hotel in Mumbles.

'Larry Murton Davies made an idiot of himself.'

'And made us look like idiots because we were with him.'

'Seeing as how he's in Italy now, he can't make either himself or us look like fools tonight.'

'Which makes you all the more determined to carry on where he left off.'

'You're being ridiculous,' Joe retorted irritably.

'You've done nothing but talk about Lily Sullivan since she gave you back your engagement ring.'

'She couldn't give it back to me because I didn't give it to her in the first place.'

'No need to be so bloody pedantic.'

'You were at the engagement party, you saw . . .'

'Your intended fiancée's real mother crawl out of the gutter she touts in, gatecrash and put an end to the proceedings,' Robin interrupted, hoping to avoid yet another exhaustive post-mortem on the event from Joe. 'You had a narrow escape, the only problem is you can't see it.'

'I refuse to stand by and watch a girl like Lily throw herself away on a lout.'

'Martin Clay is your brother-in-law, as of this afternoon.'

'The brother of my brother-in-law and that doesn't make him any less of a lout.'

Robin reined in his exasperation. He and Joe had met as Freshers at Swansea University almost three years before. And apart from an overdeveloped sense of romanticism and a puritanical bourgeois attitude to sex, Joe had proved a good and loyal friend. It was Joe's coaching that had enabled him to pass examinations with grades beyond his own capabilities and Joe had already been offered a position at the BBC on graduation, an organisation he burned to work for. Given Joe's extraordinary talents, he had no doubt his friend would rise high and hopefully take him some of the way with him. Which was why he was sitting drinking with him, instead of savouring the delights of a town-centre pub crawl with the rest of their group who had failed to persuade Joe to join them.

'Consider what you've just said,' he suggested patiently. 'You know as well as I do what most people will think when you say "a girl like Lily". And before you start on another of your tirades, remember I saw her mother – and in her working clothes. A Tiller girl wears more on stage and the woman who would be your mother-in-law if you persist in going after Lily didn't have a body any man in his right mind would want to look at. Why can't you see you're well rid of the girl?'

'Because I love her.'

'How can you, when her mother trawls the docks every night offering herself to any man with a couple of shillings in his pocket and

67

a stomach strong enough to face getting close to her for however long it takes.'

'Lily didn't even know she was related to the woman until she turned up at the party. You can't hold her responsible for someone who abandoned her . . .'

'Blood's thicker than water. As my father says to his patients, it's all in the genes. Hair colouring, eye colouring – character . . .'

'Rubbish!' Joe pronounced tersely, thinking of himself and his unknown father as much as Lily. If Robin was right, what had he inherited from the man who had walked away from his eighteen-year-old mother when she was carrying his bastard? A yellow streak of cowardice? His height? His dark hair? God forbid, his talent for writing. He wanted that to be his and his alone, not owed to some stranger who had abandoned him. He finished his pint and downed his whisky in one swallow. 'Same again?'

'Ever known me refuse?' Robin followed Joe to the bar. 'This fixation of yours for Lily Sullivan . . .'

'I told you . . .'

'You love her,' Robin chanted sceptically. 'I don't buy this one woman/one man claptrap; that's for poets and schoolgirls who've overdosed on Tennyson and Byron. There's any number of women out there who'd suit you as well, if not better, if you'd give them a chance. I'll grant you Lily's not bad looking but I've seen prettier and she hasn't one tenth of the class of Emily . . .'

'If by class you mean the money to swan off to Paris to blow a year's average wages on a shopping trip, you're right.' Joe referred to the holiday Robin's girlfriend Emily and his sister Angela were taking with half a dozen of their wealthier girlfriends.

'It's not just money,' Robin unconsciously reiterated his mother's opinion. 'It's knowing how to say the right things. How to cultivate people who matter; how to dress, how to behave . . .'

'Lily behaves a bloody sight better than Emily,' Joe defended warmly. 'She wouldn't jump into bed with a man after two dates, as Emily did with you.' Suddenly aware of people staring, he signalled to the barman. 'Two pints and two whiskies,' he ordered abruptly, resenting the grin on the man's face.

'Perhaps if you had taken her to bed, you'd have recovered from what happened at the party and got over her by now,' Robin replied, refusing to get embarrassed or angry.

'You make Lily sound like a disease.'

'The way you're carrying on about her I'm beginning to wonder. You know she's seeing Martin Clay. She could be sleeping with him . . .'

From the savage look Joe gave him, Robin wondered afterwards if he would have punched him if it hadn't been for the barman's interruption.

'Two pints, two whiskies, sir, that will be five shillings and sixpence.' The barman eyed Joe as he took his money. 'You two gentlemen all right?'

'Quite,' Joe answered brusquely.

'We don't want any trouble.'

'And there won't be any.' Taking his drinks, Joe returned to their table.

Aware the barman was watching them, Robin smiled. 'What are your pickled eggs like?'

'We don't serve bar snacks, sir. If you are hungry, may I recommend our upstairs restaurant?'

'Thank you for reminding me.' Taking his drinks, Robin carried them over to the table where Joe was sitting.

'Lily's only going out with Martin Clay to make me jealous,' Joe snapped pre-emptively as Robin pulled out a chair.

'She told you?'

'All through the wedding reception she watched me while she flirted with him. And it was the same tonight when Martin went to pick her up to take her to the Pier. She knew I was getting into the car, so she kept him on the doorstep to make sure I saw her kissing him. But she only kissed him on the cheek.'

'But you haven't spoken to her.'

'I don't have to speak to her to know what she's thinking. We were – are –' he corrected, 'that close. There's no need for words between us. I only have to look into her eyes to feel what she feels . . .'

'She is your "*ever fixed mark – the star to every wandring bark.*"'

'Mock all you like. I deserve it for expecting a *Beano*-and-*Dandy*-reading moron who is incapable of seeing further than the physical, to understand true emotion – or the poetry of the soul.'

'It is just as well some of us live in the real world.' Robin sipped his beer. 'Man cannot live by romance alone.'

'Your idea of romance is a tumble between the sheets so Emily can scratch your itch, as you down a decanter of your father's whisky.'

'Pity you haven't allowed a girl to scratch your itch. You're proof of the theory that if you don't get enough you go mad. And there's my sister pining . . .'

'I don't love Angela.'

'You don't have to love a girl to go to bed with her.' Robin suddenly felt as though he were talking to a small child, not a contemporary.

'I do.'

'There is such a thing as sex for sex's sake. It's good healthy exercise and more fun than a cross-country run.' Robin looked closely at Joe and realised that some time in the last couple of months his friend had lost weight. His face was leaner, his dark eyes sunk in purplish-black shadows that gave him a slightly crazed appearance. Perhaps he'd hit closer to the truth than he'd realised when he'd mentioned madness.

'I'm not like you, Robin.' As the passion that had sustained Joe during their argument subsided, his voice softened.

'I never thought you were.'

'Don't you see, if I don't go to the Pier, Lily may think I've lost interest in her. She knows I overheard her and the others making plans to go there tonight. And she's with Martin; if he's anything like his brother Jack . . .'

'He'll have the knickers off the gorgeous Lily before you manage to get your leg over.' Waiting for Joe to bite back, Robin drank half his whisky.

'Why do you always have to bring everything down to a crude level?'

'Because life is crude.'

'I'll go to the Pier on my own.'

'No you won't. In your state of mind you need someone with you to stop you from making a complete ass of yourself. And who knows, another couple of these' – Robin finished the other half of his whisky – 'might mellow you enough to see sense. God knows why, but my sister's still keen on you. She'll be back from Paris on Thursday and although she is my sister, I still say Angela's a better prospect for you than Lily.'

Chapter 5

AS THE WAITER helped her off with her coat, Helen studied the decor of the Italian restaurant the hotel manageress had recommended. It was smaller and far less grand than the upstairs dining room of the Mermaid Hotel in Mumbles and positively downmarket compared with the Mackworth Hotel in High Street. The walls were whitewashed; the tables and chairs simply made from planks of dark wood and the tablecloths and napkins a cheerful red gingham that suggested a country kitchen rather than the impersonal elegance she'd expected to find in a London establishment.

Her father had made a point of taking her and Joe out to eat at least once a week since he'd considered them old enough to sit at an adult table. As a result she'd never felt intimidated in even the grandest of the hotels her grandmother patronised and invited her and Joe to dine in on family state occasions. But she sensed from the look on Jack's face as he handed the waiter his coat that he was ill at ease.

'Will this suit, sir?' The waiter ushered them to a table for two, set in a corner next to the window. As Jack looked to her for confirmation, she gave him a reassuring smile.

'It will do fine.' She continued to smile at Jack as the waiter pulled out a chair for her, lit the candles on their table and shook her napkin over her lap.

'Would you like to see the wine list, sir?'

Helen reached for Jack's hand across the table. 'I'd love a lemonade, darling.'

'Do you have beer?' Jack asked tentatively, as the waiter flourished the wine list in front of him. The only places he'd ever eaten out in had been the Italian cafés of the egg, beans and chips variety in Swansea. This place with its black-suited, fawning waiters, elaborately printed menus and wine cellar was completely beyond his experience.

'We have Guinness and Worthington, sir.'

'My wife will have a lemonade and I'll have a pint of Worthington please.' Jack tried to look as though he ate out every day of the week as he took the menu the man handed him.

'The manageress of the hotel was right, the prices here aren't too bad.' Helen scanned the card as the waiter went to get their drinks.

'The set dinner is three and sixpence. You can get sausage, eggs, beans and chips in the café by the bus station for one and six.'

'But not tablecloths and waiters.' She set the menu aside. 'And this is our honeymoon.'

Jack ran his finger round the inside of his collar. It suddenly seemed too tight and the restaurant too warm for his liking. 'What are you going to have?'

'Tomato soup, lamb Italian style, and Italian ice cream, a large one with raspberry sauce. You?'

'What's lamb Italian style?'

'I have no idea,' she confessed lightly.

'It could be horrible.'

'And it could be wonderful. I won't know either way until I try it.'

He stared down at the bewildering array of cutlery in front of him. His mother never had money enough to set more than one course on the table while he'd been growing up and generally there hadn't been enough of that to satisfy his, Martin's and Katie's appetites.

'I'm starving.' Helen squeezed his hand as the waiter arrived with their drinks. 'Besides,' she whispered into his ear so the waiter couldn't hear, 'I'll need to keep up my strength if your performance today is an indication of what the rest of our honeymoon is going to be like.'

Drawing confidence from her composure in these strange surroundings, Jack looked the waiter in the eye as he gave him Helen's order and, after a moment's hesitation, asked him to bring everything for two.

'I thought you didn't want to risk the lamb.' Helen stirred her lemonade, sending the slice of lemon and ice cubes swirling around the tall glass.

'I can't have the waiter thinking my wife is braver than me.' He sipped his Worthington. It was colder than any beer he'd drunk before.

'It is only a restaurant.'

'My experience of restaurants is standing outside and reading the menu, and as I could never afford more than a plate of bread and butter in one, the café always seemed to be a better bet.'

'The way you work in the warehouse you won't ever have to count the pennies again.'

'We won't be able to eat out very often,' he warned.

'It could be our treat, say once a month.'

'And when the baby is born?'

'I'll want to stay in and look after him – and you – until he's old enough to join us.' Resting her chin on her hand, she gazed at him. 'This is wonderful. Us, eating out alone in London, with fourteen whole days to do exactly as we please ahead of us.'

'And where do you want to go tomorrow?'

'The Tower.'

'And if it's on the way, back to the hotel via Harrods.' He returned her smile.

'Admit it, you're as curious about the place as I am.'

'Worried more than curious. Their prices are supposed to be out of this world.'

'I promise not to spend more than . . . five shillings? How's that?'

'And what do you intend to buy for five shillings?'

She felt his hand fumbling for hers beneath the cover of the tablecloth. 'A tie for my husband.'

'What's wrong with the one I'm wearing?'

'You don't know?'

He shook his head.

'That's exactly why I need to buy you a new one. To start developing your taste.'

'Are you trying to change me already, Mrs Clay?' he asked seriously.

'And if I am?' Her blue eyes glittered in the candlelight.

'I'd expect a reward for submitting to your bullying.' He leaned back as the waiter brought their soup, along with a basket of small brown bread rolls.

'Perhaps I'll give you one when we get back to the hotel.'

'If it's anything like the reward you gave me when we arrived, you can make that extravagance ten shillings.'

'I'll hold you to that.'

He watched her take a bread roll and set it on her side plate before picking up her spoon. After carefully taking note of where she'd lifted it from, he followed suit.

'Don't take this the wrong way, but what would you do, if I did give up my job in London and come back to Swansea?' Judy asked, as Brian slid a tray of drinks on to their table and handed her a bottle of Babycham and an empty glass holding a cocktail cherry speared on a toothpick.

'What wrong way is there to take it?' He moved his chair, sat down and pretended to study the couples on the dance floor.

'Like I said earlier, you'd be the first to know if I do decide to take my mother up on her offer.'

'So, you are still thinking about it.' He reached for his pint of beer.

'I told you I'd give London a chance.'

'But you're not sure you want to.' He finally looked at her.

'What's that supposed to mean?'

'I have absolutely no idea.'

Her temper rose as she glared at him. 'What did you say?'

'I have absolutely no idea what I'd do if you came back here,' he explained, refusing to rise to her bait.

'You wouldn't return with me.' She was suddenly alarmed at the thought.

'To do what?' He lowered his glass back on to the table.

'Take your old job back.'

'I wouldn't get it. The brass aren't too fond of policemen who switch from one force to the other every five minutes. And if we talk any more about this tonight, we'll argue, so let's not.'

'We can't just sweep it under the carpet,' she persisted.

'We can for tonight.' He tapped his foot as the band went into a swinging version of 'Rock a beatin' boogie.' 'Dance?'

She knew he was right to want to drop the subject but she couldn't leave it alone. 'Look . . .'

'No, you look,' he interrupted, allowing his irritation to surface. 'You were the one who wanted to be footloose and fancy free. Have you changed your mind?'

She fell silent.

'Dance?' he repeated, looking towards the floor where Martin and Lily, and Katie and Sam were jiving.

As she rose to her feet, Adam barged into their table with a full pint glass sending it and their drinks rocking.

'There are plenty of girls out there looking for partners.' Brian was aware that Adam was on his fourth drink, when he'd just bought everyone else's second.

'You and Martin have staked claims on the only two worth dancing with,' Adam slurred.

Judy realised the mention of 'two' meant Katie's rejection was still a sore point. 'That's rubbish, Adam. And if you want to dance with either Lily or me, you only have to ask.'

'Brian wouldn't let you.'

'Brian doesn't own me.' She smiled at Brian as she pulled Adam on to the dance floor.

Brian had to allow that even half cut, Adam was a better dancer than he was. He and Judy looked good together, so good that a dozen or so couples stopped dancing, formed a circle around them and began to clap.

'You allowed Adam to borrow Judy.' Martin sat besides him and idly twirled Lily's empty glass, tracing the lines of the deer transfer with his finger.

'He's well on the way to getting sozzled again. I thought the exercise might help.'

'That was generous of you.'

'Judy and I were only arguing anyway. It's what we do most of these days.' Brian took the cigarette Martin handed him. 'Where's Lily?'

'Ladies. Something she didn't want me to know about snapped under her dress.' He lifted the glass of beer Brian had bought him. 'Cheers.'

'Cheers.' Brian sipped his pint again before lighting their cigarettes. 'As soon as this dance finishes, I think we should take Adam to one side and tell him what really happened, or rather didn't, between him and Lifebuoy Lettie last night. It's too late to stop him from getting plastered but it might slow his pace.'

'He won't be happy with us,' Martin cautioned.

'We can't put it off any longer.'

'I suppose not.'

'And we can always blame Jack.'

'I'd agree, if Jack had emigrated to Australia as opposed to gone on a two-week honeymoon in London.' Martin reflected that he couldn't stop playing the big brother, even now when Jack was married with his own responsibilities. 'Adam may have a temper but Jack has a worse one and I dread to think what might happen if Adam tried to have a go at him.'

'And if we allow Adam to go on thinking he jumped Lettie he

might say something to her and then we'd look like right idiots,' Brian pointed out.

'You still volunteering?'

Brian thought before answering. 'Why not. Seeing as I'm leaving tomorrow, he won't be able to get at me for a while.'

'It might be better if the three of us tell him. He can hardly take us all on.'

'I'll go with that,' Brian agreed.

'So, bearing in mind that I'm only trying to help, what were you and Judy arguing about?' Martin ventured.

'Nothing – everything – stupid niggles every couple quarrel over.' Brian looked at Judy and Adam again. 'Rock a beatin' boogie' had given way to 'Unchained Melody' played in waltz time. Adam had one hand on Judy's shoulder the other round her waist, but she was careful to keep him at arm's length. He wondered if she'd bother if he weren't around – like back in London – and she were here permanently.

'Lily and I have never had an argument.'

'Go out with her much longer and you will.' Brian turned his back to the dance floor and picked up his beer.

A shiver of foreboding ran through Martin, as he saw Joe and his friend Robin Watkin Morgan walk into the room and head for the bar. There was only one reason why Joe Griffiths would lower himself to enter a public dance hall on a Saturday night. How could he possibly compete with all Joe had to offer? And given his background and prospects, did he even have the right to try?

Jack sat on one of the chairs in the hotel bedroom watching Helen as she moved around, tidying away clothes, pushing her stockings into the laundry bag, brushing out her hair, securing it with a band and cleaning off her make-up with cold cream and cotton wool. Despite his misgivings, the meal in the restaurant had been good – very good. After three courses and two pints of Worthington he felt sated and, looking at Helen, blissfully happy and just the slightest bit smug.

'You look like the cat that's got the cream.' She picked up her toilet bag, nightdress and negligee.

'I know just how he feels. That restaurant,' he blurted uneasily, 'it was nice. Thank you for insisting we went there.'

'Are you saying I was right and you were wrong?' she teased.

'If it had been up to me, I would have looked in and walked away, and we would have ended up eating fish and chips on the street corner.'

'There's nothing wrong with fish and chips on the street corner – in between visits to restaurants,' she qualified.

'I've a feeling you're going to change the way I look at things along with my life, Mrs Clay.' Catching her round her waist, he pulled her on to his lap and kissed her. As she linked her hands round his neck and responded, he tugged her blouse free from her skirt.

'Not as much as you've changed mine, Mr Clay. And I'm surprised you can move, let alone think what you're thinking after the meal you've just eaten.'

'You're too full?' He stopped slipping the buttons on her blouse from their loops.

'No, but I was about to have a bath. Then again' – her fingers wandered to his belt – 'we could have one later.'

'Together!'

'Why not, the bath is big enough.' She was amused by the shocked expression on his face.

'What if someone sees us?'

'You heard the manageress say no one else is staying on this floor and I was going to lock the door.'

'But if anyone came up the stairs they might hear us and know we were in there.'

'We're married, Jack. It's legal.'

Picking her up, he swung her high into his arms and on to the bed. 'God, you're wonderful.'

'I know.' Pulling him close to her, she kissed him.

'You what?' Adam's eyes gleamed, ice-blue and furious, as he glared at Brian in the men's cloakroom.

'Played a practical joke on you,' Brian repeated, taken aback by the venom in Adam's voice.

'It was a stag night and I wasn't the bridegroom.'

'It was just a joke, Adam.' Turning off the tap, Martin shook his hands over the sink before drying them on the roller towel.

'Which I don't find in the least funny.'

'We were amazed you swallowed it,' Sam broke in blithely. 'Even allowing that you were out of your skull, we never thought you'd believe you'd made a play for Lifebuoy Lettie.'

'How did that lipstick get all over me?' Adam questioned coldly.

'We drew it on you.' Brian gave Martin and Sam a warning look.

'On my underpants, which I had to throw away along with my shirt.'

'You didn't need to do that,' Martin protested. 'It would have washed off.'

'You think I could have allowed my mother to see them?'

'You could have washed them yourself,' Martin remonstrated.

'Unlike you, Martin, I have a family who care about me enough to do my washing.'

'Steady on, Adam, that's uncalled for,' Brian reprimanded.

'Is it?' Adam turned on Brian. 'And what else did you do to me when I was out of it?'

'Nothing,' Brian said firmly.

'And which one of you has taken to wearing lipstick?'

'We borrowed it.' Brian shifted his weight uneasily from one foot to the other.

'From the girls.'

Given the problems between Adam and Katie, Brian decided to bend the truth. 'I told Judy we wanted it to play a joke on Jack.'

'And you expect me to believe that.'

'It's the truth. Come on, Adam,' Brian coaxed, 'if it had been one of us, you'd see the funny side.'

'But it wasn't one of you. It was me. And you stripped me in front of the girls . . .'

'The girls weren't there.' Brian leaned against the sink, as he looked Adam squarely in the eye. 'And we stopped at your underpants.'

'And which one of you bastards kissed my pants?'

'You didn't think . . . Adam, I swear none of us kissed you.' Brian was horrified that Adam could even think one of them had actually worn the lipstick. 'We drew a pair of lips on an orange and pressed it all over your chest and on your pants. And that's the absolute truth.'

'None of us touched you with anything except that orange,' Martin added solemnly.

'We'll swear it on a Bible if you want us to . . .' Sam began.

'You all still had a bloody good laugh at my expense.' Turning his back on them, Adam pulled his comb from his pocket and ran it through the styled quiff that had cost him seven shillings and sixpence as opposed to the half-crown he used to pay for his short back and sides.

'It was a joke, Adam.' Martin offered Adam a cigarette.

'A childish one,' Brian granted. 'And I admit, we went over the top with the lipstick and scent . . .'

'That I gave Katie.' Ignoring Martin's proffered cigarette, Adam was careful to keep his back turned, but Brian saw him watching them in the mirror.

'Not the bottle we splashed over you. I borrowed it from Judy along with the lipstick.' Unaccustomed to lying, Brian felt now he'd started he'd never stop.

'How about we apologise by paying for your beer for what's left of tonight and any other night you choose? Come on, mate.' Martin laid his hand on Adam's shoulder. Turning, Adam lashed out, hitting Martin's hand from his shoulder and knocking his cigarettes from his other hand.

'Hey, there's no need for that.' Concerned that Adam was about to hit out again, Brian stepped between him and Martin.

Drawing back his fist, Adam punched Brian with all the strength he could muster, sending him reeling into a cubicle. Martin realised that Adam was about to follow his punch with a kick, so he blocked Brian's body with his own, taking the kick Adam had intended for Brian on his own shin. Staggering, fighting pain and nausea, he pushed forward, forcing Adam away from the cubicle and Brian, who remained crouched double on the floor.

Adam's features contorted in ugly, naked violence as he closed his hands into tight fists. But Martin didn't see his fists, he was mesmerised by Adam's face – the face of a vicious, cowardly bully just like his father. He couldn't hit his father any more but he could hit Adam . . . Curling his right hand into a ball, he pounded it into Adam's jaw . . . and again . . . and again . . .

'Enough!' Sam yelled.

'Martin, for God's sake stop!'

Brian's command penetrated Martin's rage. Trembling, he slowly unclenched his fingers. Staring at Martin, Adam moved unsteadily from the corner he had been driven into.

'It's all right, nothing to worry about,' Sam shouted unconvincingly to a crowd of boys who gave them nervous looks before backing out through the door. Sam glanced from Martin to Adam. As they were both on their feet, he went to Brian who was still slumped in the cubicle. 'You all right?'

'Just about.' Brian took the hand Sam offered and stumbled clumsily towards him.

'You're bleeding.' Sam handed Brian his handkerchief.

'I'll survive.' Brian made his way to the mirror. His lip had split and blood was flowing down his chin. Stumbling to the sink, he filled the bowl with cold water and threw in Sam's handkerchief.

Sam went to Adam. 'That eye doesn't look too clever. Neither does your jaw. It's beginning to swell.'

'Leave me alone.' Adam shoved Sam away.

'Martin, your hand . . .'

'I'll be fine.' Nauseous, shaking from the shock of losing control for the first time in his life, Martin sank down on his heels. Leaning against the wall, he lowered his head between his legs as much to avoid looking at the others as to recover.

'Satisfied, Adam?' Brian wrung out the cloth and staunched his cut, wincing as cold water trickled into the wound.

'Satisfied! A stinking coward like you never gives satisfaction. You can't even fight your own battles . . .'

'Martin only stepped in because you knocked me off my feet,' Brian protested.

'And tried to put the boot in,' Sam reminded him. 'So I wouldn't mention the word coward again if I were you, Adam.'

'Butt out, Sam. This isn't anything to do with you,' Adam retorted viciously.

'You want to have a go at these two for playing a joke on you, have a go at me as well. I was as much a part of it as them,' Sam asserted boldly.

'You didn't duck and run when I called you to account.'

'You want a rematch you can have it.' Brian fingered his torn and bloody lip as he studied the damage in the mirror. 'Although I can't see that beating one another's brains out will accomplish anything, other than prove you're a bigger idiot than I take you for now, for wanting to do it.'

Adam lifted his fist again, but Sam was waiting for him. Catching it, he pulled him off balance and away from Brian.

'Three against one.' Adam gripped the roller towel with his free hand for support. 'The way chickens fight.'

'You threw the first punch and caught Brian off guard,' Sam countered forcefully. 'And God knows what you would have done if

Martin hadn't stepped in. You should be thanking him, not still trying to chuck your weight around.'

'Me, thank him.' Adam sneered at Martin who was still crouched on the floor.

'If you've any sense, you'll do just that, the minute you sober up,' Brian advised.

'And if I don't, you'll arrest me for punching a police officer,' Adam taunted.

'You don't know when to drop it, do you, Adam.' Brian turned away from the mirror.

'I do know it will be a long time before I forget this and in the meantime you'd all better look out.'

Brian nodded to Sam. He relaxed his hold. Shrugging him off, Adam left the cloakroom. His threat had sounded ridiculous but none of them was smiling.

Brian helped Martin up from the floor. 'You all right?'

Martin nodded unconvincingly.

'Shall we go back and join the girls?'

'You and Sam go ahead, I'll be with you in a minute.' Still shaking, Martin went into a cubicle. Before Sam and Brian could open the door they heard him retching.

'Do you realise this is not only the very first time we've lain together in a bed, it's also the longest we've been beside one another naked without anything happening?'

'Only because you've worn me out.' Helen wrapped her arm round Jack's chest and snuggled even closer.

'I've worn *you* out!'

'No tickling,' she squealed as his fingers crawled lightly over her ribs.

'Why not?'

'Because I'm asking nicely.' As he desisted she burrowed her head down on to his shoulder. 'This is nice. I've never shared a bed with anyone before.'

'Never?' he asked, amazed at the thought. 'None of your girlfriends . . .'

'Not that I can remember.'

'I've always shared with Martin, but' – he kissed her forehead as he wound his arm round her – 'you're nicer.'

'Is that meant to be a compliment?'

'I'll do better tomorrow morning when I'm not so tired.' He yawned.

Exhausted, she closed her eyes. Tomorrow morning and every morning for the rest of her life she'd wake next to the man she loved. It was a thought that stayed with her, sweetening her dreams. And when Jack woke with a start two hours later, disorientated and not knowing where he was for a moment, he looked at her face, dim in the light of the street lamp that shone through the curtains, realised she was smiling and sank back to sleep, revelling in that same certainty.

'What have you two been doing?' Judy asked as Brian and Sam returned to their table.

'Nothing much,' Brian snapped, warning her off prying.

'Funny "nothing" that splits your lip.'

'Drop it, Judy.' He held out his hand. 'Dance?'

Realising she might get more out of him once they were on the dance floor, Judy followed him.

'Dance, Katie?'

Before Katie had a chance to reply, she caught sight of Martin walking towards their table. Unlike Brian, he bore no outward scars but she only had to look at him, even in the dim lighting of the ballroom, to know something was wrong.

Leaving her seat she ran up to him. 'Martin . . .'

'I'm fine.' Martin saw Sam standing waiting. 'Go and dance with Sam, Katie.'

Knowing when to leave her brother alone, Katie gave Martin a backward glance as she walked away.

'Do you want to talk about what happened?' Lily asked, as Martin joined her at the table.

'No.'

His hands were shaking so much that Lily decided not to pursue it. She glanced over her shoulder to the bar where Adam was standing alone, drinking. Even from that distance she could see red blotches on his face, especially round the jawline. Adam saw her looking at him and gestured rudely.

'I'm sorry you had to see that.'

She turned back to Martin. 'Why should you be sorry because Adam's being childish?'

'Because he's trying to get at me through you,' he acknowledged.

'You did something to him.'

'Hit him.'

'You must have had a good reason,' she said simply.

'There's never a good reason to hit anyone.'

Knowing how much Katie abhorred violence and remembering some of the things Katie had told her about her parents' marriage, she suddenly realised Martin felt the same way. He reached for his cigarettes and offered them to her. She shook her head. She had never smoked and it said something for his state of mind that he had forgotten.

'Adam split Brian's lip,' he divulged after a long silence.

'I saw, but surely he didn't mean to do it.'

'You weren't there.' He tried to light a match, but he snapped the head without igniting a spark. Leaving the cigarette between his lips, he tossed the match aside, accidentally dropping the box on to the table. 'He meant it all right and given half a chance he would have done a whole lot more.'

She took the matches, struck one and held it up to his cigarette. 'Adam's had a few drinks . . .'

'Your problem is you always want to believe the best of everyone.'

'Is that so terrible?'

He looked into her eyes and saw concern – and something he didn't want to think about. Not after what he'd just done. 'No.' He exhaled slowly, wanting to add, 'it's one of the reasons I love you,' but he didn't because he'd never told her he loved her and after losing his temper and punching Adam, felt he no longer had to the right to.

'So what are we doing tomorrow?' She deliberately changed the subject.

'You want us to do something together?'

'I have a whole day free. I'm offering it to you, if you want it.'

A second wave of nausea swept up from the pit of his stomach and he slumped forward, resting his elbows on the table. 'After tonight, I don't think you should be going anywhere with me.'

'Because you got involved in a fight.'

'Because I hit Adam.'

'Before or after he hit Brian?' she questioned.

'After. But what difference does that make?'

'A lot.' She pulled her chair closer to his. 'Would he have hit Brian again if you hadn't stopped him?'

He looked up at her. 'I didn't wait to find out.'

'But he was still moving towards Brian,' she pressed.

'Yes.'

'Then it sounds to me as if Adam deserved all you gave him.'

He flicked the ash from his cigarette into the ashtray on the table. 'After watching the way my father carried on when I was growing up, I swore I'd never hit anyone, especially in anger.'

'And you wouldn't have, unless you had to.'

'A sensible man would have tried to reason with Adam before using his fists.'

'Only if he'd had time and it sounds to me as if you didn't.'

'I was so angry I can't remember much of what happened and that terrifies me. What if I lose my temper again with someone else? You – Katie – Jack . . .' His eyes clouded in anguish at the thought.

'You won't.'

'How can you be so sure?' he asked seriously.

'Because I know you.'

'How can you, when I don't even know myself?'

Grasping his free hand with both of hers, she tried to still his trembling. 'Martin, you're good and kind . . .'

'I'm not,' he interrupted tersely.

'I suggest we shelve this conversation until tomorrow, when we won't have a band blaring in our ears. When we'll be somewhere nice and quiet.' She hesitated as he fell silent. 'Can you think of anywhere that fits that description?'

'A few places,' he answered absently.

'Jack told me he offered you the use of his bike.'

'He did.'

'I didn't know you could ride it.'

'I have a full licence.' He stubbed out his cigarette and retrieved his hand from hers. 'I've been saving for a car. I hoped that I . . . we . . . could go out in style.'

'A motorbike is stylish enough for me,' she enthused. 'Just think, for once we can go somewhere off the bus route. Perhaps Pennard Castle or the woods around Parkmill.'

'I don't think so.'

'Because you hit Adam.'

'Because I lost control. If Brian hadn't been there and shouted at me I wouldn't have stopped . . .' He buried his face in his hands.

'But you did, Martin.' She pulled his hands away. 'Don't let a stupid quarrel with the boys spoil what could be a good day out for both of us.'

Martin turned as someone tapped his shoulder. Looking past him as if he were invisible, Joe beamed at Lily. 'Would you like to dance?'

'Sorry, Joe,' she apologised politely but firmly. 'Martin and I were discussing something important.'

'It is just a dance, Lily.' Joe's smile tightened as his eyes darkened.

'I don't mind.' Martin had no idea why he was saying the exact opposite of what he felt, or why Joe Griffiths always succeeded in making him feel as if he were still the grubby street urchin in hand-me-down clothes because his father drank away the rent and housekeeping money more weeks than he handed it over.

'Perhaps we could have the next dance, Joe,' Lily suggested.

'She wouldn't dance with you?' Robin asked Joe as he returned to the bar.

'It's all part of her ploy to make me jealous. She told me to ask her for the next one.' Joe snapped his fingers at the barman and pointed to their empty glasses.

'And will you?' Unlike Joe, Robin wasn't at all convinced that Lily was playing games with his friend.

'No.' Joe took a pack of cigarettes from his pocket and offered them to Robin. 'I'll make her wait until the first slow dance after that.'

The barman filled their glasses but Robin had to put his hand into his pocket to pay the man. Joe was too engrossed in watching every move Lily and Martin were making to concern himself with anything as mundane as paying for their drinks.

'You didn't have to turn Joe down on my account.' In trying to contain his jealousy Martin realised he had only succeeded in sounding offhand.

'I put him off on my account, not yours. We were making plans for tomorrow, remember.'

'You were the one making plans. I was trying to tell you to stay away from me because I lost my temper. Besides, you and Joe were almost engaged – if there's any likelihood of you two getting back together, don't let me stand in the way.'

'There is no likelihood,' she interrupted caustically. Taking a deep breath, she lowered her voice and continued in a calmer tone. 'Please, can't we carry on discussing tomorrow? We don't have to visit the castle or the woods. It was only a suggestion. I'd be happy to go wherever you like.'

Yet again, he pictured what he'd done to Adam and his blood ran cold. Why couldn't she see the danger of going anywhere with him? 'After what happened with Adam . . .'

'You did what you had to, Martin. It's obvious Brian and Sam don't think any the less of you for it and they're policemen. If you'd broken the law they would have arrested you, so will you please stop going on about it.'

As they tried to pick up their conversation, Martin felt as though their outing was doomed before it had begun. It wasn't just his guilt over attacking Adam. It was Joe. He felt as if Joe had invited himself along. A good-looking, wealthy, well-educated, self-assured young man with promise; how could he even consider himself a serious rival? And how could Lily fail to be in love with Joe when he so blatantly loved and wanted her?

Chapter 6

AS THE MELLOW, romantic strains of 'Autumn Leaves' filled the ballroom, Joe walked purposefully to the table where Lily and Martin had been joined by Brian and Katie. 'Would you like to dance, now?' He gave Lily a tight-lipped smile.

To his irritation she turned to Martin for approval. 'Do you mind?'

Martin shook his head, wishing he had the courage to tell her – and Joe – that he did mind . . . very much.

As Joe took her hand and swept her into his arms, Lily tried to hold back, keeping as much distance between them as possible.

'Now you've made me jump through hoops . . .'

'I haven't made you do anything, Joe,' she murmured, acutely conscious of Martin watching them.

'No?' He stared intently into her eyes, dazzlingly beautiful with tawny gold lights and the reflection of the mirror ball that hung above them. Just as he had seen them every night in his dreams since he had first danced with her in this same ballroom.

'No,' she reiterated decisively.

'I would have liked to have spoken to you this afternoon. I hoped we could have sat next to one another at the reception.'

'It made more sense for the bridesmaid and best man to sit next to one another.'

'It made no sense to me.' He guided her into the centre of the room. The lights were dim – too dim to see the expressions on the faces of the people sitting at the tables around the perimeter of the room, he noted gratefully, but not too dim to note every curve and line of her face and commit them to memory.

'Helen had a lovely day.' Lily made an attempt to move the conversation away from the personal.

'I wanted to make it our day too.'

'There is no more "our", Joe,' she said resolutely.

'I behaved badly at our engagement party. I should never have walked out on you when that woman . . .'

'My mother,' she corrected.

'You haven't seen her since?' He was alarmed at the thought that Lily might want to keep in contact and actually acknowledge her if she saw her again. From what Robin had said, he knew Lily's reputation was damaged; it would never survive further gossip.

'No.'

'I'm glad to hear it.'

'But neither can I ignore the fact that she gave birth to me.'

'It would be more sensible if you did,' he lectured.

'Possibly.' Steeling herself for what she might see, she glanced over his shoulder to her table. Brian and Katie were talking but Martin was still staring in their direction.

'Rumour has it she ill-treated you before she abandoned you. You don't owe her anything.'

'If you don't mind, I'd rather not talk about her, Joe,' she interrupted impatiently. 'That is, unless you've heard something I should know.'

'I haven't heard anything.'

'Then why ask me to dance?'

'I need a reason?'

Lily swallowed her rising irritation. 'No, but at the risk of sounding bad-mannered, I don't like discussing our engagement party – or my mother.'

'You did say when you broke off our engagement that we could remain friends.' Suddenly realising that she was looking in Martin's direction, he whirled her round, turning her back to her table so she couldn't see him any longer.

'And I meant it, Joe.' She finally gave her full attention to Joe.

'But we're not friends, are we.'

'Of course we are. We wouldn't be dancing together now if we weren't.'

'I disagree.' He gazed into her eyes, willing her to sense the depth of his love for her. 'We're not, at least not in the sense of casual acquaintances, and I don't think we can ever be that to one another again. Not after what happened between us.'

'Joe . . .'

'Hear me out, Lily. What I have to say is very simple. I love you. I never stopped loving you – not for an instant. When I walked away

88

from you that day I knew I was making the biggest mistake of my life and all I can say in my defence is that I wasn't thinking straight.' Keeping her back to Martin, he guided her into the thick of the crowd, where he sensed she'd be reluctant to make a scene. 'I have the ring I bought for you in my pocket. I planned to drive you down to Gower today after the wedding reception so I could propose to you again.'

She lifted her face to his. There was a peculiar expression in her eyes that he failed to decipher. 'At sunset, on the cliffs overlooking Pobbles.'

'You remembered.'

'That the cliffs were where you intended to propose to me the first time, yes.' She smiled.

'It would have been perfect.'

'It was just as perfect, if not more so, in the afternoon in the churchyard at Oxwich.'

'Then, although it's past sunset and this isn't a clifftop, you will take the ring back?'

'No, Joe.'

'In God's name why?' he questioned heatedly, attracting the attention of the couples dancing around them. 'I have everything. Money to give us a good start in life, good prospects . . .'

'I don't love you.'

'I don't believe you.'

'It's the truth.'

'You can't switch your feelings on and off any more than I can. You love me, Lily, perhaps not as much as I love you but you do love me,' he repeated fervently, in the hope of forcing her to accept what was so blatantly obvious to him.

'Maybe it was the thrill of having my first boyfriend, maybe it was because you were kind to me when Auntie Norah died, or maybe I wanted to be in love because I'd heard so much about it and desperately wanted it to be my turn. Whatever it was, if I ever loved you, Joe, I don't now.'

'You're just saying that to hurt me as I hurt you.'

'The last thing I want to do is hurt you,' she protested.

He either didn't hear or chose to ignore her. 'What do you want me to do? Go down on my knees and shout I love you here and now? Because if you want me to I will.'

'Please don't,' she cried, alarmed at the thought.

'If you think I haven't suffered enough, then you don't know what I've been through since you returned my ring. I'm offering you everything I have, Lily. We could have a wonderful life together. I'll graduate in a few months. I've checked with my solicitor, I'll be able to draw on my trust fund to buy that cottage we talked about . . .'

'You talked about.' She recalled how his vivid imagination could take hold once he drifted into one of his fantasies and how much she'd loved listening to him sketch out the perfect future he would build for both of them. Almost as much as she'd loved listening to the romantic stories he'd woven about her mysterious past as an abandoned evacuee. But both fantasies had been shattered by the arrival of her mother. That event had forced her to re-evaluate her identity and her life, along with her relationship with Joe, bringing the realisation that daydreams were all very well – in their place – and that place wasn't her everyday existence.

'You wanted that cottage too. The green and gold drawing room, the blue, cream and silver bedroom . . .'

'I thought I did at the time, Joe, but I was wrong.'

'You haven't changed any more than I have. I only have to look into your eyes to see you still want the same things as I do. You love me.'

'No.' She stopped dancing as the band struck the final chord. 'I'm sorry, Joe, I never meant to mislead you.' She slipped from his arms and held out her hand. 'I hope we can still be friends.'

Instead of shaking her hand as she'd intended, he held it for a moment, then pressed it to his lips. 'One day we'll be a whole lot more than friends, Lily Sullivan. And that's one promise I will keep.'

She hesitated, then realised there was little point in trying to reason with him. He'd obviously been drinking. If he remembered anything of their conversation when he sobered up, he'd understand that she had meant every word she'd said and would hopefully be too embarrassed to refer to the subject again.

Drink, Lily?' Sam offered, as she returned to their table.

'Have we time?' She laid her hand on Martin's shoulder as she sat next to him. He didn't shrug it off but neither did he return her smile.

Sam checked his watch. 'We don't have to leave for half an hour.'

'In that case, thank you.'

'Give me a hand, Katie.'

Katie helped Sam gather the boys' empty glasses and followed him to the bar.

'Dance?' Brian asked Judy, sensing emotional frost in the atmosphere.

As they made for the dance floor, Lily removed her hand from Martin's shoulder. 'You didn't mind me dancing with Joe.'

'You can dance with whoever you like.'

The silence at the table closed in around them until Lily felt she had to say something to break the tension between them. 'You know Joe and I were finished before I went out with you.'

'But he won't accept it.' It was a statement not a question.

'What makes you say that?'

'The way he looks at you. And he's here on a Saturday night when he could be with his posh university friends.'

She sat forward until her head almost touched his. 'I won't be going out with him again, Martin.'

He moved away from her as if he wanted to emphasise the emotional distance that had grown between them since the outset of the evening. 'You're free to go out with anyone you like.'

'I thought I was going out with you.'

'I haven't asked you to make any promises,' he said flatly.

'I don't feel anything for Joe . . .'

'Look, Lily,' he interrupted sternly, 'I'm an apprentice mechanic, with a temper I can't control, on wages that will barely keep me in a rented room in a basement. I don't have enough savings to put down a deposit on a second-hand car. Even when I qualify, the money won't be much better. Joe has a trust fund that everyone talks about and when he finishes university he'll start earning a salary – not wages – and ten times more than me.' Not trusting himself to look at her again, he fumbled for his cigarettes and flicked open the packet.

'Are you saying you want me to go out with Joe?'

'No!' He continued alternately to flick open and close the packet he was holding without attempting to remove a cigarette.

'It sounds like it to me.'

'I'm trying to make sure that you know I'll never be able to offer you as much as Joe Griffiths.'

'What kind of a girl do you think I am? A gold-digger . . .'

'A gold-digger would never have gone out with me in the first place.'

'Drinks, everyone.' Sam set a pint of beer in front of Martin.

'Thank you,' Martin snapped.

'Dance, Katie?' Sam asked, as she placed three Babycham bottles besides Lily's, Judy's and her own glasses.

Realising his 'thank you' had sounded like an insult, Martin muttered, 'Don't go on our account.'

'I do a mean cha-cha, as Katie is about to find out.' Sam dumped the tray holding the second and third pints of beer on the table and cha-chaed Katie away.

'Great night this is turning out to be.'

'Are you talking about you thumping Adam, or me dancing with Joe?' Lily queried icily.

'Both,' he answered honestly.

'If you want to give me the brush-off, Martin, say the word and I won't bother you again.' Terrified of what his answer might be, she crossed her fingers under cover of the table.

'I'm only telling you it'll be years before I can think of marriage and even when I do, I won't be able to give you a quarter of what Joe can — and that's without bringing my temper into it.'

'Stop going on about your temper. Everyone has one . . .'

'Face it, Lily. Boys like me don't go out with girls like you. Just look at us, you dress up to work in an office, I put on greasy overalls over old clothes to graft in a garage. You meet people — important people — every day in the bank, while I spend my days crawling under refuse lorries and buses, up to my neck in filth and oil. You make polite conversation. I hit people . . .'

'Mention that once more tonight and I'll hit you.' She rose to her feet and for a second he thought she really was going to thump him.

Taking her hand, he pulled her back down on to her chair. 'Whichever way you look at it, I don't deserve a girl like you.'

'That's a load of nonsense. And just to set the record straight I'm not looking to get married to you — or anyone.'

'Jack terrified me today. Eighteen years of age, taking on a wife and soon a baby. I couldn't cope . . .'

'No one is asking you to.' She gripped the table until her fingers hurt. 'Do you want to go out with me tomorrow or not?'

'A man would have to be insane not to want to go out with you. And I'm not mad. But you only have to look at my family. My father . . .'

'Why do I have the feeling that you're looking for an excuse to get rid of me?'

The band broke into a rousing rendering of 'Razzle Dazzle'. For once, Lily was glad she couldn't hear herself think. Taking the bottle of Babycham Sam had bought her; she tipped it into her glass. When she looked at Martin again, he was staring at the dance floor. She loved him, she was certain of it, but she felt more confused about his feelings for her than ever.

'I'm sitting on top of the world . . .'

'You'll wake the street,' Brian hissed at Sam who'd broken into song as they turned from Verandah Street into Carlton Terrace.

'I've a good voice so why shouldn't I entertain the neighbours.'

'Because it's half past eleven and most of them are in bed.'

'Sad, sad people.'

'And you're supposed to be a responsible member of the local constabulary,' Judy reminded him.

'Spoilsport.' Sam giggled, putting his arm round Katie who shrank from his touch. 'Who's coming into our lair for coffee?'

'Not me.' Katie removed his hand from her shoulders and walked up to the front door.

'Lily?' Sam glanced from her to Martin.

'Not tonight, Sam, thank you.' Lily waited until Katie unlocked the door and followed her into the house without even so much as a 'goodnight' for Martin.

'So much for their ladyships.' Sam gave an unsteady bow as the door closed behind them. 'Brian?'

'I may call in after I've taken Judy home.'

'Be careful' – Sam lowered his voice as Martin ran down the steps to their basement – 'or you too will fall prey to the wrath of a woman.'

'It's been a disaster,' Brian declared as he walked Judy to her door.

'What?' she asked carefully, wondering if he was referring to the words they'd had about her returning to Swansea.

'Tonight. Martin told me earlier that he and Lily have never had an argument, and after the last couple of hours I can believe it. Their idea of arguing is evidently not to say a word to one another. You could bottle the atmosphere between them and sell it as fog. What was it all about, anyway?'

'Don't you know?' She turned in at her gate.

'I wouldn't be asking if I did.'

'It's Joe. Didn't you see Lily's face when she was dancing with him, or Martin's as he watched them?'

'Martin's jealous of Joe?' he murmured incredulously.

'I'd say so.'

'Does he have reason to be?'

'Lily's adamant it's over between her and Joe, and I believe her. Martin's a fool if he thinks otherwise.' She stopped outside her front door. Her mother had left the lamp burning in the hall and the stained-glass panel reflected vivid blue, red and green jewels of light on to Brian's suit and face. 'You coming in for coffee?'

'It's nearly midnight.'

'I know the time, I asked if you wanted coffee.' There was an edge to her voice he found difficult to ignore.

'What about your mother?'

'She said I could ask you, but if you don't want to . . .'

'Oh, I want to, but where is your mother?' he asked warily.

'At a guess I'd say listening to the wireless or reading in bed.' Judy turned the key and stepped inside. 'Mam?'

'In the kitchen, Judy.' Her mother appeared in the doorway in a pale-pink quilted-nylon housecoat. 'I've just made some cocoa. Do you want some?'

'Brian and I would prefer coffee, Mam.'

'It'll keep you awake.'

'Not after the day we've had, Mrs Hunt.' Brian waited until Judy pulled off her gloves before helping her off with her coat.

'From what I remember weddings can be tiring affairs but not as tiring as a full Saturday in the salon, so if you'll excuse me I'll say goodnight, Brian.' Joy nodded to him and kissed Judy as she carried her cocoa to the stairs.

'Goodnight, Mrs Hunt.' Brian gave Judy's mother a cautious smile and, feeling the need to say more, added, 'I won't keep Judy up long.'

'That's good to know.' She returned his smile and he even thought he saw a little warmth in it.

Since Katie had moved in with Lily to share her bedroom they had fallen into the habit of talking over their day last thing at night. But to Lily's relief, for once Katie crawled into bed after leaving the bathroom, turned her face to the wall and closed her eyes. If she didn't fall asleep shortly afterwards, she certainly gave a good impression of it. Lily crept in beside her, switched off the bedside light, curled into a self-contained ball and contemplated the evening – and Martin.

Given his father's reputation for violence and Katie's stories of the beatings Ernie Clay had inflicted on every member of his family, she could understand Martin's concern over losing his temper and hitting Adam but not his reaction. Martin was totally unlike his father who had been feared and avoided by everyone in Carlton Terrace. She was one hundred per cent certain that he would never lash out at any man without provocation and it was unthinkable even to consider that he'd ever hit a woman or a child. When they had been children she had seen Martin ignore taunts and bullying about his ragged clothes and his family that had driven Jack to blind rage.

Was he really afraid of hurting her as he had said, or was he simply fed up with her and looking for a way to end their relationship? And what was their relationship anyway? A few dates, some good times when she had assumed he had enjoyed her company as much as she enjoyed his, but he had never told her so. What if he had been bored the whole time?

And he'd talked about not wanting to take on the responsibility of a family as Jack had done. She tried to recall everything she had said to him, not only that night but on their dates. Had she frightened him off by giving him the impression that she was only going out with him because she wanted marriage and a family? The only times she could recall discussing anything remotely related to the topic, the conversations had been concerned with Jack and Helen. Had Martin assumed that because she'd been happy to help Helen set up her home she wanted to do the same herself?

Just before sleep obliterated thought, she came to the conclusion that the only thing she could be absolutely certain of was that Martin meant more to her than she did to him, otherwise he wouldn't be so determined to push her out of his life – and towards Joe.

As Lily relaxed into sleep, Katie allowed the tears she had kept in check since she had left the warehouse to fall. Stifling her sobs in her pillows, she cried until dawn broke. She'd lost the only man she would ever love and her heart was broken.

'Your mother's mellowed,' Brian commented as Judy carried a tray of coffee and sandwiches into the living room.

'Absence and all that.' Judy set the tray on the coffee table in front of him. 'She actually admitted this afternoon that she misses me.'

'I get the impression she almost likes me.'

'Don't get a swollen head over it, she "almost likes" a lot of people.' Sitting beside him, she handed him a plate.

He opened one of the sandwiches. 'Great, pickle and cheese. Can we switch off the main light?' He turned on a sofa lamp in anticipation.

'Not until I've eaten. I like to see what's in my sandwiches.' She heaped two on to her plate.

'Didn't you make them?'

'Who else?'

'Then you should know what's in them.'

'I'm tired, I could have scraped up a spider with the pickle.'

He paused mid-bite and opened his sandwich again.

'That was a joke.'

'You think that's funny.' Realising that the banter was Judy's way of trying to cope with the underlying tension that had set in between them since he had discovered she was considering returning to Swansea, he gave her a hard look.

'It got you going, didn't it?'

He left the sofa, turned off the light and closed the door to the hall.

'Why do boys always want the light out?' she asked, as he took her plate from her hand and set it together with his own on the table.

'Possibly for the same reason girls always close their eyes when they kiss.' He sat on the sofa and pulled her towards him.

To prove him wrong she left her eyes open as he wrapped his arms round her and lowered his lips to hers.

'Always have to prove a point, don't you,' he remonstrated, as he released her.

'I wondered what it would be like to leave my eyes open for once. Do you realise this is the first time we've been alone together in anything resembling privacy since we left Swansea a month ago?'

'Yes.' He kissed her again and this time she closed her eyes, shivering as he pulled down the elasticised sleeves of her dress and exposed her bra. Slipping his hand behind her back, he unfastened the hooks. She clung to him as he laid the strapless bra on the cushion behind him and gently caressed her exposed breasts. 'You really are very beautiful. Much more than . . .'

'Who?' she snapped, instantly on the alert.

'Not who, what,' he muttered, shamefaced. 'The boys have magazines in the hostel . . .'

'Of naked girls.'

'You've seen them?' He was stunned at the thought.

'Helen used to pinch Joe's and show them to us.' Her mouth turned down in disapproval. 'They were disgusting. I can't believe you'd want to look at pictures like that, or that any decent girl would pose for them.'

'The girls are well paid.'

'No amount of money would make me strip off for a photographer.' She frowned. 'And how do you know the girls are well paid?'

'Because one of the boys in the hostel went out with a model. She told him she earns ten times her regular fee every time she works in the nude.'

'And I suppose she gave you and "the boys" a private show.'

'I never even met the girl,' he protested. 'And before you say another word, I can't avoid seeing the magazines when they're always lying around, now can I.'

'You could if you tried.'

'Isn't it enough that I don't buy them or go out of my way to find them?'

'No.'

'It's not like I have another woman,' he said defensively as she pulled up her dress.

'What would you say if I told you that Lily, Katie and I look at magazines of naked men?'

'I'd say, do whatever makes you happy.' He grinned as an image of the three of them poring over a photograph of a naked man came to mind.

'Happy – we'd die laughing. Naked men are ridiculous,' she railed scornfully.

'Oh, yes, and how many have you seen?'

Caught in her own trap, she sensed her cheeks burning. 'None.'

'Then how do you know we look ridiculous?'

'I've seen Greek statues.'

'And you think classical statues of men look ridiculous.'

'This is a stupid conversation.' She picked up her plate and took another bite of sandwich.

'You always say that when I'm winning.'

'I don't.'

'I think you need to study a naked man in depth.' Setting her plate aside again, he nuzzled her neck.

'You volunteering?' Her cheeks burned again at her audacity.

'If you reciprocate.' Sliding her dress down again, he cupped her breasts with his hands and gently caressed her nipples with his thumbs.

'Do you ever feel like going further than this?' she ventured, as his touch sent shock waves coursing through her body.

'Every time we're alone.'

An image came to her mind of Helen's and Jack's flat. Would they be able to find one like it in London? If they did, she could give up work and keep house for Brian. It wouldn't be like living in Swansea but then she wouldn't have to get up every day to face a job she hated either. 'You haven't tried recently.'

'Only because we haven't had the chance to be alone and if my memory serves me correctly, you always fight me off.'

Her green eyes glowed seductively in the muted glow of the lamp as she lifted her legs on to the sofa and moved against the cushions to make room for him to lie beside her. 'But you want to.'

He slid his body along the length of hers and kissed her again. 'It would have to be for the right reasons,' he whispered huskily. Pushing her dress down over her arms, he stripped her to the waist, pulled off his tie and dropped it to the floor.

'How many girls have you made love to?'

'Millions.' He slid his hand up her leg and rested it on her stocking top.

'I'm serious, Brian.'

His hand froze as he opened his eyes. 'What kind of a question is that?'

'You did your National Service, you were a soldier, you've been abroad. There are always girls around army camps who'll do anything for a few shillings . . .'

'Who told you that?'

'I read the Sunday papers.'

'The *People* or the *News of the World*?'

Putting the odd tone of his voice down to frustration, she continued, 'I'm only asking because I think it's time I stopped fighting you off.'

'You want me to make love to you, right here and now?'

'I've never done it and I'm curious as to what it's like. Helen . . .'

'Helen talked about her and Jack!' He removed his hand from her leg.

'All she would say was it was private between her and Jack.'

'Good for Helen.' Sitting up, he moved away from her.

'We've been going out together for months now. Don't you think it's time we made love?' Kneeling beside him, she pulled the skirt of her dress from beneath her and tugged it over her head.

The breath caught in his throat. She was very beautiful and temptingly desirable dressed in only a lace waist petticoat, suspender belt, panties and stockings. But something in her eyes made his blood run cold. It was almost as if one of the models from the magazines was with him, not his girlfriend of the past few months. 'If I did, would you insist on marrying me afterwards, or move on to the next thrill?' he asked coldly.

She stared blankly at him. 'I can't believe you just said that.'

'Do you realise you asked me to make love to you without once mentioning that you love me.'

'You know I love you. I told you this afternoon.'

'That was this afternoon, when you also told me you were thinking about leaving London to come back here. I don't know where I am with you, Judy. And, frankly, the last thing I need at the moment is to satisfy your curiosity by indulging in a bout of meaningless sex.'

'That's a horrible thing to say.'

'But true. And it's made me realise that this isn't the time or place for what we've just been doing, not with your mother upstairs.' Leaving the sofa, he retrieved his tie from the floor and pulled out the knot.

'If my mother is all you're worried about, she won't disturb us.'

'I'm more worried about you than your mother.' He looked back at her as he fastened the buttons that had worked loose on his shirt. 'Hasn't anyone told you lovemaking is just that, making love, an expression of your feelings for one particular very special person?'

'But I do love you, Brian, you know that.'

'That was an afterthought if ever there was one.' He reached for the door handle.

She couldn't understand why he was angry or what she had done wrong. He had more or less admitted he liked looking at naked girls, she had taken most of her clothes off and yet he was walking away from her. 'I'm prepared to give you everything and you're turning me down because you won't make love to me until we're married, is that it?' she asked in confusion.

He looked at her as if she were a stranger. 'You really don't understand, do you?'

'No. You asked me to marry you . . .'

'Months ago and you said no.'

Her eyes rounded in alarm as he opened the door. 'Don't go . . .'

'I told your mother I wouldn't keep you up late.'

'But what about us? We haven't decided anything . . .' Her voice tailed off as a cold shiver ran down her spine.

'We have hours to talk about us on the train tomorrow, Judy; that is, if you are going back to London. And if you're not, I rather think any decisions will have been made.'

'But we won't be alone on the train like we are now.' Making no attempt to cover herself she went to him and tried to kiss him.

'No.' He pushed her gently down on to the sofa. 'Not now, and certainly not with you in this mood.'

'What mood? I love you . . .'

'You're so mixed up you don't know what you want, London or Swansea, me or any man who'll show you what sex is like. I don't want to have to get married like Jack, forced into it because there's a baby on the way. I want to get married because I love the girl, she loves me and we've made a decision to spend the rest of our lives together. Not because the girl sees marriage and a family as a way out of a job she can't get to grips with.'

'It wouldn't be like that . . .'

'Do you think I'm so stupid I can't work out that the only reason you're mentioning marriage now is so you can give up work?'

'I love you,' she protested in a small voice.

'I'm sorry, much as I want to, I don't believe you.'

'So what happens now?' Forced to accept that he wasn't going to touch her again, she reached for her dress.

'That is entirely up to you.'

'You want us to carry on as we have been, with both of us working all the hours of the day and night, hardly ever seeing one another . . .'

'And we'd see so much more of one another if you came back here.' He stepped into the doorway. 'If you can't see a future for us together, I'd rather you told me now, Judy, before I waste any more time making plans that aren't going anywhere.'

Her heart missed a beat. 'You want us to stop seeing one another?'

'It might be an idea until you decide what you really want out of life.'

'And if I decide I want you?'

He looked carefully at her. 'You'd continue to put up with a city and a job you hate just for me.'

She hesitated. 'I just need time . . .'

'I won't wait for ever, neither will I let myself be used by you or anyone else, Judy. Just one last piece of advice. Whatever happens between us, don't go asking any more men to make love to you when you're not sure whether you love them or not. In my experience that's how girls get reputations they'd rather not have.' He gave her one final piercing look before he walked away.

'The kettle's not long boiled, there's instant coffee and bread and cheese in the cupboard,' Sam greeted Brian as he walked into the basement kitchen.

'Where's Martin?' Brian asked, as he made himself coffee.

'He went straight to bed when we came in.'

'Happy days,' Brian mused sardonically.

'Not for him and Lily, or you and Judy by the look on your face,' Sam diagnosed as Brian sat in the only other easy chair.

'You know girls.'

'Unfortunately not as well as I'd like to.'

'If you take my advice you'll stay away from them.'

Sam handed Brian the sugar bowl. 'From where I'm sitting, it doesn't look like you're taking your own advice.'

'I may soon be forced to.'

Sensing a depressing conversation about to start, Sam left his chair. 'I'm for bed. See you in the morning.'

'I'll be here,' Brian answered absently, as he swung his feet on to one of the kitchen chairs.

Chapter 7

RECOGNISING MARTIN'S SILHOUETTE behind the stained-glass panel in the front door, Lily ran down the passage in the hope that he had called to tell her he would like to spend the day with her after all, but he looked anywhere but at her as he backed down the path.

'Come in.' She opened the door wider.

'I can't. Brian is catching the two o'clock train.'

'I know, Judy told me. Haven't you even the time to step inside?' she asked, as Joe walked out of his house and waved to her.

'No. Sam suggested we take Brian for a pint down the Rose before Sunday dinner. Mrs Hunt's invited us.'

'She's invited Uncle Roy, Katie and me too.'

'Then I'll see you there. About today . . .'

'Yes,' she broke in eagerly.

'The weather isn't really good enough for us to go anywhere.' He held out his hands as if to emphasise the slight drizzle that was dampening the air and greying the pavement.

'No, I suppose it isn't,' she agreed reluctantly.

'See you at Mrs Hunt's, then.'

'Yes, see you there.'

Martin didn't even look back as he turned down the steps to his basement.

'Chicken or pork?' Roy asked Joy as he picked up the carving knife and set about the two roasts she had placed in front of him.

'Chicken, please.'

'Katie, Judy?'

'Chicken, please.'

'And for me, Uncle Roy.' Lily placed a bowl of mashed potatoes on the table.

'Joe?'

'I don't mind either, Mr Williams. Whichever is the least popular will be fine.' Joe glanced at Lily in an attempt to gauge her mood, but she followed Joy back into the kitchen.

Sensing that everyone would be feeling a little flat after the wedding, Joy had invited Roy and John Griffiths and their respective households together with Martin, Sam and Brian to Sunday lunch. When they all accepted she bought a joint of pork to complement the large chicken she had ordered from her butcher. Pleading a heavy workload, John Griffiths had dropped a note through her door early that morning to say that he wouldn't be able to join her, but Joe would.

Roping Katie and Lily in to help her and Judy in the kitchen, Joy had been concerned by how subdued all three girls had been. There had been none of the usual banter as they had prepared the vegetables and Katie, especially, looked pale and heavy-eyed. Reluctant to pry, Joy hinted that if any of them wanted to talk to her they could, but the silence had only intensified as the girls retreated even further into themselves.

'If you take in the apple sauce, Lily, I think that's it.' Joy glanced around the kitchen to check she hadn't forgotten anything as she ladled gravy into a jug from a pan on the stove. Picking up the sauceboat, Lily led the way back into the dining room and slipped on to a chair between Roy and Joe who had engineered a seat next to hers.

Roy said a brief grace, tureens and plates were passed, the salt cellar and pepper pot travelled from one end of the long table to the other and the whole time Judy fought the urge to scream. Every time she looked up, she caught Brian watching her, but the only conversation between them was of the 'pass the salt' variety and she was too embarrassed by the events of the previous evening to attempt anything more.

Sam said a great deal, most of it to Katie who, when she replied at all, did so in monosyllables. Joe was too busy staring at Lily to say much beyond complimenting Joy on her cooking. Martin ate silently, neither looking at nor saying a single word to anyone, so it was left to Roy and Joy to direct what little discussion there was.

Martin was the first to break up the party. As he finished his main course he pushed back his chair from the table. 'That was wonderful, Mrs Hunt, a real treat. Would you mind very much if I left now?'

'There's loads more food, Martin . . .'

'I couldn't eat another thing, Mrs Hunt, thank you.' Rising to his feet, he replaced his chair beneath the table.

'Not even the apple crumble and custard I've made?' Joy had noticed that Lily and Martin were avoiding one another and Joe's smile was broadening, and wondered if Lily had gone back to Joe.

'I've never had much of a sweet tooth and I have to study for my City and Guild finals. They start the week after next.' Martin folded his linen napkin and set it neatly beside his plate.

'Of course, if you have work to do. I'll see you out.'

'Don't disturb yourself, Mrs Hunt, I'll see myself out.' Martin left the room and seconds later the front door closed behind him.

'Anyone want any more meat, vegetables, potatoes or gravy?' Joy asked.

'I wouldn't mind a few more roast potatoes please, Mrs Hunt.' Sam beamed at Katie as he pushed his plate towards his hostess.

'My mother would have a fit if she could see me now.' Helen took the ice cream cone Jack handed her and sat on a park bench.

'Why?' Jack watched as she licked all round the edge of her cone to stop it from dribbling.

'Because I'm eating in public.' She imitated Esme's drawl: 'Like common street riff-raff.'

'I warned you that I'd bring you down to my level when I married you.'

'I'm glad you did.'

'Warn you?'

'Marry me, you idiot.' She grabbed his arm and planted a kiss on his cheek.

'Steady with that cone; that's a brand-new sports coat you're about to rub icecream into.'

'I wasn't about to do any such thing.' She sat back and stared up at the bright blue cloudless sky. 'Do you think the weather's as perfect as this in Swansea?'

'If it isn't, it will be when we get back.'

'Just think, all our Sundays are going to be like this from now on. Walks and ice cream in the park, nothing to do . . .'

'Except change nappies, feed the baby, wash his clothes, rock him to sleep, play with him, teach him to crawl, then walk, play football – I never did make a good job of that with Katie. She's a terrible footballer.'

'You remember Katie as a baby?' she asked in surprise.

'I was three but I can remember her being born.'

'This is going to be the first baby in our family since me.' She had a sudden panic attack. 'What if I don't cope? Some women don't . . . I read about one the other day. She abandoned her baby on a doorstep . . .'

'I forbid you to read any more stories like that.' Demolishing the last of his cone in two bites, Jack wiped his fingers on his handkerchief and handed it to her. 'You'll be fine, sweetheart.'

'I wish I had your confidence.'

'My mother used to say there's nothing to babies. Feed one end, clean up the other and they'll be happy.'

'I didn't need to hear that when I'm eating.'

'You all right?' he asked anxiously as she paled.

'Morning sickness.'

'It's three o'clock.'

'Looks like I've got all-day sickness.'

'Want to walk back to the hotel?'

'Please.'

'If you're ill I could try and get us a taxi.'

'I don't feel that bad' – she looked up at him mischievously – 'but a lie-down before dinner might be nice.'

Everyone sitting at Joy's table was relieved when the last vestiges of apple crumble and custard had been eaten. No one lingered. Brian left to finish his packing and Judy went up to her bedroom to do the same. Roy made for the parlour to fix a broken window sash and Katie and Lily persuaded Joy to go with him, promising to bring them both a cup of tea when they'd finished clearing the table and washing the dishes.

For once Joy didn't argue, deciding if something was bothering the girls it might be as well to leave them on their own so they could talk it out, but she had reckoned without Sam and Joe. Both hung back after she left the room, Joe in the hope of renewing his conversation of the night before with Lily and Sam in search of an opportunity to ask Katie to go out with him.

'If you need a slave to wash the dishes, I'm your man.' Taking the tray Katie had brought in from the kitchen, Sam set it on the table and began stacking plates and bowls on to it.

'We can manage,' Katie protested, as Joe left his chair, picked up a tureen of cabbage and made a beeline for the kitchen.

'The least I can do after that magnificent meal is help clear up.' Refusing to be deterred, Sam carried on scraping and stacking bowls.

'Here, let me take those from you, they look heavy.' Joe snatched the meat and Yorkshire pudding trays from Lily. Misjudging their weight, he almost dropped them. Steadying them against his chest, he smudged the pale-grey cashmere slipover he was wearing with grease.

'Someone's going to have fun trying to get that stain out.' Lily cast a critical eye over the damage as she took two clean Pyrex bowls from Joy's cupboard.

'Our housekeeper's good at laundry.'

'No wonder, you must give her plenty of practice. It still might be an idea to go home and change. If you put that slipover into cold water it will prevent the stain from setting.'

'Now I'm a mess, I may as well stay and help you until this lot is cleared away.' Dumping the trays in the sink, he began to run the hot water.

'Take the trays out of the sink and stack them on the stove,' Lily ordered.

'I'm going to wash them. They're far too heavy for you and there's no sense in both of us getting into a state.'

'You don't know much about washing up, do you?'

'It's that obvious?' He gave her a sheepish smile.

'If you're intent on learning how to do it, clear and clean the sink, fill it full of hot water, add a couple of spoonfuls of soda and start with the cleanest things first, which in this case will be the glasses, then the dessert plates and cutlery, then the dinner plates and cutlery. The oven and meat trays can wait until last.'

'Yes, ma'am.' He gave her a mock salute. 'But won't the water be very dirty by then?'

She wondered if he was deliberately playing the fool in an attempt to make her look like an idiot. 'It will do to get off the worst of the grease. You can always run a fresh bowlful afterwards.'

'Clear a space, heavy load coming through.' Sam burst into the kitchen with the tray, Katie trailing in his wake. 'Good to see you already at it, Joe. Shall I dry?' He picked up a tea towel as Joe removed the first of the glasses from the sink of hot water he had run and placed them on the draining board.

'Fine by me, is that all right with you, Lily?' Joe asked, as Lily removed the remainders of the meat into the Pyrex bowls.

Lily glanced across at Katie, who was scraping the leftovers into the pigswill bin. Realising her friend was no more comfortable with Sam's attempts at flirting with her than she was with Joe's, she nodded agreement. 'And seeing as how the two of you are so set on clearing up for us, we'll skive off and see if we can help Judy upstairs.'

'I'm sure she can manage . . .'

'So am I, Joe,' she interrupted sweetly, covering the Pyrex bowls with plates and stowing them on the cool marble slab in the pantry. 'But it will give us the chance to have a last gossip. Let us know when you've finished and we'll come down and make Mrs Hunt and my uncle that cup of tea. Do you want a hand to untie your apron, Katie?'

'You left Sam and Joe with the washing up?' Judy started to laugh as Lily closed the door.

'It was Lily's idea.' Katie sat on Judy's bed.

'I didn't hear you object.' Lily joined Katie on the bed.

'Serve them right for being so pushy.' Judy rummaged in her handbag for her make-up. 'I wish we had all afternoon so we could have a really good chat, like the old days.'

'The old days?' Lily raised her eyebrows. 'I'm not forty yet.'

'God, imagine being forty.'

Lily thought about it for a moment. 'I can't.'

'You two will be married like Helen. You'll have four children apiece and I'll be good old spinster Auntie Katie.' There was a trace of bitterness in Katie's voice that Lily had never picked up on before.

Judy sat on her dressing-table stool. 'By "old days" I meant before I went to London.' She made a face as she studied her reflection in the mirror. 'I'd give anything to be able to stay here with you two.'

'Then stay,' Katie said suddenly.

'For two pins I'd take you up on that.'

'I could find two pins.' Katie examined her nails. Since her father's death she had stopped biting them and the novelty of actually having nails she could polish hadn't yet worn off.

'I talked to my mother about coming back here for good again this morning. It's tempting but I should work out my notice at the BBC in case I ever need a reference from them.' Judy tipped her make-up out on to a glass tray.

'If you work for your mother you won't need a reference,' Katie pointed out logically.

'And Brian?' After revealing Judy's doubts about life in London to him the day before, Lily had to steel herself to ask.

'I told him how much I hated my job and living in the hostel when he came to tea yesterday afternoon.'

'Was that because of what I said to him at Martin's?' Lily felt guilty at the thought.

'Yes.'

'I'm sorry.'

'Don't be, I should have told him weeks ago.' Judy unscrewed the top from a bottle of foundation.

'If he was upset it's only because he's besotted with you.' Lily left the bed and moved restlessly to the window.

'I'm not so sure.'

'You didn't hear some of the things he said about you on Saturday afternoon when you left to clear out your wardrobe.'

'That was before he brought me home from the Pier last night.' Judy paused for a moment. She wanted to talk about what had happened between her and Brian but there was no way she could tell even her closest friends the full, mortifying details. 'We had the most awful row.'

'What about?' Katie asked.

'I'm not quite sure,' Judy prevaricated, still raw from Brian's rejection. She would have given anything to erase all memory of the humiliating episode from her memory. 'What about you and Martin, Lily? Neither of you said a word on the way home from the Pier, or over lunch, come to think of it.'

'Martin and I are just friends.'

'Pull the other one.' Judy dabbed spots of foundation along her forehead and down her nose.

'We haven't been going out together anywhere near as long as you and Brian.' Lily sat on the windowsill.

'But Martin adores you,' Katie broke in defensively. 'I know him, Lily, he's loved you for years.'

'Love is a pretty strong word to use after a few dates.'

'But you do like him?'

Lily looked back at Katie. She looked small and a little lost sitting alone on Helen's bed. 'I wouldn't have gone out with him if I hadn't liked him.'

'Then everything will be all right between you, you'll see.'

'You won't say anything to him, will you?' Lily was alarmed at the thought that Martin might think she'd appealed to his sister to intercede between them on her behalf.

'About what?' Katie picked up Judy's teddy bear and cuddled it.
'That I've talked to you about him.'

'You haven't said anything other than you like him and I think he's gathered that much himself by now.' She watched Judy shake more foundation on to her fingertips. 'You always make putting make-up on look so easy.'

'It's just practice. And before you ask any more about Brian and me, I haven't a clue where I am with him. Last night he suggested I should take some time to think things over and let him know how I feel about staying in London or coming back here after I've made my mind up.'

'That sounds like good advice.'

'Don't you dare take his side, Katie Clay!'

'What side? You admitted yourself on Friday night that you weren't sure whether you loved him or not.'

Judy smoothed the tinted cream over her chin and cheeks. 'He said yesterday that he wanted to talk and we'll have four hours to do it in on the journey back, more if there's delays like there were on the way down.'

'And if he asks you to marry him?' Lily smiled.

'Whatever he wants to talk about, I guarantee it's not a proposal,' Judy dismissed firmly. 'Not after last night.'

'But if it is, what would you say?' For all her protestations that she didn't want to get married, Lily couldn't help wondering what she'd say if Martin asked her that very special question.

'I haven't a clue but "no" would definitely come into it,' Judy lied as she pretended to concentrate on her make-up. She had never told the girls that Brian had proposed to her before they'd left Swansea or that she'd turned him down.

'I don't believe you. If I had to bet on which one of us will get married next I'd put all my money on you,' Lily mused thoughtfully.

'I haven't changed my mind about not getting married before I'm thirty.' Judy had repeated the sentiment so often she began to wonder if she meant it. Marriage to any man would mean giving up her independence – not that independence in London was worth holding on to. But Brian had said so many harsh, hurtful things . . .

'Given time, Brian might change it for you.' Lily looked down at the garden and wondered if Martin was really studying as he had said he would.

Judy set aside the foundation and reached for her rouge. 'Katie's a witness. I bet ten bob that you'll race to the church the minute Martin asks you.'

'Given his reaction to Jack and Helen getting married, I'd say he's of the same opinion as Katie and preparing for a lifetime of bachelorhood.' Not even knowing if Martin would ask her out again, Lily tried to make a joke of his reluctance.

After checking that her rouge and foundation had been evenly applied, Judy closed her eyes and puffed a delicate coating of powder over her face. 'I feel as if I'm getting ready for a funeral.'

'If going back to London makes you feel that bad then don't go,' Katie cajoled again, hating the thought of Judy disappearing for months on end.

'Don't tempt me.' Judy blotted the lipstick she'd applied with a ball of cotton wool before applying another coat.

'Just tear up your ticket and unpack. I'll help.' Katie looked at the suitcase Judy had placed by the door as if she couldn't wait to open it.

'You'd be better off cashing in your ticket,' Lily advised, 'you might even get enough back to buy another set of underwear from the warehouse.'

'You two aren't helping one bit, do you know that?' Moistening a block of mascara, Judy combed it through her lashes.

'You'll be back in the summer.' Lily looked around the room. Although Judy had left a few childhood keepsakes and toys on her shelves, it had taken on a cold, impersonal air, as if the walls somehow knew they were no longer permanently lived in.

'I've booked out the first two weeks in July . . . that's if I'm not back before.' Judy opened her purse, checked her ticket, pushed her hairbrush to the bottom of her handbag, refilled and slipped in her cosmetics bag and closed it. 'And in the meantime you two could always come and see me.'

'In London?' Katie eyes rounded at the thought.

'The hostel has camp beds friends can rent out for a shilling a night. There isn't room for two beds in my room but if you decide to come at the same time I could ask one of the other girls to put one of you up.'

'I thought you didn't speak to the other girls,' Lily said artfully.

'Some are better than others. And perhaps I exaggerated their unfriendliness — just a little,' Judy confessed.

'Won't the warden mind?' Katie asked.

'Not as long as you pay for your food.'

'The pigswill?'

'You've too good a memory, Lily,' Judy reproached her. 'Some meals aren't too bad, some are terrible but we could always eat out. There are a few cafés around the area that aren't too expensive.' She looked earnestly at her friends. 'Write to me.'

'We have been.'

'But write to me more often,' she pleaded. 'I have a feeling this visit is going to make my homesickness worse than ever.'

'Judy,' Joy shouted from downstairs.

'My mother always panics about time.' Judy pulled on her gloves. 'You and Brian walking to the station?'

'He complained so much about the weight of my suitcase I ordered a taxi.'

'We could come down and see you off,' Lily offered.

'I'd rather say goodbye here.' Judy hugged Lily, then Katie. 'Give Helen my love when you see her and tell her I know she'll be busy but if she could find time to write to me, even just a note, I'd be grateful.'

'We will.' Lily and Katie followed her downstairs.

'The taxi will be here in five minutes,' Joy fussed. 'Have you . . .'

'I have everything, Mam.' The doorbell rang and she opened the door.

'You fit?' Brian looked tall, dark and handsome in the suit he had worn to the wedding, a white shirt and a green tie she hadn't seen before.

'Just about.' She met his steady gaze and her knees turned to jelly. Leaning against the doorpost for support, she considered what she was returning to. Her lonely life in the hostel in London, the work she neither enjoyed nor was particularly good at, the tedious train journey in front of her – the scathing and humiliating observations Brian had made the night before. 'I'm sorry, Brian.'

'For what?'

As he looked at her she saw that he already knew. 'I'm staying here.'

Picking up his suitcase, Brian turned his back and walked away.

'You're sure you're all right.' Martin eyed Brian with concern as they waited on the platform for the London train to arrive.

'I'm fine,' Brian answered testily.

'It might be just as well Judy's staying here,' Sam chipped in, trying to think of something positive to say. 'It was obvious you two weren't getting along all that well and now you'll be free to go out with any girl who takes your fancy . . .' He fell silent as Martin kicked his ankle.

'No need for tact or tragic looks.' Brian adopted a cheerful tone that was at odds with the bleak expression in his eyes. 'It's not the first time I've lost a girlfriend and I dare say it won't be the last. I survived before and I'll survive now. As Sam has just said, there's plenty more in London.'

'That's the spirit. Cigarette?' Sam offered.

'No thanks, the train will be here any minute and I've enough to carry.'

'Brian!'

The three of them turned to see Judy thrust a penny platform ticket at the guard at the gate. As he took it from her, she ran towards them, her coat thrown carelessly over her shoulders, her feet squelching in bedroom slippers that had become soaked along the way.

Martin and Sam moved away as she charged up to Brian.

'You will write,' she gasped as she caught up with him.

Brian wished he'd taken Sam up on his offer of a cigarette as he looked at her. It would have given him something to do with his hands.

'Brian . . .'

'If you've anything to say to me, Judy, you know where to find me,' he said quietly, wishing the train would come.

'I'm sorry . . .'

'So am I.' He picked up his suitcase as the signal clanked down and the train finally steamed into the station.

Chapter 8

MARTIN GLANCED UP from the mechanics manual he was attempting to study as Sam walked into the kitchen in his uniform trousers and shirt, carrying his tunic. 'I didn't know you were on duty.'

'A week of nights, starting tonight,' Sam complained. 'The downside of getting yesterday off for the wedding and there's a stain on this damn sleeve the sergeant's bound to spot at inspection.'

'Spot remover in the dresser drawer, tea in the pot.' Martin closed the manual. Before he had spent an hour staring at diagrams he had been fairly confident that he knew all he needed to know about Ford engines. Now all he was sure of was there was a great deal he hadn't covered – or had it been that he was too concerned about the strained silence between himself and Lily to concentrate?

Sam glanced at his watch as he rummaged among the mess of elastic bands, pencils, rules and tubes of spent glue in the drawer. 'Fortunately, I'm ahead of myself. I don't need to be at the station for another hour, so it's yes to that tea.'

'You expect me to pour it for you?' Martin asked indignantly.

'You do it so well.'

'Liar.' Martin picked up a tea towel from the table and flung it at Sam, catching him on the side of the face.

'That stung.' Sam tossed it back on to the table. 'Do you think Brian will be all right?'

'Difficult to say.' Martin took a clean mug from the dresser and set it next to his on the table. 'He was pretty fond of Judy.'

'Stupid bugger.'

'Him or Judy?'

'Both of them for quarrelling.' Sam found the bottle of stain remover and placed it and the sleeve in the sink. 'How's the swotting going?'

'It's not.' Martin poured out two mugs of tea.

'That's because you're whacked. If I were you I'd get some fresh air before an early night.' He winked suggestively. 'Take the gorgeous Lily for a long walk down a dark alley.'

'You've been talking to her,' Martin broke in suspiciously.

'Not since lunch in Mrs Hunt's and you were there.'

'You said something to her after I left.'

'"Where do you want me to put the leftover mashed potato?" And forgive me for forgetting her reply,' Sam answered carelessly. 'I told you, Joe and I washed up.'

'You didn't say anything to her about me?'

'Not that I can remember.' He eyed Martin. 'Why the Spanish Inquisition.'

Martin sugared his tea and pulled his cigarettes from his shirt pocket.

'Don't tell me you two haven't made it up since last night.' Sam poured a little of the stain remover on to a corner of a tea towel and dabbed at the sleeve.

'There's nothing to make up,' Martin said dismissively.

'No?' Sam questioned sceptically. 'It was obvious you two had had a spat from the mournful silence on the way home.'

'That stuff stinks.' Taking the stain remover, Martin screwed the top back on the bottle.

'Stinks maybe, but it's done the trick.' Sam held up his tunic and shook it out, before hanging it on the back of a chair.

'I'd hate to be a criminal in Swansea tonight. You'll gas them before you arrest them.'

'And I hate to see two mates in trouble on the same day.' Sam picked up his mug.

'I am not in trouble.'

'If Lily got the wrong end of the stick about what happened with Adam I could explain,' Sam offered generously.

'What's to explain?' Martin laid a cigarette next to Sam's mug. 'I lost my temper.'

'Lucky for Brian that you did.'

'He would have managed.'

'I doubt it.' Sam poured milk into his tea and heaped in three spoonfuls of sugar. 'That kick you took on your shin was aimed at his stomach. I've seen what that can do. It's not a pretty sight and the mopping up can take hours. Which reminds me, how's your leg?'

'Bruised.'

'You should get it checked by a doctor.'

'It's fine,' Martin snapped irritably.

'You're not feeling guilty about clocking Adam, are you?' Sam flicked his lighter and lit Martin's cigarette before his own.

'I was so mad I didn't know what I was doing. If you and Brian hadn't been there to stop me I could have killed him.'

'Adam's not that much of a wimp. Once he'd got his wind back he would have given as good as he got.' Sam settled comfortably in one of the easy chairs with his tea.

'That's not the point. Suppose I lose my rag with someone else, you – Lily . . .'

'You only lost your temper with Adam because Brian was threatened. And you weren't the only one who saw red. If I could have got between them before you, Adam wouldn't have stood a chance.'

'That's because you're a trained police officer.'

'Forget training. I lost my cool just like you. But, unlike you, I'm not frightened of losing it.' He hesitated, then asked, 'Is it because of your father?'

'What do you know about my father?' Martin bristled defensively.

'I've heard stories.' Sam swung his legs on to the seat of one of the kitchen chairs.

'The people in this town never let up. He's dead and buried.'

'People love gossip.' Sam inhaled on his cigarette. 'And from what I've heard he gave them plenty to talk about.'

'He was a vicious bastard, end of story,' Martin said shortly, with the intention of putting an end to the conversation.

'Are you afraid of losing your temper because he was always losing his?' Sam questioned with uncharacteristic insight.

Martin drew heavily on his cigarette. 'Probably,' he conceded grudgingly.

'One, I've lived with you for over a month now and you can take it from me, you're a good guy. Two, people who are aware that they are likely to lose their temper take care to keep it under control except under extreme provocation. And if what Adam tried to do to Brian last night doesn't come into that category I don't know what does. And three, I've seen you with your sister and Lily. You'd slit your own throat before you'd touch a woman in anger.'

'I wish I had your confidence.'

'Find it, Martin. Because the way you are now, you're too scared to

115

take what life is offering you on a plate and that's sad.' Sam looked him directly in the eye. 'As much for the gorgeous Lily as you.'

'The gorgeous Lily has Joe.'

'I watched Joe and Lily today and she doesn't look at him the way she looks at you.'

A glimmer of a smile appeared on Martin's face. 'You think so?'

'I know so,' Sam pronounced decisively, 'so why don't you go upstairs and ask her if she feels like a walk. And while you're there, put in a good word for me with your sister.'

'You want to go out with Katie?' Martin looked at him in surprise.

'I'd like to, but she doesn't seem to know I exist.'

'She's shy, particularly with men.' Martin hadn't spoken to Katie about her relationship with John Griffiths since the night she and John had told him they would marry as soon as his divorce was finalised. He wanted his sister to be happy but he couldn't help feeling that Sam would make a more suitable husband for her than a man more than twice her age.

Misunderstanding Martin's silence, Sam sought to reassure him. 'If you're worried about my intentions, they are strictly honourable. They'd hardly be anything else when we all live in the same house. And if that's not good enough for you . . .' He grinned wickedly. 'Remember, I saw what you did to Adam.'

Lily sat back and watched Katie flick through the *Sunday People*. She stared at various pictures and articles but from the blank expression on her face Lily doubted whether a single image or word was registering. Setting aside the stocking she'd repaired with one of her own hairs, she reached for the kettle. 'Do you fancy a cup of tea?'

'I suppose we ought to think about laying the table,' Katie answered, in a tone that suggested she wanted to do anything but.

'If we do, it'll only be for us. Mrs Hunt had a list of jobs a mile long for Uncle Roy, so he'll be eating tea over there.'

'Perhaps we should invite Judy over.'

'She made it clear she wanted to be alone for a while. I think we should respect that, at least for today.'

Katie thought about what Lily said and knew she was right. One look at Judy's face when she had returned, soaked and dejected, from the station had been enough for her to realise that there was nothing she or anyone – aside from Brian and he was on his way to London – could do for Judy. When something as devastating as losing the man you love happened, there was no comfort. Since John had told her he no longer wanted to see her privately, a sick, desolate feeling had set in, draining all pleasure from life. It made no difference where she was or whom she was with, she couldn't shake it.

'But there are the two of us and we should eat.' Wishing Katie would talk about whatever it was that had upset her, Lily turned on the tap and filled the kettle.

'Has your uncle said anything to you about what's going to happen to the house and us when he marries Mrs Hunt?' Katie asked, wondering if she should start looking for other lodgings.

'Only that they won't be marrying before the summer at the earliest.'

'Anyone in?'

'In the kitchen, Marty,' Katie called, as he knocked on the connecting door between the basement and the house. 'Did you see Brian?' she asked, as soon as he walked into the room.

'Sam and I caught up with him at the station. He didn't say much but he seemed upset.'

'So was Judy.' Katie leaped to her friend's defence.

'She was the one who wanted to stay here,' Martin reminded her.

'It's Judy's and Brian's problem and I think we should leave them to sort it out without interfering or gossiping about them. Tea?' Lily reached for the cups.

'No, thanks. As I've been in all afternoon I wondered if the two of you fancied a walk.'

'I'm so tired I'd curl up and drop off on the pavement,' Katie said flatly.

'Lily?'

'I'd like to. You sure you don't mind being left alone, Katie?' Lily was already untying her apron.

'No, I want to wash my hair anyway.'

Lily looked at the kettle she'd just put on to boil. 'I'll make us all tea when I come back.'

'Not for me, I'll grab a sandwich after you've gone. I promise,' Katie added in response to Lily's concerned look.

Lily turned to Martin. 'I'll brush my hair and get my coat.' As Lily left, Katie lifted the kettle from the stove and closed the hob.

'You all right, sis?' Martin asked.

'Just tired.'

He debated whether or not to try to push her, but before he had made a decision, Lily returned and he thanked his lucky stars that he'd picked a girlfriend who didn't take hours to doll up. A touch of lipstick, a brush through her hair and a coat, and she was ready. 'We won't be long, sis.'

'Please don't hurry on my account. As soon as my hair is dry I'm going to bed. I really am tired.'

He kissed Katie's cheek before following Lily to the door.

Joy knocked before opening her daughter's bedroom door. 'Do you feel like talking?' she asked, tactfully remaining in the doorway.

'There's nothing to say.' Judy screwed the damp handkerchief she was holding into a ball as she looked up from the bed.

'You will have to telephone the BBC and the hostel.'

Judy choked back her tears. 'I'll do it first thing in the morning.'

Joy thought for a moment, choosing her words carefully. 'It's not too late to change your mind. You could catch an early train and be in London before your afternoon shift starts at the BBC.'

Judy shook her head.

'Judy, I know you, how impetuous you can be. It seems to me that you've rushed thoughtlessly into this . . .'

'I've made the right decision, Mam. I'm sure of it. I was desperately unhappy in London.'

'You never said,' Joy reproved. 'If you had, we might have been able to do something about it.'

'Like what?' Judy challenged.

'Perhaps found you another hostel to live in.'

'It would have made no difference.'

'Well,' Joy conceded, 'if you're absolutely sure you've made the right decision there's nothing I can say.'

'I am absolutely certain that I want to stay in Swansea,' Judy reiterated tearfully.

'And Brian?' Joy probed gently. 'He must have thought a great deal of you to give up his job and follow you to London.'

'Whatever he thought of me then, he doesn't think the same of me now.'

'Then it's over between you two?'

Judy remembered his harsh words as he had rejected her suggestion that they make love. *You're so mixed up you don't know what you want, London or Swansea, me or any man who'll show you what sex is like. I don't want to have to get married like Jack, forced into it because there's a baby on* the way. *I want to get married because I love the girl, she loves me and we've made a decision to spend the rest of our lives together. Not because the girl sees marriage and a family as a way out of a job she can't get to grips with.* 'Yes, Mam, it's over.'

'I'm sorry, Judy, if there's anything I can do . . .'

Sitting up, Judy scrubbed her tears with the damp handkerchief. 'Start looking for that second salon tomorrow.'

Stepping into the room, Joy hugged her. 'If you'll take over the Monday half-price pensioner clients tomorrow I'll see if I can sign a lease by teatime. But I warn you, they all want to look the way they did when they were sixteen, even down to the crimped knife-edge waves, so don't go trying any Doris Day soft curls on them.'

'Where are we going?' Lily asked Martin as they turned out of Carlton Terrace into Craddock Street.

'The beach,' Martin answered decisively. 'After clouding my brain with mechanics all afternoon I want to breathe fresh sea air.'

A blast of freezing wind hit them as they rounded the corner into Mansel Street. Lily put her head down and pulled up her collar. 'By fresh I take it you mean Arctic.'

'Spring doesn't seem as close as it did yesterday. Want to put your hand in my pocket?' he ventured, unsure of the reception his suggestion would receive after their argument in the Pier.

'That depends what's in your pocket.'

'A half-eaten tripe and onion sandwich. My pet mouse . . .'

'You've been spending too much time with Brian.' Relenting, she slipped her gloved hand into his, relishing the intimacy – and the warmth as he closed his fingers round it and pushed both their hands into the deep pocket of his overcoat.

'He does have a weird sense of humour,' he conceded, as they headed down Christina Street towards the Kingsway.

Knowing she was on dangerous ground didn't prevent her from risking a reference to the fight. 'Which is presumably why Adam hit him.'

'It wasn't just Brian's fault, we were all to blame,' he admitted, shouldering his share of the responsibility. 'Brian just happened to be closest when we told Adam what we'd done.'

'And what was that exactly?'

'Played a silly joke on him on Jack's stag night.'

'With scent and lipstick.'

'How do you know?' He wondered if Jack had told Helen what he'd done and she'd had time to mention it to the girls before leaving the Mackworth.

'I was there when Jack came upstairs and asked Katie for them. I told him then that the bridegroom was supposed to be the target on stag nights, not his guests.'

'The bridegroom didn't like having his beer spiked with vodka,' Martin said in an attempt to justify what Jack had done.

'So Jack played the joke, and you and Brian took the punishment.' She quickened her pace so as to keep up with him as they left the Kingsway for St Helen's Road.

'Neither of us took much punishment. Sam held Adam back when he tried to have a second go. And you are not to say a word to Adam as to who the real culprit was. It will only make him boiling mad again, possibly enough to confront Jack when he comes back.'

'Sometimes I wonder if you boys ever grow out of the fighting in the playground stage,' she said crossly, hating the thought of Martin and Brian fighting anyone, especially Adam who was one of their crowd.

'If I was ever into it, I'm not now. I'll never hit anyone again,' he pledged grimly.

'Not even if they are trying to hit you?'

'Especially, if they are trying to hit me,' he reiterated. 'Lily, about last night . . .'

'Forget last night. I have.' Afraid he'd try to pick an argument with her again, she tried to move the conversation on. By inviting her to take a walk with him he'd proved that he didn't want to finish with her – unless he intended to give her the unpleasant news now. She shivered at the thought.

'You're cold.' Taking off his scarf, he wrapped it round her neck, drew the ends towards him and pulled her close enough to kiss the tip of her freezing nose before walking on. 'Unfortunately I can't forget last night and I doubt Adam will either.'

'I hope you're wrong. I hate quarrels and you've always got on well together.'

'And us?' He looked keenly at her as they stopped to cross the Mumbles Road. 'Do we get on well together?'

She looked into his eyes. They were dark, serious in the cold late-afternoon light. 'What do you think?'

'Before last night I would have said yes.'

'I asked you to forget last night.'

He removed her hand from his pocket as they crossed the Mumbles Road. 'The evenings are getting lighter.'

Dismayed that he'd moved the conversation on to the impersonal, she murmured, 'I've noticed.'

'It was dark at half past five a month ago. In a few weeks it will be warm enough to swim.'

'Auntie Norah used to say "Never cast a clout until May's out"'.

'My mother wouldn't let us in the sea before June either, but Jack and I used to sneak off and swim in our underpants and dry them in the coalhouse afterwards. Mam could never understand why they were always black and sandy.' He smiled at one of the more bearable memories from his childhood.

'We used to borrow costumes from Helen. She always had half a dozen spares, and her mother didn't watch her the way Aunt Norah used to watch me, or your mother and Mrs Hunt watched Katie and Judy. On Saturday afternoons we'd pretend to go to the pictures and catch a bus to Limeslade. Given the freezing Mays we've had over the years, and the fact that we were too scared to go home until our hair dried, it's a wonder we didn't catch pneumonia.'

'So' – he grabbed her hand again as they stood at the top of the steps that led down to the beach – 'now we've established we both misbehaved when we were children, will you come swimming with me?'

'Not next week.' Was the casual question meant as an invitation to carry on going out with him until the weather was warm enough for swimming?

'But you'll be able to make that outing we talked about, next weekend?'

Confused by his present warmth after his offhand manner of that morning and the night before, she wondered if he was doing the one thing dreaded by all girls and written about at length by agony aunts in women's magazines: 'taking her for granted'. Deciding caution was the best option open to her she said, 'If you want me to.'

As they reached the bottom step that led down to the deserted sands he pulled her into the shelter of one of the shops built into the arches under Victoria Bridge. Closing his hands round her back, he pressed the full length of his body against hers. Her head began to spin and not only from the breathtakingly bitter wind. His lips were warm, he smelled of scents she was becoming familiar with, Coal Tar soap,

Vosene shampoo and Old Spice aftershave. His body was hard, unyielding even through layers of clothes, arousing new – and in view of what had happened to Helen – frightening sensations. But as he undid the buttons on her coat she didn't want him to stop. Not even when his hands closed over the front of her sweater and he caressed her breasts through layers of cloth.

'I'm sorry.' A faraway look stole into his eyes as he removed his hands and released her.

'For what?' She hoped he was about to apologise for some of the things he'd said the night before, not the most passionate embrace they'd shared.

'Dragging you out in weather like this. Your face is blue.'

Taking care not to show her disappointment at the prosaic pronouncement after his passion of a moment before, she turned her back to him. 'Once we start walking, I'll soon warm up.'

'Where do you want to walk to?'

'Mumbles.' She looked at the lights nestling in the wooded curve of the bay.

'Nothing will be open when we get there.'

'We don't always have to go somewhere.'

'No, we don't.' He followed her as she left the shelter of the shops and struck out towards the tide line. It lapped high, leaving only a narrow stretch of sand to walk on. As they scrunched along a crust of blackened seaweed, pebbles and debris, the wind scudded into them, damp and gritty with a salt spray that stung their faces and knotted Lily's hair, bringing tears to her eyes and numbing her body, even through her coat.

'Look, Lily, you know I'm fond of you,' he confessed suddenly.

'After last night and this morning I wasn't too sure.' Tired of fighting the wind, she turned her back to it and looked out to sea. The sun was no more than a smudge of light on the horizon. Dusk was falling rapidly around them. As navy and purple shadows crept upwards from the beach shrouding familiar landmarks, they took on new and peculiar shapes. Only the sea remained constant, a vast, gleaming, blue-black pool crested by short-lived bursts of white foam.

'But I'm not like Jack. The thought of marriage scares me to death . . .'

'I told you last night I'm not looking to get married, Marty.' She smiled in relief. He was finally talking to her about the reasons behind his strange moodiness.

'But you will want to – one day, I mean?'

'At the moment I have a good job, a great boyfriend . . .'

'Great?' He returned her smile.

'Fantastic.'

He pulled her towards him. 'I look at Jack and Helen all starry-eyed and happy, then I look around at the couples in the street who've been married for years and I can't help wondering if they started out that way too and, if they did, what went wrong. There's Helen's mam and dad . . .'

'Their divorce is hardly a surprise,' Lily interposed. 'According to Uncle Roy they've led separate lives ever since they married, him in the warehouse, her in the Little Theatre. And they are such different people. Mrs Griffiths, well she's Mrs Griffiths,' she said guardedly, trying to conceal her dislike. 'Even Helen says she's always been more interested in her friends and fashion than her own family. And Mr Griffiths is more of a one for the quiet life. He seems to enjoy his work and helping people . . .'

'Point taken,' he interrupted, not wanting to think of all the reasons that lay behind John Griffiths's kindness to his sister. Despite Katie's insistence that nothing had happened between them until she had been working in the warehouse for some time, he remained deeply suspicious.

'Why don't you try looking at the happy people in our street instead of the unhappy ones,' Lily suggested. 'From what I can see there's not much difference between the way Helen and Jack feel about one another and my Uncle Roy and Mrs Hunt.'

'No, but your Uncle Roy and Judy's mother haven't been married for years.'

'But they will be, and happily,' she countered stubbornly.

He linked his hands round her neck and pulled her even closer. 'If good wishes were wings I believe you'd have the whole world flying.'

She clung to him for a few minutes, resting her head on his shoulder. 'I know you don't like talking about your father,' she began cautiously, 'but Uncle Roy told me that he was different before the war. He thinks something must have happened to change him.'

'My mother used to try to tell me the same thing,' Martin released her and looked towards Mumbles. 'I didn't believe her then and I don't now.'

'Don't you remember what he was like before he was called up?'

'I was seven when he went away and if there were any good times

123

they've been overshadowed by what came later. Whenever I think of him, I wish I'd done something to stop him from beating Mam.'

'Like what, Marty?' she asked, sensing and wanting to alleviate his pain. 'You just said, you'll never hit anyone again even if they hit you.'

'I would have made an exception in his case. You have no idea what it was like to live with him day in day out. Terrified of what he'd do next – and which one of us he'd pick on. Dreading him having a go at me and hating myself whenever he had a go at one of the others because it wasn't me.'

'Katie told me you stopped him from hitting your mother after you came home from National Service. Before then you were a child who would have got badly beaten if you'd tried.'

'Better me than my mother.'

'There wasn't a choice, Marty,' she said firmly. 'It would have been you *and* your mother.'

'You have an answer for everything, don't you,' he said softly as he reached for her hand.

'No, but since my mother gatecrashed my engagement party I do know there's no use fretting over the past. It can't be altered no matter how much you wish some things had never happened. All you can do is get on with life.'

'Is your mother the reason you broke off your engagement to Joe?'

She glanced down, only just able to make out the veins of blackened coal dust in the gloom that covered the waterlogged sand. Another few minutes and it would be too dark to see them, or their footprints that held for the barest fraction of a second before being obliterated by the welling sea water.

'Sorry, I had no business asking that.' He dropped her hand, furious with himself for allowing his jealousy to surface. And it wasn't simply jealousy. Lily had been engaged to Joe. Everyone accepted that engaged couples could 'go further' than couples who were simply 'going out' or 'courting' and he wasn't even sure he and Lily had breached the barrier between going out and courting. Every time he thought of Joe and Lily or saw them together, he tortured himself by imagining the things she had allowed Joe to do her. There were bound to have been kisses – and touches. How far had her petting gone with Joe? Had she taken off her clothes –

'Yes, you do have a right to ask that.' Her declaration broke in on his thoughts. 'And I don't mind talking about it.' She was elated that

Martin had finally made an admission that he was resentful of her 'almost' engagement to Joe. 'But as it's freezing, do you mind if we carry on walking?' She took his arm as she stepped close to him. 'You were there, you saw how shocked Joe was.'

'And you.'

'I was horrified,' she agreed.

'Why?' He slipped his arm round her shoulders. 'You're not responsible for your mother. She didn't bring you up. You didn't even know she existed until that day.'

Drawing even closer to him, she wrapped her arm round his waist. 'At the time I honestly thought that because she'd given birth to me I wasn't good enough – not just for Joe, but any decent company. Then Uncle Roy explained that every one of us is worth exactly the same as the next person, no matter where we come from, or what airs and graces we try to adopt. It's the life we make for ourselves and what we give to others that's important, not our past, or how much or how little money we may have.'

'You really believe that.'

Once again she realised just how insecure and vulnerable he was. 'Anyone who's thought about it for more than five minutes has to, Marty. Otherwise what we have is more important than who we are and that kind of thinking would turn the world upside down – not to mention put the criminals who make their money dishonestly on top. Sorry,' she apologised, 'I sound exactly like Uncle Roy on one of his rants.'

'That still doesn't explain why you broke off your engagement to Joe.' He set the conversation firmly back on course.

'That's so simple I thought you would have realised by now. I didn't love him.'

'Then why did you agree to marry him?'

'Because he proposed to me on the day Auntie Norah was buried. Uncle Roy was wonderful but I felt very alone – and frightened of the future. I had no idea what was going to happen to me. Joe offered me security and a ready-made life as his wife. I didn't have to do anything except say yes and I'm ashamed to say I was too much of a coward to turn him down. Later, after the party, I realised I'd accepted him for all the wrong reasons.'

'You never loved him?' Halting, he stood in front of her and linked his arms round her waist.

She wanted to say 'not in the way I love you', but unsure how he'd respond after his declaration about marriage, she settled for, 'I only thought I did at the time. There's nothing between us now, nor will there be again.'

He kissed her once more, then, leaving one hand round her waist, led her on. As they neared the village, he spotted lights burning in the Italian café. 'Buy you a coffee?'

'The café's open?' she asked.

'The lights are on.'

'It will be warm in there.'

'And then we take the train back.'

'Lazybones.'

Once again silence fell between them, but it was devoid of strain and tension. He wondered why he couldn't always be like this, simply take what life offered and be grateful for it, like Lily. Instead, he seemed doomed always to question any happiness it brought, too terrified to enjoy it, in case it would be snatched away.

Chapter 9

'I'VE ASKED ANN to clear the out-dated files from the system,' John informed Katie as he returned from the warehouse floor early on Monday morning with one of the assistants from Ladies Fashion. Taking the girl aside, he pointed to the bank of filing cabinets set between his office and Katie's desk. 'Remove every file that hasn't any papers documenting transactions in the last year and place them in alphabetical order in the cupboard in the corridor. If you're not sure about anything ask Miss Clay.'

'I will, Mr Griffiths.' Smiling nervously at Katie, Ann opened the top drawer in the first of the cabinets as John disappeared into his office and closed the door. Katie managed a brief nod, before continuing to type a letter John had given her that morning, the first he'd written out instead of dictating it.

She knew exactly why John had brought Ann into the office and it had nothing to do with overcrowded filing cabinets. He could no longer bear to be alone with her and that knowledge hurt. More than she would have believed possible. She finished her letter and began another. By the time she had cleared her typing in-tray she had made a decision. Glancing at her watch, she looked at Ann.

'It's time for mid-morning tea, Ann. Go down to the canteen, ask them to set a tray for three and bring it up here, please.' As the girl left, Katie rose from her desk and went to John's office door. Lifting her hand, she rapped on it with her knuckles.

'Come in.'

Katie deliberately left the door open as she walked into John's office. 'Could I have a word, please, Mr Griffiths?'

'Of course, Miss Clay.' Not trusting himself to look at her, he kept his attention fixed on the letter he had been trying to read.

'If it won't cause too much inconvenience, I'd like to leave half an hour earlier tonight. I'll work through my lunch hour tomorrow to make up the time.'

'Take all the time you want, Katie, there's no need to make it up.' He set aside the letter but still avoided looking at her.

'I'd get behind if I didn't.' She moved aside as Ann entered with a tray. 'Set it on the table in the reception alcove, please, Ann, and pour it out. Mr Griffiths takes milk and two sugars, I just take milk.'

'Yes, Miss Clay.'

Standing back so Ann could walk out ahead of her, Katie murmured, 'Thank you, Mr Griffiths.'

As Katie returned to her desk, John looked from her to the young girl who brought his cup of tea. Ann was probably only a month or two younger than Katie but there seemed to be years and a wealth of experience between them. Experience he had given Katie, which he was finding it impossible to forget – or totally regret.

Joy stood in the street and looked through the window of her salon. Judy was engrossed in combing out old Mrs Jones's hair, coaxing it into a style that had been the absolute height of fashion a quarter of a century before. Judy didn't look happy but there was no trace of the tears she'd shed the previous day – and night. Two other elderly clients were sitting under the hairdryers and the junior was washing the hair of a third. As all the customers were smiling and talking animatedly, her daughter had evidently coped. Pushing open the door, Joy called out, 'Good afternoon, ladies,' as she walked in.

'And a good afternoon to you, Mrs Hunt.' Mrs Jones, who could be cantankerous when she chose, beamed at her. 'Your daughter's a lovely little hairdresser, quick too,' she added, making Joy feel as though she had always been tardy in doing her hair.

'I'm glad to hear you're satisfied, Mrs Jones.'

'Lacquer, Mrs Jones?' As Judy glanced at her mother in the mirror she realised she was watching her.

'Please, Judy, it's well worth the extra sixpence.'

Judy covered Mrs Jones's face with a cardboard shield and picked up the plastic squeezy bottle of lacquer. Holding her breath, she squirted it liberally over the waves she'd pinched into shape, only stopping when they were thoroughly coated with a shiny crust.

'Beautiful, Judy, just the way I like it,' Mrs Jones complimented her, reaching for her handbag. 'Same time next week, all right?'

'Mam?' Judy looked at her mother.

'You'll probably get me, Mrs Jones.' Joy went to the desk and flicked through the pages of the appointment book.

'Judy's not come back to work for you, then?' Mrs Jones asked, fishing for gossip she could pass on to her neighbours in Hanover Street. Despite all her quizzing, Judy had refused to tell her why she'd returned from London so suddenly. And she had pretended not to hear her when she had asked after her young man, the policeman.

Joy smiled at Judy as she took the half-crown Mrs Jones handed her. 'We're opening another salon, in Mumbles, Mrs Jones. I've just signed the lease on it. The decorators and plumbers are moving in there tomorrow and if I can get the equipment delivered by Saturday we'll be opening first thing on Monday morning.'

Joe paid the barman for the pint of beer and cigarettes he had bought. The windows in the pub were set too high for him to see out of if he sat at a table, so he pulled up a stool and perched at the bar. Fortunately, at this time of day he'd never found the pub busy. Four old men sat crouched around the table nearest the fire, playing dominoes. A couple of labourers from one of the building sites on the Kingsway had laid claim to the darkest corner, but as both started nervously every time a shadow darkened the glass in the doors he wondered why they'd bothered to come in, as they were obviously feeling far too guilty to enjoy their drink.

He opened his cigarettes and looked towards the double doors. The top halves of both were glazed, giving him a clear view of the bank opposite. It was almost five o'clock. The bank had been closed for an hour and a half. On Friday, the first of the staff had left about this time but he knew from the number of times he'd sat at this same bar that Lily was always one of the last. She had recently been promoted secretary to the assistant manager. Not an entirely good move from what she had told Helen, because the man was a stickler for rules, regulations and procedure, and insisted on both his and her desk being as clear as possible at the end of every day.

He sipped his pint. There was an odd metallic tang to the beer but he couldn't stay in the pub without a drink and he always felt men, particularly those who frequented pubs in the afternoon, looked sideways at anyone who ordered orange squash in a bar.

The bank door opened and he was instantly on the alert. Two girls walked out, arm in arm, wearing bright purple headscarves and identical green duster coats. From the back they could have been twins. Chattering, they headed in the direction of the bus station.

He glanced at his watch again before lighting his cigarette. If the bank timetable was running true to form, Lily should be out in the next twenty minutes. He checked his pockets for the peppermints he had bought earlier to disguise the smell of the beer. They would serve coffee and cake in the Kardomah until six. Lily would be tired after her day at work and, after what Martin had said about his finals yesterday, he assumed he'd be too busy for the next week or two to take Lily out. What girl could resist a casual invitation originating from a chance encounter in the street with a friend? Hopefully not Lily.

Katie left the warehouse at half past four. Walking into the nearest newsagent's she bought a copy of the *Evening Post*. Turning to the Situation Vacant column she scanned it before leaving the shop. Monday was usually a sparse day but there were two advertisements that caught her attention. Folding the paper under her arm, she left the shop and headed purposefully for High Street.

'Lily, how amazing to see you here.'
    'Hardly, Joe.' She eyed him suspiciously. 'I work here.'
    He glanced behind her to the bank as if he hadn't noticed the building. 'So you do.'
    'You'd forgotten.'
    'I'm just a bit preoccupied. Exams and all that.'
    'Nice seeing you.'
    As she turned to leave he touched her arm. 'Have you time for a coffee?'
    'After Saturday night I'm not sure that's a good idea.'
    'I want to apologise. I . . . I had too much to drink. I behaved like an idiot. I would have said something at Mrs Hunt's yesterday but there were too many people around.'
    'Apology accepted.'
    'We are still friends?'
    She hesitated for a fraction of a second. 'Of course.'
    'Then have that coffee with me to celebrate.'
    'I should go home.' She sounded half-hearted, even to herself. Katie was never home before seven o'clock and frequently later on a Monday, Wednesday and Friday because they were her overtime nights. And she didn't want to call in on Judy without her. Her uncle was on afternoons and wouldn't be home until ten at the earliest, and Martin had warned her last night that he would be swotting all week

and most of the next for his exams, and he'd make up for his absence after he had sat the last one.

'How long will a quick coffee with a friend take?' Joe smiled disarmingly and she relented.

'One quick coffee.'

'If we go to the Kardomah they may have some of those chocolate cream cakes you like.' He almost offered her his arm, then thought better of the idea. The more distant and gentlemanlike he behaved, the more likelihood there was of her trusting him and building a foundation on which he could re-establish their relationship.

'And you, of course, hate.' She laughed, referring to an evening when he had met her from work, taken her to the café and eaten four of the cakes himself.

'No lady should remind a gentleman of his failings or fondness for sticky cakes.' His smile broadened as he pushed the café door and held it open for her.

Martin was walking through town on his way home when he glanced into the Kardomah and saw Lily sitting at a table close to the window with Joe. She was drinking coffee and smiling at him while he talked expansively, using his hands as much as his mouth.

He felt as though someone had plunged a knife into his stomach and twisted it. Stepping into the shelter of the porch of a children's clothes shop opposite, he continued to watch them, contrasting Joe's immaculately cut, black-and-white houndstooth sports coat and black trousers with the grease- and oil-stained jeans and jacket he was wearing. Joe and Lily looked perfect together. Like the young couples in the advertisements in glossy magazines, who lived in beautifully furnished homes and bought all the right products.

'Excuse me, young man.'

As he moved to allow the middle-aged woman to pass, he caught a glimpse of the contemptuous expression on her face. He was what he looked, a filthy labourer. Putting his head down, he charged round the corner. Who was he to tell Lily who she could and couldn't see? Last night she had insisted that it was over between her and Joe – that there was nothing left between them. Had she remembered him telling her on Saturday night that there was no way he'd be able to marry or support her and decided to give Joe another chance after all?

For all Lily's declarations that she didn't love Joe, perhaps he should bow out. Despite his hopes to the contrary it was obvious she didn't love him — if she did, why was she with Joe now . . .

Then he realised he didn't have to bow out because Joe was already seeing her again. The only wonder was why Lily had agreed to go for a walk with him last night after his behaviour on Saturday night. Kindness — or did she feel sorry for him? The thought that the only emotion he evoked in her was pity hurt. But when he compared himself with Joe Griffiths he really couldn't see why else she would even stop to give him the time of day.

Either of you thinking of going to the Pier tomorrow night?' Judy looked at Katie and Lily as she settled herself in the window seat of Lily's kitchen.

Lily shook her head. 'Martin's too busy swotting and I don't want to go without him.'

'You seen him this week?' Judy took the tea Katie handed her.

'Beyond shouting "Good Luck" when we pass in the street, no.'

'What about you, Katie?'

'I don't want to go to the Pier full stop.'

'What a trio we make, one boyfriend between the three of us and he's too busy to go out.' Judy gazed at the raindrops sliding down the window-pane as she stirred her tea.

'You still haven't heard from Brian?' Lily passed Katie the sugar bowl.

'No, nor am I expecting to.'

'Don't you think you should write?' Katie suggested. Certain that Judy loved Brian, she couldn't understand why she wasn't doing everything she could to remain close to him. She would have thought a dismal, lonely hostel life in London a small price to pay for an occasional shared evening with John.

'To say what? "I'm sorry I left London to return to Swansea"?'

'You must miss him.'

'A lot.' Judy swung her legs up on to the seat and curled them beneath her. 'But much as I hate to admit it, I'm not cut out for the high life of glamour at the BBC, more like the tedium of running a small local salon, which I start doing first thing on Monday morning.'

'Is it ready?' Lily asked, surprised.

'It is. You wouldn't believe how hard my mother has worked this week to make sure it would be and if you aren't too busy to take a trip down Mumbles tomorrow you can see it for yourself.'

'I'd like that.' Katie sat in the easy chair opposite Lily.

'Ice creams on me afterwards,' Lily offered.

'So' – Judy looked around the room – 'it's back to girl evenings, exactly where we were two months ago before I went away.'

'Not quite,' Katie corrected. 'Helen's married and Lily has Martin.'

'You and I are footloose and fancy free.'

Katie tried not to think about John as she parried Judy's forced smile. At that moment she would have given everything she had and twenty years of her life to be closeted with John, discussing what they would do as soon as his divorce was finalised.

'Mr Griffiths.' Katie left her desk as John entered the reception area of the outer office. 'May I have a word, please?' She glanced at Ann, who was removing the last files from the bottom drawer of the third cabinet. The girl had taken nine and a half days to clear three four-drawer cabinets; a task she could have accomplished in a fraction of the time.

'No problems, are there, Katie?' John forced himself to look at her and once he started he couldn't stop. Her face was unusually pale beneath a light layer of impeccably applied make-up, but dressed in a bottle-green costume complemented by a freshly laundered cream cotton blouse with starched collar, she looked as though she'd stepped from the pages of *Vogue*. The floor supervisors in the warehouse had told him that she took a keen interest in fashion and cosmetics, not only asking them for hints and tips, but also their opinion on what suited her and didn't. It was to her and their credit that she looked as good as she did.

'No, Mr Griffiths.' She followed him into his office and stood before his desk. 'I'd like to leave at three o'clock this afternoon.'

He heard the outer office door opening and closing, and assumed Ann was carrying another load of files to the cupboard in the corridor. 'You took some time off last week.'

'I made up the time then, as I will now.'

'I am not concerned about the time. May I ask where you're going?'

'A personal matter.'

'If it's anything I can help with . . .'

'It isn't, but thank you for asking, Mr Griffiths.'

'Katie . . .'

'Yes.' She leaned expectantly towards him and he retreated to the window.

'Have you checked Ann's progress with the filing cabinets?' He didn't want to know. He simply wanted to keep her in his office for as long as possible. Being close to her, inhaling her perfume, being able to look in her eyes, brought the strangest mix of emotions including pain, yet it was still preferable to not being with her.

'She's slow but thorough.'

They both started at a knock on the door.

'Come in,' he shouted impatiently.

'A Mr Davies is downstairs, Mr Griffiths. He's asking to see you on urgent personal business. I did enquire, but he wouldn't tell me what it was.' Ann tried to imitate Katie's professional manner but she only succeeded in sounding faintly absurd, like a child play-acting at being an adult.

Katie went to the door. 'Shall I show Mr Davies in, Mr Griffiths?'

'Please.'

She left, closing the door softly behind her.

Wishing his solicitor had chosen any other time to call, John sat at his desk and lifted the pile of letters Katie had typed in front of him. Unscrewing the top from his fountain pen he scanned the top one and signed it. Then the next and the next, dropping them one by one into the out-tray, all the while conscious of Katie's perfume lingering in the room. He hadn't even liked essence of violets until she had begun to wear it.

He only had to close his eyes to conjure every line of her slender figure, to see her eyes lighting her face when she smiled, the graceful walk that sent his heart rate soaring every time she stepped near him. *A personal matter!* He had been the one to exclude her from his life. He had no right to pry, yet the only personal matters he wanted Katie Clay to have were ones that related to him. He reminded himself of all the reasons why he shouldn't see her privately; his age; his ugly, crippled body; Esme – and her vicious, vindictive nature. It might be painful to see and work with Katie every day but he simply couldn't bear the thought of the alternative – not to see her at all.

'And how did the last exam go?' Sam asked as Martin stepped down into their kitchen and closed the door behind him.

'It went.' Exhausted as much by tormenting thoughts of Joe and Lily as the exams, Martin sank down in an easy chair.

'Put your feet up; I'll make you a cup of tea.'

'Why are you being nice?' Martin questioned suspiciously as Sam filled the kettle.

'Because I thought you might want to include me and Katie in your plans to celebrate with Lily tomorrow night.'

'And who says I'm celebrating with Lily tomorrow night?'

'You're not taking her down the Pier?'

'There's a class booze-up to mark the end of the exams.'

'You prefer to go out with the boys than Lily?'

'I haven't thought about what I'm doing yet,' Martin muttered. If he joined the boys on their night out he wouldn't have to face Lily and that meant postponing a decision on the jealousy that had gnawed destructively at him ever since he had seen her with Joe.

'We could take Judy. You never know, she might be able to appease Adam,' Sam coaxed.

'I doubt she's forgotten Brian that quickly.'

'Has he mentioned her in his letters to you?'

'No.' Martin had the feeling that Brian had only written to him in the hope that he would mention Judy. He had told him about the salon Joy had opened, because he had heard about it from Katie when she had come down to collect his washing in the week, but he had said nothing else, simply because since he had started his examinations he hadn't seen anything at all of Judy and very little of Lily or his sister.

'So what do you say?'

'I'll let you know what I decide tomorrow.' Taking his notebook, Martin left the kitchen for his bedroom and closed the door.

'Smart secretary you have there, John,' Mark Davies observed as Katie deposited a tea tray on John's desk and closed the door on them.

'I know, but I doubt you came here to compliment me on my staff. Take a seat.' John pulled out a chair.

'I had a telephone call from Richard Thomas half an hour ago. Esme is withdrawing her petition for divorce.'

John stared at him in disbelief. 'She can't do that! I've admitted adultery.'

'She can do it because she's the petitioner.' Mark lifted one of the cups of tea from the tray. 'Richard also mentioned that Esme asked you to consider a reconciliation.'

'She asked, I considered, I refused.'

'When?'

135

'After Helen's wedding.'

'And you didn't think to tell me?'

Stung by the reproach in Mark's voice, John explained, 'As I had no intention of doing anything of the kind, I didn't think it was important.'

'Your wife suggests a reconciliation when you're in the middle of divorce proceedings and you don't think it's important enough to mention to your solicitor!'

'It's not as if she's had a change of heart,' John said impatiently. 'It's simply that her friends in the Little Theatre don't regard divorcees as socially acceptable. Could my refusal affect the divorce?'

'What divorce?' Mark asked flatly.

'You can't be serious.' John frowned. 'Esme has agreed to a settlement. Everything's sorted.'

'Was being sorted. We had your wife's verbal agreement but she has signed nothing and according to Richard Thomas, she is not going to.'

'What can I do?' John pleaded.

'Tread very carefully. If she comes to see you make sure you're never alone long enough for her to state that a reconciliation has taken place between you. And if she insists on moving back into the matrimonial home . . .'

'I'll change the locks.'

'If you fail to keep her out, move somewhere else.'

'And in the meantime, you'll try to speed things along.'

'Frankly, John, I don't hold out any hope.'

'Esme has had affairs . . .'

'Anything you can prove?' Mark interrupted.

'No,' John conceded grimly.

'We'd need proof to bring a counter petition, and even if we had we'd be placed right at the bottom of the queue again. You could be stuck in the courts for at least another two years.'

'There has to be something we can do.' John felt sick at the thought of remaining tied to a woman he neither loved nor respected and who had nothing but contempt for him.

'I could try asking for a formal meeting with Esme and Richard Thomas. If they agree, it will be up to you to try to persuade her to change her mind.'

'If it's a question a money . . .'

'In my opinion you've already made her a far too generous offer.'

'Money means nothing to me.'

Mark pushed his half-drunk cup of tea aside and left his seat. 'As long as you remember there's no guarantee she'll agree to a meeting. You'll be careful with Esme until you hear from me, won't you.'

'That's one piece of advice I don't need,' John assured him, as he showed him to the door.

'I can't believe we've been here for fourteen days.' Helen flung back the sheets and rolled naked to the edge of the bed as Jack returned to their hotel bedroom from the bathroom.

'Not even when you consider everything we've done?'

'Like visit the Tower, Westminster Abbey, Harrods . . . and' – she smiled beguilingly – 'the huge advances we've made in getting to know one another.'

He looked down at her. 'Stop teasing, you know what it does to me to see you like that.'

'Yes.' She held out her arms to him.

'We have to pack if we're going to be out of here by eleven.'

'All done.' She slipped her hand between his thighs.

'I'll need another bath.'

'We can have one together.' She glanced at the clock. 'We've plenty of time before breakfast.'

'If you carry on like this when we get home, I'm never going to want to leave you to go to work.'

'Then it's just as well I'm the boss's daughter.'

Stripping off his dressing gown he lay beside her. As his lips travelled over her throat and down to her breasts she fought a sudden and unexpected twinge of pain but their lovemaking was far too important to interrupt for yet another bout of morning sickness. Pulling him close, she kissed him back with a ferocity that drove all thoughts of trains and timetables from both their minds.

'Sure you don't mind?' Martin asked Lily, willing her to tell him what was going on between her and Joe.

'Of course not,' She hid her disappointment behind a smile. 'Judy and Katie were only saying yesterday they wanted to go to the pictures. *Seven Brides for Seven Brothers* is on in the Albert Hall.'

'That's all right, then.'

'What about Sunday? You did say you wanted to go down the Gower.'

'I'm not sure,' he hedged. 'Jack will be back tonight . . .'

'I understand.' She didn't understand at all. He was pushing her away just as he had the last time they had gone to the Pier and that was the last thing she had been prepared for after their discussion on the beach.

'See you.'

'Yes, Martin.' She closed her front door as he went to the basement steps. 'See you,' she echoed dismally.

'What's wrong?' Jack watched, alarmed, as Helen grimaced. 'And don't say morning sickness. It's five o'clock in the afternoon.'

'I have a pain.'

'Where?'

'In my stomach, but I'm sure it's nothing. It comes and goes . . .' She blanched as a stronger stabbing pain took hold.

'You taken anything?'

She shook her head. 'I didn't like to, not with the baby.'

'I wouldn't have thought an aspirin could hurt him.' He looked out of the window. They'd just left Cardiff. There wasn't another station until Bridgend, at least half an hour away. 'If you'd said something earlier we could have got off the train.'

'Not when we're returning home from our honeymoon,' she protested tearfully as another pain shot through her. 'I want tonight to be perfect. Our first meal together in our first home . . .'

'I'm going to ask the guard if there's a doctor or nurse on board.'

'Don't leave me,' she begged.

'I can't sit and watch you go through agony.' He went to the door and opened it. A man was standing in the corridor looking out through the window. 'Please, could you find the guard for us.' Jack looked back at Helen. 'My wife is ill.'

Lily sat between Katie and Helen in the back row of the Albert Hall and tried to concentrate on the film. Howard Keel was singing well, the colour was wonderful, the dancing terrific, and the film must have had its amusing moments because the people around them laughed from time to time but all she could think about was Martin. Why had he cooled towards her again? Was it something she'd said or done – should she ask him or hope he'd come round and tell her himself?

Carefully unfolding a bag of sweets she'd bought so as not to rattle the paper, she turned to offer Judy a peppermint cream. Even in the gloom she could see tears trickling down her cheeks.

Deciding against disturbing her, she looked at Katie. If anything her cheeks were even wetter. Perhaps it was just as well they'd decided to see a musical, not the melodrama *The Night My Number Came Up* at the Castle. None of them would have survived the experience.

'There's no doctor or nurse on the train.' The guard peered apprehensively at Helen who was crouched double with her eyes closed. 'We'll be in Bridgend in five minutes. I could call an ambulance as soon as we get there.'

'No,' Helen gasped in pain. 'I want to go home.'

'Swansea's another half-hour away, sweetheart,' Jack pleaded, 'and the pain is getting worse.'

'No, it's not.' As a spasm subsided, she smiled weakly with relief. 'And I'm sure it's nothing serious, probably just something I've eaten.'

'If you don't mind me saying so, miss, I think your young man is right. I'd go for that ambulance if I were you. Better safe than sorry.'

'I'm her husband,' Jack corrected.

'Sorry, sir. Do you want me to call an ambulance when we get to Bridgend?'

Helen shook her head. 'No, I want to go home to my own doctor.'

'I'll look in again in five minutes. If you change your mind, let me know.'

'Let me take the guard up on his offer,' Jack pleaded as he sponged Helen's face with eau de Cologne and a flannel he'd taken from her toilet bag.

'I want to go home,' she gasped, fighting pain again as the train pulled into the station.

'You're insane and I'm just as bad for listening to you.'

'But I love you.' She tried to hold his hand as the train pulled out, but her fingers wouldn't respond. Black spots wavered in front of her eyes. The tide of pain was no longer ebbing and flowing within her. She *was* pain. Nothing existed outside the blinding haze of agony that enveloped her, hot, burning, consuming her entire being. She focused on Jack's face, white with strain, almost unrecognisably grave. It was too much effort to keep her eyes open. She would close them – just for a moment.

'Helen!'

Jack's voice, shrill with anguish, yet muted as though he were on a boat and she at the bottom of the sea, echoed through her pain. She struggled to open her eyelids but they no longer responded.

'Helen!' His voice grew harsher. She could hear him, feel him tapping her hand but, strangely distanced from the whole proceedings, she could neither respond nor stop herself from sliding effortlessly downwards through thick grey swirling waters to a blissfully pain-free place where she could truly rest and nothing mattered – not even Jack.

Chapter 10

'I TOOK THE liberty of asking the station master in Neath to call for an ambulance to meet us in Swansea, sir.'

Jack nodded dumbly, his attention fixed on Helen. As she'd fainted a pinched look had settled around her nose and mouth, reminding him of his mother the last time he had seen her, battered and too weak to fight for life in Swansea Hospital. As a child he'd been convinced that he would never love any woman as much as he loved his mother. She'd cared for him and done everything in her power to protect him from his father, and the fact that she had tried far outweighed his pain on the frequent occasions when she hadn't succeeded.

He rubbed Helen's hand vigorously and stared intently into her face, willing her to open her eyes, but she remained comatose. He loved Helen every bit as much as he had loved his mother but in a different, more intense way and he couldn't endure the thought of losing her too. It was his fault Helen was ill. It had to be. All the stupid things he'd done: thieving; fighting; hurting people; making love to her – his love was a curse that killed . . .

'We'll be in Swansea in five minutes, sir.'

'She's cold. Very cold.' Jack continued to rub Helen's hand. 'You are sure there's no doctor or nurse on this train.'

'Quite sure, sir. We've asked in all the carriages.' The guard laid a reassuring hand on Jack's shoulder. 'I'll be back in a few minutes. I'm just going to check that all the arrangements to get her off the train run smoothly.'

Jack didn't even realise the man had left. All he could think of, all he could repeat in his mind, was, 'Please God, don't let her die. Please God, don't let her die.' Because if she did, he simply wouldn't be able to bear it.

Joe took the glass of punch one of his fellow students had ladled out for him and walked out of the french windows of the Head of the

University's English Department's bungalow into his small but immaculate garden. It was laid out like a thousand others, a path and washing line stretched from one end to the other, flanked by two squares of lawn edged by daffodils meticulously planted at four-inch intervals. He turned and glanced back through the windows after he had crossed the lawn. The house was packed with students, all, including Robin, on their best behaviour, sipping punch, nibbling twiglets and cheese biscuits, and making polite, meaningless conversation. He invariably felt at his loneliest and most isolated in a crowd and would have been happier indulging in a solitary walk along the beach but when a student was invited to attend one of Mr Edwards's soirées they refused at their peril. Believing that he was developing the social skills his undergraduates would need when they left the rarefied atmosphere of the college for the wider world, it had never occurred to Huw Edwards that some of his young guests might not think his cider cup and sparse refreshments the height of sophistication.

'Bored, Joseph?' His tutor, Hilary Llewellyn, joined him.

'Just taking a quiet moment to admire the garden.'

'I didn't know you were a horticulturist.' She gazed at the daffodils. 'Do you think Huw uses a ruler when he sets out his bulbs?'

Uncertain whether she was joking or not, he looked her in the eye and she smiled.

'Do me a favour, turn your back to the house.' As he did, she stepped in front of him and tipped the contents of her glass on to the daffodils. 'Thank you, I only hope it doesn't kill them.'

'I had no idea lecturers felt press-ganged too.'

'Swift demotion for all non-attendees,' she replied. 'By the way, that last piece of work you did on Thomas Hardy was excellent. Another straight A to add to your collection. You do know the hopes of the entire department are pinned on you to get a first.'

'I hope I live up to your expectations.'

'Don't try being modest; it doesn't become you. Do you have a cigarette you can spare? I've run out.'

'Of course.' He pulled the gold cigarette case his grandmother had given him for his twenty-first birthday from his inside pocket and flicked it open. Hilary Llewellyn was about the same age as his mother but she couldn't have been more different. She dressed as if she didn't give a damn about clothes, usually in shapeless black skirts and sweaters and coloured stockings, and he had never seen her without the large pair of men's horn-rimmed spectacles that had a habit of slipping to the end of her nose. Her fingernails were clipped short and remained unpolished, and she wore her hair scraped into a tight knot that emphasised her sharp, angular features. The first time he'd seen her tall figure striding into a lecture theatre he'd thought her intimidating, but in the three years she'd lectured him and the year she'd been his personal tutor he'd discovered a kindness behind her innate professionalism. She alone in the English Department had the knack of being friendly with her students without being overfamiliar. She treated everyone the same, student or fellow lecturer, as though they were her equals, and unlike some her colleagues never tried to conceal her passionate support for a Socialism that bordered on Communism.

As she never mentioned the time before she had lectured in the university or discussed her personal life, all sorts of rumours circulated about her. That she'd been a secret agent during the war, that she'd lost all her immediate family in some ghastly tragedy, that she wrote steamy novels under a pseudonym and was a passionate advocate of free love – although no one had ever actually seen her with a man who wasn't a colleague or student.

'I needed that.' Throwing her head back, she blew smoke upwards at the darkening sky. 'Any parts of the course you're not confident with?' she asked briskly.

'None. Apart from . . .' He hesitated.

'The Brontës?' she supplied.

'It's obvious?'

'Only because of the look on your face when I gave you a B for your essay on *Wuthering Heights*.'

'It's still the only B I've ever had.'

'You deserved it for underrating female writers. No one can excel at everything and some' she shook her head at Robin as he strolled out to join them – 'like our Mr Watkin Morgan here, excel at nothing.'

'It's a practised art, Miss Llewellyn,' Robin replied nonchalantly.

'You may practise it but I wouldn't call it an art.' She lifted her empty glass. '"Once more unto the breach . . ." Much as I enjoy your company, I'd better return before Mr Edwards notices my absence. The revenge of a department head can be mean-spirited and time-consuming.'

'Leave her to us now, son.'

'I'm going with her.'

'Not in my ambulance, you're not. Now, stand back and let us do our job.' Concerned only for the welfare of their patient, neither the ambulance driver nor his mate had time to spare for Jack.

'She is my wife.'

'I don't care if she's the Queen of Sheba, son. There's no passengers travelling in this ambulance.'

The guard who'd arranged for the ambulance to meet the train took pity as the driver pushed Jack aside and asked, 'Where are you taking her?'

'Swansea General.'

He touched Jack's arm. 'I'll get a taxi for you, sir. You'll be there before her. Do you have enough money . . .'

'Money . . . yes.' Jack looked around in confusion as the driver and his mate lifted the stretcher Helen was lying on into the ambulance. 'But I haven't got Helen's luggage . . .'

'Don't you worry, sir. I'll check your cases into Left Luggage and bring the tickets to the hospital.' The guard whistled at the row of waiting taxicabs. Opening the door as the first in the queue pulled up alongside them, he pushed Jack into the back seat. 'Swansea Hospital and see if you can get there when that ambulance does.'

'Thank you for a most entertaining evening, sir.' Robin shook Mr Edwards's hand vigorously as he backed out through the door.

'Such a shame you and Mr Griffiths have to leave so early . . .'

'Unfortunately there was no one else to pick up my sister from the cinema, Mr Edwards, and my father won't allow her to travel on a late bus out of town on a Saturday.'

'I quite understand.'

'Goodbye, sir.' Practically pushing Joe behind him, Robin left the house and walked down the path.

'Are we really picking up Angela?' Joe asked as Robin opened the door of his sports car.

'Don't be an idiot.' Robin slid into the seat and slipped his key into the ignition. 'But I couldn't have stayed in there for another minute without screaming. Fancy a game of pool and a drink at my place?'

'Why not.' Joe glanced at his watch. Lily would still be in the Albert Hall. He'd watched her go in earlier with Judy and Katie, and taken comfort in the knowledge that she wasn't with Martin. 'I have nothing better to do.'

* * *

'I wasn't expecting to see you still here, sir. I thought I'd have to leave these with the receptionist.' The guard handed Jack a tea-stained envelope. 'Your Left Luggage tickets,' he explained.

'I can't find anyone who knows anything about my wife.' Jack opened the envelope. 'I must owe you . . .'

'Nothing, sir. It's all part of the service. You can pick up your luggage whenever it's convenient.'

'You must be out of pocket.'

'Not me, sir. I'd like to stay but my lift's waiting. There's a nurse who doesn't look as if she's doing much. Why don't you ask her about your wife.'

'Thank you,' Jack called back, as he took the guard up on his suggestion and charged up to the nurse. 'My wife is here . . .'

'This is Casualty,' the staff nurse barked officiously. 'If she's a patient she'll be on a ward. You'll have to go to the main entrance . . .'

'She was brought in by ambulance,' Jack interrupted.

'When?'

'Over two and a half hours ago.'

'Then she's most probably on a ward. All enquiries should be made at Reception at the main entrance.'

'They sent me here. Her name is Helen Griffiths – Clay . . . She was taken ill on the London train. I know the ambulance brought her straight here. Please, couldn't you find out . . .'

'This is a hospital casualty area, not an information bureau.'

Jack had never hated a stranger as much as he hated this self-important nurse at this moment. 'She must be somewhere . . .'

'Our primary consideration is the welfare of our patients, not their relatives.'

'There has to be someone who can tell me where she is.'

'Have you enquired at the Casualty Reception desk?'

'Twice, they told me to take a seat.'

'Then I suggest you do so.'

Unable to close his mind to images of Helen lying white-faced, unconscious and abandoned on a stretcher in a forgotten corner of this maze of antiseptic-smelling, impersonal corridors and cubicles, Jack was at breaking point. 'For how much longer?' he pleaded.

'We are *very* busy.' As the nurse turned away, a swing door to the right of the desk opened. It closed quickly but not before Jack saw four staff nurses standing idly gossiping. His hands were already clenching into fists when a young doctor, grey-faced from lack of sleep, white coat flowing behind him, stethoscope dangling from his neck, ambled into the area. Heading for Reception, he buttonholed the woman behind the desk.

'Is anyone with Mrs Clay?'

'Me!' Pushing past the nurse, Jack ran up to him. 'How is she? Can I see her?'

Barely able to keep his eyes open, the doctor squinted at Jack. 'And you are?'

'Jack Clay, her husband.'

'Husband?' The doctor gave Jack a dubious look.

'We were on our honeymoon . . .'

'Then you're not from Swansea.'

'We are,' Jack answered irritably, wondering what that had to do with anything. 'Helen is going to be all right, isn't she?'

'She's in theatre.'

'I don't understand . . .'

'We're not sure what is wrong with her, Mr Clay.'

'You're operating and you don't know what's wrong with her!' Jack reeled at the prospect of a surgeon slicing open Helen's perfect body.

'Your wife's symptoms could be related to any one of a number of conditions. Her personal possessions have been sent down to the main Reception desk. I suggest you pick them up, go home and telephone us in the morning.'

As he walked away, Jack grabbed his arm. 'Please, I must see her.'

'That is impossible. She could be in theatre for hours and even when she comes out she'll be sent to recovery, and relatives are only allowed to visit patients on a ward.' The doctor was a final-year medical student. He'd been on duty for over thirty hours. All he wanted was his bed and he felt totally unequal to dealing with a distraught husband who looked as though he should be playing football in the street, not going on honeymoon. He closed his hand over Jack's and removed it.

'Please, I can't just walk away . . .'

'You've left your details at Reception?'

Jack nodded.

'You have a telephone number where you can be contacted?'

'Yes.'

The doctor was surprised. Not many people, let alone newlyweds, were on the telephone. 'If there's any change we'll be in touch. If you haven't heard anything by morning you can call us. There's no point in telephoning before.'

Jack stood rooted to the spot as the doctor left. An image of Helen lying butchered on a slab flooded his mind. The waiting area grew misty, wavering around him as a peculiar buzzing filled his ears.

'You can get to main Reception down that corridor.'

'Sorry, I . . .'

Realising he hadn't taken in a word she'd said, the nurse repeated, 'Main Reception, to pick up your wife's clothes.'

'Yes . . . yes, thank you.' Forgetting his earlier antagonism towards the woman, Jack forced himself to put one foot in front of the other. Helen was in theatre and there was nothing he could do for her except pick up her clothes. Just as he and Martin had picked up his mother's when she'd died among strangers in this same building.

'Another pint?'

Martin shook his head. 'I've had enough.'

'Last time we're inviting you to a booze-up, mate.' As his fellow apprentice went to the bar, Martin picked up his coat and left the Antelope. Crossing the road, he walked down to the beach. A cold breeze ruffled the waves as they slurped in between the pebbles on the foreshore but the stars shone down from a clear, cloudless night sky and he decided to walk home. Aware he'd been a wet blanket, he wished he hadn't joined the others to celebrate the end of the exams and done what Sam had suggested, taken Lily out and – and what? Asked her outright about Joe?

'Thought it was you.' Sam stepped out of the darkness to join him. 'Going home?'

'Yes.'

'Bit early to leave a celebration, isn't it?' Sam fell into step beside him.

'Didn't feel in the mood for drinking. Anyway, you're a fine one to talk. Looks like you've cut your evening short too.'

'Only because I had to,' Sam said sourly. 'I'm on nights, remember.'

'I forgot. So where have you been?'

'Fish and chip shop with a mate and I couldn't even join him for a pint afterwards. The duty sergeant has a nose like a bloodhound and he plays merry hell if he smells booze on anyone's breath at the start of a shift. But I have two days off starting tomorrow. How about we take the girls somewhere?'

'Have you asked them?' Shivering, Martin fastened the top button on his overcoat.

'Nope.'

'Why not?'

'Because I'm afraid that if I ask your sister to go out with me on a date she'll say no, whereas a foursome with you and Lily puts a different connotation on the situation.'

'Jack and Helen will be back tonight.'

'So?'

'They may have made plans that include us for tomorrow.'

'You're not going to help me with Katie, are you?'

Martin smiled. 'No.'

'I'd help you if you were after my sister.'

'I thought you didn't have one.'

'I don't.'

'A word of advice.' Martin reached into his pocket for his cigarettes. 'If you're after Katie, the first thing you should know about her is she despises people who try to get others to do their dirty work for them.'

Loaded with his own and Helen's suitcases, and a brown-paper carrier bag marked *Patient's Property*, Jack walked unsteadily up Craddock Street and rounded the corner into Carlton Terrace. There were no lights on in Helen's house or Roy Williams's house or basement. Dropping the cases, he checked his watch, peering at the hands in the twilight. It was half past nine. Seven and a half hours since he and Helen had boarded the train out of London. If only they had caught the mid-day train as he had wanted to instead of eating that last meal in the Italian restaurant. Helen would have been safely in Swansea when the pain started and he would have got her into hospital that much sooner.

Martin would be down the Pier with Lily and the others. Roy Williams would be on duty or in the White Rose. John Griffiths – he suddenly realised he had to tell Helen's father where she was. Stumbling under the weight of the cases, he staggered to Helen's front door and rang the bell. The sound reverberated hollowly down the passage, echoing through the empty rooms.

He sank down on the step. He'd given Martin his door key when he'd left, so he and Sam could use it as a spare, and he didn't have a key to the Griffiths's basement. He had told Helen there would be plenty of time to get a copy cut from hers when they came back from honeymoon.

Feeling as though he were prying, and hating himself for it, he opened the carrier bag. Helen's hat shone, a splash of white in the gloom, on top of her neatly folded gloves and handbag. Beneath them was her blue costume. He brushed his hand over the silk and Helen's favourite perfume, Bond Street, wafted into the cool night air, bringing tears to his eyes. Struggling to compose himself, he replaced the gloves and hat and removed her handbag. The gold push clasp was fiddly, doubly so when the darkness prevented him from seeing what he was doing, and he was afraid of using force lest he break it. How Helen would laugh if she could see him now – defeated by a girl's handbag.

It took him ten minutes to work out that the clasp had to be swung back to release the catch. Lifting out a small red leather purse he had seen Helen use a hundred times in London, he set it on the step next to him. As he delved into the bag his fingers closed over her gold-plated powder compact, then he brought out a gold-cased lipstick, comb, small hairbrush, a tiny bottle of perfume, a lace-edged handkerchief, a card of hair clips – all intensely personal possessions he felt he had no right to touch. Swallowing hard, he slipped his hand inside again. The bag was empty. He peered inside but it was too dark to see. He felt around the silk lining. Surely she would have her keys. He shook the bag and heard a metallic rattle.

They were folded into a buttoned-down pocket sewn into the lining. He took his time over replacing everything, trying to imagine Helen's reaction if he had to tell her he had lost any of her precious possessions. But the only image he could conjure with any clarity was her lying unconscious on the stretcher being loaded into the back of the ambulance.

Rising from the step, he realised he was shattered. He ached as if someone had been using him as a punchbag and there was a sharp pain between his eyes that stabbed deeper every time he moved his head. He walked back through the gate and climbed down the steep flight of steps to the basement. He tried both keys on Helen's ring, the lock turned when he inserted the second. He reached out and switched on the light before stepping down into the kitchen.

Closing the door behind him he sank on to a chair. The fresh paintwork and Formica kitchen cupboards sparkled back at him. The room even smelled new — new and clean and antiseptic. Helen had been in the flat scrubbing and cleaning the moment the builders left so they'd have an immaculate home to return to. Taking the carrier bag, he rose to his feet, made his way to the bedroom and switched on the light.

He stowed Helen's white court shoes in the bottom of her wardrobe. Her handbag and gloves he placed on the bedside table. Then he reached for a hanger for the costume. He slipped the jacket on to it, only to drop it back on the bed. He simply couldn't bring himself to shut it in the wardrobe; it would feel as if he were relegating Helen herself to a cupboard — and the past.

He sat on the bed and ran his fingers over the eiderdown that Brian and Judy had bought them, although he suspected that, like him, Brian had little say in the presents he bought with Judy. So much money, time and effort had gone into making the basement a perfect first home. But he couldn't help wondering if he and Helen would ever live in it.

'Helen, Jack, are you down there?' John Griffiths called out, as he unlocked the door that connected the main house to the basement.

Slumped on the bed, Jack rubbed the back of his hand across his eyes. To his amazement they were wet. 'Only me, Mr Griffiths,' he answered, rising as he heard John's step on the stairs.

'I saw the light . . .' John stepped into the passage; looked up and down the corridor and realised the rest of the flat was in darkness. 'Where's Helen?' When Jack didn't reply, he said, 'You two haven't had a stupid quarrel, have you?'

'No, Mr Griffiths, it's nothing like that.' Jack swallowed hard as he looked at his father-in-law. 'Helen is in hospital.'

'John Griffiths, enquiring about Mrs Helen Clay . . .' John's voice rose precariously as his patience wore thin. He had been on the telephone for over twenty minutes and during that time he had been passed from one member of the hospital staff to another. First the night porter, then the night casualty receptionist who'd connected him to two ward sisters who both insisted they hadn't heard of 'Mrs Helen Clay'. At the third ward his call had been diverted to, he'd spoken to a student nurse who'd told him to hold for a staff nurse who finally conceded that there was 'a Mrs Helen Clay on the ward', but as she wasn't authorised to take calls from relatives she would get sister to speak to him.

'Night sister speaking.'

Controlling his irritation, John repeated, 'I am enquiring about Mrs Helen Clay.'

'And you are?'

'John Griffiths, her father.'

'Her husband is down as next of kin.'

'He is with me. Would you like to speak to him?'

'Frankly, Mr Griffiths, with a ward to run I would rather speak to neither of you.'

'Can you tell me if my daughter is out of surgery?'

'Yes.'

'And?' he pressed angrily.

'She is as well as can be expected.'

'What does that mean in plain English?'

'It means what I said, Mr Griffiths. Considering she has had a major operation, she is as well as can be expected. If there is any change we will contact you.'

The line went dead. Jack jumped up from the stairs where he'd been sitting as John replaced the receiver on its cradle.

'"As well as can be expected considering she has had a major operation." At least we know she is out of theatre.'

'Did they say when we can see her?'

'No, but they said they'll be in touch if there's any change. If they don't, I'll telephone first thing in the morning.' He patted Jack reassuringly on the shoulder. 'You look exhausted. Why don't you try to get some sleep.'

Jack thought of the pristine flat downstairs waiting for Helen and him to move in. 'I couldn't – not in the basement.'

'There's Helen's room.'

'I couldn't sleep there either.'

'Do you want to go back to your brother's?'

'If you don't mind, Mr Griffiths, I'd like to stay here in case the hospital does ring.'

'I don't mind,' John said wearily, 'but I warn you, our sofa has to be the most uncomfortable that's ever been made.'

John didn't draw the curtains in the living room so he could watch the street. Every time he heard a footfall, he went to the window, hoping it would be Martin or Katie. Since he had telephoned the hospital, Jack had retreated into silence, refusing all offers of food and drink although he was sure he hadn't had anything since leaving London. If he couldn't get him to eat perhaps Martin could.

He jumped up as he heard a familiar voice. Walking to the front door, he opened it and shouted, 'Martin?'

'Yes, Mr Griffiths.' Leaving Sam, Martin walked up the short path to John Griffiths's front door.

'Jack's here.'

'Did they have a good time . . .'

'Helen's in hospital.'

'What!'

'What's happened?' Judy and Lily ran up to them but Katie hung back behind her brother rather than face John.

'Helen was taken ill on the train,' John divulged. 'She's in hospital.'

'Do you know how she is, Mr Griffiths?' Lily asked.

'Neither Jack nor I succeeded in getting any sense out of the hospital. All we know for sure is that she's had major surgery.'

'Can we see Jack?' Katie refused to meet John's eye.

'Of course.' He held the door open for Martin and Katie, then looked at Sam, Judy and Lily. 'I don't want to stop you from coming in but I don't think there's anything any of you can do tonight.'

'You'll telephone if there is,' Lily pleaded.

'I promise.'

Surprised to see lights on in the house when he returned from Robin's at one in the morning, Joe unlocked the door and walked into the living room to find his father, Katie and Martin sitting in silence. 'Who died?' he joked, not noticing Jack slumped in the corner of the sofa behind the door until he stepped into the room.

'Helen was taken ill on the train, she's in hospital,' John said flatly. 'They said they'd telephone if there's any change.'

Joe stopped in his tracks. 'Is it serious?'

'They won't tell us anything.' His father gave him a warning glance before looking at Jack.

'God, how awful. Jack, I'm so sorry.'

Jack shrugged his shoulders, not trusting himself to speak.

'But she is going to be all right.'

'Hopefully.' John adopted an optimistic face for Jack's sake. 'We'll find out more in the morning. If you're making yourself a drink, mine's a whisky.'

'Jack, Martin, Katie?' Joe enquired as he poured his father a generous measure. 'We've brandy, gin, port, sherry . . .'

'Nothing, thank you.' Jack sat forward, rested his elbows on his knees and stared at the floor.

'No thank you, Joe,' Katie said.

'I couldn't face a drink either.' Martin was finding it a strain to be in the same room with Joe.

'I could make you tea or coffee if you prefer, and sandwiches . . .'

They all shook their heads.

'There's no point in us all staying up to wait for a telephone call that might not come.' John took the whisky Joe handed him. 'Why don't you go to bed, that way one of us will have a clear head in the morning.'

John left his chair and limped to the standard lamp as the first pewter-hued rays of dawn filtered through the crack between the curtains. Switching off the light, he pushed aside the drapes and looked outside. There was a slight mist, portending a fine day and he noticed the leaves unfurling on the shrubs on the bank opposite. Spring was giving way to summer. Turning, he looked at Katie and Martin. They had insisted on staying with Jack but both of them had fallen asleep in the small hours, Martin in one of the chairs, Katie curled beside Jack on the sofa. Jack, like him, hadn't closed his eyes all night.

'Tea?' he mouthed quietly.

Jack nodded.

Glad to leave the oppressive atmosphere, John went into the kitchen and filled the kettle. As he lit the gas Jack, looking even more haggard, drained and exhausted than when he had found him in the basement the night before, joined him.

'Katie and Martin still asleep?' John set cups and saucers on a tray.

'Yes, I managed to move without disturbing her.' Jack rubbed his arm where his sister's head had rested most of the night. He hadn't minded the numbness that had led to pins and needles; it had helped keep him awake, ears straining for a telephone call that he hadn't known whether to wish for or not. 'Can I telephone the hospital, Mr Griffiths?'

John glanced at the clock. 'You can try but I doubt they'll tell you anything at this time in the morning.'

'Thank you.'

'You know the number?'

'They gave it to me last night.' As Jack searched his pockets for the piece of paper the receptionist had given him along with Helen's clothes, the telephone rang, startlingly loud in the hushed house. He charged down the passage and lifted the receiver.

'Is Jack Clay available?'

'Speaking.' Jack's hand was shaking so much he could barely hold the telephone.

'Will you be able to meet Mrs Clay's doctor at nine o'clock this morning?'

'Yes – how is Helen . . .'

'Nine o'clock,' the voice repeated.

Jack looked up to see Joe standing in his dressing gown and pyjamas on the landing. Martin and Katie were in the doorway of the living room. He turned to John. 'The doctor will see me at nine o'clock.'

'And Helen?'

'They wouldn't tell me any more.'

Chapter 11

MARTIN STEPPED BACK as Lily opened her door. 'I can't stay.'

'Not even long enough for me to ask how Helen is?'

Taking Lily's comment as a reproach, Martin joined her in the hall. 'Jack left with her father for the hospital a few minutes ago.'

'She is going to be all right, isn't she?' Lily asked anxiously.

'Jack hasn't even been told what's wrong with her. You know what they're like in hospitals.'

'No.' She opened the door to the parlour, but he remained in the hall. 'I haven't had much experience of them.'

'They never tell the family a thing until they absolutely have to.'

'If there's anything I can do . . .'

'Thank you, but there isn't anything that Katie or I can do,' he broke in, making her feel as though she were trying to push herself where she wasn't wanted. 'About today . . .'

'Even if we'd made firm plans, we could hardly go off on a jaunt with Helen ill.'

'I hoped you'd understand.'

Lily almost said 'and I hoped you knew me better' but with Helen ill and him worried about Jack, it was hardly the time to confront him about his attitude to her. 'Mrs Lannon is making breakfast. You're welcome to join us.'

'None of us felt like eating this morning so Katie's preparing something for when Jack and Helen's father come back. I ought to stay with her – just in case Jack or the hospital telephones.'

'Give Katie my love and remind her I'm here if she needs anything.'

'She'll probably call in later, even if she decides to stay with Jack again tonight.' He looked at her for a moment and she thought he was going to say something else, then he turned and left.

At ten minutes to nine John and Jack were shown to a row of wooden chairs in the corridor outside the female surgical ward. They sat side by side, too concerned about what might be happening to Helen to attempt conversation. John glanced impatiently at his watch after he could have sworn they had been there several hours. The hands pointed to twenty past nine.

Footsteps echoed further down the corridor but none came near them. After another ten-minute wait he rose stiffly from his chair and massaged his damaged leg. His scars were aching and he was muscle-bound after sitting up all night. Pacing uneasily, he was careful to keep within sight of Jack who blanched paler with every passing second.

'Mr Clay.' A middle-aged nurse stood in front of Jack's chair. 'The doctor will see you now.'

They were shown into an office that smelled of hospital disinfectant. The walls were painted institution green, the woodwork brown, matching the linoleum on the floor. A young man sat surrounded by files, scribbling notes at a desk.

'Mr Clay and . . .' The nurse looked inquisitively at John, uncertain whether to admit him.

'John Griffiths, I'm Mrs Clay's father.'

'Thank you, staff. Take a seat. Be with you in a moment.' The doctor waved his hand without looking up from the notes he continued to pen as they sat on the only two spare chairs in the room. He continued to write for another five minutes, which John monitored using the second hand on his wristwatch. Eventually the doctor sat back and blotted the page he'd been working on. Avoiding looking at them, he slowly and laboriously screwed the top on his fountain pen, removed his spectacles and finally – because he couldn't delay any longer – turned to them.

Judging by the difficulty the man appeared to have in focusing, John wondered if he could see them without his glasses, then he realised the doctor didn't want to see them. He was keeping the interview as impersonal as possible because he had bad news and was stalling for time while he debated how to break it.

'How is Helen?' Jack began, unable to wait a moment longer.

'As well as can be expected.'

John gritted his teeth – that damned phrase again.

The doctor cleared his throat. 'She was very ill when she was brought in; frankly, it was touch and go whether she'd survive. But although I'd advise caution, I am fairly optimistic that she will make a recovery.'

'She will be all right?' Jack urged, clearly unable to make much sense of what the doctor had said.

'She is still poorly. I was told she was on honeymoon.'

'We were returning home from London.' Jack wondered what exactly the doctor meant by 'poorly'. It sounded more like something Mrs Lannon would say than a professional.

'You are aware that she was pregnant.'

'Yes.' Jack turned ashen as he realised the implication of the 'was'.

'She had a tubal pregnancy.'

'I don't understand, doctor,' John said shortly, trying to force the man to explain the facts in language that he and Jack could comprehend.

'The baby was developing in a fallopian tube outside the uterus. There was simply no way it could survive and by lodging in the tube it almost killed the mother. Her condition was acute by the time she reached here. She must have been in pain for hours. It would have been better if she had come in as soon as she was taken ill.'

'You could have saved the baby?' Even Jack's lips were white.

'The baby was never viable. But by coming in sooner she might have been spared considerable pain and discomfort.'

'We were on a train.' Jack took the doctor's comments as criticism and wished he had listened to the porter and insisted they leave the train at Bridgend. 'Was there anything we . . . I could have done to stop it from happening?'

'Only brought her in sooner. That might have resulted in less radical surgery but it would not have affected the outcome. A small percentage of babies develop in the fallopian tubes outside of the uterus. We have absolutely no idea why and cannot predict or prevent it from happening.'

'But she will make a full recovery.' John willed the doctor to say something that would wipe the guilt-ridden expression from Jack's face.

'Clinically, given sufficient rest and care, and barring complications, that is the most likely scenario.'

'There could be complications?' John pushed.

'None I can foresee. She was also suffering from uterus unicornis.'

Jack turned to John, not the doctor.

'We're laymen, doctor. What does that mean?' John demanded.

'It means, Mr Griffiths, she had only one fallopian tube. We had no choice but to remove it. As a result she will never have a child.'

157

Bleak-eyed, Jack stared blankly at the wall above the doctor's head. John was the first to recover. 'Have you told her?'

'Her condition is too acute for anyone to discuss it with her.' The doctor rose to his feet and opened the door. 'Your daughter will be hospitalised for approximately four weeks, Mr Griffiths.'

John realised the doctor couldn't wait to be rid of them but he also wanted answers to the questions he knew Jack would ask when he recovered from the initial shock. 'Can we see her?'

'There would be no point; she is still heavily sedated. But there is visiting this afternoon. Possibly then, sister will allow one visitor for a short time provided they take care not to upset the patient.'

'Does my daughter know that she has lost her baby?'

'No, apart from being barely conscious, as I said, she is far too ill for anyone to discuss her condition with her. Now, if you'll excuse me I have patients to attend to. The nurse will see you out.'

John drove straight from the hospital to the warehouse. 'We need to sort a few things,' he explained in answer to the confused look on Jack's face. 'There are too many people back at the house. All well-meaning, but you need to make some decisions before you see them.'

Jack followed him up to the office suite and sat on the sofa in the reception area. John joined him a moment later with a bottle of whisky and two glasses. 'Just one,' he poured out two measures. 'We've both had a shock.'

Jack drank it as if he were obeying orders. John realised his son-in-law was in a stupor and doubted much of what the doctor had said had registered.

'Practical things first.' John sat opposite him. 'You're going to need somewhere to live while Helen's in hospital.'

'I couldn't live in the flat. It's Helen's. She chose everything. She was looking forward to using all the new things. I would mess it up.'

'You can live upstairs with Joe and me. There's three spare bedrooms in the attic if you don't want to sleep in Helen's room.'

'I'd rather move back in with my brother.'

'That's a good idea,' John conceded. 'You'll need company. And as for work . . .'

'I might take an hour or two off if they let me visit Helen during the day, Mr Griffiths, but please don't stop me from coming in here. I have to do something . . .'

'Whatever you do, Jack, your job will be kept open for you. I didn't get around to telling you, but it's not only me that's pleased with the progress you've made since you joined us. The stockroom manager was only saying last week how willing and quick to learn you are.' John refilled both their glasses and screwed the top back on the bottle. Left to his own devices he might have been tempted to empty it, but there was visiting that afternoon – for Jack if not for him. And given his present state, Jack would need someone to drive him there. 'You heard what the doctor said about not telling Helen she's lost the baby.'

'Or can't have any more,' Jack murmured wretchedly. He'd been offered a glimpse of something he hadn't even known he'd wanted and just as he'd not only become used to the idea, but actually started to look forward to having a family of his own, it had been snatched away. That curse again. Him bringing grief and misery to everyone he loved.

'Nothing that's happened is your fault, Jack.' John had to repeat himself before he could be sure that Jack had heard him.

'Helen wouldn't have been pregnant if it wasn't for me.'

'And you faced up to your responsibilities and married her,' John reminded him. 'Didn't you hear the doctor say this happens in a percentage of cases? That they have no idea why and can't stop it from happening?'

'But I made Helen carry on working and she saw to everything in the flat . . .'

'No one's ever made Helen do anything she didn't want to in her life. And you saw to all the decorating and heavy work. If she saw to the rest it was because she wanted to. And as for working, being an office clerk is hardly grafting like a navvy.'

'If she'd rested . . .'

'The doctor said it would have made no difference,' John interrupted firmly.

'I should never have brought her back to Swansea. I should have made her get off the train in Bridgend . . .'

'It would have made no difference. She would still have lost the baby.'

'But she might have . . .'

'Jack, look at me,' John ordered, waiting until Jack lifted his head. 'Nothing you did or didn't do caused this to happen.'

'I wish I could believe you.'

'You had better start trying, because if you see Helen this afternoon looking the way you do now, she is going to know something is wrong and that could prevent her from recovering as quickly as she might.'

'I have to tell everyone . . .'

'If you want, you can leave that to me.'

'It's bad enough she lost the baby and she's ill. But not being able to have any more.' Jack set his mouth into a grim line as he fought to suppress the tide of emotion that threatened to overwhelm him.

'How about I tell everyone she's lost the baby and leave it at that? No one else need know she can't have children unless she chooses to tell them.'

Jack nodded dumbly.

John laid his hand on Jack's shoulder. 'I think you know that I wasn't thrilled when you told me Helen was going to have your baby.'

'An ex-Borstal boy doesn't make the best son-in-law.'

'But you do, Jack. And I want you to know that I'm proud and pleased that Helen is married to you, because I'm confident that somehow you'll find the strength to see both of you through this.'

If Jack heard him, he made no sign. Unequal to dealing with Jack's misery as well as his own, John cleared the glasses and whisky, and reached for his car keys. 'We'd better be going.'

'You'll tell everyone we've lost the baby?'

'I'll tell them, Jack.' John locked the door and followed him out of the building.

Refusing all offers of help and breakfast, Jack packed the clothes Helen had hung in the wardrobe in the flat into his battered suitcase. Taking it, and the case he'd brought back from London, he left the basement by the front door; locking it with the key he'd taken from Helen's handbag.

Primed by John, Martin was waiting. He couldn't conceal his amazement at the difference a few hours had made to his brother. Jack looked dazed and suddenly years older.

'Mr Griffiths told you.'

'Yes.'

'That Helen's lost the baby,' Jack continued, checking that Martin knew what he and John had decided and no more.

'I'm sorry, Jack, I know how much you were looking forward to being a father.'

'Perhaps this is fate's way of telling me I would have made a lousy one,' Jack answered, succumbing to a bout of self-pity.

'You would have made a great one. And when Helen recovers . . .'

'Does anyone else know?' Jack broke in swiftly.

'Mr Griffiths told Roy Williams and Mrs Hunt, and they've probably told Lily and Judy by now. I told Katie and Sam. I didn't think there was any point in trying to keep it a secret with Helen in hospital.'

'There isn't.'

'Here, let me.' Martin reached for one of the cases.

'No.' Jack kept his grip on both of them.

'Mr Griffiths said you wouldn't eat breakfast. I could cook us something. There's bacon and eggs . . .'

'I'm not hungry.' Jack glanced from the dresser to the table, evading his brother's eye. 'I need to be alone for a while.'

'Katie . . .'

'She's here?' Jack eyes clouded with exhaustion and Martin realised he simply couldn't face people, not even him or their sister.

'No, but she told me to tell you she'll be upstairs all day if you want to see her.' He paused, searching for something to say. 'Everyone wants to help, Jack, they're just not sure how.'

Jack nodded as he opened the door to the passage.

'Roy Williams has invited us upstairs for Sunday dinner.'

'Mr Griffiths is driving me back to the hospital at two o'clock.'

'I could make us beans on toast. Just the two of us, you won't have to talk if you don't want to.'

'Don't bother.'

'You have to eat,' Martin insisted. 'If only for Helen's sake. It won't help if you make yourself ill.'

'I'll put my clothes away first.'

Relieved at the small concession, Martin watched his brother walk to the room they'd shared. Jack slammed the door behind him. The noise reverberated through the house, rattling the casement windows.

'They must have heard that at the other end of the terrace.' Sam opened the door of the second bedroom and joined Martin in the kitchen.

'The wind probably caught it.' Martin knew it hadn't, he also knew he hadn't fooled Sam.

'You going upstairs for dinner?'

'No, Jack can't face company and I want to stay within kicking distance.'

'You won't mind if I do?' Sam asked clumsily, trying to be tactful.

161

'No.'

'If there's anything I can . . .'

'He's my brother and there's nothing I can do.'

'Bloody bad luck.'

'Bad luck!' Martin echoed uncomprehendingly.

'I don't mean about Helen losing the kid, that's rotten but if it had to happen, it would have been better if she'd been taken ill a couple of weeks ago. Then Jack wouldn't have had to marry her.'

Martin was too stunned by Sam's attitude to reply. It was only later, after Sam had left for upstairs and he was opening a tin of beans, that he realised the truth in what his flatmate had said. If Helen had been taken ill a couple of weeks ago it would have been an entirely different situation. He could only speculate as to whether Jack would have wanted to marry Helen, or Helen Jack, if there hadn't been a baby to force them into it.

'Mrs Griffiths is still unavailable, Mr Griffiths. I have your messages and I will give them to her when she comes in.'

The clipped tones of his mother-in-law's housekeeper irritated John even more than they had done the night before. 'Have you any idea when she'll be home?'

'No, sir.'

'She must have said . . .'

'It was a spur-of-the-moment decision, Mr Griffiths. Mrs Green . . .'

'Dot?'

'As I was saying, sir, Mrs Green had plans to visit friends for the weekend and Mrs Griffiths joined her at the last minute.'

'And you have no idea where they've gone.' John didn't bother to conceal his scepticism.

'Neither of them confided in me, sir.'

'And her mother doesn't know where she is.'

'Madam is unwell. Mrs Griffiths takes care not to burden her with anything that might prove stressful, like the telephone ringing every couple of hours.'

'Well, let's hope madam's condition doesn't worsen while her daughter is away and can't be contacted,' John bit back angrily, before hanging up.

'Only one visitor,' the sister warned as Jack and John returned to the ward that afternoon. 'And no more than ten minutes. Mrs Clay is very weak.'

'Jack, you go ahead. I'll be outside.'

'The last cubicle on the right,' the sister directed, 'and be careful not to upset her. The doctor did tell you not to mention the baby.'

Jack nodded.

'Ten minutes.'

Jack flinched as the thick crepe soles on his brothel creepers squeaked on the rubbery linoleum. He tried not to look in the other cubicles as he made resolutely for Helen's but it was difficult. Vases filled with brightly coloured spring flowers stood, bizarrely at odds with the wan, sick patients in the beds.

He had tried to imagine Helen 'acutely ill' but none of his imaginings had prepared him for the reality. She lay between scaldingly white sheets, as white and still as a marble sculpture in the Glyn Vivian Art Gallery. The only splash of colour was her blonde hair spread out on the pillow above her head and even that looked paler than usual.

Tiptoeing in, he jumped at the noise from his own shoes as he stood beside the bed. He would have liked to hold her hand but they were both tucked beneath the sheet and he didn't dare disturb the pristine bed-making. As he watched, her eyes flickered open. When she saw him, she tried to smile. He had to lean over to catch what she said.

'It's all right, Jack, you don't have to worry any more. The pain has gone.'

'I'm glad you called, Lily,' Joy Hunt said as she opened the door to her. 'Judy's upstairs, sorting out her bedroom. She'll be glad of some company.'

'I called to invite her over because Katie doesn't want to leave the house in case either of her brothers needs her.' Lily braced herself. 'You have heard about Helen?'

Joy nodded as she saw tears in Lily's eyes. 'Come on now, none of that.' She hugged her. 'I spoke to John earlier; he told me that Helen's going to recover.'

'I know.' Lily fumbled in her pocket for her handkerchief.

'Helen and Jack are going to need their family and friends more than ever, and knowing you, love, you'll be top of their list of friends.'

Lily wiped her eyes and stuffed her handkerchief in her pocket. 'I'll go up and see Judy.'

'It's horrible and unfair. They were both so happy and Helen was looking forward to having the baby.' Judy lifted the underclothes she'd arranged in neat piles on her bed and dropped them into her chest of drawers to make room for Lily to sit on the bed.

'Jack was just as excited as Helen about the baby. She told me that he had even talked about teaching him – he was sure it was going to a boy – to play football.'

'But it has to be worse for Helen. She's the one who went through all the pain of actually losing the baby and having an operation. I hate to think of her lying in hospital among strangers. She must be feeling desperate.' Judy slammed shut the last drawer in the chest. 'There has to be something we can do.'

'Beyond making sure Katie is all right, and helping her to look after Jack, not much,' Lily said bleakly.

'Helen will need things in hospital and there'll be small things like her washing to be done.'

'Your room looks like you've never been away.' Lily moved the conversation away from Helen and Jack because she was in serious danger of crying again.

Judy looked around. 'It does, doesn't it?' Her cosmetics and toiletries were back on the dressing table; she'd replaced her precious collection of Wade porcelain animals on the shelves above her bed and lined up her books between a pair of heavy wooden bookends on the windowsill. Picking up a box filled with scraps of newspapers that she'd used to wrap and store her ornaments in, she placed it by the door.

'No second thoughts about coming back for good?' Lily went to the window and glanced through the titles of Judy's books.

'Not about leaving London.' Judy sat on the dressing-table stool and picked up her hairbrush.

'And Brian?'

Judy brushed back a few stray hairs. 'As I haven't heard a word in two weeks, I assume he's forgotten me.'

'You don't really believe that.'

'I don't know what to believe.' Judy faced Lily. 'If I tell you something, will you promise not to tell a living soul?' She waited until

Lily nodded agreement before continuing, 'I offered to sleep with Brian the last night he was here and he turned me down.'

Speechless, Lily stared at her.

'He said I wanted him as a way out from a job I didn't like.' She opened the drawer in her dressing table and took out a framed photograph that had been taken at a police dinner dance. Brian was standing beside her, his arm round her waist. They looked happy, relaxed and well-dressed, she in a grey satin shirtwaister with a full skirt, he in a dark suit, white shirt and tie. 'I tried to tell him I love him, but he wouldn't listen. I don't think he believed me.'

'It must have been a misunderstanding . . .'

'You weren't there, Lily.'

'No matter what he said to you then, I'm sure that deep down he knows how you feel about him,' Lily consoled.

'He said I was only curious about sex.'

'I should think everyone who hasn't experienced it is,' Lily observed honestly.

'You too?' Judy looked at her.

'Of course.'

'Have you and Martin . . .'

'I've only just started going out with him.' Lily didn't want to discuss her relationship with Martin, even with Judy, until she knew exactly how he felt about her.

'Will you?'

'I don't know. Perhaps, in time, if things go right between us,' she answered vaguely.

'He hasn't asked you to marry him?'

'No.'

'Brian did before we went to London.' Judy looked at her hairbrush as she set it back on the tray on her dressing table. 'I refused even to accept an engagement ring from him. I said all the things I always say whenever anyone brings up the subject of marriage; that I wanted a career and independence, and I wouldn't even think about settling down until I'm thirty. Things I've said so often I didn't stop to think whether I believed them or not. Then when I came back here, saw Helen, Jack and their flat, and heard her talking about the baby I was unbelievably envious. Brian had asked me to marry him – granted not since we'd been in London – and I imagined myself in the same position as her, living in a flat instead of the horrid hostel, with a baby and Brian coming home every night – well, days sometimes, given the shifts he works – and it seemed so much better than sticking with a job I hated. That makes me sound as if I only wanted him for what he could give me but it's not just that. I really do love him, Lily. I know that now. And he doesn't believe me and I've lost him.' She bit her lip to stop it from trembling.

'You have to write to him.'

'And tell him what?' Judy choked back her tears.

'Exactly what you've just told me, starting with you love him,' Lily advised.

'You think I'll get him back?'

Lily's silence answered her. Even if she could sort out her problems with Brian and convince him that she had loved him all along, how could she possibly get him back when he was in London and she in Swansea?

'You telephoned, John?' Esme succeeded in injecting a heavy hint of reproach into her formal manner.

'I did,' John agreed tersely, retreating into frigid politeness.

'The last time we met, you informed me that you only wanted to communicate with me through our respective solicitors.'

'I was referring to matters relating to our divorce.'

Her tone lightened as she slipped into a role she had always played well – that of the seductress. 'You've reconsidered my suggestion of a reconciliation?'

'No.'

'Then what possible reason can you have for harassing mother's housekeeper? You know mother is unwell . . .'

'Yes,' he interrupted angrily. 'And it amazes me that you went away for the weekend without leaving a telephone number where you could be contacted in case of emergency.'

'I did.'

'The housekeeper insisted she didn't know where you were.'

'I told her I didn't want to be bothered with non-urgent matters,' she replied carelessly.

'Like your daughter's health.'

John could hear Esme breathing at the other end of the line but when she finally spoke her voice was harsh, clipped. 'Helen's ill?'

'She collapsed on the train yesterday afternoon when she and Jack were returning from honeymoon. She's in Swansea General. They had to operate. They think she will recover but she has lost the baby.'

'There is no baby!'

'Not any more.'

'The fool! I told her not to rush into this marriage.' As the import of John's news sank in, she turned furiously on him. 'You should never have arranged the wedding so quickly.'

'Given the circumstances, I'm glad I did.'

'Even after this?'

'Especially after this,' John replied resolutely.

'I'll call and see her.'

'They won't allow visitors again until Wednesday evening.'

'I'm her mother. I'm next of kin.'

'Jack is next of kin, Esme,' he corrected. 'If there is any change in her condition they will contact him.'

'You will let me know if there is any news?'

'I will leave a message with your mother's housekeeper.'

If Esme saw the irony in his remark, she didn't comment on it. 'Shall I wait for you to call, then?'

'If you are really interested in Helen's condition, I suggest you telephone here late on Wednesday after Jack has visited her, or the warehouse on Thursday morning. Goodbye, Esme.'

Leaving the hall, he went into the living room and opened the cocktail cabinet. Pouring himself a large whisky he turned to see Joe sitting, reading. 'It's not like you to spend a Sunday evening at home.'

'With everything that's going on with Helen, I didn't feel like company.' Joe closed his book.

'Would you like a whisky?'

'Please. It's no better between you and my mother?'

'As you heard.' John poured Joe a glass of whisky and handed it over. 'How's the studying going?'

'According to my tutor I'm still on course for a first. I realise you're being optimistic for Jack's sake but how is Helen, really? Is she going to recover?' Joe was almost afraid of what his father might say. He and Helen had fought since cradle days but underneath all the bickering he'd discovered that he was surprisingly fond of her.

'The doctor's cautious. She's going to be in hospital for at least a month but with luck, care and rest he said she should get well.'

'There are no complications?'

'Such as?' John looked keenly at him.

'She will be able to have other children?'

When John didn't answer, Joe read the expression on his face. 'That is tough to take at her age.'

'Not a word to anyone,' John warned.

'Does Jack know?'

'The doctor told us, but no one else knows, not even Helen. It's Jack's and Helen's business, Joe, and no one else's. You won't tell anyone?'

'Of course not.' Joe tried to imagine being told that he could never have children. It was one thing to crack jokes about wanting dozens, or never wanting any at all, quite another to discover that the decision had been taken out of your hands and you didn't even have one to make.

Chapter 12

'TEA?' SAM ASKED Jack who was shaving in front of the sink in their basement kitchen.

'Please, three sugars and milk.'

'I remember – and although I'm on days the rest of this week, it doesn't mean I'm taking over breakfast,' Sam warned as he cut a couple of slices of bread. 'It'll be your turn to make it tomorrow.'

'I should have been out of the house ten minutes ago.' Martin charged in, grabbed the tea Sam had just poured and picked out his working boots from a line to the right of the door. 'You people with an eight-o'clock start don't know you're born. It's murder having to clock on at seven.'

'Try working shifts and see what that does to your social life with the gorgeous Lily.' Sam opened the door to the postman's knock and took a bundle of letters and a box from him. 'Thank you.' He dumped everything on the dresser. 'Another cake from my mother. I swear she thinks people in Swansea are still on wartime rations.'

'If that's one of her fruit cakes, long may she think it.' Martin finished tying one bootlace and started on the other.

'Two letters for me.' Sam sniffed the envelopes. 'And neither perfumed.'

'You expecting one?' Martin asked.

'I live in hope. Here's one for you, Jack, I'm sorry.' Sam had received his National Service call-up papers three years before and recalled what they had looked like.

Dropping his razor, Jack wiped his chin and opened the letter.

'When?' Martin asked, reading the return address on the discarded envelope.

'I've to report for a medical a week on Monday.'

'Get your doctor to write a letter telling them you've just got married and your wife is in hospital,' Sam suggested. 'They're bound to delay it on compassionate grounds.'

169

'You think so?' Jack asked hollowly.

'Talk to John Griffiths.' Martin finished lacing his boots. 'If anyone can sort it out for you he can. I have to go. My boss threatened to keep me on for an hour without pay if I'm late again this month. See you tonight.' He looked back anxiously at his brother as he opened the door.

'Is Mr Griffiths in?' Jack stuck his head round the door. Although Katie was his sister and John Griffiths his father-in-law he still felt diffident about venturing from the warehouse stockroom into the rarefied atmosphere of the office.

Katie glanced down at the small switchboard next to her. 'He's on the telephone.'

'Do you know if he's rung the doctor yet about my National Service?'

'If you take a seat, I'll ask him when he's finished his call.'

After checking his overalls were clean, Jack sat on the chair in front of her desk.

'Would you like a cup of tea while you're waiting?' It felt odd to ask her brother the question but, constrained by Ann's presence and John's reserve, she felt the need to be even more businesslike than usual.

'No, thanks. You all right?' he asked, noticing how pale and drawn she looked.

'Just tired.'

'I wish you'd gone to bed on Saturday night.'

'I wouldn't have slept even if I had.'

'Jack.' John opened his office door. 'I was just going to send for you. Can you organise some tea, Ann.'

'Not for me, please, Mr Griffiths. Have you spoken to the doctor?' Jack questioned impatiently.

'Yes. Come into the office.'

'Can Katie come too? It will save me having to repeat everything.'

John turned to Ann. 'Go down to the canteen and get tea.' He looked at Jack. 'You sure you don't want any'

'I'm sure.'

'For three, please, Ann.'

John waited for the girl to close the door. 'The doctor's already spoken to someone and he'll give you a letter to take to your medical. He's fairly confident you'll qualify for a month's postponement.'

'A month! That's just when Helen will be coming out of hospital. She'll need looking after . . .'

'In the meantime we'll try for longer.' John sat on the edge of his desk. 'It's not ideal, but it's the best we can hope for at the moment.'

'Thank you, Mr Griffiths.'

'You failed your last army medical, Jack.' Katie tried to raise his spirits.

'I had a broken arm.'

'You both look tired. Why don't you take the rest of the afternoon off,' John offered.

'There's a lot of stock to be shifted downstairs, Mr Griffiths.'

'And I have letters to type.' Katie opened the door. 'I'll get Ann to bring in your tea, Mr Griffiths.'

Between Sunday and Wednesday visiting, Jack felt as though he were sleepwalking. He drove to and from the warehouse with John, accepted meals from Martin and Sam that he left uneaten on his plate and spent the intervening time lying on his and Martin's bed staring at the ceiling. The only time his life drew sharply into focus was when he called the hospital and the message was always the same: 'Mrs Helen Clay is as well as can be expected', followed by 'we'll inform her you telephoned, Mr Clay'.

All he could think about was Helen and how miserable she must be, sick and alone in unfamiliar surroundings, cared for – if that was the right word – by officious nurses. Whatever the time of day or night, he wondered if she was awake and, if she was, whether they had told her about the baby – and that there wouldn't be any more. He thought he knew everything there was to know about her, but try as he might he couldn't envisage her reaction to the blow.

Refusing John's offers to take time off work, he checked the stores against shop-floor stock levels and, mindful of John's directive that 'Goods not on display are goods that can't be sold', filled every conceivable gap in the warehouse. Working through his breaks, he set out women's pom-pom slippers on the boys' boot rack, fur coats on the girls' school-wear rails and Royal Albert china in the catering supplies section, unaware that for the first time since he'd begun work in the warehouse, his supervisor and the stockroom manager were double-checking his every move.

By three o'clock on Wednesday he had dropped more goods on the floor than he had set out on display and John insisted he take the rest of the afternoon off to prepare for his visit to the hospital. Wishing time away, he slipped on his coat and walked back to Carlton Terrace via town and the open-air market. He wanted to buy Helen something special but as he wandered among the stalls nothing caught his eye. Even the flowers seemed to be conspiring against him. Bunches of garish tulips filled the flower vendors' buckets, grating with his mood like clowns at a funeral. Eventually he bought a pot of pale-yellow primroses in a basket, but even as the woman wrapped it for him he caught himself looking around for something better.

John Griffiths had reminded him to sort out clean underwear and nightdresses for Helen the night before but, unable to face the flat, he had asked Katie to pack a case for her. Lily and Judy had helped, and they had found other things they maintained Helen needed: soap, talcum powder, scent, skin cream, toothpaste, shampoo, handkerchiefs, make-up, brush and comb. The weekend bag they filled weighed more than the suitcase he had taken on his fortnight's honeymoon in London.

He wandered back through the stalls and picked up the largest box he could find of the Regency Candies Helen liked. He paused before a fruit stall. Fruit was supposed to be good for invalids. Would she have recovered enough to eat any? He bought a bag of apples and pears and a bunch of bananas just in case.

Half an hour later he made his way to Carlton Terrace with two heavy bags. He knew he had bought enough fruit for the entire ward but he had to show Helen he cared. And as he couldn't think of anything more constructive, he decided he could always bring back what she didn't want. That had to be better than not taking something she couldn't possibly do without.

'Only two visitors to a bed,' the sister barked as John followed Jack into the ward. 'One . . . two.' John pointed at himself, then Jack, but the sister didn't smile at his weak attempt at humour.

'Mrs Clay's mother is with her.'

John took a deep breath. He should have anticipated that Esme would turn up eventually after his telephone call. There'd be nothing she'd like better than playing the role of martyred wife, discarded by her husband, yet still prepared sacrificially to nurse her sick daughter. He checked his watch, the hands pointed to five minutes to the hour. 'I thought visiting started at seven.'

'Your wife had an appointment at six thirty to discuss your

daughter's condition with the doctor. He suggested it might be beneficial for Mrs Clay to see her mother right away.'

'Helen can't stand her mother.'

As the sister gave Jack a severe look, an agonised cry echoed down the ward. Dropping the bags, Jack charged towards Helen's room. Her mother was sitting in an armchair she'd pulled close to the bed. Helen had turned her back to her. Curled on her side, she was sobbing into her pillow. Ignoring Esme, Jack sat on the bed and gathered her in his arms.

'Mrs Clay, we will not hold ourselves responsible for the consequences if you do not lie flat at all times. Mr Griffiths, only two visitors per patient. And Mr Clay, visitors are not allowed to sit on the bed. Your germs . . .'

'As we're married, Helen will have to get used to them.' As Jack gently lowered Helen back on to the bed, John stacked the bags he had dropped next to it. When he finished, he spoke to Esme. 'Helen and Jack need privacy.'

The sister glared at John. 'I will not have my patients upset . . .'

'Please sister, let Jack stay.' Helen dug her nails into Jack's shoulder as though she was afraid the sister was about to drag him away from her.

'Esme.' John held the door open.

'Five minutes, Mr Clay,' the sister warned as John followed Esme out.

'I haven't seen my wife since Sunday,' he protested.

'You do want her to get better.'

'And out of here.' Jack concentrated on Helen, smoothing her hair away from her face and wishing they were somewhere – anywhere else, and alone.

'She had to be told.' Esme lifted her chin defiantly.

'And you decided you had to be the one to do it.' John folded his arms across his chest as he confronted Esme in the corridor.

'I am her mother.'

'Did you have the doctor's permission?' John asked.

'He had already told her that she had lost the baby. It was self-evident. The girl has a massive, disfiguring scar . . .'

'Did he ask you to inform her that she would never have a child?' he reiterated coldly.

'He agreed she had to be told.'

'Today?'

'No woman would want information like that kept from her,' Esme blustered. 'Especially a woman in Helen's position, tied to a man by circumstances that no longer exist. Don't you realise this means she can divorce Jack Clay? Richard says . . .'

'Richard Thomas!' he exclaimed. 'I can't believe you discussed our daughter's personal life with that man.'

'You've never objected to my discussing our personal life with him.'

'He's handling your divorce.' Noticing a couple of porters staring at them, John retreated to a bench in an alcove that afforded a little more privacy.

'He is my family's solicitor, which is why I discuss *family* problems with him,' Esme asserted, standing before him as he lowered himself on to the bench

'Don't you think you should have talked to Helen first?'

'She is a child.'

'A married child,' he reminded her.

'Who could soon be free to choose a young man with better prospects and background than Jack Clay.'

'You suggested this to her?' He gazed at her, wondering if she knew just how close he was to losing his temper with her.

'We discussed what she already knew. That Jack only married her because of a child that no longer exists. That a boy with his background will want children to satisfy his ego and as she can no longer give him any, she should leave him and start looking for someone more suitable. A man with a career who needs a hostess . . .'

'My God, Esme, don't you ever think of anything besides money and social standing?' he enquired contemptuously.

'All I want for Helen is what every mother wants for her child. The absolute best. Something you, with your ridiculous insistence on living in Carlton Terrace, never understood.'

'If you really want what's best for Helen I suggest you leave Helen and Jack to sort out their own problems.'

'And entrust Helen's future to a boy like Jack Clay? Don't be ridiculous.' Opening her handbag, she removed her gloves and proceeded to put them on; smoothing the soft brown leather over each finger until it formed a second wrinkle-free skin on her hands.

John watched, trying to see her as a stranger might. A once

beautiful, middle-aged woman, who knew how to take care of herself and make the most of her fading attractions. He couldn't deny her looks or her charm – when she chose to exercise it – but he had suffered too much from her scheming and snobbery to see her objectively. 'The last thing Helen needs right now is you interfering in her life.'

'It appears to me that is exactly what she does need. I leave her with you and she gets mixed up with a Borstal boy. Ends up pregnant at eighteen . . .'

'It is a little late for recriminations.'

'I agree. But I intend to make sure there won't be any need for them in future. I'm Helen's mother, John. You can't stop me from visiting her here and when she leaves I intend to take care of her, either in your house or mother's. It makes no difference.'

'It will to me – and Helen.'

'This time I intend to make sure things are done my way.'

'Before you make too many plans I suggest you consult with Helen and Jack.'

'Don't worry, I intend to.' She buttoned her coat, walked past him and out of the door.

'Katie, Lily and Judy packed your case. They all send their love and letters and get well cards.' Jack placed them on Helen's locker. 'There's clean nightdresses and soap and woman's stuff.' He lifted one of the bags he'd brought closer to Helen's bed. 'And I bought you some flowers.' He unwrapped the basket of primroses. 'Regency Candies, I know you like them. Everyone wanted to send you something. There's magazines and . . .' He looked into her eyes and realised she wasn't listening to him.

'I'm sorry about the baby,' she whispered. 'I know how much you were looking forward to having a son and now . . .'

Forgetting the sister's directive, he sank down on the bed beside her again. 'It doesn't matter.'

'How can you say that? It was our child.'

'The doctor told me there was no way it could have lived.' Blotting the tears from her eyes with his handkerchief, he kissed her gently on the lips. 'Don't be angry with me for caring about you more than a baby that never lived. I can't bear to see you like this.'

'My mother told me I won't have any more children – ever!'

Caressing her shoulders, he held her close to his chest. 'It doesn't matter.'

'It does. Jack, don't you understand . . .'

'All I understand is that I can't live without you,' he interrupted fervently. 'The only thing that's important to me now is that you get well.'

'I should have listened to you on the train. Let them take me to a hospital in Bridgend.'

'It would have made no difference.' Slowly, haltingly he told her what the doctor had told him and John. And all the while he was thinking of what Martin had said before the wedding. *Doesn't it scare you? A wife and in a few months a baby. Your life mapped out for you.*

'I love you.' He murmured the trite phrase, wishing there were something more he could say that would prove just how important she was to him.

Helen dried her tears but her eyes looked bruised and anguished as she turned to him. 'My mother said you'd want children.'

'Not without you. And your mother's an old witch.'

She smiled in spite of her pain. 'I can't believe you still want me. I have an enormous scar.'

'It will fade.'

'I'm ill . . .'

'You'll get better.'

'It could take months.'

'I don't care if it takes years. I need you; I'm lost without you. You're my girl, remember.'

'Please don't let my mother come here again.'

'I'll talk to the doctors.'

'Will you?' She looked at him in wonder.

'I promise.' A lump rose in his throat. They had lost their child and he was determined they were not going to lose one another. But how would she feel when he told her he was going to have to spend the next two years away from her?

'Mr Clay.' The sister loomed in the doorway.

He moved from the bed to the chair. 'I didn't hear the bell.'

'Your wife . . .'

'Wants me to stay with her as long as possible.' He turned back to Helen. 'And that is exactly what I intend to do.'

A late lecture on Thursday prevented Joe from waiting for Lily outside the bank, but to his delight he saw her turning the corner of Carlton Terrace as he returned from the university. Running to catch up with her he said, 'Have you heard there's a good film on in the Plaza?'

'I dare say.' Lily didn't break her stride.

'You won't come with me?'

'No.'

'And that's your last word on the subject?'

'I'm . . .'

'I know, going out with Martin,' he interrupted flatly.

Trying not to think about the last three weeks when she'd scarcely seen him, she murmured, 'That's right.'

'Probably just as well,' he acknowledged, trying to keep the conversation light. 'I should do some revision. The finals are only a couple of weeks away.'

'Then it sounds as if the last thing you should be doing is inviting people to go to the pictures with you.'

'You're not people and the cinema's more fun than revision.' He walked with her to her gate. 'Come to think of it, anything's more fun than revision.'

'You will get your degree?' she asked, knowing how important it was to him.

'So my tutors tell me.'

'And then you're going to Cardiff to work for the BBC.'

'Not until the autumn. I intend to enjoy one last summer of freedom on the Gower.'

'Lucky you.' She opened her handbag and rummaged around for her keys. They had an annoying habit of always sinking to the bottom.

'You have holidays?'

'Only two weeks.'

'When?'

She gave him a sharp look.

'I'm only asking.'

'Possibly July.' Her boss had tried to pressurise her into booking her holiday dates earlier that day, but she had refused, wanting to speak to Martin first in the hope he would be able to take some time off that would coincide with hers.

'Helen should be fit by then. If I borrow a boat we could go sailing together.'

'That would be nice.' She showed the first signs of enthusiasm since he had accosted her.

'She'll need cheering up if Jack's away,' he added, sensing her change of attitude. 'You have heard.'

'That he received his call-up papers? Yes, Katie told me.'

'Jack hasn't told Helen yet.' He watched as she pulled her key from her bag. 'I'm sorry I couldn't persuade you to come to the cinema.'

'I'm not. I have a mountain of mending and ironing to do.' She smiled as Martin ran up the steps of his basement. 'Martin . . .' Her smile faded as he charged past her. 'Can't I talk to you for a minute?'

'I'm late.'

'Then, when you come back?'

'I've no idea when that will be. I'm going to the pub – it's a leaving do for one of the mechanics.' His feet pounded over the pavement as he raced round the corner.

'Perhaps we should both take a leaf out of Martin's book.' Joe went to his front door.

'What do you mean?' she questioned defensively.

'Forget duty and go down the pub. See you around, Lily.'

'Yes, see you around,' she echoed, as a sick feeling of foreboding stole through her stomach.

Lily was walking towards the kitchen when there was a knock on the door that closed off the internal basement staircase from the rest of the house. She opened it to find Sam, in his police uniform standing on the stairs.

'I confess I saw you coming in and as Katie's out . . .'

'You're watching us!'

'Only from the best of motives. I did debate whether to bring a cup to borrow some sugar, but decided honesty is the best policy. Can we talk?'

'We are talking.'

'I'd talk better over a cup of tea.'

'Men only ever think of their stomachs,' she grumbled. 'Next thing you'll be telling me is you want a sandwich.'

'No sandwich, as Martin's out I've volunteered to cook for Jack, that's if I can prise him out of his bedroom.'

'He's shut himself into his bedroom?'

'Seeing as how he heard today that one month's postponement of his conscription is all he's going to get on compassionate grounds, I think he's entitled to sulk.'

'Poor Jack and poor Helen, nothing seems to be going right for them.'

'Perhaps they're getting all the bad luck they're ever going to get in one go.' He sat at the kitchen table while Lily set about making the tea. 'Is Katie likely to be long?'

'All she said this morning is that she wanted to clear some work because she's taking tomorrow morning off.'

He glanced at the clock. Katie was rarely home before six thirty and it was that now. He had at least half an hour and ten minutes should be enough to find out what he wanted to know – if Lily would tell him. 'Has Katie a steady boyfriend?' he blurted out awkwardly.

'That's a bit personal, Sam.'

'If she's free I'd like to ask her out.' He reached for the sugar bowl and sugared the empty cup she'd placed in front of him. 'But I heard that her and Adam . . .'

'That's been over a long time.'

'I'm glad. With things the way they are with Adam . . .'

'You boys are idiots,' she declared indignantly.

'I'll not argue with that but to go back to Katie. I've tried to let her know I'm interested but she hasn't picked up on my signals.'

'You could try the old-fashioned approach,' she suggested.

'What's that?'

'Forget signalling and ask her outright for a date.'

'I have. She told me she wasn't interested.' He pushed his cup towards her so she could fill it.

'Then you've had your answer.'

'But it's not just me, is it. It's all boys.' He reached for the milk. 'What happened between her and Adam? Something must have. He's obviously still miffed with her and she can't seem to stand the sight of him.'

She set the teapot on its stand and took the chair opposite his. 'The only thing I know that happened between Katie and Adam is that she told him she wasn't interested in going out with him any longer after a few dates.'

'At least he got a few dates in. If she gave me the same chance I wouldn't blow it.'

'I'm not sure he did, "blow it" as you put it.'

'She's a pretty girl.'

'And you can't understand why she isn't overwhelmed by your attentions.'

'As I told Martin, they are strictly honourable.' He passed her the sugar bowl. 'They could hardly be anything else, seeing as how I'm sharing rooms with her brothers.'

'You've discussed Katie with Martin?'

'I mentioned that I would like to go out with her.'

'And what did he say?'

'That she's old enough to make her own decisions.'

She sipped her tea. 'That sounds sensible.'

He sat back and looked at her. 'I heard her father beat her mother to death.'

'You shouldn't listen to gossip.'

'Then it's not true?'

'In a way,' Lily admitted cautiously. 'He did beat her and she ended up in hospital where she died.'

'Is that why Katie doesn't like men?'

'You'll have to ask her that, Sam.'

'Then you won't help me.'

'Katie's one of my closest friends,' she said firmly, wanting to discourage him. 'I feel disloyal just having this conversation with you. If you want to know anything more, you'll have to talk to her yourself.'

'Every time I go near her she runs a mile.'

He looked so crestfallen that Lily relented. 'What were you going to cook for Jack tonight?'

'Sausage and chips.'

'As tonight's Mrs Lannon's night for visiting her sister I do the cooking and as it happens I bought sausages. Why don't you bring yours up here and we'll eat together. But mash, not chips. It's easier to reheat when my uncle comes in after his shift.'

'If you weren't Martin's girlfriend I'd kiss you.'

As he went haring downstairs to get Jack, Lily filled the sink with water and threw in a couple of pounds of potatoes. She only hoped she hadn't given Sam any false hope. Katie had always been reticent to talk about herself, even more so since she had broken off with Adam. For all she knew there could be another boy, but if there was she simply couldn't work out when Katie saw him.

'You will tell Martin?'

'That you want to see him, no matter how late he comes in,' Jack chanted mechanically as he left the dining room. 'I won't forget, Lily. Thanks for the meal. All Martin and Sam can cook is chips.'

'I heard that,' Sam shouted from the kitchen.

'You were supposed to,' Jack called back.

'You're cooking tomorrow.'

'You like my tinned soup and sliced bread that much?' Jack opened the door to the basement stairs.

'I have to wait up for Uncle Roy anyway . . .'

'I won't forget to tell him, Lily,' Jack assured her.

'And in case I don't see you . . .'

'I'll give Helen your love on Sunday.'

'She really is getting better.'

'She'll be better still when I get her out of that hospital.'

'Tell her Katie and I are storing up all the gossip.'

'I will.' He gave her a small smile. 'And thanks again for the meal, even if all this attention does make me feel like a charity case.'

'None of us thinks of you like that. It's just that . . .'

'You want to do something for Helen, you can't and I'm the next best thing.'

His candour embarrassed her. 'Look after yourself, Jack. If not for yourself, then because Helen needs you.'

'Goodnight.'

Lily waited until he closed the door before returning to the dining room. Straightening the tablecloth, she relaid the table for her uncle. As she busied herself with clean cutlery and crockery, she could hear Sam and Katie in the kitchen. She made a conscious effort not to listen to what they were saying but she couldn't help noticing that Sam – not Katie – was doing most of the talking.

'But you will be going to the Pier next Saturday?'

Katie kept her eyes focused on the sink as she stacked the last plate on the draining board. 'Possibly, if Lily and Martin go.'

'And the chances are if Martin goes, I'll be going with him and as we'll all be together anyway. I just don't understand why you won't let me take you.'

'Because if you did, it would be like we were going out together.'

'But we are going out together,' he persisted stubbornly.

'Only in a crowd.' She untied her apron and hung it on the peg behind the door.

'And that's how you see me, one of a crowd.'

'I don't want a boyfriend, Sam.'

'Just a friend.' He couldn't keep the derision from his voice.

'Yes, please.'

'Hellfire and damnation!' He slammed the plate he'd just dried on top of the stack of clean ones. 'I can't even have a good quarrel with you. You're just so . . . nice,' he finished in exasperation. He wanted to reach out and stroke her face, or at the very least hold her hand but he sensed her almost physically recoiling from him. 'You won't mind if I keep trying?' he continued in a gentler tone.

'If by trying you mean asking me out again, I'd prefer you not to.'

'So, no matter what, you'll never go out with me.'

'It's not you, Sam. I like you, I really do.'

'You could have fooled me.'

'You're fun to be with.'

'As a friend.' He summoned his courage and dared to ask the question he had put to Lily earlier. 'Is there someone else?'

'There's no one,' she answered, wishing with all her heart there were.

'Then there's no reason why I shouldn't keep trying to change your mind.'

'I won't.'

Drying the last dish, he flung the tea towel on to a chair. 'Will you dance with me on Saturday?'

'If we're both down the Pier and you ask.'

'Katie Clay, I swear I'll wear you down if it's the last thing I do.'

'Find another girl to say things like that to, Sam, please.'

'I warn you.' He gave her his most gallant smile. 'I'm used to getting my own way.'

'So am I, Sam.'

His smile turned to a scowl as he closed the door behind him.

Chapter 13

'THAT WAS GOOD.'

'There's more sausage and potato, if you want it,' Lily offered.

'No thanks, love, I've eaten too much for comfort as it is.' Roy loosened his belt and sat back in his chair as Lily cleared his plate. 'This afternoon shift is a killer. I feel as though it's six, not eleven o'clock. But you don't have to sit up with me. You have work in the morning.'

'I told Jack to ask Martin to call up when he comes in. He's gone to a leaving do for one of his workmates.'

'Problem?' He frowned.

'No.' She carried his plate and cutlery into the kitchen and stacked them neatly next to the frying pans. As it wasn't worth running a sink full of hot water for so few dishes she decided to leave them until the morning and wash them then along with the breakfast things.

'I've been meaning to ask, is it serious between you two,' he asked, as she returned to the dining room.

'No, it's just that my boss wants me to book my summer holidays and I hoped that Martin and I could take some time off together.'

'In my day it was the boy who did the chasing.'

'You think I'm chasing Martin?' she asked hesitantly.

'Aren't you?' He crossed his long legs in front of him as he leaned back in his chair and reached for his pipe.

'Martin asked me out, not the other way round.'

'That was weeks ago, love. Things change.'

'And you think he doesn't want to go out with me any more?'

'That's an odd question, considering you wanted to spend your holidays with him a moment ago.' Taking out his tobacco pouch, he began to pack the bowl of his pipe.

She sat in one of the easy chairs next to the fire and looked into the flames. 'I'm not sure what he thinks of me.'

'A lot, judging by the amount of time he spends here.'

'I'm not so sure.'

'I know you, love. Something is wrong. Tell me to mind my own business if you like, but if it's anything I can help with, all you have to do is ask.' Leaving the table, he sat in the chair opposite hers.

'It's nothing I can put my finger on, Uncle Roy. I just can't make Martin out. One minute he's telling me he can't support a wife and the thought of marriage scares him to death, the next he's inviting me out for a walk. Then, just when I think we're getting really close, he starts ignoring me.'

'You asked him to marry you?'

She laughed at the shocked expression on his face. 'No. The last thing I want to do at the moment is get married and I told him so.'

'So he brought up the subject.'

'Out of the blue, right in the middle of the dance at the Pier.'

'Before or after Jack got married?'

'The same day,' she murmured thoughtfully.

'Perhaps Jack getting married put the thought in his head and he's angry because he can't afford to support a wife like little brother,' he diagnosed cautiously.

'If you're right, then the last thing I should do is suggest we take our holidays together.'

'It might be better to let things run their course in their own time, love.' Finally satisfied with his pipe, he flicked his lighter and lit it. 'At the risk of sounding like the ancient mariner, you're both very young.'

'Helen's my age, and Jack is three years younger than Martin.'

'I don't think you can consider them a good example.' As he puffed away, clouds of blue smoke wreathed around his head. 'I wish Norah were here. She'd know exactly what to say and how to say it. I've a tendency to speak my mind and think about what I've said afterwards.'

She sat back and looked him in the eye. 'What do you really think about Martin and me going out together?'

'I think it's fine as long as you enjoy one another's company and have a good time.'

'You don't think it will last.'

'A moment ago you said you didn't want to get married.'

'I don't – yet. But who knows, maybe in the future I'll change my mind.'

'And who's going to change it for you, Martin or Joe?' he asked perceptively.

'Not Joe.'

'That sounds very definite for a girl who almost got engaged to him.'

'I didn't know him then.'

'And you do now.'

'Enough to realise we're poles apart. Oh, he's nice enough, but he's a dreamer.' She gazed back at the fire, recalling nights when she and Joe had sat before the fire in this same room, studying the flames and imagining shapes in them – fairy tale castles, wicked witches, glowing caverns of rubies populated by goblins, nothing was too wild or fanciful for Joe.

'And you're too old for dreams now, I suppose.' Without waiting for her to answer he continued, 'I've had a soft spot for Martin and Jack ever since they were nippers. Who wouldn't, after seeing the way Ernie treated them, but having a father like that creates problems. You must have noticed the way both of them – and Katie – keep their distance. Live more within themselves, as it were, than most people.'

'Katie I'd agree with, but Jack loves Helen.'

'Yes, he does. I only hope he has the sense not to smother her with it.'

'You think it's difficult for Jack, Martin and Katie to relate to other people,' she said slowly, trying to consider the implications for her and Martin if her uncle was right.

'I think they haven't seen much of what you and I would call a normal life, love. In my opinion – and it is only an opinion and I could be wrong you should take things very slowly with Martin. Let him set the pace.'

'And not try to push him into spending his holidays with me.'

'Not unless he suggests it first, love. That doesn't create a problem for you, does it?'

'No.'

'I could take some time off and we could go somewhere . . .'

'No, Uncle Roy.' His unselfishness was so generous and character- istic that she left her seat and kissed the top of his bald head before curling at his feet and resting her head against his knee. 'You have your wedding and honeymoon to arrange. Judy said if her mother can organise cover for the Mumbles shop she intends to take a couple of weeks off early in July. I'll take the same fortnight off as her. If Katie can do that too and Helen's well enough to join us it will almost be like old times. We'll be able to spend all day together, gossiping, visiting the beach, shopping . . .'

The doorbell rang.

'That will be your young man.' He smiled at her as she rose to her feet. 'Don't talk too long. You look tired.'

'I am. Goodnight.' She kissed his cheek.

He patted her hand. 'Sleep tight. We must have a talk soon – about the wedding.'

'We must.' She hesitated as the doorbell rang a second time. 'Nothing urgent, is there?'

'Nothing that can't wait, love.'

Martin was walking away when Lily opened the door. He turned back to see her framed in the doorway, the light shining like a halo round her dark hair. The breath caught in his throat. Jack and Sam had joked that Lily couldn't live without him for five minutes but he knew different after seeing her in the Kardomah with Joe and again tonight. It was obvious Joe had walked her home from work and he was certain she only wanted to see him to tell him she was taking back his ring.

'I'm sorry, Marty, I didn't mean to keep you waiting.'

'Jack said you wanted to see me.'

'Yes.' She opened the door wider. 'Come in.'

'It's late.'

'My uncle's here and you'll be just as quick walking down the inside staircase.' Relenting, he stepped inside.

'I feel a bit of a fool, I did want to see you but . . .' She gave him a nervous smile. 'It's not important. Not any more.'

'You sure?'

'Yes,' she answered awkwardly.

'You must have thought it was important at the time.' He braced himself for her rejection.

'It was just a small thing. My uncle helped me to think it through. See you tomorrow.'

'If you want to,' he answered carelessly, deliberately affecting an offhand manner in response to her refusal to tell him about Joe.

'If you're busy . . .'

'I've been offered overtime.'

'Some other time, then. Sorry to disturb you.'

'Goodnight, Lily.' Utterly miserable, he watched her run up the stairs.

'Someone's going to look smart tomorrow.' Lily returned from the bathroom to see one of Katie's favourite costumes hooked outside the wardrobe door. Pale-grey, trimmed with black, it was one of the few outfits Katie possessed with a straight skirt. Beneath it, she had set out a pair of plain black leather court shoes trimmed with grey buckles, black gloves and handbag, and a tiny black hat, cut at the back to accommodate a chignon.

'I hope so.' Katie sat in front of the dressing table and pushed her hair back with a band before smearing her face with Pond's skin cream.

'Special day?'

'Promise you won't tell anyone.'

'Promise.'

'I've an interview.'

'For a job?' Lily couldn't have been more astounded. 'I thought you were happy at the warehouse.'

'I am – was.' Katie curled her feet on the stool, rested her head on her knees and hooked the hem of her nightdress round her toes.

'But not any more.'

Katie shook her head.

'Want to talk about it?'

Katie hesitated. She hadn't told a soul about her affair with John Griffiths except Martin and he had point-blank refused to discuss it. But Martin's refusal hadn't prevented her from sensing his disapproval. She hadn't even told him of John's decision not to see her in private again because she knew he'd not only be relieved but would also try to persuade her to spend time with boys her own age – like Sam. But she couldn't go on bottling everything up and Lily had never divulged a secret she had entrusted to her, not even when they had been children.

'I can't work with John any more.'

'You mean Mr Griffiths?'

'Yes.' Tears ran cold and wet down Katie's face. She brushed them away with her fingers but not before Lily saw them.

'I don't understand. I thought you got on well with him. He tells everyone you're the best secretary he's ever had . . .'

'I love him.'

Lily dropped the dressing gown she was about to hang on a hook at the back of the door.

'I couldn't help it. He's a wonderful, kind, gentle, thoughtful man. I've never met anyone like him. And it is love, not a childish crush.' She almost dared Lily to say otherwise.

Lily sank down on the bed. 'Have you told him?'

'Yes. And the awful thing is, although he says he loves me, because he's married he won't see me outside office hours any more and I simply can't bear to carry on working for him. You've no idea what it's like to be with him every day and pretend he means no more to me than any other boss would.' She looked across at Lily. 'Please say something, even if it's only that you're horrified.'

'I'm not horrified but I am surprised.' Realising she was cold, Lily climbed into bed and pulled the sheet and blankets to her chin. Suddenly everything made sense: Katie's refusal to continue to see Adam after only a few dates; her insistence on going out as part of a crowd never one of a couple; her long silences and secretiveness. 'Have you told anyone else how you feel?'

'Martin knows. John told him he loved me and wanted to marry me when his divorce was finalised the night my father died.'

'What did Martin say?'

'He wasn't pleased. There's the age difference for a start. And although John and Mrs Griffiths are divorcing they are still legally married, so Martin was upset about that. And because I work for John, Martin accused him of taking advantage of me. Trying to buy me by giving me a job when no one else would, driving me back and for to work, allowing me to open a clothing account in the warehouse.'

'I can see how Martin would think that.'

'But it wasn't like that between us, Lily,' Katie protested. 'I was the one who told John I loved him, not the other way round. I was the one to kiss him first. If it was seduction it was me who seduced him.'

Before that moment the idea of Katie as a seductress would have brought a smile to Lily's face, but not now, when she faced the full intensity of Katie's passion. Whether Katie loved John Griffiths or not, one thing was crystal clear, she believed she did and Lily knew exactly what it felt like to fall in love with someone who didn't love you back.

'And now, somehow Mrs Griffiths has found out about us . . .'

'She said something?'

'To John at Helen's wedding. And because he's afraid she'll spread gossip that will hurt Helen and Joe as well as bring up my name in court, he won't see me alone any more.'

Lily opened her arms as Katie climbed into bed beside her. Hugging her, she wondered why life wasn't the way they had imagined it would be when they were growing up. Then it had seemed so simple. All a girl had to do was meet the perfect man – preferably in a ballroom – fall in love and, after an idyllic courtship, marry him and make a perfect home for him to come home to every night. Eventually they'd have one or two children and live happily ever after. She was certain it had never crossed any of their minds that the man might already have a wife and be twenty years older. Or that one of them would have a miscarriage and be separated from her husband by National Service, or the man could live too far away to iron out any misunderstandings.

And her? Should she settle for Joe because he loved her, even if she could never love him back the way she loved Martin, who didn't seem to want her the way she did him? Was it possible to grow to love someone after marriage? Or perhaps more important, forget someone else?

'So what did your lady love have to say?'

'Nothing.' Undoing the top buttons on his shirt, Martin pulled it over his head and tossed it on to a chair.

'That I find difficult to believe.' Jack plumped up his pillow, rested on one elbow and looked at his brother.

'It's the truth.'

'There's no need to snap my head off.' Jack softened his tone. 'Things not going so well between you and Lily?'

'There's nothing going on between me and Lily.' Unbuckling and unzipping his trousers, Martin stepped out of them and dropped them on top of his shirt.

'You two are finished?' Jack asked in surprise.

'We never got bloody started.' Martin pulled his pyjamas from beneath his pillow. 'Now, if you don't mind, it's late and I have to get up early in the morning.'

As Martin switched off the light. Jack lay on his back and stared at the ceiling. He was aware his brother was as wide awake and dejected as he was; he only wished they could talk about it.

'I made love with John and I'm not sorry,' Katie whispered into the darkness that shrouded Lily's bedroom after they had turned off the bedside lamps. 'A marriage certificate would make no difference to the way I feel about him.'

'So that's why you said what you did, when Judy asked Helen what it's like to sleep with a man.'

'It's the most wonderful feeling ever, if you love him.' Katie shrank further beneath the bedclothes. 'But it's impossible for me to carry on working with him the way things are between us now.'

'Where's the interview?'

'Lewis Lewis.'

'They have beautiful things in there.' Lily recalled some of the clothes and fabrics she'd seen on her last window-shopping trip.

'They do,' Katie agreed. 'The manager showed me over the store and the staff discount is generous. Not as generous as the warehouse, but then few people are as kind as John.'

'What's the job?'

'Secretary to the manager,' Katie said proudly. 'When I put in an application I never thought I'd get an interview but I've passed the first selection process. Tomorrow's the big day and they're only interviewing three girls.'

'Have you told Mr Griffiths?'

'Only that I want the morning off. If I get the job John's going to find out soon enough. If I don't, I'll have to keep looking and I'm dreading it either way. If I get it I'll have to leave the warehouse and never see him again – well, not every day and no more than a quick hello in the street. And if I don't get it I'll have to carry on as I am, and I'm not sure how much longer I'll be able to stand it.'

'You're shivering. Shall I get another blanket?'

'Is that all you can say?' Katie waited for Lily to comment on the secret that had weighed so heavily on her.

'Other than I won't tell a soul and I'll always be here to listen.'

'You're not shocked?'

'Just sad it didn't work out for you.'

'John did say if I was sure I still loved him after his divorce was finalised I could talk to him again then. But I think he only said it because he expects me to go off with someone younger, like Adam Jordan or Sam.'

'Which you've obviously no intention of doing.'

'Do you think he meant it?' Katie asked eagerly. 'That he wasn't just saying it to let me down gently?'

'I don't know. But he's going to have to talk to you if you get that job tomorrow. If half the things Helen said he told her about your secretarial skills are true, he's going to be devastated at losing you.'

'As a secretary,' Katie murmured disconsolately.

'I can understand him not wanting you to be any more until he's free.'

'Like everyone else around here, you're afraid of the gossips.' Katie turned over restlessly.

'As you suggested, I'm sure he's only thinking of your reputation.'

'I couldn't care less what people say.'

'You would if the gossip hurt John, Helen and Joe, or trade at the warehouse.'

'You're right, I would. But I love John so much it hurts.' Impulsively she hugged Lily before settling back on to her pillows. 'Thank you, you've no idea how much it means to have someone I can talk to about this.'

'Any time.' Lily closed her eyes.

'Just one thing,' Katie said quietly. 'Don't invite Sam for any more meals for a bit.'

'You knew.'

'He's been nagging me for weeks to go out with him. When he told me earlier that I had a loyal friend in you, I guessed he'd been pumping you for information and you wouldn't tell him anything.'

'He's persistent and keen.'

'Not as keen as Martin is on you.'

'I'm not so sure about that.'

'I am. It'll be great to have you as a sister as well as Helen. Goodnight.'

'Goodnight.' Lily turned over. Contrary to what she had suggested to her uncle earlier, she wasn't too old for dreams. She only wished they could be about something more realistic than castles in the air — like Martin.

The telephone rang a dozen times in the outer office before John remembered that Katie was taking a couple of hours off that morning. Cursing Ann for not picking it up, he left his office and limped over to Katie's desk. 'John Griffiths,' he snapped, as he lifted the receiver.

'Mark Davies here, John.'

'Just a minute, Mark.' John looked at Ann who was on her hands and knees, going through the files in the bottom drawer of one of the filing cabinets. Doubting the girl would ever finish the task, he wished he'd picked out someone else to do it. 'Take a twenty-minute break in the canteen, Ann.'

'Shall I bring you back a cup of tea, Mr Griffiths?' She brushed the dust from her skirt as she rose from her knees.

'Please.' He waited until she had left the office, then asked, 'You've made some headway with Esme, Mark?'

'Unfortunately not. But I had a telephone call from Richard Thomas half an hour ago. Your mother-in-law died early this morning.'

'I'm sorry to hear that, although we were never close.'

'He asked if you, Joe and Helen would be at the funeral. He'll be reading the will after the interment.'

'Are Helen and Joe beneficiaries?'

'He didn't say. What he did say was that Esme would appreciate your support for the next week or so.'

'I don't need him, or Esme, to remind me to attend my children's grandmother's funeral.'

'I think he had more support in mind than that, John. He mentioned that Esme still wants a reconciliation.'

'No chance.'

'That's what I said. You'll tell Joe and Helen that Richard Thomas wants them to attend the will reading?'

'I'll tell Joe. Helen won't be fit enough to leave hospital for at least another week.'

'I'm sorry, I heard she was ill. You'll pass on my condolences?'

'I will. Thank you for calling, Mark.' John looked up as the door opened and Katie walked in, looking extremely smart and, to his eye, heartbreakingly beautiful.

'Thank God you're here.' He smiled at her with relief, without thinking what he was doing or saying. 'That stupid girl hasn't even sense enough to pick up the telephone when it rings.'

'I'm sorry, Mr Griffiths.' She hung her coat on the stand.

'It's hardly your fault, Katie. I was the one who picked Ann out from the shop floor.' Leaving her desk, he looked back at her. 'Is anything the matter?' He was perturbed by her manner. She had become overtly formal in her approach since he had told her he could no longer see her privately, but he thought he could detect a new uneasiness.

'I would appreciate a word in private, Mr Griffiths.'

'Then you'd better come into my office.' This time, he noticed, she closed the door behind her.

'I have been offered another position and I'm handing in my notice.'

'You've accepted another job?' His blood ran cold at the thought of losing her altogether from his life.

'Yes.'

'Why didn't you discuss this with me?'

'Because I knew you'd try to persuade me to stay.'

'I thought you were happy here.'

'I was.'

'If you want more money . . .'

'I don't want your money!' she exclaimed, horrified that he should even think she was leaving the warehouse for mercenary motives. 'I won't be getting any more in Lewis Lewis than I get here. In fact, they were amazed that you were paying me so much.'

'Then why go?' he pleaded urgently.

'Because I can't carry on seeing you, day in day out, all the while treating you as though you mean no more to me than any other person here. I can't bear it . . . I simply can't . . .' As she struggled to compose herself, she saw him looking towards the door.

Almost as though on cue there was a knock. She instinctively reached for the notepad and pencil on John's desk as he called, 'Enter.'

Ann bustled in with a tea tray.

'Thank you. Put it on the desk,' John ordered abruptly.

'Is there's anything else, sir?'

'Nothing, thank you, Ann. We have some confidential work in hand, so I'd appreciate it if you'd go down to the shop floor and assist the supervisors for the rest of the day.'

'Yes, Mr Griffiths.'

Katie and John sat in silence until they heard the outer office door opening and closing.

'You will give me a reference?' Katie asked.

'A glowing one, if that's what you want.'

'It's the last thing I want,' Katie whispered.

'Then don't go.'

'I can't stay while things remain as they are.'

'Do you think I'm happy with the situation?'

'If you're not, why can't we . . .'

'No!' he broke in harshly. 'I refuse to risk your reputation on my account. You're young; these should be your best years and I won't allow you to waste them on me.'

'They are wasted without you.'

'Katie.' His voice softened as he looked at her. 'You don't know what you're asking. How can you, when you've scarcely begun to live. I don't even have a name to offer you and if I did, who's to say you'll feel the same way about me a month from now.'

'I'll love you until the day I die.'

Coming from anyone other than Katie the declaration would have sounded melodramatic. 'You haven't even tried to find happiness with someone else, have you.'

'There's no point when I know I can't be happy without you.'

Leaving his desk, he limped to the window and looked out, trying to summon strength enough for both of them. 'Nothing's changed. I still refuse to risk your reputation by carrying on a hole-in-the-corner affair that should never have started.'

'You're sorry it happened.'

He turned back to her. 'How could I be when you gave me the happiest moments of my life, but I won't sleep with you again while I remain married to Esme and at the moment she is refusing to divorce me.'

'You could divorce her.'

'My solicitor has warned me that if I try it could take years and even then there's no guarantee I'd succeed. She is a bitter, twisted woman who is terrified of losing her social position and ending up alone and ostracised. She feels she has nothing to lose by exposing us and she won't hesitate to do it, Katie, if she thinks it will get her what she wants.'

'You.'

'The last thing she wants is me.' He smiled grimly. 'But she does want the money and respectability marriage gives her.'

'And you,' Katie asked seriously. 'Do you still want to divorce her?'

'More than ever but she wants us to carry on living together for appearances' sake, both of us leading separate lives.'

'If that's what she wants, we could . . .'

'I'll not make you my mistress, Katie,' he broke in decisively.

'Not even if it's what I want?' she begged.

'Not even if it's what you want,' he echoed dismally. He reached out and touched her face with his fingertips. 'Perhaps it was an impossible dream from the beginning.'

'But you'll still try to divorce Mrs Griffiths.'

'My solicitor holds out little hope that I'll succeed.' He turned back to the window. 'I wish I were free right now to offer you everything I have, but I'm not.'

'I don't want anything from you except your love.'

'You have that.'

'Not the way I want it. I couldn't care less about respectability and I couldn't love you any more if you were free. A marriage certificate is only a piece of paper . . .'

'Which a woman like Esme can use to destroy our lives.'

'Only if we let her.'

'God, Katie, I'd give anything to see the world the way you do. But I know what scandal can do in this town.'

She moved behind him and put her arms round his waist. For one blissful moment he leaned back against her, then he turned, intending to push her away, but her hands moved upwards. Linking her fingers round his neck, she pulled his head down to hers and as their lips met he forgot Esme, the divorce, the age difference between them, even his disfigurement. She loved him more completely than he had ever believed it possible for a woman to love a man and it made him feel omnipotent. As if he could fight the entire world and win.

The telephone rang, shattering the moment. Hating himself for being weak enough to take what Katie so innocently and lovingly offered, John extricated himself from her arms and reached for the receiver. 'Yes.'

'The Ekco television rep is here, Mr Griffiths. You said you wanted to see him when he next came in.'

'I'm busy at the moment, Dennis. Offer him coffee and tell him I'll be down as soon as I can.'

'You don't want me to send him up, Mr Griffiths?'

'No, Dennis, I don't want you to send him up.'

Katie handed John her handkerchief as he replaced the telephone. 'You have lipstick on your cheek.'

John went into the cloakroom and used her handkerchief to scrub his face clean. Reluctant to see anyone until he had regained his equanimity, he remained in front of the mirror. Was it his imagination or were there more grey hairs at his temples? Had his scars always been so ingrained or were they deepening with age? He raised his hands to brush back his hair and caught sight of the withered claw that had almost been consumed in the fire. Then he thought of Katie, young, fresh, perfect . . . it couldn't last between them – could it?

Taking a deep breath, he checked his face again before rejoining Katie in the office. She was sitting at her desk.

'That was insane. Anyone could have walked in on us.'

'Don't ask me to be sorry or promise that it won't happen again because I'm not sorry and I do want it to happen again.'

He held her look for a moment. 'I'm the one who's sorry and I understand now why you have to leave. How soon do Lewis Lewis want you to start?'

'I told them I have to give two weeks' notice.'

'Two weeks!'

'It's what's on my contract.'

'It doesn't give me much time to replace you.'

'Everyone in Swansea has heard how good the conditions are here. There are plenty of experienced secretaries who'd jump at the chance of working for you.' She knew the inference that he only wanted her to be his secretary would hurt; yet she twisted the knife in the hope that even now he'd change his mind about allowing things to go back to what they had been.

'Place an advertisement in the *Evening Post* in the morning. Run it by me before you submit the copy.'

'Yes, Mr Griffiths.' He was so close, all she had to do was reach out to touch his hand. As if he knew what she was thinking, he retreated. 'You'll work your notice.'

'Yes, Mr Griffiths.'

'You have holidays coming.'

'I don't mind losing them.'

'I'll pay you.'

'I don't want your money.'

'It's all I have to give you and it's not as if you haven't earned it. You'll be hard to replace.' He finally looked at her. 'And I don't just mean as a secretary.'

'Then don't let me go.'

'I have to, Katie, for both our sakes.'

Showing more strength than he would have given her credit for a few months before, she picked up the notepad, returned to her desk and began to draft the advertisement.

Chapter 14

'SO YOU'RE HELEN'S husband.' The middle-aged woman looked Jack up and down, as though he were a foul-smelling specimen on a fishmonger's slab.

Despite the fact that he was wearing a brand-new black suit, white cotton shirt and black tie John had insisted he buy, on the grounds that the Italian mohair suit he had worn for his wedding was unsuitable for a funeral, Jack felt distinctly second-class as he nodded an uncomfortable agreement.

'A welshcake, Mr Clay.'

'No, thank you.' Jack politely refused the housekeeper's offer. He was having enough problems trying to balance the teacup and plate of sandwiches she had pressed on him as soon as he had walked through the door of Helen's grandmother's house for the traditional post funeral 'tea'. He glanced through the open drawing-room door into the dining room of the house that had assumed manor house proportions to his inexperienced eye. It was packed with people but he could see no sign of his father-in-law.

'Joseph, darling, you poor, poor boy. We were simply devastated when we heard the sad news, weren't we Robin, Angela?'

Jack watched as a middle-aged woman bore down on Joe. After embracing him she moved along, making room for her children to speak to him, and Jack recognised Joe's friends, Robin and Angela Watkin Morgan, from Lily's and Joe's ill-fated engagement party.

'Helen's mother tells me John found a job for you at the warehouse.'

'Yes.' Jack glowered at the elderly man who'd accosted him, resenting the implication that he needed someone to 'find' him a job as if he were incapable of landing a job on his own merit.

'We haven't been formally introduced. I'm Richard Thomas, the family solicitor.'

As the man offered a handshake, Jack looked round for somewhere he could dump his cup and saucer. Seeing his predicament the man lowered his hand. 'There's no need to stand on ceremony. You will be at the reading.'

'The reading?' After a family service in the house, a second interminable one that seemed to last years in a cold, grey, damp church and a third mercifully short one at the graveside, Jack had hoped the formalities were over.

'The will,' Richard explained. 'I asked John to gather the family in the library in one hour.' He looked around the room. 'By then everyone should have moved on. Funerals are rarely protracted affairs when the deceased are as elderly as Mrs Harris.' Seeing Jack's confusion he explained, 'Most of her friends, if not all, have gone before.' As he sauntered off, Jack spotted John standing alone in the doorway. In his eagerness to reach him he spilled most of his tea over the carpet. Embarrassed, he rubbed his foot over the stain, hoping no one had noticed.

'So that's your brother-in-law.' Angela Watkin Morgan studied Jack from his shiny black shoes to the gleaming Brylcreemed tip of his styled quiff.

'You've met Jack before,' Joe reminded her.

'I most certainly have not. I'd remember someone who looked like him.'

'Why?'

'He's extremely good-looking. In a rough and ready, coarse, working-class sort of way,' she qualified. 'Bit Marlon Brando. The sort of man who'd sweep a girl off her feet and out of her knickers before she knows what's hit her and' – she smiled knowingly – 'give her an alarmingly good time. But then your sister's experience rather bears that out.'

'Excuse Angie, she has a vivid imagination she overdoses with romantic potboilers.'

'I do not read potboilers.'

'What's *Forever Amber* if it's not a pot-boiler?'

'A historical novel.'

'The way you were dribbling at the mouth when you read it, I'd say history was the last thing on your mind.' Robin by-passed the tea tray the housekeeper was carrying and liberated a couple of sherries from a tray on the sideboard behind him. Handing one to Joe, he murmured,

'No disrespect to your grandmother, but why do they never have whisky at funerals?'

'Because it would be bad form to get pie-eyed in the middle of the afternoon.' Angie snatched Robin's sherry from him and downed it in one. 'So, you going to introduce me?' she demanded of Joe.

'To Jack?'

'No, the King of Siam.'

'After what you just said about him, no.'

'Because you don't trust him.'

'You.'

'Spoilsport. I lo-ove married men. They are so vulnerable, especially when their wives are away — or in hospital.'

'That's my sister's husband you're talking about.'

'Dear Joe.' She brushed the tip of her fingers over his cheek. 'Always the prehistoric prude. Never mind, I can introduce myself.'

To Joe's annoyance she strolled over to Jack and took the plate and teacup from his hands.

'Take no notice. Angie's making a habit of trying to shock people.' Robin reached for the sherry tray again.

'Looks like she's succeeding,' Joe observed, as he watched her take Jack's arm and lead him into the next room.

'You going drinking with the boys in the Vivs tonight?'

'That would be bad form on the day of my grandmother's funeral.'

'As Angie says, you're prehistoric.' Robin leaned against the wall. 'Tomorrow?'

'I have work to do.'

'Saturday?'

'Perhaps,' Joe answered, his mind clearly elsewhere.

'You're not thinking of going down to the Pier again.'

'I like it there,' Joe retorted, instantly on the defensive.

'The gorgeous Lily might not dance with you again.'

'She will.'

Robin drank his sherry and took two more from the tray. 'These are both for me,' he said, as Joe held out his hand. 'With you for a friend I need them.'

'Helen's a lucky girl.'

'You think so?' Jack wondered how he could get rid of Angela without appearing downright rude.

'Not for being in hospital, silly.' She giggled, leading him out through the french doors towards the shrubbery. 'For having you for a husband.'

'I'm lucky to have her for a wife.'

'How sweet, a couple who are not cynical about marriage. And they say love is going out of fashion. Do you think it is?'

Jack looked down at her. 'I think you're talking a lot of nonsense.'

'But, darling, nonsense is the only thing worth discussing these days.' Leading him behind a large oak tree, she pouted her lips in a fair imitation of Doris Day and waited expectantly for a kiss.

'Only for people who have nothing better to do.' Removing her hand from his arm he returned to the house.

Richard Thomas sat behind the desk that had been Esme's father's and studied the people assembled on the rows of chairs before him. He pretended to rearrange the piles of papers in front of him, although his secretary had set out everything to his exact instructions earlier. Almost fifty years of being a solicitor hadn't diminished the buzz of excitement he derived from will readings – when there was a sizeable estate at stake.

The beneficiaries invariably attempted to look solemn, grief-stricken and disinterested, as befitting people mourning the loss of a beloved relative, but few managed to achieve it. He had even begun to recognise the types. The stalwart, sacrificial servants who had given the best years of their lives to caring for a cantankerous elderly employer, were usually at pains to point out they expected nothing, although he sensed that they generally had expectations of a valuable something. Few managed to look gleeful at modest bequests and he doubted whether Mrs Harris's housekeeper would be delighted with her lot in a few minutes.

Then there was the immediate family. If the deceased was a widow or widower and there was more than one child, the ensuing arguments over who got what had been known to result in civil suits, which decimated the estate and benefited his firm. There were no siblings here, but he could sniff a potential suit. The question was, did he want to take it?

'Are you sure you want me here, Richard?'

John Griffiths's question concentrated Richard's mind. This was his moment and he would allow no one else to take control. 'If you'll bear with me, John. Shall we begin.' As no one spoke, he indicated a pile of envelopes set out on a table to the side of the desk. 'These are copies that have been made for the beneficiaries of Mrs Harris's estate. After the reading, you may take the envelope bearing your name and study the document at your leisure. My office will be pleased to answer any questions you may have. But I think you will find everything quite straightforward. Mrs Harris took pains to keep everything simple and legally watertight.'

Wondering what he was doing there, Jack gazed out of the window as the solicitor droned on in a tedious monotone. Helen had told him about her grandmother's house, of Sunday visits, teas on the lawn, picnics she and Joe had taken down to the beach that stretched, vast and inviting, below the garden, but he had never imagined anything as grand as this. It emphasised the social divide between them even more than the rented basement flats in Carlton Terrace that he had lived in all his life and her 'upstairs existence' as the daughter of a family that actually owned a house. A sharp intake of breath drew his attention to what Richard was saying.

'. . . My housekeeper, in recognition of years of devoted care and service, five hundred pounds.'

Five hundred pounds! The most he had ever saved in his life was five. Five hundred pounds would buy a decent house, yet the woman didn't look pleased. As she pulled a handkerchief from her skirt pocket and blotted her eyes, he wondered if she was too grief-stricken to realise her good fortune.

'To my niece, Dorothy Green, the sum of two thousand pounds in recognition of her frequent visits and sincere enquiries after my health.' Jack smiled as he looked at Helen's Aunt Dot. She at least looked pleased – and surprised. He was glad. He and Helen owed her a lot for recommending their honeymoon hotel and paying their first week's bill. 'To my son-in-law, John Griffiths, I bequeath a life-time interest in my investment properties in the Sandfields area of Swansea, in recognition of the care he has taken of my grandchildren.'

John evinced all the astonishment Jack had expected to see on the housekeeper's face.

'To my granddaughter, Helen, the house, land and full estate I inherited from my sister, Julie, to do with as she wishes and, after her father's death, my investment properties in the Sandfields.' Jack noticed that Richard Thomas paused and peered at him over the top of his spectacles but as Helen had never mentioned an 'Aunt Julie' and he had no idea what 'investment properties' were, the bequest meant absolutely nothing to him.

'To my daughter, Esme, my fur coats, the painting of Three Cliffs Bay executed by my late husband, her father, all the jewellery in my rosewood casket and no other pieces.'

Everyone in the room turned to Esme. She was sitting bolt upright, her attention fixed on Richard. Only her hands, twitching nervously in her lap, betrayed her emotion.

'To my grandson, Joseph Griffiths, I leave the entire residue of my estate. This includes all my personal possessions and jewellery in the hope that he will find a woman worthy of wearing pieces I treasured for their family not monetary value.'

The room was silent but the inference was obvious. No one could be certain what Mrs Harris's definition of a worthy woman had been. But they were all left in absolutely no doubt that she did not regard her daughter as such.

'Your bequest will be forwarded to you in cheque form, within twenty-eight days.'

'Thank you, Mr Thomas.' The housekeeper gave the solicitor and Joe a venomous look before rising to her feet, picking up her handbag and stalking as majestically as her insignificant stature would allow to the door.

As she closed it behind her Richard looked expectantly at the others gathered in the room. Dorothy Green was still looking stunned by her genuinely unexpected good fortune, John was wearing a distinctly suspicious expression – as well he might. Jack Clay succeeded in appearing dangerous, bored and bemused all at once. Forewarned by his grandmother, Joseph had received sufficient hints of his forthcoming inheritance to remain, outwardly at least, composed. And then there was Esme.

Tight-lipped, unnaturally pale, a stranger might have been forgiven for believing she was putting on a brave face to conceal her grief but he knew her well enough to realise she was having difficulty in keeping her temper in check.

'Are there any questions?' After a moment's silence he said, 'Then all that remains is for me to thank you for your patience.' Shuffling the papers on the desk in front of him into a neat pile, he pushed them into a file and returned it to his briefcase.

'Richard, if I might have a word in private.'

'Yes, John. Joseph, you will wait until I have spoken to your father.' Taking his briefcase, Richard opened the door behind him and led the way into the morning room that overlooked the garden and the beach. The lightest and arguably the most beautiful room in the house, Esme's mother had claimed it as her own, furnishing it in blond wood art deco furniture and pastel-shaded William Morris fabrics. Placing his case on a side table, Richard settled into a fan-back cushioned sofa with the proprietary air of a man perfectly at home. 'Cigar?' He opened an engraved gold case and offered it

'No, thank you.'

'You are surprised that Mrs Harris remembered you in her will.'

'Astounded.' John lowered himself into a chair opposite Richard. 'Could it be an oversight? A clause left in by mistake dating from the time of my marriage to Esme?'

'That will was signed two weeks ago. The witnesses were her doctor and the local vicar. She chose them because she was concerned that someone' – Richard gave John a significant look – 'might attempt to challenge the document on the grounds that she was failing in health and faculties.'

'Was she?' John asked shrewdly.

'I drew up every clause of that document according to her specific instructions.' Flicking an elaborate and expensive gold lighter that matched his cigar case, Richard lit his cigar. 'At no time did I, the vicar who called every day to give her spiritual guidance, or the doctor who attended her during her last illness doubt that she was of sound mind.'

'As sound as the investment properties she left me and Helen?' John enquired cynically.

'They are in need of some repairs.'

'And the rents are fixed at a level that makes those repairs uneconomic,' John diagnosed.

'Depends on what you mean by uneconomic. The way property prices have been rising the last few years, they should make a sound investment for Helen.'

'Which I cannot sign over to her.'

'I am not conversant with your daughter's finances, John, but I wouldn't advise making them over to her as they are, unless she intends to liquidise Julie Harris's estate and realise her stocks and shares, or has considerable savings to invest on a long-term proposition.'

John sat back and studied the magnificent view. 'I knew the old lady disliked me. I had no idea how much.'

'You do her an injustice, John. She has left her entire estate to your son.'

'*My* son, Richard?'

The inflection wasn't lost on Richard. Momentarily disconcerted, he opened his briefcase and removed several files, piling them on the table beside his chair. 'Given the circumstances, I feel I must warn you, should you refuse this bequest, you will leave yourself open to litigation.'

'You'd sue me?' John asked in surprise.

'Not me, Helen.'

'My own daughter? Don't be ridiculous.'

'Any competent solicitor would advise her to do just that, should you refuse to accept the bequest.'

'Helen would have more sense than to follow that kind of advice.' Anxious to put an end to the interview, John asked, 'How many houses are there?'

'Fourteen.'

'Am I right in thinking that you have already had an estimate for the necessary repairs?'

'Mrs Harris did commission one.'

'How much?'

'The actual figure escapes me.'

'A rough estimate will do.'

'I really can't remember.'

'You have the details of the properties.'

Richard made a great show of thumbing through the files on the table. 'Regrettably, I don't seem to have brought that particular file with me. You can pick it up from the office.'

'Send it on.'

'There's the matter of Helen's bequest. I'll need to see her.'

'She's in hospital.'

'Esme did tell me. I sent her a letter yesterday terminating her employment with us.'

Given Richard's ruthless nature, John had been expecting the news, but not while Helen was still in hospital. 'Because she's sick?'

'Unfortunately we needed to fill her post.'

'You could have hired a temp.'

'Wouldn't do to have just any girl come in off the street and handle confidential client files. We pride ourselves on our discretion and service. I did, however, enclose a cheque to cover severance pay which, given the short tenure of Helen's employment with us, I hope she'll find generous. Is she well enough to receive visitors?'

'I'd rather you left it until she's completely recovered,' John rejoined tersely.

'You have no objection to my forwarding her an inventory of her inheritance so she can study it? I'll need a signed acceptance as soon as possible.'

'None.'

'That is one file I do have.' Richard handed him a large envelope sealed with wax. 'You will deliver it, seal unbroken?'

'I will. I'll send Joe in.'

Richard peered over his spectacles as he opened a file and flicked through the papers. 'There's no need for you to wait to drive him back to town. I'll give him a lift when we've completed the necessary paperwork.'

'Joseph, you don't mind waiting a moment longer, do you.' Before Joe had time to answer his mother, Esme brushed past him and John, entered the morning room and closed the door behind her.

'Are you driving back through Sketty, John?' Dot asked.

'Yes. Would you like a lift?'

'Please, if it's not too much trouble.'

'My pleasure.'

'John.' Dot lowered her voice as she drew him towards the window. 'Have you given a thought as to what's going to happen to Esme?'

'In what way?' he asked warily.

'She is living here at the moment. I have no idea what Joe intends to do with the house . . .'

'I see what you mean.' He recalled Esme's threat to move back into Carlton Terrace and felt more strongly than ever that he could never live with her again – on any terms.

'I just wanted to say that given the situation between the two of you, if it will help in any way she is welcome to stay with me.'

'That is very kind and generous of you, Dot.' John meant it. Dot's cramped flat above her hat shop was barely big enough for one and Dot knew as well as he did that Esme wasn't easy to live with.

'You'll remember my offer?'

'I will.' John looked around. 'Where is Jack?' he asked Joe.

'Taking a walk in the garden.'

'You have a lot to go through with Mr Thomas. He said he'd give you a lift back to town but if you'd rather I waited, I will.'

'There's no need. You take Aunt Dot and Jack back.'

'I'll wait with Jack in the garden. I've always loved the view of the beach from there.' Dot tactfully withdrew, leaving John and Joe alone.

Joe crossed his arms, stood back on his heels and looked around the room. His grandfather had died two years before he'd been born, but given the state of his library a stranger might be forgiven for assuming he'd just popped out for a stroll. A fire burned in the grate, just as it had done every day from the first of October to the last day of June since his death. His pipes, tobacco pouch and pipe lighter were set out neatly on a rack on the mantelpiece. An array of pens, pencils, sharpeners and ink bottles were arranged on his desk tray, even his heavy tweed winter coat hung on a hook on the back of the door. 'I crept in here once when I was about five years old. Grandmother caught me looking at the books. For a few minutes I really thought she was about to beat me to death.'

'What kind of books were you looking at?'

'I was too small to lift down the ones on the high shelves.' Joe caught John's eye and they both smiled. 'You knew he had a penchant for the risqué.'

'He died before I met your mother but I recognised some of the titles on my first visit.'

'Grandmother actually allowed you in here?'

'She gave me the grand tour so I could see for myself that culturally and socially your mother's family was infinitely above mine.'

'I wondered why you never joined us on visits.'

'Your grandmother didn't want me here and I didn't want to come.'

'I used to hate visiting here. The house seemed so still, so silent, it reminded me of a museum. Every time I moved as much as a finger, I was ordered not to fidget or touch anything. When Helen and I were older it wasn't so bad because we could escape to the beach. Grandmother insisted we visit at least twice a month but she was only happy when she knew for certain that we were out of the house and garden, and couldn't disturb her, the arrangement of her treasured possessions or, horror of horrors, break them. Even now, after a day of funeral services, I find it hard to believe she's not going to walk in and reprimand me for daring to enter this hallowed sanctum.'

'It's yours now, Joe. You can do what you like with it.'

Joe surveyed the room. 'I'd like to get rid of all this dark furniture and brown carpet, and put some colour in, but most of all I'd like to make it a happy family home.'

John knew he was thinking of Lily and their broken engagement. 'It will be too far for you to travel from here to Cardiff if you take that job at the BBC.'

'I know, but now that the place is mine I'm loath to give it up.' He walked to the window. 'Just look at the garden, the view, the beach, all that space. Can you imagine growing up here?'

John smiled at his enthusiasm. 'Yes. I can see that it could be a children's paradise.'

'Half of this should be Helen's.'

'Your grandmother made provision for her.'

'I didn't think Aunt Julie left much.'

'There's the house in Limeslade for a start and before you go worrying about Helen talk to Richard Thomas and see exactly how much you are inheriting.'

Joe looked at him in surprise. 'You think there could be debts?'

'Like the houses your grandmother left me, the residue of her estate might prove a mixed blessing.' He glanced out of the window and saw Jack and Dot standing at the bottom of the garden talking. 'I'll see you back at the house.'

Joe hesitated, then blurted, 'Thanks, Dad.'

'What for.'

'Bringing me up the way you did. It couldn't have been easy for you. Knowing I was another man's son.'

'You're my son, Joe, and you always will be.' Hearing Esme shouting at Richard in the morning room, he was glad to open the french door and step out into the cool, clear air.

'She can't leave me destitute . . .'

'If you don't want your husband, son, cousin and half of Langland to hear you, Esme, I'd advise you to lower your voice,' Richard interposed. 'Your mother did not leave you destitute. She knew the terms of your divorce settlement.'

'That's John's money, not hers. She had no right to cut me out of her will. She left more to her housekeeper and niece than me,' she railed bitterly. 'This is my home . . .'

'And it is now your son's,' he interrupted coolly.

'I'm instructing you to challenge the will.'

'On what grounds?'

'Health. She was a sick, confused old lady who didn't know what she was doing.'

'Even if I could, I wouldn't.'

'You're refusing?' Esme glared at him.

'I drew up the will, Esme, and it was patently obvious to everyone who knew her that your mother knew exactly what she was doing.'

'You're not the only solicitor in Swansea.'

Pulling a file from his briefcase, he said, 'You're welcome to take your business elsewhere.'

'And tell my new legal adviser that you suggested this will in favour of Joseph to my mother because he is your son?'

'You'd have to prove it in public court.'

'There are blood tests.'

'Which can only prove a child is not related to a putative father. That might benefit John Griffiths and possibly strengthen his case for divorce proceedings but it would prove nothing against me. You'd only succeed in creating a scandal that would implicate your son, as well as yourself.'

'You're forgetting you. What would your clients say if they knew you had seduced the eighteen-year-old virginal schoolgirl daughter of your best friend, your own goddaughter, when you were forty-five years old?'

'They'd say the one-time virginal schoolgirl daughter's divorce deranged her mind twenty-one years later. Everyone knows how cruel the female menopause can be.'

'You bastard!' she hissed vindictively.

'Try fighting this, Esme, and you'll find out just how much of a bastard I can be,' he threatened.

'You influenced my mother . . .'

'Into leaving you her fur coats, jewellery and your father's painting. If it hadn't been for me, you wouldn't have inherited that much.'

'Even I know a small bequest leaves a beneficiary in a worse position to challenge a will because it means they weren't inadvertently overlooked. And you also know she only left me her costume jewellery. I doubt it's worth tuppence halfpenny.'

'There is such a thing as sentimental value,' he said heavily.

Incensed by his composure in the face of her loss of self-control, she flounced out of the room, slamming the door behind her.

* * *

'I'm sorry to have inflicted a family funeral on you so soon after your wedding,' John apologised to Jack as he drove towards the Uplands, after dropping off Dot outside her shop in Eversley Road.

'It was boring, not upsetting. It might have been different if I'd met the old lady.'

'You think you might have liked her?'

'Not from what Helen has said.'

'She could be a tartar,' John conceded. 'Aren't you curious about Helen's inheritance?'

'It's hers, not mine.'

'You are married.'

'I didn't marry her for any inheritance . . .'

'I know that, Jack, and so does Helen.' John made a mental note to tread more carefully when it came to Jack's pride in future. Hopefully Ernie Clay's violence had been buried with him but he thought he recognised traces of his temper in Jack's outburst. 'All the same, it will be nice for the two of you to have the house. It overlooks Limeslade beach. I've only been there once. But the one thing I do remember is the garden. It wasn't that big but it was beautiful.'

'There's a house?'

'Four-bedroomed, if my memory serves me correctly. Helen's Aunt Julie died four years ago. I had no idea she left her house to Helen's grandmother but if it's been empty all that time it may need some work doing to it.'

'If it's only decorating I could do it,' Jack began enthusiastically. 'I didn't make too bad a job of the flat.'

'You made a very good one.'

'And Limeslade's only a couple of miles from the centre of town and the warehouse. I have my bike . . .' Jack faltered as he realised he had only a few more days of work before he had to report for National Service.

'Two years will go quickly,' John sympathised, reading his train of thought. 'And in the meantime Helen can organise any changes she wants to make.'

'When she's well enough.'

'It may give her something to get well for, especially when she finds out you have to leave.' John changed gear as the stream of traffic slowed. He glanced at Jack, sitting hunched in the passenger seat, and wished he could take some of the burden from him. But like everyone else, Jack and Helen had to find their own way in life; he only hoped that despite the two-year separation they would be able to find it together.

Joe stared in disbelief at the figures on the sheet of paper. 'These are right?'

'Correct as of yesterday. Your grandmother inherited considerable property. The only criticism that could have been levelled at her is that she was a little too cautious in her investments. However, time has proved that her circumspection was well-founded. If you'll sign here and here, this paper is for the house, this for the stocks, the bonds, the shares . . .'

Joe took the sheets Richard handed him and read them through quickly before signing his name at the bottom of each page. 'I can't understand why she left everything to me. There's Helen and my mother . . .'

'Your grandmother wanted you to inherit her estate to ensure the house remained in the family. She took great comfort in the thought that one day you would take your grandfather's place as head of the household. And she did make provision for your sister. Your Aunt Julie's estate is not as substantial as your grandmother's but it is not insignificant either.' Gathering the papers together, Richard returned them to his briefcase.

'And my mother?'

'Your grandmother was aware of the generous divorce settlement your father has made her.' Richard offered Joe a cigar. 'Some things can wait but I would like to discuss this house with you. Have you thought what you're going to do with it?'

'Live in it.'

'Immediately?'

Joe shook his head. 'Not immediately. I have my finals and then there's the job at the BBC . . .'

'Then may I suggest you rent it out on a short-term lease, say six months to start with, renewable every three months after the initial contract? That would give you an income sufficient to take care of the overheads on the place, plus money to set aside to finance any repairs over the next few years. It would also enable you to reclaim the house and move in at three months' notice.'

'Wouldn't it be difficult to find tenants who'll agree to those terms?' Joe tried to pretend he was enjoying the cigar. He wasn't, it tasted bitter and not at all as he'd imagined an expensive cigar would.

'No, this is a prestigious property. In fact, I received an enquiry from someone this morning. I'm not at liberty to say who it was as yet, but I assure you the party is wealthy, respectable and well thought of in the literary world. Would you like me to go ahead and see if I can close the deal?' Joe thought for a moment. It would be months, possibly even years, before he would be in a position to take possession of the house. 'Yes, please.'

'Now that's done you should celebrate your new status as one of the wealthiest young men in Swansea. I could introduce you to my club.'

'No, thank you, Mr Thomas.'

'You have another appointment?'

'I'd like to look around the house for a while.'

'I understand. It's difficult to take in all at once. I'll wait for you.'

'I'd rather you didn't,' Joe said resolutely.

'You'll have to get home.'

'The telephone is still connected. I'll call one of my friends when I'm ready.'

Resenting his dismissal, Richard handed Joe a file. 'Your papers. Go through them carefully and if there's anything you don't understand I will explain it to you.'

Joe took them. 'Thank you, Mr Thomas.'

'I'll see you soon, Joseph.' Richard opened the door that connected the morning room to the hall. He'd hoped to avoid Esme, but she was hovering at the front door, brandy glass in hand, obviously waiting for him and Joseph to finish their business.

Setting down her glass, she refilled it, slowly and deliberately, with a large measure before opening the cupboard and handing him his coat and hat. He took them, checked the level in the brandy bottle, which had been full before the funeral, and left.

Chapter 15

JOE OPENED THE french windows of the morning room and stepped out on to the terrace. The stone Victorian planters were bright with masses of red and white tulips and the red, white and pink buds on the rhododendrons and azaleas that filled the shrubberies bordering the garden were coming into bloom. The lawns had been cut, dressed and spiked ready for summer. His grandmother's orders? Or had the gardener continued to work to the best of his capabilities in the hope that the new owner would keep him on?

He looked down at the beach and imagined walking there with Lily, and later their children. Throwing balls for the children and sticks for the dog. The floppy-eared golden retriever he had always wanted and his mother had never allow him to have . . .

'Congratulations, Joseph.'

He turned to see Esme standing behind him. 'That seems to be an inappropriate word to use on the day of grandmother's funeral.'

'Even when she's made you a very wealthy young man?' She picked a few wrinkled brown leaves from the ivy that climbed past the french windows to the first-floor balcony. 'You'll be needing a housekeeper. I could stay on, supervise a daily and look after the place for you.'

'Mr Thomas advised me to lease it until I'm ready to live here myself.'

'Lease this house!' She couldn't have been more shocked if he'd suggested burning it down.

'On a renewable contract. He explained that I could reclaim it at three months' notice whenever I wish. He has a tenant in mind.'

'And when this tenant wrecks the furniture, ruins the decor . . .'

'I intend to change it when I finally move in,' he cut her short. 'Until then, leasing it out will give me an income to cover the overheads and pay for any repairs that need doing.'

'It's easy to see who you've been talking to. You even sound like Richard Thomas.'

'He *is* our family solicitor.'

'And like him, all you see when you look at this house is an "investment" property to be milked for even more money for your overflowing coffers.'

Joe looked out over the bay to the glittering sea. 'It means a lot more than that and I'd like to live here one day but not as it is. It's decorated to grandmother's taste, not mine.'

'It's full of things, mine, your grandparents' . . .'

'Take whatever you like.'

She froze as realisation dawned. 'When is this tenant moving in?'

'As soon as it can be arranged. I've told Mr Thomas to go ahead.'

'And where am I supposed to go?' Her eyes blazed furiously.

He recalled what Richard Thomas had told him about his grandmother ensuring his mother was well provided for. 'You have the divorce settlement and the monthly allowance Dad . . . John Griffiths has made you.'

'You consider that enough? After you've just been left my mother's entire estate?'

'Mr Thomas . . .'

'To hell with bloody Richard Thomas.'

He moved away from her, hitting his back against the balustrade. It was the first time he had heard her swear. Then he saw her sway and realised she had been drinking. 'Mr Thomas told me grandmother wanted me to inherit her estate to ensure the house remained in the family.'

'And the generation in between your grandmother and you?'

'I don't know what happened between you and grandmother . . .'

'You happened between me and my mother,' Esme interrupted bitterly.

'I didn't ask to be born.'

As he uttered the stock phrase of the peeved child, Esme's face contorted into pure hatred. 'If your father had been allowed his way you wouldn't have been. I should have listened to him . . .'

'Who was he?' A cloud blocked out the sun, snatching the warmth of the afternoon light from the terrace. He shivered as the temperature dropped.

'Isn't it obvious? The man who made damned sure you inherited everything my mother had to give. The man who looked after your trust fund . . .'

'Richard Thomas is my father?'

'I . . . I . . .'

'Richard Thomas!'

The impact of Joe's disgust mitigated the effect of the brandy. Esme opened her mouth but, stunned by the intensity of Joe's revulsion, no words came.

'Richard Thomas is old enough to be my grandfather. He was probably older than your father. He was your godfather . . .'

'I was only eighteen,' she whispered hoarsely. 'I went to a convent school. We weren't told anything about men or life in those days. Richard knew that and took advantage of me. I was upset, lonely, my father had just died . . . Joseph . . .' Too late Esme realised she was calling to his back as he ran away from her down to the beach.

'Lily! Over here!'

Lily looked around as she left the bank but couldn't see anyone she knew until the passenger door of a red sports car parked in front of her swung open and Joe leaned out. 'Come for a drive.'

'Joe, I can't . . .'

'Please, Lily, I've had a foul day,' he pleaded desperately. 'I need to talk to someone and you know me better than anyone else. Just half an hour,' he begged. When she didn't step any closer, he added, 'Is Martin so terrified you'll run off that he won't even allow you to talk to your friends?'

'Of course not. He's just sensitive about my seeing you.'

'I only wish he had cause to be. Please' – he looked at her through anguished eyes – 'if you never talk to me again, spare me a few minutes now.'

She had never seen Joe so fraught or distressed. 'Just a drive?'

'Even if I wanted to make it more, I've had such a disgusting day that I'm not up to anything else.'

'I should have remembered. Jack said your grandmother's funeral was today. I'm so sorry, Joe, I meant to write a condolence letter to you and Helen . . .'

'Stop apologising and get in.'

Waving goodbye to a couple of the girls who worked with her and wishing the car weren't quite so flamboyant, Lily finally climbed in, bundling her wide skirt and petticoats around her legs so they wouldn't bunch round the gear stick. 'Has your father changed his car?'

'For this?' He shook his head as he drove off. 'Nice thought, but unfortunately not. I borrowed it from Robin on the off chance you'd come with me.'

'To where?'

'Somewhere we can talk.'

'You must have a place in mind.' She untied the scarf she was wearing from round her neck and placed it over her head, knotting it beneath her chin in the hope of saving her French pleat from disintegrating in the breeze that whipped across the open top of the car.

'How about Langland?' He drove past the Guildhall and out on to the Mumbles Road.

'To your grandmother's house?'

'She left it to me.'

'Joe, I don't want to go there with you.'

He kept his attention fixed on the road. 'Don't worry; it's the last place I'd take you. My mother is living there. For the moment,' he added, relishing the power he had to evict her and hating himself for being small-minded enough to enjoy it.

'Then why go to Langland?'

'We can walk on the beach and talk. It is public.'

'And you want your mother to see us.'

'God, no.' He turned the wheel abruptly and swerved into a car park alongside the waterfront, incurring an angry horn blast from the car behind. Driving into a parking bay, he turned off the engine.

'That wasn't very sensible.'

'I'm not feeling very sensible.' His hands shook as patted his pockets in search of his cigarette case.

'What's happened, Joe?' she asked quietly.

'My grandmother has left me her entire estate – well, almost, but what she didn't leave me wasn't worth having.' He sat back and stared at the beach. The tide was at its furthest point, exposing a vast stretch of mudflats populated by small boys and ardent fishermen digging for lugworm. He watched them for a moment. 'I told you about my trust fund.'

'That wasn't part of what your grandmother left you?'

'Oh, no.' He adopted a mocking tone. 'You can have absolutely no idea just how wealthy your companion is. According to the family solicitor, "the wealthiest young man in Swansea".'

'And you brought me here to boast about it.' She depressed the door handle.

'No! Lily,' he called out to her as she left the car. 'What do you think I am?'

'At this moment I'm not sure.'

'Lily . . .'

Turning, she ran down on to the beach.

He lit a cigarette and inhaled deeply before climbing out of his seat and locking the car. She was running so quickly it took him a few minutes to catch up. Arriving behind her, he gripped her arm to slow her down.

'If you picked me up from work to tell me how much you've got, and how mad I'd be to turn you down again, you're talking to the wrong girl, Joe Griffiths.'

'It's nothing like that, Lily. Please.' Steadying her, he forced her to face him. 'Do you remember one night not long after I asked you to marry me, when I discovered John Griffiths wasn't my real father?'

She calmed down enough to murmur, 'Yes.'

'And I told you I went to see my mother and she insisted it was her secret and she would never tell me who had fathered me? Well, today she changed her mind. My father is the family solicitor, Richard Thomas.'

She stared at him in disbelief. 'Helen's boss, the one we met at Robin and Angie's party?'

'The man Helen christened "sneaky old grubby eyes".'

'Judy, not Helen, coined that expression,' she muttered, not thinking about what she was saying. She couldn't have been more shocked. Richard Thomas was old enough to be Joe's grandfather and the only time she had met him he'd sent shudders down her spine. Helen had told her that every girl who worked in the solicitor's office, including her, hated being alone in a room with him because whenever he looked at them they felt as though he were mentally undressing them. 'Are you sure? I mean, he's ancient and nothing at all like you, not in looks or ways.'

'For that at least, thank you. But consider the alternative: I take after my mother.' Discarding his cigarette, he ground it into the sand with his shoe.

'You're your own person, Joe.' She led the way back towards the sea wall.

'I wish.' He sat beside her and stared at the sea. It looked colder, greyer than the sea in front of his grandmother's house in Langland – not his grandmother's, his.

'You just said it, Joe, one of the wealthiest young men in Swansea. You can do anything you want.'

'With the trust fund my real father has looked after for years. How can I be sure it only holds what my great-aunt invested for me, not Richard Thomas's conscience money for abandoning my mother when she was pregnant with me? And as if that's not enough, he also drew up my grandmother's will and, according to my mother, persuaded my grandmother to drop everyone else in the family in favour of me.'

'Your mother's upset.' Lily gripped his hand in an attempt to stop him from shaking. 'She couldn't have known what she was saying; she's just lost her mother . . .'

'You don't know my mother, the only thing she's upset about is losing free board and lodging at one of the best addresses in Swansea.'

'That's a dreadful thing to say.'

'My mother's a dreadful person.' Pulling one of his hands free, he extricated his cigarette case from the inside pocket of his suit jacket. 'Joe . . .'

Opening his case he offered her a cigarette. When she refused, he pushed one between his lips and lit it. 'Don't you realise Richard Thomas could have been fattening my trust fund with his money for years – for all I know the fund could even have been his idea in the first place. He was my mother's godfather, the confidant of everyone in the family including my grandmother and aunt. Old enough to have fathered my mother and . . .' Sickened by the thought of his mother and Richard Thomas – together – he covered his mouth with his fist.

'Have you talked to Mr Griffiths about this?'

'How can I? He's never known who my real father was. He'll be as devastated as I am.'

'Do you think Mr Thomas knows that you're his son?'

'He knows.' He drew heavily on his cigarette. 'My mother made that much clear when she told me she suspected him of topping up my trust fund and influencing my grandmother to leave everything to me, to spite her.'

'Why on earth would she think Mr Thomas would want to spite her?'

'Because when she discovered she was pregnant, he wanted her to get rid of me and she wouldn't.' His hand shook so much he dropped his cigarette. 'Presumably, as I'm now here and not to be got rid of, he's decided a wealthy bastard is less of an embarrassment than a poor one.'

Lily sensed his rage, burning hot, painful – and destructive. 'You can't let this blight your life, Joe.'

'How can I touch a penny of my trust fund or my grandmother's estate knowing that bastard probably rigged it?'

'You have to ask him if he has.'

'What's the point?' He took his lighter from his pocket and flicked on the flame. 'If he says yes I'll feel as if my inheritance is tainted and if he says no I won't believe him.'

'You could hand over all your affairs to another solicitor and ask him to check everything. If Richard Thomas has given you money, you don't have to touch it.'

'Always the practical one.' He looked at her as he returned his lighter to his pocket. 'Would you take the money if Richard Thomas were your father?'

'He's not my father so I don't know how I'd feel.'

'Would you take money your mother had earned by selling herself down on the docks?'

His question hurt, not because she wanted to pretend her real mother was anything other than a prostitute but because he had reminded her of her parentage – yet again. 'You're forgetting my mother only came looking for me to get money out of Uncle Roy. She practically sold me to Auntie Norah.'

'I'm sorry . . . I didn't mean . . . Oh God!' He ran his hands through his hair, rumpling his curls. 'I'm so confused I don't know what I'm saying or doing. I begged you to come with me because you're the one person I can talk to about this and now I've upset and humiliated you. Lily, I'm sorry . . .'

'I'll get over it,' she said flatly.

'You're nothing to do with your real mother.'

'I know that, Joe.' Untying the scarf from her head, she replaced it round her neck. 'I only wish everyone else realised it.'

'Do people bring it up? Because if they do, I'll . . .'

'You're the only one who brings it up.' Her hair was caught painfully at the nape of her neck. Reaching up, she pulled out her hair clips and shook it free. 'Uncle Roy and I haven't mentioned her since the day of our engagement party. Helen, Judy and Katie asked about her. After I told them what I knew, they said they were sorry and that was the end of it as far as they were concerned. But every single time I talk to you my mother comes into the conversation.'

'I only mentioned your mother because I finally discovered who fathered me and hoped that because you had been through a similar experience you would understand how I feel.'

'Seeing as how my mother is a common prostitute and your father a wealthy solicitor, I fail to see the connection.'

'I don't want Richard Thomas to be my father any more than you want a prostitute for a mother.'

'He's a wealthy, important man, Joe.' She brushed sand from her skirt. 'He has influence in the town. He could help you when you leave university.'

'He also abandoned my mother and me,' he pronounced bitterly.

'He must have had his reasons. He could have been married already.'

'As it happens he was. He's had the same wife for forty-odd years,' he admitted, 'but that doesn't excuse what he did.'

'Perhaps the trust fund was his way of keeping in touch with you, in which case you can't accuse him of totally abandoning you. And your mother did marry another man.'

'Only because Richard Thomas deserted her.'

'I think you're making assumptions when you don't know the facts.' Leaving the wall, she stood in front of him. 'You have to talk to him and your mother.'

'Why should I give either of them the time of day?'

'Because if you don't you'll drive yourself crazy.'

'When I last talked this over with John Griffiths, he suggested that my father might have been one of my mother's set, a student or someone too young to get married and support a family.'

'And you would have preferred that.'

'Frankly, yes, anyone other than a lecherous bastard old enough to be my grandfather.'

'Do you remember how you used to say that I was the last surviving member of the Russian royal family, the daughter or granddaughter of a child smuggled out by an Irish nanny?'

'I had to explain away the surname of Sullivan somehow.' He almost smiled at her.

'And as you didn't even have a surname to explain away because you had John Griffiths's you thought you could have been the son of an intellectual, a film star, a member of the royal family . . .'

'I confess I had my fantasies, but then you know all about those. The castles, or rather cottages I built in the air.' He changed the subject before she could mention Martin. 'So what would you do in my position?'

'First, I wouldn't forget who brought me up.'

'My mother . . .'

'Think of what it must have been like for her, Joe. Pregnant with an older man's baby, unmarried . . .'

'I'll never forgive her,' he broke in sternly.

'For giving birth to you when Richard Thomas wanted to "get rid" of you . . .'

'That doesn't alter the fact he's trying to buy me now.'

'You don't know that for certain and you won't until you talk to him.'

'I wish he didn't have money and position. I'd have more respect for him if he'd been a common labourer who'd had the decency to marry my mother.'

'That's easy to say after you've had all the advantages of a comfortable upbringing, including a university education.'

'Yes, it is.' He followed her example and rose from the wall. 'And you're right, I do have to see him if only to find out if he did influence my grandmother's will and put money into my trust fund.'

'And if he did?'

'I won't touch a penny of it.'

'And your grandmother's house?'

'Give it to Helen.'

'You can do that, but Richard Thomas will still be your father.'

'Then what do you suggest I do?'

'About your trust fund and grandmother's estate, whatever you want. About Richard Thomas, talk to him and accept the fact of him, even if you decide never to see him again.'

'Like you with your mother.'

'Like I said, Joe, I can't ignore who my mother is, but I can stop myself from getting angry or feeling embarrassed.'

'I wish I could be like you.' He looked into her eyes, tawny gold in the evening sunlight.

'Everyone's their own person. You have to make your own life.'

He reached for her hand and kissed her fingers. 'How could I ever have been foolish enough to let you go?'

'You didn't let me go, I went and we're friends now, remember.'

As he hugged her and felt her heart beating next to his, he did remember – just long enough to keep their embrace chaste.

* * *

Restless, needing to talk to someone, disappointed not to find Lily at home and knowing Judy wouldn't be back from Mumbles for another half-hour, Katie found her way down to her brothers' basement. Knocking on the door, she walked in to find Sam alone in the kitchen.

'Tea,' he offered, pouring boiling water into the teapot.

'No thanks, I was looking for Martin.'

'He's working late.'

'So he is. I forgot.'

'Jack's in. He's changing to go down the hospital.' Pushing a cup in front of her, Sam handed her the milk and sugar. 'You look beat. Tough day at work?'

'Yes.' Without thinking what she was doing she sat at the table and poured milk into her teacup.

'Tea's ready,' Sam announced as Jack burst through the door juggling a bright-red tie while trying to push studs into his collar.

He glanced at the clock. 'I've only ten minutes.'

'Mr Griffiths will wait for you.'

'We want to get to the ward before Helen's mother.'

'Is she visiting her as well?' Katie asked.

'Not if we can help it.' He frowned at his sister. 'You all right? You look a bit peaky.'

'That's just what I said. How about we go for a walk on the beach, get some fresh air and meet Jack in Joe's ice cream parlour after visiting?'

Before Katie could refuse, Jack said, 'That sounds like a great idea. I can always do with some company after visiting. I hate having to leave Helen in that place when the bell rings, as much as she hates having to stay there.' He screwed his tie into an unwieldy knot. 'Bloody thing! And you didn't hear that.' He stood still as Katie pulled it free from his collar. Smoothing it between her fingers, she knotted it neatly. 'Thanks, sis. I didn't want to see Helen wearing a black one. Big night tonight, the doctor's rounds were this morning and she was hoping they'd give her the all clear to leave before the weekend.'

'Does she know yet that you have to report for your National Service on Monday?' Sam opened a tin of biscuits and foraged through the mess of broken digestives in the hope of finding a hidden chocolate cream.

'I talked it over with her father. We thought it would be best to tell her when she gets home.'

'She's going to be devastated,' Katie murmured.

'Do you think I like having to leave her just as she comes out of hospital?' Jack glanced at the clock again. 'I'll give the tea a miss, Sam. See you in Joe's.'

Katie glared Sam as the door closed. 'This is not a date.'

'Absolutely. Just a walk, an ice cream and your brother takes you home. But you have to admit it's criminal to stay indoors on an evening like this, particularly after a day at the office. I don't know what yours is like but I don't believe a breath of fresh air has stirred the hallowed chambers of the police station in years. See you in half an hour,' he called after her as she went to the stairs.

'Three-quarters, I need to change.'

'You look fantastic as you are.'

'I should hope so. These are my working clothes. I'm going to put on a pair of pedal-pushers.'

'Twenty minutes out front.' His heart sank. He'd hoped that perseverance would eventually wear Katie down. But it didn't seem likely when she was 'dressing down' to go out with him.

'You're up.' Jack beamed as he walked down the ward with John Griffiths to find Helen sitting in a chair next to her bed, which had been moved into the general ward the week before.

'Not only up, I can stay out of bed all day, walk around and bath myself. And' – her smile had a trace of the old mischievous Helen – 'the doctor says, if I'm good, I'll be discharged on Friday morning.'

'It will be wonderful to have you home.' Jack sat beside her.

'I'll even give Jack Friday and Saturday off to look after you.'

'You meany, Dad. Why only Friday and Saturday?'

'In the meantime you can study this.' John gave Jack a guarded look as he handed Helen the envelope that Richard Thomas had entrusted to him.

She picked suspiciously at the wax seal. 'What is it?'

'A list of everything your Aunt Julia left to your grandmother when she died. Your grandmother's left it to you.'

'The house overlooking Limeslade beach.' Her eyes shone with excitement.

'And everything else your Aunt Julia owned.'

'Including the furniture?'

'Apparently so. Richard Thomas wanted to talk to you about it but I told him he'd have to wait until you are out of hospital.'

'Thank you.' She shuddered at the thought of her boss's wet lips and slack mouth. 'I'd hate him to see me in my nightdress.'

'Helen, he's old enough to be your grandfather.' John looked around for a chair.

'And a horrible, greasy, lecherous . . .'

'He hasn't done anything to you, has he?' Jack broke in anxiously.

'Not unless you count looking at me as if he can see through my clothes.'

'If I'd known that, I would never have let you work for him.' Jack flushed as his temper rose.

'"Let me!" You may be my husband, Jack Clay, but you don't own me.'

'Save your quarrelling for situations you can do something about.' John lifted out a stool from under the bed and sat down next to Jack. 'And as you're no longer working for Richard Thomas it's all a bit academic.'

'He fired me!'

'He told me this afternoon that he's filled your position.'

'It's just as well,' Jack declared. 'You couldn't have gone back for months and that was before you told me he was after you.'

'I didn't say he was after me. I said he looked at me . . .'

'Jack's right, love,' John intervened, in an attempt to stave off an argument. 'You need to rest and get your health back.'

'Now the two of you are ganging up on me.'

'Jack needs all the support he can get to keep you in order,' John joked, trying to lighten the atmosphere.

'Neither of you is going to turn me into a housewife. I'd go mad . . .'

'Come on, Helen,' Jack coaxed, 'it's not as if you even liked working for Richard Thomas. You were always on about how much you hated it. This could be an opportunity to do something you really want – when you're well.'

'Just like a man. "Do what I want" when I've no training for anything other than office work.'

'Actually, I have a proposition.' John propped his stick against Helen's bed. 'I was going to bring it up after you came home. But now might be as good a time as any. You could work for me.'

'As a junior under Katie! Thanks but no thanks.'

'Not in the office. Do you remember those underclothes you

wanted for your trousseau that the buyer insisted wouldn't sell in Swansea?'

'And then went like hotcakes,' Helen crowed.

'It made me think that the warehouse could do with another buyer. A young person with an eye for young people's fashion.'

'This isn't a "let's feel sorry for poor Helen and find her something to do", is it?' she asked suspiciously. 'Because if it is . . .'

'This is a "yesterday morning I overheard a couple of young girls telling their mothers that they wouldn't be seen dead in our summer range of sports clothes."'

'I told you they were dire when they came in.' Helen smiled at Jack as he squeezed her hand between his own. 'Your range of ladies' fashions isn't too bad, apart from the underclothes, but the buyer hasn't a clue when it comes to teenagers.'

'So, will you consider my offer?'

'I don't have to. If you're serious about updating the range, the answer's yes,' she qualified.

'But I'll not allow you to start in the warehouse until you are one hundred per cent recovered,' John warned.

'It wouldn't hurt for me to take a look at the suppliers' catalogues . . .'

'When you're well, not before.' John kissed her forehead as he left the stool and pushed it back under her bed. 'Now, if you two will excuse me I have to meet someone.'

'Amazing how you always have to meet someone halfway through visiting,' Helen commented.

'I have a warehouse to run.'

'From the White Rose.'

'She's better, Jack, she's beginning to insult me again.' John gave her another kiss before limping off up the ward.

'He looks tired,' Helen said, watching her father walk out.

'We've had a tiring day.' Jack lifted her hand to his lips and kissed it.

'Was the funeral awful?'

'Long.'

'In one way I feel terrible, not being able to go, but in another I'm glad I didn't have to sit in the house for hours with my mother and grandmother's friends while you, Joe and my father were at the cemetery.'

'The service in the church went on for ever.' He closed his fingers round her wedding ring.

'Did my mother talk to my father?'

'Not that I saw.'

'Funny, it hasn't occurred to me until now, but he's going to be lonely after the divorce.'

'No more than he is now, or when your mother lived with you. She was never at home.'

'But Joe and I were. And Joe will be leaving for Cardiff at the end of the summer. Do you think he'll get married again?'

'Your father?' he asked, surprised by the thought.

'Why not?' she questioned. 'He deserves to have someone nice to look after him, especially after being married to my mother.'

'You want a stepmother.'

'I want my father to be happy.'

'You'll only be downstairs . . .'

'It would be crazy to pay my father rent for the flat when we own a house. I can't wait to show it to you. You can see the sea from almost every room. Two minutes and you're on the beach. There's a huge living room, a big kitchen, four bedrooms, a garden. It's absolutely perfect,' she gushed enthusiastically. 'I know you're just going to love it.'

'Before you have us moving in, your father thinks it's been empty for a few years, in which case it may need some work doing to it.'

'You don't want to live in Limeslade?'

'There'll be plenty of time to look the house over and decide what to do about it after you've left here,' he answered evasively.

'I suppose so.' She looked earnestly at him. 'We won't end up like my parents, will we, Jack? Quarrelling, divorcing . . .'

'Not if I have any say in the matter.'

'It's just that . . . without children . . .' She fell silent, as both of them were suddenly aware of the woman in the next bed listening in on their conversation.

'You'll be home on Friday. We'll talk then,' he whispered.

'I can't wait.' She grabbed his hand with both of hers. 'What is the flat looking like?'

'Exactly as it did the last time you were in it.'

'You haven't been living there.'

'I moved back in with Martin.'

'Why? You would have been more comfortable in the flat. It has all our things. Everything you need, it's our home . . .'

'I was afraid I'd mess it up without you.'

'Oh, Jack.' The tears that had hovered perilously close to the surface ever since she had emerged from the anaesthetic to find she had lost their child began to fall again. Conscious of heads turning in their direction, he handed her his handkerchief.

'I'm sorry. I promised myself before you came that I wouldn't cry. And now look at me.'

'I'd be howling like a baby if I had to spend a month in this place.'

'Mr Clay.' The ward sister appeared at the foot of Helen's bed. 'I see you've managed to upset your wife again.'

'No, sister, it's my fault . . .' Helen began.

'It's best you leave, Mr Clay,' the sister interrupted sternly.

'No!' Helen protested.

'Mr Clay.'

'Please, sister,' Helen begged, her tears falling again despite her frantic efforts to control herself.

'How about I just hold her hand and don't say a word.' Jack parried the sister's glare.

'Any more tears, Mrs Clay, and we'll have to reconsider doctor's decision to discharge you on Friday.'

Jack glowered at the sister until she moved away. He leaned forward under pretence of picking up a coin he'd deliberately dropped to the floor.

'No one will be able to tell me to leave you after Friday, love, even if I have to break you out of here.' The irony of his declaration struck home as he recalled the railway warrant he'd received that morning.

She smiled at him through her tears. He lifted her hand to his lips and kissed it again. 'Love you,' he mouthed silently.

'Love you back.' She blotted her tears as the bell rang.

Seeing the sister watching him, he left his chair. 'See you on Friday. I'll be here the moment they let you out.'

'I'll count the minutes,' she murmured hollowly as he walked away.

Chapter 16

MUCH TO SAM'S annoyance, Katie wasn't the only one waiting for him outside the house three-quarters of an hour after she left the basement. Judy was standing alongside her, both of them dressed in sweaters and pedal-pushers with their hair in ponytails as if they were going to the beach instead of an outing he'd hoped would turn into a date. Feeling a fool in his suit, shirt and tie, he thought things couldn't get any worse until Katie spotted Adam walking up St.Helen's Road, from the direction of the Bay View pub. Stepping in front of him, she blocked his path. 'Hello, Adam.'

Adam glanced warily from her to Judy to Sam, before nodding an acknowledgement.

'We're going for an ice cream. Why don't you join us?' Katie invited.

'I don't make a habit of going where I'm not wanted,' Adam growled.

'If we hadn't wanted you to come with us I wouldn't have asked you.' She looked at Sam. 'This quarrel between you boys is stupid.'

'You don't know the first thing about it,' Adam refuted.

'Katie's right.' Judy came to her friend's defence. 'We were all having fun before it started. And now you aren't talking to one another. Come on, Adam, can't you put whatever happened down to you boys having one drink too many?'

'You think that's all there is to it?' he asked angrily.

'I know better than anyone that Brian can be a clown after he's had a few drinks, but from what I can gather none of you behaved like saints at Jack's stag party or afterwards at the Pier,' Judy said pointedly.

'She's right, Adam. We all behaved like idiots. What say you we shake and make up?' Sam held out his hand.

Adam hesitated for the barest fraction of a second before taking Sam's hand and shaking it.

227

'Ice creams on me.' Sam led the way into the parlour. 'Katie, Judy, what flavour would you like?'

'Strawberry, please.' Katie delved into her handbag for her purse. 'But I'll pay for my own.' She handed him a shilling.

'I'll have chocolate.' Judy found a couple of sixpences in her pocket and handed them over.

'Right, independent misses. Find a table for five.'

'Why five?' Adam followed Sam to the counter.

'We're meeting Jack after hospital visiting.'

'I thought perhaps you and Katie or Judy . . .'

'Katie and I aren't anything,' Sam said sourly. 'I only wish we were. And as far as I know, Judy's only separated from Brian by distance.' He cornered an assistant. 'One strawberry ice, one chocolate . . . What are you having, Adam?'

Lily glanced at her watch. 'It's almost eight o'clock. Katie and Mrs Lannon will be wondering where I am.'

'Not your uncle?' Joe settled back in the driving seat, linked his hands behind his head and studied the view.

'He's on afternoons, so he won't be home until eleven.'

'You could telephone,' he suggested.

'I have things to do.'

'Like washing your hair.'

Lily looked at him and realised he was teasing. They had parked on the cliff edge of the car park between Mumbles and Limeslade. Behind them was the big Apple Kiosk where Joe had bought them a scratch meal of crisps, lemonade and Tiffin chocolate bars; although to his annoyance she had insisted on paying for her share. In front was a breathtaking vista of sky, sea and, in the distance, the Devonshire coast.

'Nothing could be more important than watching this sunset,' he said appreciatively. 'Have you ever seen such jewelled colours? They could have been mixed on the palette of a Renaissance painter. And that gigantic, colossal sun! Its dying embers look as though they're about to ignite the sea. I think that's how it will appear at the end of the world.'

'And when is that going to be?' she enquired drily.

Turning, he gazed into her eyes. 'Never, because this one moment is ours for ever.'

She looked back out to sea. Below them faint cries and snatches of conversation drifted upwards from teenagers playing the halfpenny shove machines in the Pier's amusement arcade. Above them gulls circled, screeching before they swooped down to the sea in their relentless hunt for food.

'It is a perfect sunset, Joe. But it is also just like a hundred others.'

'How can you be so prosaic? It's unique because it is the first we've seen from here together.' He moved one of his arms, resting it on the back of her seat behind her head.

She sat forward, preventing him from putting his arm over her shoulders. 'And in Robin's sports car. Shouldn't you be getting it back to him?'

'Not until morning. I arranged to pick him up and drive him to college. He's at a party tonight.'

'Weren't you invited?'

'I wasn't fit company for anyone.'

'Except me,' she observed wryly.

'Not many people are as understanding or forgiving as you.'

'I really do have to go, Joe.' She dropped her empty crisp packet into the paper bag that held the remains of her Tiffin bar.

'Because Martin's class finishes at nine and he'll be home at half past?'

'Martin tried his finals last week so his evening classes have finished.' She suddenly realised the significance of what he'd said. 'You know the time of Martin's classes?'

'Only because Robin and I occasionally pick his sister and Emily up from their evening classes,' he lied.

'I thought they were at art college.'

'They are.'

'And they study in the evening?'

'Some girl thing or other,' he muttered dismissively in an attempt to hide just how closely he watched Martin's movements – and hers. 'So.' He finally moved his arm from behind her head. 'You want to go home.'

'Yes, please.'

'Straight home?'

'Straight home,' she repeated firmly.

'I haven't thanked you properly for listening to me. Let me buy you dinner. The upstairs dining room in the Mermaid serve a steak and kidney pie that tastes like home cooking should and never does, and an ice cream gateaux that melts on the tongue like a slice of heaven.'

'Not tonight, thank you,' she refused politely.

'Soon.'

'I don't think so. It would be too much like old times.'

'They were good times – or didn't you think so?'

'They were old times, Joe. Now I'm with . . .'

'Martin. I know. Tell him I'm grateful for allowing me to borrow you. Thanks to you, I now have a plan of action and the determination to confront Richard Thomas.'

'Don't do it before your finals.'

'Why?' He gunned the ignition.

'Because it's not worth risking upsetting yourself. It could affect your exams.'

'They'll be over in two weeks.'

'That's such a short time, it gives you all the more reason to wait.'

'You're right, as always.' He smiled at her. 'You know it is criminal to leave that sunset . . .'

'Drive,' she ordered, tying her scarf over her hair again. 'Are you going to tell Mr Griffiths about Richard Thomas?'

He pushed the car into reverse gear and backed out of the parking spot. 'I'll think about it. I know it will hurt him but I've never kept any secrets from him before and I see no reason to start now. And it's not as though it will cause any more friction between him and my mother. The situation couldn't be worse.' Changing into first gear, he drove towards the main road.

'I'm sorry.'

'So am I.' Turning right at the main road, he headed back towards Mumbles. 'But no one can colour the whole world rosy.'

'It would be nice if we could.'

'I won't forgive you for making me leave that sunset.'

'There'll be others.'

'For us?' he asked seriously.

'No, Joe.'

'You can't blame a fellow for trying.'

As Jack left the ward, a nurse entered it. On impulse, he looked back as she pushed through the swing doors. Helen was still sitting in the chair where he'd left her, tears running unchecked down her cheeks. The door swung shut in his face. It would be so easy to push it open, run over to her, scoop her into his arms and . . .

'Mr Clay.' The sister tapped his shoulder.

'I'm leaving.' He fought the urge to tell her to go to hell for Helen's sake.

'Doctor would like a word. You can wait in here.' She ushered him into a tiny office dominated by an enormous desk.

Angered by the assumption that no one's time was as important as that of the hospital staff, he moved a pile of papers, perched on the edge of the desk and resigned himself to watching the clock. After twenty minutes the sister returned with a middle-aged man in a white coat. Closing the door, she leaned against it as if trying to block his escape.

Without acknowledging his presence, the doctor elbowed past and settled behind the desk. Still ignoring him, he lifted out the files in the in-tray and scanned them.

'You're, Mr . . .'

'Jack Clay.'

'Mrs Helen Clay's husband,' Jack interrupted, incensed that the sister had spoken for him.

'Ah, yes, Mrs Clay.' Taking care to avoid direct eye contact, the doctor muttered, 'She's had a serious operation. Very serious indeed.'

'I know.'

'It's not only the stitches on the outside that you can see. There are many, many more on the inside.' He spoke slowly as though Jack were a child capable of understanding only the simplest of concepts. 'She'll need rest and care – a lot of care. Regular meals, early nights . . .'

'She'll get it.'

'And no hanky-panky, eh.'

'Hanky-panky?' Jack repeated in bewilderment.

'No marital relations for at least six weeks,' the sister elaborated.

'Not until she receives the all clear from us in the outpatients clinic.' The doctor returned to his papers.

'Given your age and men's natural predisposition, it would be a wise precaution for you and your wife to sleep in separate bedrooms for a month or two,' the sister advised bluntly.

Jack looked pointedly at the sister's left hand. 'You are not married.'

'I am a nurse and I am speaking medically. If you force yourself on your wife you will damage her.'

'I don't need to be told how to care for my wife.' Jack's temper, along with his voice rose precariously.

'We are giving you sound medical advice. Ignore it . . .'

'And I don't need you to lecture me on the obvious.' He realised he was shouting, but he was too incensed to calm down. 'I would never do anything to hurt Helen . . .'

'You say that now but you may feel differently when you get her home.'

'She will receive the best possible care I can give her until Sunday.'

'And after Sunday?' the sister enquired.

'My father-in-law will take over.'

'You are leaving your wife?'

'I've been called up to do my National Service.'

A hubbub of voices echoed in from the corridor. Someone banged on the door. The sister barged into Jack as she tried to make room to manoeuvre it open. Before she pulled the door back six inches, Jack saw Helen lying on the floor surrounded by nurses. Grabbing the door, he slammed it into the sister and rushed out. Pushing two of the nurses aside, he knelt beside her and took her head gently into his lap. She was pale – so pale that he held his breath and stroked her face gently. Then he saw the flutter of a pulse at her neck and began to breathe again. 'You are going to be fine, sweetheart,' he insisted, wanting to believe it. 'Just fine . . .'

'I can't understand where Jack's got to.' Katie trailed her spoon around the inside of her empty ice cream dish before pushing it into the centre of the table.

'Perhaps they gave him an extra half-hour with Helen.' Sam stacked her bowl inside his.

'If they're letting her out on Friday, it's more like they're giving him instructions on how to look after her,' Adam suggested. 'My father and I had to sit through a half-hour lecture from the ward sister before they let my mother out after her appendix operation and even then they sent a battery of nurses in and out of the house at all hours of the day and night to make sure we'd understood their instructions and weren't doing anything we shouldn't.'

'That's probably it,' Judy agreed.

'As there's no sign of him, how about I get us all a coffee?' Sam offered.

'My shout.' Adam left his chair. 'Give us a hand, Judy.'

'I'll be over when you're served.'

'Do you girls like having men dance attendance on you?' Sam gibed, as Adam went to the counter alone.

'No,' Judy snapped.

'Seems like it to me.'

'We weren't the ones who suggested a walk and an ice cream.' Katie reminded him.

Sam smiled in an attempt to diffuse their irritation. 'You didn't have to. Your charms did it for you.' His smile broadened as Katie scowled. 'Even now, when you're trying to look angry, you're irresistible.'

'I can see it's time I helped Adam with the coffees.' Judy left her chair.

'Perhaps, like Judy, you prefer Adam to me,' Sam suggested to Katie.

'Unlike you he does know how to take no for an answer.'

'And that's an advantage.' Taking the dirty dishes, he stacked them on an empty table behind them.

'Definitely, as far as I'm concerned.'

'You really don't like men, do you?'

'I'm not interested in going out with one.'

'At the moment.'

'Ever.' She left her chair and waved to Jack as he walked in. He saw her and made his way to their table.

'You look as though you've lost a shilling and found a penny.' Sam pulled out a chair for him. 'Everything all right with Helen?'

'No.'

'She's not worse . . .'

'I'm not sure. I don't think so,' he reassured Katie, 'but she can't stop crying and the bloody . . .'

'Any more of that language and I'll call the police,' the manager threatened.

'Sorry,' Jack apologised as he sat down. 'The doctor and the sister wanted a word with me about looking after her when she was discharged . . .'

'Told you.' Adam set two coffees on the table and stood back to make room for Judy who was carrying two more. 'Coffee?' he asked Jack.

Jack shook his head as he lit a cigarette.

'They might throw you out, especially after that language,' Sam warned.

'All right.' Jack nodded to Adam, totally forgetting that Martin had mentioned he'd quarrelled with him, Brian and Sam, in his concern for Helen.

'You were telling us that you were talking to the doctor,' Katie prompted.

'I explained that I'd only be taking care of Helen until Sunday because I'd received my call-up for National Service. I think she must have overheard me on her way to the bathroom, because she fainted in the corridor.'

'You're sure she only fainted?' Judy asked.

'I don't know. She was very pale but she was definitely breathing. The . . .' He eyed the manager who was watching him and moderated his language. 'They threw me out. I tried to stay, but the sister called a couple of porters. I tried arguing with them but it became ugly and I decided a fight wouldn't help Helen.'

'Did they say you could telephone?' Katie pushed her coffee in front of him.

'Tomorrow morning. She's my wife and I'm not even allowed to ask how she is.' He pulled heavily on his cigarette.

'Look on the bright side,' Sam commiserated, 'she'll be out on Friday.'

'If she's recovered.'

'If it was just a faint, it's not serious. My mother kept passing out all the time for the first month after her operation.' Adam returned with more coffee and, realising Katie was the only one who didn't have a cup in front of her, handed it over.

'You'll have a couple of days together, Jack,' Katie consoled him.

'And at least a week's leave after your training,' Sam handed him the ashtray. 'Maybe more if they send you overseas.'

'And then I won't see her for two years.'

'That might not happen. Look at Adam.'

'Look at Adam what?' Adam bristled, anticipating another insult.

'You spent the whole of your National Service in this country,' Sam reminded him.

'I was the exception rather than the rule.'

'I'm not sure Jack wanted to hear that.' Sam looked at Jack who was so deeply sunk in misery that he'd stopped listening to them.

'I know Helen.' Katie laid her hand over her brother's. 'She'll bounce back from this, you'll see.'

'The operation, or me being away for two years?' Jack enquired acidly.

'Both.'

'I hope you're right.' Jack ground his cigarette butt to dust in the ashtray.

'I am, you'll see.' Katie tried to sound optimistic but she didn't really believe it. John was in Swansea, and working in Lewis Lewis's she'd be able to see him, albeit from a distance. But even now when they still worked together, seeing wasn't enough for her, and she didn't know how she was going to cope without being able to talk to him – even about inconsequential work matters – on a daily basis. If she were suddenly to discover he was going away, possibly even abroad for two years and there was no likelihood of seeing him during all that time, she simply wouldn't want to go on.

'You're leaving this car in the street?' Lily asked Joe in surprise as he parked outside his house.

'You want me to put it in the living room?' He looked quizzically at her. 'Even if I could get it through the door, it wouldn't fit in the hall . . .'

'Don't be silly, you know I meant the garage.'

'There isn't room for two and my father's car will be there.'

'Then you'd better put the top up in case it rains.'

'I intended to.'

'Thanks for the drive.' She opened the door.

'You're going, just like that.'

'You want me to give you notice?'

'Just the chance to say thank you.'

'You've already said it.'

'I can say it again. Look . . .' Momentarily lost for words, he stared into her eyes. They glowed luminous in the twilight. Magnificent, beautiful eyes that had first attracted him to her. No matter how many times he looked into them, they held a fascination that seemed to encompass her entire personality. He loved her wholly, deeply and profoundly to the half-agonising point where he felt himself defined by his feelings for her. She was the first thing he thought of in the morning and the last image his mind clung to before sleep overtook him at night. She stole into his day and night dreams. How could she not realise that every breath he took, every plan he made, was for her?

'Look?' she reiterated expectantly.

He searched for the right words. 'I know we're only friends but can we do this again?'

'The next time you want to talk to someone, you know where to find me.'

'Not just talk. Go for a drive, a walk . . .'

'Perhaps,' she murmured distractedly. 'There's Martin.' Opening the door, she ran up the street to meet him.

A knot of jealousy tightened and twisted in Joe's stomach, flooding his mouth with bile as he watched Lily greet Martin. He didn't want to look at them but couldn't stop himself. She was smiling. Was it his imagination, or was there more warmth in her face now than there had been all evening?

Slowly, gradually, her smile grew strained as Martin looked from her to the car. Instead of the hug he'd braced himself for, Martin turned his back on her and headed in his direction. 'Just can't leave her alone, can you, Joe!'

Lily grabbed the arm of Martin's torn and oil-stained denim jacket as he lunged forward. 'There's nothing between Joe and me any more. We're just friends . . .'

'Friends!' Martin spat out the word as if it were a profanity.

'Friends,' she repeated quietly, still clinging to his arm.

He looked at her for an instant, then at Joe. Clenching his hands into fists, he turned on his heel and ran down the steps to his basement.

'I'm sorry, Lily.'

'It's all right, Joe, he just lost his temper. I'll talk him round.'

'If it will help I'll go with you.'

She shook her head. 'It wouldn't, but thank you for the offer.' Leaving him in the car, she walked up the path to her front door.

'You're late, Lily.' Mrs Lannon emerged from the kitchen as Lily hung her coat and hat on the stand. 'Your tea is in the oven, although heaven only knows what state it will be in after all this time. Burned to a crisp, I don't doubt.'

'I've eaten, Mrs Lannon, but thank you for the thought.'

'Well, I must say it would be more thoughtful of you if you told me when you're going to be out in future. And for how long. It will save me the trouble of making meals you can't be bothered to eat, and all the worry that Katie and I . . .'

'Katie's in?'

'She went down to Joe's ice cream parlour with Judy and Sam. I think they're going to meet her brother after visiting.'

Lily was sure that Katie hadn't told Mrs Lannon every detail of her planned movements but she said nothing beyond a vague, 'I see.'

'Don't you want anything? A cup of tea at least? I know what you young girls are like. Dashing about here, there and everywhere, filling yourself with all sorts of rubbish, never taking time to sit at a table and eat a proper meal.'

'I don't want anything, thank you, Mrs Lannon.' Lily was conscious she was clipping her words. She had to try harder – learn patience like Katie. Mrs Lannon's constant carping and prying never set her friend on edge the way it did her.

'You haven't said where you've been.' Mrs Lannon crossed her arms and waited to hear.

'A friend was in trouble and needed someone to talk to.'

'Would that be a girlfriend?'

'Just a friend, Mrs Lannon.'

'You're not thinking of going downstairs at this time of night,' she warned disapprovingly, as Lily opened the basement door.

'It's not that late and I need to see Martin.'

'He's alone down there, you know. I just heard the door bang.'

'It could have been Sam or Jack.'

'They're still out with Katie. Besides, I saw Martin walk down the steps.'

Lily realised that if Mrs Lannon had seen Martin walking down the steps she must have been standing in the front parlour window and that meant she must also have seen her and Joe arrive in Robin's car and Martin shouting at Joe. 'I won't be long.'

'Your uncle won't like you being alone in that flat with your young man,' Mrs Lannon called after her. 'It's not right for a girl your age to be with a boy that close to his bedroom . . .'

'Uncle Roy would understand.'

'There'll be gossip.'

Lily finally bit back, 'Not if you don't tell anyone.'

'Leave the door open . . .'

Suspecting that Mrs Lannon wanted the door left open so she could eavesdrop, Lily drowned out the rest of her directive by banging on the door that connected to the basement. When it didn't open, she tried the handle. It didn't surprise her to find it unlocked because the boys never bothered to pull the bolt on the inside. Stepping into the passage she shouted, 'Martin,' but there was no reply.

She glanced into the kitchen. The light was on, but it was empty. The door in front of her was Sam's bedroom, the door to her right at the end of the passage the bedroom Jack and Martin shared; both were in darkness. Closing the door and thrusting the bolt home to stop Mrs Lannon from following her, she walked down to Martin's door and knocked gingerly on the glass pane before noticing that the back door was open.

The light was on in the garage at the bottom of the garden. As her uncle had never owned or taken any interest in cars, he had practically given it over to the boys. Jack used it to store and work on his motorbike and Martin as a workshop where he cleaned and repaired the car components his boss allowed him to bring home.

Martin glanced up as she opened the door, then quite deliberately looked down at the makeshift workbench he had cobbled together from an old table and a couple of tin trays. Usually he bathed and changed out of his work clothes as soon as he came home, but he was still wearing his stained denim jacket, jeans and old, worn shirt.

She stepped inside and closed the door lest Mrs Lannon was watching from the kitchen window. 'If I'd known you were that jealous of Joe, I would never have gone for a drive with him.'

'You're free to go wherever you please, with anyone you want to be with.'

'There's no one I'd prefer to be with rather than you.' It was the closest she'd ever come to admitting that she cared for him but he continued to polish the rust from a piece of metal as if his future depended on the shine he put on it. 'Martin, please, say something.'

'What is there to say?' He finally looked at her.

'I bumped into Joe after work . . .'

'And not for the first time,' he broke in angrily. 'I've seen you together before. Talking and holding hands in the Kardomah.'

'I've had the occasional coffee with Joe in the Kardomah,' she acknowledged, 'but I never held his hand. Not after I broke our engagement.'

'No?' he challenged. 'Think back a couple of weeks.'

'I didn't hold his hand,' she protested.

'And he's walked you home from work. I've seen you coming up the street together.'

'You make it sound as if Joe and I planned our meetings.'

'Don't you?' He glared at her, daring her to say otherwise.

'No!' she exclaimed vehemently. 'And if seeing me in the Kardomah with Joe bothered you, why didn't you say something at the time?'

'Because I was waiting for you to tell me that you'd gone there with him.'

'If I didn't, it was because I didn't think it worth mentioning.'

'You go to the Kardomah with your fiancé and didn't think it worth mentioning to your boyfriend.'

'Ex-fiancé, and if you don't want me to see him again I won't.'

'Why, Lily? He has it all, fancy car . . .'

'It's his friend's.'

'But he has enough money to buy one just like it if the mood takes him. Just as he has prospects and a trust fund to give you everything I can't.'

'We've been through this, Martin,' she reminded him hotly. 'It's you I'm going out with, not Joe.'

'Were going out with.'

'You're finishing with me?' Her throat went dry. She leaned against the wall.

'You'll ruin your jacket.'

'Then I'll have to clean it,' she snapped.

'Knowing what Jack's like when he's working on his bike, it could be covered with oil.'

'For heaven's sake stop fussing about my clothes.'

'People like you shouldn't come near grease monkeys like me. Here.' Ignoring her outburst he wiped down an old stool with a rag, covered it with his handkerchief and handed it to her. As she took it, their fingers touched. He jerked back as if he'd been scalded.

'Do you think so little of me that you'd believe I'd go out with Joe when I'm going out with you?' she asked as she sat down.

'It doesn't matter what I think about you any more, does it.'

'It does to me,' she said impatiently. 'I can't understand why you think I want to get back with Joe.'

'It's obvious.'

'Not to me. Joe's a friend. He came to me tonight with a problem . . .'

'What kind of a problem?'

'His problem and it has nothing whatsoever to do with me, or you. He wanted to talk . . .'

'And there was no one else he could talk to.'

'He probably would have gone to Helen if he could have, but she's in hospital.'

'He has a father, his posh university friends . . .'

'But he came to me,' she countered. 'I'm sorry if that upsets you, Martin. He offered to come here to try to explain . . .'

'I bet he did.' He finally set down the piece he'd been working on. 'It's the end of a long day, Lily. I've been working since seven this morning and I haven't had tea.'

She watched as he tidied away the sandpaper and dusted his bench. One of them had to say it. All she had to lose was her pride and that was a small price to pay if it meant holding on to him. As he walked to the door to turn off the light, she steeled herself for rejection and whispered, 'I love you.'

He paused, without turning to look at her.

'It's you I love, not Joe,' she repeated, leaving no room for misunderstanding.

He finally switched off the light, plunging the garage into darkness.

'Did you hear me?' She followed him outside.

'Yes.' He swung the bolt across the door.

'And?'

'I don't know how you can. I've a foul temper. I hit people . . .'

'Not people, only Adam and he deserved it.'

Still refusing to look at her, he busied himself with the padlock on the door. Petrified that he was about to rebuff her, she gazed up at the stars. It was a clear, cloudless night. Millions upon millions of dazzling diamond pinpricks of light shone around a perfect crescent moon. Dizzy with apprehension – and wonder – she almost lost her balance.

Catching her, Martin pulled her back against his chest, wrapped his hands round her waist and brushed his lips across the top of her head. 'I don't understand how you can love someone like me.'

'Neither do I after the way you just behaved.' She turned and kissed him and, as his lips met hers and the length of his body pressed against hers, all doubts and uncertainties dissipated. He might not have repeated her words but his embrace gave her all the reassurance she needed.

'Are you absolutely sure?' He looked into her eyes as he finally released her.

'Absolutely. You?'

'I love you so much it hurts.'

The kitchen window banged open above them. 'I can see you, Lily Sullivan. Come in this house this instant, or I'll tell your uncle what you've been up to.'

'We're not doing anything illegal, Mrs Lannon, so I doubt he'll arrest us,' Martin called back.

'Your behaviour is disgraceful . . .'

'Would you rather I kissed her behind the shed where you couldn't see?'

'Martin Clay . . .'

Neither Lily nor Martin heard another word. Lost in the moonlight, they kissed again, clinging to one another as if they'd just invented love.

Chapter 17

'EVERYTHING GO ALL right?' John looked up from the *Evening Post* as Joe walked into the living room.

'I think so. Why?' Joe asked suspiciously.

'You've been a long time and I didn't mean that as a criticism. Whisky?'

'Please.' Joe sat down. 'I met Lily from work and took her for a drive in Robin's car.'

'Then you two are . . .'

'Just friends.' He looked at John. 'You'll be glad to know that I'll be able to afford my own car now so I won't need to borrow Robin's — or yours.'

John handed him a glass of whisky. 'Then your grandmother's estate was worth having.'

'According to Richard Thomas, I'm officially one of the richest — if not *the* richest — young men in Swansea.' He watched John carefully as he mentioned Richard's name, but there was no flicker of knowledge that suggested John knew the man was anything other than the family solicitor.

'I'm happy for you, Joe.'

'It will take a while to sink in. Do you mind if I take this' — Joe held up the whisky — 'upstairs? I have some studying to do.'

'If you're hungry, Mrs Jones left a fish pie in the kitchen.'

'I'll forage later.' Joe took his glass and climbed the stairs. Switching off the landing light, he walked into his bedroom, leaving it in darkness. The curtains were open and light flooded out from their dining room and next door's kitchen windows, shining down on Martin and Lily locked in one another's arms below him in the garden. He continued to stand at his window, watching every move they made, all the while hating himself for being unable to walk away.

Katie knocked discreetly on the back door. 'Jack's upset and Mrs

Lannon's hysterical. Judy's trying to calm her down but she's threatening to give your uncle notice, Lily.'

Lily slipped her arms round Martin's waist. 'Kiss me again, quick.'

'Tomorrow.' Martin wrapped his arm round Lily's shoulders and faced his sister. 'Why is Jack upset? Helen's not worse, is she?'

'He doesn't know. She overheard Jack telling one of the doctors he was leaving on Sunday to do his National Service and fainted, but they turfed him out of the hospital before she came round.'

'Don't worry, sis, I'll look after him.' He smiled at Lily. 'See you tomorrow?'

'Yes.'

His smile widened as he went to the door. 'We should quarrel more often.'

'You and Martin quarrelled?' Katie asked, as she led the way up the basement stairs.

'Our first.'

'But you've made it up.'

'As you saw.'

'I'm glad.'

'Glad enough to brave Mrs Lannon with me?' Lily whispered as they reached the top of the stairs.

'That's a lot to ask.'

'Please, she's always preferred you to me,' Lily pleaded, as she opened the door to the hall.

'Only if you stand between us, so I can run if I have to,' Katie compromised.

Esme walked restlessly from bedroom to bedroom, switching lamps on and off, standing at the windows and straightening the drapes, studying the garden and sea views as if she'd never seen them before and wasn't likely to again; all the while wondering when, if ever, she'd be back.

Finally, she descended the curved oak staircase, allowing her fingers to linger over the banister and thinking it strange that she had never noticed just how fine the carving was before. The drawing room was furnished with antiques that had been her father's pride and joy. He had courted experts and frequented auction houses, making it his business to find out when the best pieces would come up for sale and always insisting on detailed provenance. If she had inherited the place she would have swept them aside, ripped out the picture and dado rails, done away with the coving and painted the walls in bright modern colours, purple, orange, rich crimson and blue . . . but then, the house wasn't hers. It was Joseph's and he would prefer to allow strangers to live in it rather than his own mother.

As she left the drawing room for the dining room, her heels echoed hollowly over the wood block flooring, raising goose bumps. Although she'd grown up in the house and moved back in after she'd left John, it was the first time she'd actually spent a night alone in the place. The housekeeper had packed her bags and left less than an hour after Richard had read the will. Her mother had joined her father in his grave . . . and she . . . what was to become of her?

Richard, John and Joseph expected her to move into the flat above the shop on Newton Road that John had signed over to her as part of the divorce settlement. She hadn't set foot in the place but she knew it would be small and noisy. How could she make a new life for herself there, without status or friends, after living in this house? And how like men to expect her to do so, after they had destroyed every dream and ambition she'd ever had.

Richard had killed her aspirations of drama college and a glittering stage career by impregnating her and, as if that weren't enough, influencing her mother to leave her estate to Joseph so she'd remain a pauper. John had blighted her best years by stifling her in domesticity and forcing her to live in town, effectively removing her from the social circle she had been born into. And Joseph – the son she had sacrificed so much for – wouldn't even allow her to stay on as his housekeeper.

The injustice of her position burned, intolerable, humiliating. She could either move out meekly as they wanted her to, or she could fight back. Show all three of them they couldn't pension her off to a trade address in Newton Road just because it was convenient for them to have her out of the way. That she still had some control over her life – and theirs.

'Carrying on with Martin Clay in full view of the whole street . . .'

'What's going on,' Roy enquired mildly, as he walked into the kitchen just as Mrs Lannon's indignation was mushrooming into hysteria.

'Your foster daughter and Martin Clay making love in the back garden in front of the whole street, that's what's going on.' Mrs

Lannon crossed her arms over her tightly corseted bosom and stared angrily at Lily.

'In the garden?' Roy raised his eyebrows as he looked from Judy and Katie, who had retreated into the corner, to Lily.

Noticing that he was finding it difficult to keep a straight face, Lily fought to suppress a smile. 'We quarrelled, so we kissed and made up.'

'It was disgusting,' Mrs Lannon railed. 'Everyone could see . . .'

'Surely, only if they were looking out of their back windows, Mrs Lannon,' Roy interposed.

'You condone what she did!'

'No.' Unlike Lily, Roy realised his housekeeper would have a field day with the gossips if he sided with his foster daughter.

'See,' Mrs Lannon crowed. 'Your uncle is as shocked by your behaviour as I am.'

'Apologise to Mrs Lannon, Lily.' Roy's voice was stern but there was a twinkle in his eye that took the sting from his directive.

'Sorry, Mrs Lannon.'

'What was that?' Mrs Lannon said loudly.

'I said, I'm very sorry.'

'That's fine for you, Lily Sullivan. But Martin Clay shouted the rudest things . . . and me old enough to be his mother.'

'I'll ask Martin to apologise to you,' Lily promised.

'Not by going down into that flat again tonight, you won't.' She stepped in front of Roy. 'I warned you, Mr Williams. You give these girls far too much leeway. They'll end up like that Helen Griffiths . . .'

'Lily's apologised, Mrs Lannon. I think that's enough for one night, don't you?' Roy broke in sharply.

'Well, as long as you don't expect me . . .'

'I only expect you to do what I pay you for, Mrs Lannon, run the house. Now if there's nothing else that's important, there's something I have to discuss with Lily.'

'You need a woman's help . . .'

'It's private family business, Mrs Lannon.'

'There's your supper . . .'

'Lily can cook it. I'm sure you're tired after your long day,' he added in a tone he hoped would put an end to further argument.

'Who wouldn't be. This isn't a small house . . .'

'And we're all very grateful for the job you do.'

'I'm sure.' Sniffing hard, Mrs Lannon picked up her handbag from the kitchen chair and stalked out.

'Do you really want to talk to me, or did you just say that to get rid of Mrs Lannon?' Lily asked as the door closed.

Holding his finger to his lips, Roy stole lightly to the door and opened it suddenly. His housekeeper was standing in the dining room fumbling in her handbag. 'Have you lost something, Mrs Lannon?'

'I thought I'd mislaid my pills but I have them after all.'

'I'm so glad.' He remained in the doorway.

'I'll say goodnight, then.' Flustered, she went into the hall.

'Goodnight,' he called after her, only returning to the kitchen when he heard her step on the stairs.

'Sorry, Uncle Roy,' Lily apologised, as he closed the door.

'You know what she is, love, try and be a bit more careful around her for your own sake.'

'And Martin's. What on earth did he say to her?' Katie pulled a chair from the table and sat on it.

'That Uncle Roy wouldn't arrest us because we weren't doing anything illegal.'

Judy and Katie burst out laughing.

'Mrs Lannon's definition of illegal is anything people enjoy,' Judy said as soon as she could speak.

'I'd love to know why she doesn't annoy you as much as she annoys me.' Lily looked at Katie.

'Because I don't let her.'

'How can you ignore some of the things she says?'

'Because she's a lonely old women whose only interest in life is other people's business.'

'Katie's right, love.' Roy settled in his favourite easy chair next to the range. 'It's best to take no notice of her.'

'That's easier said than done.'

'But you'll try.' He smiled persuasively.

'For you, not her.' Lily opened the pantry and checked the stocks. 'How does bacon, eggs, beans, tomatoes and fried potatoes sound to you?'

'Like you know how to look after a man. Judy, I think your mother would like a word with you.'

'You two have fixed the date?' she guessed.

'I'm not saying anything.'

'See you tomorrow.' She ran to the front door.

'Do you need any help, Lily?' Katie asked as she returned to the kitchen after seeing Judy out.

Katie looked so drained that Lily shook her head. 'Not to fry a couple of bits and pieces.'

'Did you want to talk to me as well, Uncle Roy?'

'No, love.'

'Then you won't mind if I have an early night.'

'You're not sickening for something, are you?' Roy questioned solicitously as Katie went to the door.

'Just concerned about Jack and Helen. She found out tonight that he's leaving on Sunday.'

'Anything I can do to help?' He reached for his pipe.

'Not unless you can persuade the army to let Jack off National Service.'

'If I could, I would.'

'I'll try not to disturb you when I come up.' Lily lifted down two frying pans and a saucepan from the cupboard.

'The way I feel, I'd sleep through an earthquake. Goodnight.'

'So,' Lily picked up the conversation where she'd left off before Roy had disturbed Mrs Lannon's eavesdropping. 'Do you really want to talk to me?'

'I think I'd better, before Mrs Lannon paints you as the scarlet woman of the neighbourhood.'

'Martin and I were only kissing . . .'

'Not that kind of talk.' He flushed with embarrassment as she cracked two eggs into a basin. 'I know you haven't forgotten how Norah brought you up.'

'As if I could.' She dropped a knob of lard into one of the pans, waiting until it melted before laying four rashers of bacon and the eggs on top. 'I won't disgrace you, Uncle Roy, I promise.'

'That goes without saying, love. But I hope you were serious about trying not to annoy Mrs Lannon even if it means sneaking around and keeping whatever it is you do with Martin out of her sight.'

'Like kissing.'

'Especially kissing.' He grinned.

'Do you think she was born old?' she questioned seriously.

'Probably, unlike Joy and me. Judy guessed right. We've fixed a date with the Register Office. The second Saturday in July.'

'Auntie Norah would have been over the moon.'

'And you?'

'I couldn't be happier for you and Mrs Hunt.' Abandoning the frying pans, she gave him a bear hug.

'That's why I need to talk to you. Nothing's been decided as yet, but Joy suggested it makes more sense for me to move in with her than the other way round. She has her home just the way she likes it and it's taken her years to get it that way. The last thing she wants is all the fuss of a move while she's setting up another salon.'

'But this is your home, Uncle Roy. Won't it be hard for you to leave?' Lily tried not to think selfishly about her and Katie. If her uncle sold the house they would have to look for a bedsit . . .

'It was my home, Lily. But even when I was a boy my mother and Norah put their stamp on it more than my father and me. Not that I'm complaining, it's what women do. They can't help it and as it makes for more comfort for us men in the long run, we put up with it.'

'Are you leaving me and Katie here with Mrs Lannon?' She tried to sound positive, but Roy could see she was horror-struck at the thought.

'How serious is it between you and Martin?'

'He told me he loved me tonight.'

'Did he, indeed.'

'Yes.' She glanced at him before checking that everything was cooking properly, but it was difficult to read the expression on his face.

'Then you'll be getting married?'

'Not that serious.' She placed the bread on a board and cut a couple of slices.

'Then you won't be getting married.'

'We haven't even talked about it but I'm in no hurry. Auntie Norah always used to say twenty-five was a good age to marry, young enough to have children and old enough to have had all your flings.'

'That's Norah.' He smiled fondly at her memory as Lily arranged a plate and cutlery on the table. 'When she died there were a few things we didn't discuss because I thought they'd best be saved for later and now that later is here.' He left his chair and washed his hands under the tap. Knowing better than to hurry him, Lily handed him a towel. 'This house is yours.'

'Mine!' She dropped the spatula into the frying pan, sending globules of fat spattering over the hob.

'When my mother died she left everything jointly to Norah and me. Then Norah married. A year later war broke out. Her husband wanted her to have something to fall back on if anything happened to him. This house is big enough to take in lodgers and he decided Norah could make a living that way if she had to. He thought it was important she had her independence. None of us knew what was coming and there was no guarantee that either of us would survive. So, to cut a long story short, he bought me out. I invested the money and did very nicely by it. Then, after Norah's husband was killed and you came along, Norah suggested, and I agreed, that if anything happened to her, you should have the house. That way you'd never be without a home.'

Lily sat down.

'Bit of a shock.'

'You and Auntie Norah gave me so much when I was growing up and now this. I don't know what to say. Thank you sounds so – inadequate.'

'I've a feeling it's going to be a bit of a mixed blessing, love. I agree with Joy that it makes sense for me to move in with her, but you and Katie are too young to be left on your own.' He sat at the table.

'You and Mrs Hunt will only be ten doors up if we need anything,' she said eagerly. 'And we won't. You'll see that Katie and I . . .'

'Are capable young ladies,' he interrupted. 'But, there's Mrs Lannon.'

'We never needed her.'

'There was gossip, love,' he reminded her. 'I'm a bachelor, not related by blood to either of you.'

'And now you'll be leaving, so there won't be any more talk.' Remembering the bacon and eggs, she leaped out of the chair and rushed to the frying pan.

'There'll be plenty if you give Mrs Lannon notice and I move out while you and Katie carry on living here with Martin and Sam in the basement.' He handed her his plate.

'We could brick up the connecting door.' She heaped the bacon and eggs on to it and laid it before him.

'You think a few bricks will stop the gossips?'

'Probably not.' Scooping the tomatoes, potatoes and beans into bowls, she set them on the table.

'Especially with things the way they are between you and Martin. You and Katie could move in with Mrs Hunt and me . . .'

'And spoil your honeymoon? Never.' She buttered the bread she'd cut.

'Judy will be there.'

'She could move in with Katie and me . . .'

'Only if you give the boys notice.'

'Where would they go?' Filling the frying pans with cold water, she put them in the sink to soak. 'Rooms around here are like gold.'

'So we have a problem.'

'Unless Mrs Lannon stays,' she conceded, 'but Katie and I could never afford to pay her out of what we earn.'

'No, you couldn't, but then would you want her to keep house for you?'

'I've said all long that Katie and I could do the cooking and the housework. We don't need her.'

'Except for her respectability.'

'You've an idea, haven't you?' Taking the tomato sauce from the pantry, she handed it to him.

'I have heard she's had an offer to rent her house and she's considering it.'

'Then we'd be stuck with her.' She joined him at the table.

'You could offer her the top floor as a lodger, not housekeeper, and if you wanted to, you could make some extra money by renting out the other two bedrooms to a couple of girls.' He took a large bite of bread.

'Like Judy.'

'Like Judy,' he echoed, smiling at her transparent plotting to give him and Joy privacy, 'and with Mrs Lannon on the premises no one would dare spread rumours about any shenanigans with the boys.'

'But I would have to be nice to her.' She made a face.

'It's worth thinking about, love.'

'I will.'

'About the house and the rent the boys have been paying. It's in an account in your name. There's probably enough there to pay for improvements to the basement like John Griffiths did next door. And if there isn't, there's also the money Norah left you.'

'It seems wrong to touch it.'

'Norah wanted you to have it. In the meantime I'll check exactly how much rent money is in the account. But if you do decide to go ahead with the improvements, it would mean the boys moving out, at least temporarily, while they're being done.' He helped himself to tomatoes. 'Something else for you to think about, love.'

'No one else knows the house is mine, do they?' she asked suddenly.

'No.'

'You won't tell anyone, will you, Uncle Roy.'

'You'd rather everyone carried on thinking the place is mine?'

'For the time being.'

'If that's what you want.' He pointed at the food on the table. 'You going to help me with any of this?'

'I ate earlier.'

'Then go up to bed.'

'The dishes . . .'

'We still have a housekeeper.' He grinned. 'For the present. Let her do them in the morning.'

'So what did you and Martin quarrel about?' Katie murmured from the depths of the bed, as Lily returned to their bedroom from the bathroom.

'Joe. I bumped into him after work. He had a problem and needed to talk to someone.'

'And you volunteered.'

'We're just friends.' Brushing out her hair, Lily plaited it and fastened the end with a rubber band.

'But Martin doesn't believe it.'

'He does now.' Climbing into bed, Lily switched out the light.

'I'm glad.'

'What's wrong, Katie?'

'Nothing,' Katie answered.

'You might be able to fool your brothers and Uncle Roy, but not me.'

'I got the job in Lewis Lewis.'

'Have you told Mr Griffiths?' Lily questioned.

'Yes.' Katie paused for a moment. 'He said he'll give me a good reference.'

'Oh, Katie.' Lily gave her an enormous hug.

'You seem to be everyone's favourite agony aunt today, me, Joe . . .'

'Want to talk about it?'

'What is there to say? I don't want to leave the warehouse, John doesn't want me to go, but he's too afraid of the things Mrs Griffiths will say if he keeps me on, so I've no option.'

'And after his divorce?' Lily tried to say something that would give Katie hope if not comfort.

'That could be so far in the future neither of us dares think about it.'

'I am so sorry.'

'As my mother used to say, it's no good wishing for the moon on a stick. Every moment I spent with John was so perfect it was almost as if I was too happy. Deep down I think I knew it couldn't last.'

'Pictures tomorrow night?' Lily suggested, in an attempt to distract her.

'What's on?' Katie asked uninterestedly.

'A good Cowboy and Indian at the Plaza, according to the girls in the bank. It's about an Indian chief, Crazy Horse. Victor Mature's in it.'

'I can't stand Victor Mature.'

'There's a musical in the Albert Hall.'

'*Calamity Jane*. I've seen it.'

'It's a crying shame to go to the pictures in summer anyway. Let's go for a walk to Mumbles.'

'The boys will want to join us, and Sam and Adam are driving me mad.'

'You've seen Adam?' Lily asked in surprise.

'I got him and Sam to shake and make up tonight.'

'Good for you, I hate quarrels.'

'It wasn't that hard.'

'Sam and Adam won't bother you if Martin and I are there.'

'The sight of you two spooning makes it even worse. Besides, if Helen is coming out the day after tomorrow, someone should get the flat ready for her and although Jack might try, I can't see him making a proper job of it.'

'It's immaculate.'

'Last time I was sorting Helen's clothes I noticed it could do with a good dusting and running the carpet sweeper over the rugs.'

'Then Martin and I will help.' Pushing her pillow into shape, Lily turned over in the bed.

'If he finds out you volunteered him for that, you two will have another quarrel.'

'No, we won't. Besides, Jack should be there to make sure we put everything back right.'

'As if he'd even know,' Katie said dismissively. 'He'd just get in the way.'

'Then you and I can do it and Martin can take him for a drink.'

'I suppose so.'

'If you want to be by yourself . . .'

'Not in John's house,' Katie broke in. 'Although the flat is separate, it is still his house and if Mrs Griffiths found out that we were alone there at the same time, she might say something to Joe or Helen. What did your uncle want to talk to you about?'

'He and Mrs Hunt have set the date, it's July.'

'That's nice for them.'

'Yes,' Lily agreed. Either Katie was too preoccupied to think about the implications for them, or too distracted to ask about it, so she let the matter drop.

'Sorry I'm such a moaning Minnie,' Katie apologised.

'You've every reason to be.'

'Don't you know sympathy is the worse thing you can give a moaning Minnie?' Katie lay on her back and linked her hands beneath her head. 'But thank you for being a friend and maybe soon sister-in-law.'

'Definitely not soon. Goodnight, Katie.' Lily closed her eyes. Within minutes her breathing became shallow and regular. Katie continued to lie still and unmoving lest she disturb her. All she could think about, all she could visualise was John's face as he had pushed her away from him. And she was still thinking about him as the shadows lightened from dark to pale-grey and the first rays of morning stole through a chink in the curtains.

Mark Davies extracted an envelope from a file and slid it across the desk towards John as he walked into John's office. 'I received that this morning from Richard Thomas.'

'What does it say?' John pushed the letter he'd been reading aside.

'Read it for yourself.'

'You wouldn't be my solicitor if I didn't trust you, and I have a warehouse to run.'

'Esme is giving you formal notice that she is about to move back into your house.'

'She can't. She . . .' He fell silent as he studied the expression on Mark's face. 'She can?'

'According to this, she left the matrimonial home to nurse her mother.'

'That's rubbish!'

'And your daughter is about to be released from hospital and will need nursing care that only a mother can provide.' Mark sat down.

'Helen will never stand for Esme nursing her.'

'Helen is eighteen, legally a minor . . .'

'A married minor,' John reminded him.

'That's another thing. Esme is citing Helen's pregnancy and your permission for her marriage to . . .' Mark opened the letter and scanned the page for the phrase he wanted ' ". . . a boy of criminal tendencies and persuasion" as an example of your unsuitability to have custody of the children.'

'Custody! Joe's twenty-one, Helen's eighteen.' John left his desk. 'What does she really want?'

'On the face of it, what this says; to move back into the matrimonial home.'

'And if I refuse?'

'At this stage it's wiser to keep talking.'

'Talking doesn't seem to be bringing me any closer to a divorce.'

'You have told me everything?' Mark looked him in the eye.

John's blood ran cold as he recalled Esme's threat: *Don't think I'm going to do nothing while you let Katie Clay move in* . . . 'You think there's something else you should know?'

'Have you another woman tucked away somewhere?'

'I've already admitted adultery,' John answered evasively. 'You fixed it up, remember.'

'A technical adultery with a professional, which is of little use if Esme's prepared to forgive you and take you back when she is the one who is supposed to be suing for divorce. And you can't sue her without grounds, and desertion's no good when she's offering to move back in with you.'

'There has to be something you can do to make her change her mind about dropping the petition,' John urged.

'Legally there's nothing. But for the life of me I can't see what she hopes to gain from her refusal to give you a divorce when you're so set on it.'

'Public sympathy, the respectability that comes with being a wife, even an unwanted one.' John paced restlessly to the window and looked out over the yard. A lorry had just come in and the warehouse staff were unloading a consignment of Dansette record players and radiograms. 'We could try upping the settlement.'

'I'd advise strongly against that. As I keep telling you, it's already far too generous for a wife without dependent children.'

'But if it is simply a question of money . . .'

'There is no mention of money in the letter, John. Just a request – sorry, a demand – you reinstate her as your wife.'

'And if I refuse to do so?' John turned his back to the window and looked at Mark.

'I can't understand Richard Thomas putting his name to a letter like this,' Mark mused, not really listening. 'If it should get out that he directed a client to reject such a generous settlement . . . of course, that's it – the settlement. We could write to them, stating that your offer will remain on the table for, say, only one more week. If Esme persists in refusing to press ahead with her petition for divorce after that time, you'll withdraw it and her monthly allowance, in favour of drawing up your own petition.'

'And if she still refuses to go ahead?'

'Then we'll do exactly that,' Mark said flatly. 'Withdraw your settlement offer, stop her allowance and set about lodging another petition. Adultery would be the simplest. If you're certain she's had lovers I'll get a private investigator on to it.'

'And in the meantime?'

'I don't understand.'

'Esme has to live off something.' John limped back to his chair. 'Her mother left her practically nothing.'

'I thought you wanted to get rid of the woman. She's screwed you for every penny she can get and more.'

'It seems so – drastic.'

'It is drastic,' Mark agreed.

'There has to be something else we can do.'

'Nothing that I can think of.'

John recalled the venomous look on Esme's face when she had threatened to expose Katie. Remembered what it had been like to live with her . . . and how it would be if she moved back into their house. But she had been his wife, even if only in name for over twenty years, the mother of his daughter . . . 'No.'

'You can't be serious, John.'

'I am.'

'Even though Esme's trying every foul underhanded trick to get you back?'

'Let her try.'

'It could get bloody.'

'Knowing Esme, I've no doubt it will,' John said philosophically. 'But the answer's still no. I won't leave her destitute.'

'Then prepare for the worst.'

'I have been,' John said grimly, 'almost since the day I married her.'

Chapter 18

'JUDY.' ADAM CHARGED up the steps of his parents' basement and ran after her as she left her house. 'You walking to your mother's hairdresser's?' He took hold of her arm as he dived under her umbrella.

Resenting his familiarity, she quickened her pace. 'No, I'm catching the Mumbles train to go to the new salon, and I only have twelve minutes to get to the Mumbles Road.'

'Don't suppose you feel like coming to a dinner dance with me tonight?'

'You suppose right.' She felt that if she went out with Adam it would be like a public admission that she and Brian were over, and even if they were, it was something she wasn't ready to face or deal with – not yet.

'It wouldn't be like a date or anything,' he explained. 'It's a formal Civil Service do; the girl who was going with me is in bed with tonsillitis. I've bought the tickets and hired a dinner jacket. All I need is a fairly presentable partner in an evening frock.'

'I'm flattered,' she rejoined caustically.

'You know you're more than presentable, please, Judy . . .'

'Ask Katie.'

'After she told me to get lost?'

'If it's not really a date . . .'

'She still wouldn't come.'

'You're probably right.' She looked up and down Mansel Street to check there was no traffic coming before crossing the road.

'I'd ask Lily' – he crouched down, in an attempt to keep his head under cover as she lowered her umbrella – 'but Martin's so besotted with her, he'd never lend her out to another bloke, and with Helen married and in hospital, out of all my friends that leaves . . .'

'Me.' She stopped and looked at him, finding it difficult to believe that someone as tall, blond, blue-eyed and good-looking as Adam Jordan was having difficulty in finding a girl to go to a dance with him.

'The girl I was going with works in the office next to me. We're sort of serious,' he acknowledged coyly. 'But if I told her I was taking an old friend whose boyfriend is also a friend of mine and away in London she wouldn't mind. She knows the tickets cost a bomb and there's no way I'd get my money back at this late stage.'

'So it really wouldn't be like a date,' she murmured.

'Definitely not,' he asserted, sensing her weakening. 'You'd be doing me a favour. The tickets were twelve and six . . .'

'Each?'

He nodded. 'Now do you see why I'm desperate.'

'All right,' she agreed, 'as long as I pay my own way.'

'I wouldn't hear of it. I'd lose the money if you didn't come.'

'Then the drinks are on me.'

'I won't argue with that.' He smiled at her. 'You have a posh frock?'

'I'll dig one out.' As she returned his smile, she recalled a time before Brian had moved to Swansea and into her life when the prospect of going to a dinner dance with Adam Jordan would have sent her heart rate soaring. 'Now I really must go.'

'Pick you up at six thirty,' he shouted as she ran across the Kingsway. Despite the rain, he was still smiling as he headed up the road towards his office. Brian had told him that Judy had given him the scent and lipstick the night of the stag party. He had also more or less admitted to painting the kisses on him including the one on his underpants and, according to Sam, Judy was still Brian's girlfriend. He had given fair warning the night they'd come to blows in the Pier. Brian would soon learn that he wasn't the only one who could play a practical joke.

'They said she's well enough to come out, Jack,' John reassured him as he turned off the ignition. He had parked his car as close to the entrance of the hospital as he dared, but he could barely make out the doors through the rain that sheeted down, flooding the gutters and puddling the pavements.

'It's just that after Wednesday . . .'

'Helen has to dress and I have to get back to the warehouse before the fashion buyer doubles our regular order with the Italian knitwear rep. Every time he lays on the charm, her common sense deserts her.

So, for both our sakes, go in there, boy.' Turning, he lifted an umbrella from the back seat of the car. 'And take this. You're going to need it. You've got her clothes and coat?'

'Katie packed Helen's case.'

'Then Helen should have everything she needs.' John gave a final encouraging smile as Jack opened the door, pushed up the umbrella and ran round to the boot of the car.

'That is gorgeous,' the nurse complimented as Helen fastened the button on the waistband of the skirt that hung loosely round her waist and lifted her jacket from the case Jack had brought in. 'Is it real silk, Mrs Clay?'

'Yes, it is.' Helen smiled weakly. The staff had mellowed considerably during her convalescence and she had long since realised that their outwardly cold officious manner was merely a mask they donned whenever they felt relatives were hindering a patient's recovery. And how like Jack to bring her the costume she had been married in. If it hadn't been for the clean underclothes, new stockings and fresh handkerchief, she would have believed he hadn't unpacked the clothes that had been sent out when she'd been admitted.

The nurse fingered the cloth. 'It really is lovely and heavenly colours. Wherever did you get it?'

'My father's warehouse.'

'Griffiths's wholesale?' the nurse asked.

'How did you know?'

'Someone said you were related.'

Helen looked despairingly at her hair in the mirror. It hung, lank and greasy to her shoulders.

'Your husband brought a hat,' the nurse suggested encouragingly. 'I could put your hair in a bun if you like.'

'Please.' Helen sank on to the chair next to the bed. It wasn't simply that she was too tired to cope with having to dress and make decisions about her hair and make-up; now that she was finally about to go home, she was stunned to discover that she didn't want to leave. For four weeks the ward had been her entire world; first the poky little booth with its peeling and stained institution-green painted walls at the end of the corridor nearest the nurses' station. Then this curtained cubicle. And the whole time she'd been incarcerated she'd hated the place. The lack of privacy, the smells, the boredom, the regime, the brusque, no-nonsense senior staff and the trainees straining to prove their efficiency, and all the while she'd longed to be home. Not the pristine flat that had been prepared for her and Jack but her bedroom in her father's house where he, with the daily's help, had nursed her through all her childhood ailments from measles, through mumps to chicken pox. Yet now, when she was minutes away from leaving, she was almost afraid to go. It was confusing – made no sense – and she couldn't even begin to understand it.

'There.' The nurse handed her a mirror. The bun was neat but it did nothing to disguise the fact that her hair needed washing. 'Shall I pin on your hat?'

'Please.' Helen opened her compact and dabbed at her nose. The powder clung, pasty and lumpy, emphasising ugly patches of dry skin.

'Here, let me.' The nurse took her mascara brush from her and dipped it in her water glass, to wet it. 'It will be washed before it's passed on to someone else,' she explained in reply to Helen's bemused glance.

Helen rubbed the brush over the block and brushed on a coat. Like the powder it clumped, sticking her lashes together. Even her lipstick seemed to conspire against her, coating thickly over her lips, giving them an oddly greasy appearance.

'You look wonderful.' The nurse placed the white hat she had worn for her wedding on her head and secured it with her pearl-headed pin.

'All ready?' The sister pulled the curtain; opening it wide, when she saw Helen sitting dressed in the chair. 'And not a moment too soon, Mrs Clay, your husband's getting fractious. I think he's convinced we want to keep you here. Evans,' she called to one of the trainees. 'Check Mrs Clay doesn't leave anything behind.'

'Yes, sister.'

'Thank you for everything,' Helen murmured mechanically as the nurse packed her comb and hairbrush into her vanity case.

'Just doing our job.' The nurse smiled.

'Dab of scent.' The trainee handed her a bottle.

Unscrewing the top, Helen removed the rubber stopper, held her finger over the neck and tipped the bottle upside down, before perfunctorily dabbing her finger on her wrists and neck.

'I can't see that you've left anything.' Closing the drawer and door on the locker, the trainee took the bottle and stowed it in Helen's vanity case.

'Your coat.' The nurse held it out and Helen slipped her arms into the sleeves.

'The porter's waiting, staff.'

'Coming, sister.' The staff nurse helped Helen up as a porter pushed a wheelchair towards them.

'I can walk.'

'Not out of here, you can't.' The sister nodded to the porter. 'Her husband is in the visitors' room next to the office. 'Take care of yourself, Mrs Clay.'

'And good luck,' the staff nurse added.

Too overcome to answer and ashamed of the tears that were falling from her eyes yet again, Helen nodded as the porter laid the vanity case on her lap and lifted her suitcase. To the cries of her fellow patients' good wishes he steered her out of the ward and into the corridor.

'Mrs Griffiths.' John's daily cleaner retreated into the hall at the sight of Esme on the doorstep.

Esme walked past the woman. 'Could you carry my cases upstairs?' she asked the taxi driver who was standing behind her. 'Second door on the left.'

'Mr Griffiths didn't say anything about you coming back, Mrs Griffiths,' the cleaner said, as she found her voice. 'Your room's not ready; the bed's not even aired . . .'

'The electric fire will soon rectify that.' Esme gave the daily a tight smile as she opened her handbag and removed her purse.

'That will be five shillings, ma'am.' The taxi driver tipped his hat as he returned downstairs. Esme handed him two half-crowns, then, after a moment's hesitation, added a shilling tip.

'Thank you.'

Closing the door behind him, Esme shrugged off her lightweight pale-blue mackintosh and hung it on a hanger on the stand. 'Is Helen's room ready?'

'Jack, Martin, Katie and Lily from next door spent all yesterday evening cleaning the flat in the basement.'

'It is quite out of the question that Helen move in there. I spoke to her doctor this morning. She needs peace quiet and absolute rest, and she's not going to get that with Jack Clay around. If you get the electric fire, you can put it in her room first.'

'Mr Griffiths . . .'

'Like all men, he means well, but' – Esme looked around the hall before opening the door to the living room – 'it's obvious he's allowed this place to go to rack and ruin since I've been away.' She faced the daily head on. 'First things first, the electric fire in Helen's room. Set the mattress on its side. I'll bring in the bedclothes when I've checked the state of the airing cupboard.'

'You look great.' Jack bent over the wheelchair and kissed Helen's cheek.

'Bet you'll be glad to get her home,' the porter commented.

'You can say that again.' Pocketing the pills and prescription the sister had given him for Helen, Jack took the suitcase from the porter and held the umbrella over the chair with his free hand as the man pushed Helen out of the foyer towards the car.

John left his seat and opened the back door. Helping Helen into the car as Jack lifted her cases into the boot, he asked, 'How are you feeling?'

'Wobbly,' she admitted, ashamed of her weakness. 'And strange.'

'Strange good or bad?'

'Everything seems so cold, bright, colourful and'– she looked around – 'big.'

'That's only to be expected after you've been cooped up in an overheated hospital for the best part of a month.'

Jack folded the umbrella and tossed it on top of Helen's suitcase before slamming the boot shut.

'You sitting in the front with me, or in the back with Helen?' John climbed into the driver's seat.

'The back, Mr Griffiths.'

Under pretence of adjusting the rear-view mirror, John watched as Jack sat beside Helen and reached for her hand. She allowed him to fold it between his, but she continued to glance nervously around her, as if the world were suddenly too vast for her to take in. He gunned the ignition and switched on the windscreen wipers. 'Jack's got the flat all ready for you, love.'

'I'd rather go home.'

Struck by the panic in her voice, he looked at Jack who was staring at him in the mirror.

'Whatever Helen wants, Mr Griffiths.' Jack wrapped his arm round Helen's shoulders.

'Home it is, then.'

'Telephone call for you, Miss Sullivan.' Miss Oliver, the manager's secretary, interrupted Lily as she was taking her morning tea break in the staff room. 'You know the manager's policy on private calls during office hours. Emergencies only.'

'Yes, Miss Oliver. I'm sorry, but I've told my uncle and my friends I'm not allowed to receive calls.'

'Then we'll assume it's an emergency, shall we? You can take it at your desk.' Miss Oliver relented, granting that as it was the first private call she could recall Lily receiving at work, it might well fall into the category of 'emergency.'

'Thank you, Miss Oliver.' Lily carried her teacup to the sink.

'Leave that, Lily. I'll wash it with mine.' Marion, one of the typists, offered.

'Thanks.'

'Go on, quick, it might be the love of your life.'

Blushing, Lily walked through the office to her desk and picked up the receiver. 'Lily Sullivan.'

'Anyone would think I wanted to speak to the queen, the palaver they put me through to get to you.'

'Who is this?' she asked.

'Don't you recognise my voice?'

'No.'

'And I thought we were friends.'

'Joe, what are you doing telephoning me here? The bank doesn't allow private calls . . .'

'I had to do something to speak to you,' he broke in impatiently. 'If I didn't know any better I'd say you were avoiding me. Every time I've seen you the past couple of days you've either been with Martin or Katie . . .'

Lily glanced at her watch, there were only a couple of minutes of her tea break left and she dare not allow the call to run into her working time. 'What do you want, Joe?'

'I had no idea you could be a Miss Snappy Boots.'

'I'm in work. Did you telephone for a reason?'

'To invite you to my graduation ball.'

'I'm going out with Martin.'

'Surely he can spare you for one evening. I'm in desperate need of a date.'

'Ask someone else.'

'I don't want to. Please, Lily, it's important to me that you come. You know how hard I've worked . . .'

'No, Joe.'

'It's Martin, isn't it. He doesn't like you talking to me.'

'It's me, Joe, not Martin.' She sank down on to her chair. 'I don't want to go anywhere with you that could give the wrong impression about us.'

'To who – Martin?'

She saw Miss Oliver watching her through the glass partition. 'I have to go, Joe. Goodbye.'

John stopped the car outside his house and turned to Helen. 'I'll help Jack get you inside and see you settled . . .'

'I don't need any help from you or Jack,' Helen countered irritably. 'I've been walking around the ward now for over a week.'

'And you fainted last Wednesday.' John intercepted a perturbed look from Jack, who'd retrieved the umbrella and walked around to the driver's side of the car to open the door for Helen.

'I'm not likely to do that again. Unless there's something besides Jack's National Service that you two are keeping from me.'

'I promise you there's nothing.' Jack offered her his hand.

'Don't rush me.' She winced as the skin over her operation scar stung when she tried to leave the car. The doctor had assured her that it wasn't serious, simply her body adjusting to the healing process. But the memory of the agonising pain that had landed her in hospital was too recent and raw for her to ignore any hurt.

'I'll take your cases into the house while you get yourself together.' Handing John the umbrella, Jack lifted Helen's vanity case and suitcase from the boot and carried them to the front door. It was open, the tiled floor in the inner porch sodden and slippery with rain. Dropping the vanity case on to his knee so as not to wet it, he reached for the doorknob but the door opened before he touched it. He stepped inside and saw Esme.

'Jack.' Esme's hand fluttered upwards to pat her blonde permanent wave as she acknowledged him.

He noticed an uneasiness in Helen's mother that would have escaped him only a few short weeks before. A pulse at her temple throbbed beneath a heavier coating of make-up than he had ever seen her wear. Her mouth set into a thin line as she clenched her jaw and her eyes glittered, hard and bright, as she focused on a point somewhere to his right.

'You can leave Helen's cases here.' She indicated a spot at the foot of the stairs. 'The daily will take them up.'

Jack dropped them wordlessly.

'Is Helen going to stay in that car all day?'

Turning, he walked back to the car. John had helped Helen out and for all her assertions of independence she was clinging to his arm.

'Mrs Griffiths is in the house.' Jack eased Helen's hand from his father-in-law's arm on to his own.

'You've brought my mother back to look after me?' Helen would have fallen to the pavement if Jack hadn't put his arm round her waist to support her.

'No!' John looked at his front door.

'Then why is she here?'

'If we go inside we'll find out,' Jack muttered. The street was deserted but given the number of open skylights, he was aware that any number of people could have been listening.

'I am not going into that house while she's there,' Helen insisted adamantly.

'You need to get out of this rain.' Taking the umbrella from his father-in-law, Jack tried to shield Helen from the worst of the downpour.

'I am not going in while she's there,' Helen reiterated.

'Then go down to the flat.'

Helen thought of all the wedding presents waiting to be used, the rooms she had taken so much time and trouble to plan, the set of baby clothes she had sneaked in secretly with her trousseau and hidden in one of her handbags because she couldn't resist them. 'No!'

'Then get back into the car or go next door. If you don't get out of this rain you'll catch pneumonia.' It was the harshest speech Jack had made to her since she'd been in hospital and it had the desired effect.

'You have the keys to your and Martin's place?' she asked.

'Yes, but it's hardly comfortable.'

'It will do until my mother leaves.'

'She'll insist on seeing you, Helen, even if you hide next door. If not today, then tomorrow or next week. All you'll do is delay the inevitable.' Dreading yet another confrontation, John looked at the front door again, but if Esme was listening she was keeping out of sight.

'I won't see her.'

'That's your decision but she'll probably accuse Jack and me of keeping you from her.'

'Let her,' Helen countered defiantly.

'Legally, you're still a minor,' John reminded her.

'I'm married.'

'A married minor but still a minor,' John pointed out quietly. 'She could go to court to get access to you and then you'd have to explain to a judge why you don't want to see your own mother.'

'You expect me to talk to her? After everything she's said and done to me and Jack? She's hateful, I detest her,' she burst out furiously. 'Just the thought of being in the same room as her makes me sick.'

'Then tell her just that, love, and I'll do my best to make sure she never tries to see you again.'

'We're all getting soaked,' Jack reminded them, as Helen stood, staring at her father.

'If I see her now, it will be for the last time.'

'I can't promise you that, love,' John answered honestly.

'But you won't let her back in the house.'

'That I can promise.'

'How lovely to see you, Helen. But you are so pale. And you were so long leaving the car. Are you in pain?' Esme enquired in a nauseatingly sweet voice as, leaning on Jack's arm, Helen finally entered the house.

'No. I didn't want to come in because I didn't want to see you.'

Conscious of the daily upstairs in the bedrooms and John and Jack in the hall, Esme forced a smile. 'You don't know what you're saying, darling. You're upset . . .'

'I am only upset because you're here.'

'Helen, darling . . .'

Shrugging off her mother's hand with a force that alarmed Jack, Helen screamed, 'Go! Now! None of us wants you here.'

'Darling, you're hysterical . . .'

'Get out!' Helen's voice dropped to a whisper. 'Please, just get out.' Her anger dissipated as she burst into tears.

'I have your bedroom all ready.' Esme tried to push Jack aside but he stood firm, keeping his grip on Helen's arm. 'If you'll allow me to help my own daughter upstairs, Jack . . .'

'No!' Helen tried to push Esme away from her, but weakened by enforced bed rest she had no strength to make more than an ineffectual gesture.

'Esme, for Helen's sake, please leave.' John lifted his wife's mac from the stand.

'Don't be ridiculous. I'm her mother.'

Helen swayed on her feet as her eyes flickered closed. Scooping her into his arms, Jack shouldered the living room door open and carried her in. John picked up the telephone and began dialling. Esme followed Jack, watching from the doorway as he lowered Helen to the sofa. As soon as he was certain she was secure, he kicked the door, slamming it in Esme's face.

'Mrs Jones.'

The daily appeared on the landing, as John replaced the telephone receiver. 'Yes, Mr Griffiths.'

'Did you let Mrs Griffiths into the house?' John was speaking to the daily but he was watching Esme.

'Yes, Mr Griffiths.'

'Please don't do so again,' he ordered. 'She no longer lives here.'

'How dare you . . .'

John held up his hand to silence Esme as the daily moved back. 'Please stay, Mrs Jones.'

'Sir . . .'

'I'd take it as a personal favour. In future the only people you will allow into this house are Joe, Helen, Jack and myself. Do I make myself clear?'

'I know you and Mrs Griffiths have a private problem, Mr Griffiths,' the daily faltered. 'I hope you understand, sir, but I'd rather not get involved.'

'Unfortunately it is not private and although it might be embarrassing for you, I'd appreciate it if you remained with me until my wife leaves the house as I may need you as a witness.'

Remembering who paid her wages the woman replied, 'Yes, Mr Griffiths,' and stayed on the landing.

'And just in case you have a key, Esme, I'll call a locksmith at the first opportunity and order him to change all the outside locks.'

The doorbell rang, John opened it and ushered in the doctor.

'Where is she?'

'In the living room.' John opened the door, closing it after the doctor had entered the room.

'I should be with her.'

John blocked her path. 'I think you've done quite enough for one day.'

He stood watching Esme, aware that she was as conscious of Mrs Jones's presence upstairs as he was. He heard the doctor speak and Jack's muffled reply. After ten long minutes they heard Helen whimpering. The three of them continued to stand, silent, immobile, until the door opened and the doctor emerged.

'How is she?'

'Not good, John. She came out of the faint in a state bordering on hysteria. I had to sedate her. By rights I should send her back to hospital.'

'Then why don't you . . .'

Ignoring Esme, the doctor continued to address John. 'I'll be back before evening surgery to check on her again.'

'Thank you.'

'Jack told me he's leaving on Sunday. I can't promise anything but I'll make a couple of phone calls and try to get him a week or two's grace.' The doctor closed his bag.

'He's already had a month.'

'It's worth a try.' The doctor slipped on his coat.

'Absolutely,' John agreed.

'Keep a close eye on Helen,' he warned. 'She should sleep until late afternoon. But if she comes round to another attack like that, send for me straight away. If you can't get hold of me, then telephone for an ambulance.'

'Surely it is only hysteria.'

The doctor acknowledged Esme's presence for the first time. 'Hysteria can be dangerous, Mrs Griffiths, especially for a young girl recovering from the mental and physical trauma of the surgery your daughter has undergone. I don't know what's gone on here and I don't want to know, but Helen told me she doesn't want to see you and it was you who upset her.'

'I am her mother . . .'

'Believe me, now is not the time to try to resolve any differences you may have with your daughter.'

Esme looked from the doctor to John. 'The only problem I have is my husband setting Helen against me.'

'I've given you my professional opinion,' the doctor said coolly. 'Precipitate another attack like that one and you risk severe consequences for Helen. At the very least I'll have to return her to the hospital.'

'It seems to me that she shouldn't have been discharged today,' Esme challenged.

'And it seems to me that you should leave her alone until she has regained her health, Mrs Griffiths.' The doctor opened the door and looked at the teeming rain. Setting his hat on his head, he turned up his collar. 'You will telephone if she has another attack, John?'

'Of course and thank you.'

The doctor ran to his car.

Jack opened the living-room door and looked out into the hall.

'You wanted something?' Esme questioned.

'To carry Helen up to bed.'

'Give us a few minutes.' John waited until Jack closed the door again. 'Goodbye, Esme.'

'Shall I get your cases for you, Mrs Griffiths,' Mrs Jones called down.

John looked at his wife in disbelief. 'You brought luggage?'

'I had to move out of mother's . . .'

'So that is what this all about. You had to leave your mother's house and thought you could move back in here.'

'I was thinking of Helen.'

'Really?' he queried cynically.

'Where else am I supposed to go?'

'You have the shop and flat in Mumbles. If you don't want to live there, you have the rent from the shop and the allowance I pay you, which is sufficient to rent almost any house in Swansea.'

'Not like mother's in Langland.'

John refused to take the bait. 'Shall I call you a taxi?'

'I'll do it.'

'Take the first one you can get. Helen should be in bed and we can't risk carrying her upstairs while you are still in the house.'

'Joe, can you spare a moment?' Hilary Llewellyn asked as her students began to file out after their final tutorial before their examinations.

'Of course, Miss Llewellyn.' Joe hung back as Robin signalled that he'd wait for him.

When the room was empty apart from Joe and herself, Hilary closed the door and sat behind her desk. 'We need to discuss your work.'

'There's nothing wrong, is there?' Joe watched as she flicked through a pile of assignments on her desk.

'You tell me.' Extracting an essay he recognised as his, she slapped it in front of him. A large, glaring C had been etched on the front page in red ink. 'What's going on, Joe?'

He looked apprehensively from the essay to his tutor. He knew exactly what was going on. He had written that essay on the Brontes the morning after he had watched Martin and Lily kissing in her back garden.

She picked it up and handed it to him. 'Some students believe a C is adequate – after all, it is a pass, just – but it is totally unacceptable for a student of your intelligence, breadth of thought and capabilities to present work of this standard.'

'I'm sorry,' he stammered.

'I'm giving it to you now, so you can take another long hard look at it. If you'd care to rewrite it over the weekend and get it to me first thing on Monday morning, I'll mark it by Tuesday. I know it won't affect your degree and that you'll be studying for the examination but if this' – she tapped the paper contemptuously – 'is an indication of the standard you'll present at your finals, you had better prepare yourself for a third.'

'Yes, Miss Llewellyn.' Taking the essay, he folded it into his inside pocket.

'One more thing,' she said, as he went to the door. 'In my opinion you should also take a long hard look at the company you are keeping as well as your assignment. Robin's amusing enough, but there'll be plenty of time for drinking and parties after your finals.'

Feeling well and truly chastised, he nodded to her as he left.

'Sorry I didn't come back at lunchtime, Katie,' John apologised, as he walked into the warehouse office.

'I was just about to telephone your house to see if you were there.' She picked up her notepad and left her desk.

'There's been no problem, has there? The knitwear rep . . .'

'I sat in on the meeting and stopped the floor supervisor from doubling our normal order.'

'Thank you.'

He seemed so distracted that she asked, 'Helen isn't any worse, is she, Mr Griffiths?'

'It's a long story but she's all right now, or as all right as anyone can be when they've just come out of hospital.' Not daring to look at her, he opened the door to his office. 'Thank you for seeing to everything here. As I have some confidential work calls to make, you and Ann can leave early.'

'I'm behind with the mail because of the meeting. There are still two letters to suppliers that need typing.'

'They can wait until tomorrow. You will be in tomorrow?' he asked anxiously.

'It is my last day.' Katie opened her drawer and removed her typewriter cover. Sliding it over her machine she tidied her desk, then picked up her handbag.

'See you in the morning, Ann, Miss Clay.'

'Goodnight, sir.' Ann left before Katie but Katie didn't linger.

'Goodnight, Mr Griffiths.'

'Goodnight, Miss Clay.' John waited until Katie had closed the door, then checked the time on his watch. Picking up the telephone he dialled his solicitor's number. As he'd hoped, the secretaries had left for the day, but Mark was still working. 'Mark, John Griffiths here . . . that matter we were discussing the last time I saw you . . . Yes, something has happened . . . No, not over the telephone. I'll meet you at the Mackworth in twenty minutes. We'll discuss it then.'

Chapter 19

'HAS MY MOTHER gone?' Helen asked fretfully as she opened her eyes to see Jack sitting reading in a chair beside her bed.

He set aside his book. 'Your father put her into a taxi seven hours ago.'

'I've slept that long.' She turned on her side and looked at him. 'I can't believe I spent my first afternoon at home sleeping.'

'You obviously needed the rest.' Jack omitted all mention of the sedative the doctor had given her, as he uncovered a tray on her bedside cabinet. 'Doctor's orders, you're to eat little and often.' Shaking a towel over the front of her nightdress, he plumped the pillows behind her head, helped her sit up and put the tray on her lap. 'Chicken rolls Mrs Jones made specially, so you'd better finish them all. The bread's fresh, I bought it this morning in Eynon's before we picked you up, and there's a trifle Mrs Hunt brought for you.'

'Aren't you eating?'

'Mrs Jones made me a meal earlier.' What he didn't tell her was the meal consisted of sandwiches he'd eaten while watching her sleep because he couldn't bear the thought of her waking up alone.

As she cut one of the rolls into two, a tear fell from her eye and hit the tray. She dropped the knife. 'I don't know what's the matter with me.'

'You've been ill, you're weak, it's going to take time for you to get well.'

'And you can stop being so bloody nice. I can't stand it.'

'Language.' He grinned.

'I mean it, Jack,' she snapped. 'You didn't marry me for this.'

'For better for worse,' he reminded her.

'And all you're getting is the bloody worse.'

'Hey, I meant it about the language.'

'You've turned choirboy all of a sudden?'

'Swear all you like with me.' He steadied the tray as she fumbled under her pillow for her handkerchief, 'but if Mrs Jones or Mrs Lannon hears you, it will be all over town that Jack Clay has brought that nice, well-brought-up Helen Griffiths down to his level.'

'I couldn't give a damn.'

'Eat your rolls,' he prompted as she found her handkerchief and blew her nose.

'No.'

'I want you to get better and you won't do that until you start eating.'

'I'm too skinny for you now.'

'No, sweetheart.' He took a deep breath as he looked her in the eye. 'But you have lost a lot of weight.'

'And you wanted me to be fat. Fat with our baby . . .' Anger melted into misery as her tears began to fall again. He lifted the tray from her lap and removed it to the bedside table. Sitting next to her on the bed, he opened his arms but she shrank away from him. 'You would never have married me if it weren't for the baby and now there won't be any. Ever!'

'I would have married you no matter what.'

'No, you wouldn't have,' she contradicted fiercely.

'I love you.'

'How can you? I'm ugly and skinny and I'll never have any children . . .'

'We can adopt.'

'And they'll be queuing up to hand over a baby to an ex-Borstal boy like you.' Tired of him and her father trying to make everything come right for her when it couldn't – not ever again – she wanted to hurt him and she succeeded. She saw it in the tense lines that appeared round his mouth and the way he clenched his fists.

'Helen, we have so little time . . .'

'And whose fault is that?'

'You think I want to do my National Service?'

'I think you can't wait to get away from me.'

Biting his lip he looked towards the window.

'See, you can't even deny it,' she taunted.

'There's no point in trying to talk to you when you're in this mood.'

'I'm tired. I want to sleep.'

'You should eat first.'

'I don't want to.' Wriggling back down into the bed, she turned her face to the wall.

'Helen . . .'

'Go away and take the tray with you.'

'I'll sit with you.'

'You'd disturb me. I'd rather be alone.'

'Mrs Jones won't be happy that you didn't even take one bite of her rolls.'

'Tell Mrs Jones to go to hell.'

'The luscious Lily brushed you off again. So, what's new.' Robin sat back, nursing his pint of beer in the bar of the Antelope Hotel in Mumbles.

'I shouldn't have telephoned her at work.' Angry at his tutor's criticism of his essay and angrier still with himself for giving her cause for complaint, it had taken more persuasion than usual for Robin to get Joe to join him for a drink after college.

'She hung up on you?' Robin asked.

'She couldn't talk,' Joe answered evasively.

'Is she still seeing that other chap . . .'

'I told you, it's just a ploy to get me jealous.'

'Then give her a taste of what she's dishing out. Take another girl to the graduate ball,' Robin advised. 'I know half a dozen who'd throw over their dates if they thought they had a whiff of a chance. And that's without bringing Angie, who would dance naked on hot coals for you, into the equation.'

'I'll see Lily tonight.'

'You've made a date with her?'

'We live next door, for Christ's sake.'

'I remember,' Robin murmured softly in an attempt to defuse Joe's irritation. 'So, what are we doing tonight?'

'Studying.' Joe drank half the beer in his glass.

'You don't need to.'

'I most definitely do.'

'Come on, Joe, you got one C grade in three years. Big deal. Everyone's aware you know as much as the lecturers,' Robin consoled. 'Besides, that old adage about swotting too close to an exam is right. You'll risk addling your brains. My father had the pool cleaned out and filled last week. It's a bit cold but perhaps a swim in chilly water is what you need to clear your head.'

'Of what?' Joe asked suspiciously.

'Extraneous information superfluous to exam requirements.'

'And where did you get that phrase from?'

'Thompson.'

'He's an ass,' Joe dismissed.

'An undisputed ass,' Robin agreed, 'but unlike some, he's not putting the cart before the horse.'

'And that means what, exactly?'

'There you go, dusting off your righteous indignation again.' Robin finished his whisky chaser. 'All I'm saying is you're worried about which girl to invite to the graduate ball before we've even sat the examinations.'

'I know who I want to invite.'

'And you're going completely the wrong way about getting her.' Throwing his head back Robin went into Shakespearean declaiming mode, and quoted, '"The art of life is the avoidance of the unattainable."'

'That's Saki – and Lily is not unattainable.'

'I never said she was, and Saki got it wrong. Women flock around men they consider beyond their reach. Take Uncle Robin's advice, become unattainable and Lily will come running so fast she'll bowl you over.'

'I've already invited her to the ball.'

'She hung up on you.'

'How did you . . .'

'You just said.' Robin slipped his hand into his inside pocket and brought out his cigarette case. 'What you have to do now is put her out of your mind and concentrate on your exams. Before we've sat the last one she'll be pulling her hair out by the roots thinking you've forgotten all about her and the invitation to the ball. And by then I guarantee she will have bought the dress, matching shoes, stole, jewellery and booked a hair appointment.'

'Not Lily.'

'Then she's like no other female I've ever met.'

'And you, of course, have met them all,' Joe said caustically.

'I hope to God not.' Robin thumbed open a packet of cigarettes he'd bought along with the drinks and began to transfer them to his case. 'Lighten up. It will happen for you, just as it did me with Emily. I chased her for . . .'

'A whole hour.'

'It took a couple of days for me to get her naked,' Robin divulged.

'And now you're crowing that you're set for life as well as the ball. Well, bully for you.'

'Wrong on both scores.'

'You're not taking Emily to the ball?' Joe turned to his friend in amazement.

'I haven't decided.'

'You bought two tickets.'

'That doesn't mean Emily's coming with me.' Crumpling the empty packet into the ashtray, Robin offered Joe a cigarette.

'You two have been going out together – for what?'

'Long enough for her to take me for granted and I don't like it.' Robin lit his cigarette before tossing his lighter to Joe.

'So, if you don't take Emily, who's the unlucky lady?'

'There's a hot little redhead in second-year History.'

'Thompson's girl.'

'As was.'

'You've made a play for her.'

'Gave her the full Robin experience last night.' Robin sighed theatrically. 'She loves the car but then all girls do. Take another tip, get one like it and the gorgeous Lily will be the one doing the fawning.' He raised his eyebrows. 'She wears pale-pink knickers.'

'You got into the redhead's knickers on the first date?'

'Her, out of them,' Robin clarified. 'She is a natural redhead. You can take my word for it.'

'Does Emily know she's history?'

Robin glanced around. 'Keep your voice down. Emily's not history.'

'You can't go out with two girls at once.'

'Says who?' Robin challenged.

'Decency.'

'God, stick a broad-brimmed black hat on your head and you'd make a perfect Puritan.'

'But two girls . . .'

'They complement one another. Thanks to my expert tuition, Emily's experienced in servicing a man's needs. The redhead' – he shook his head fondly – 'is ripe, fresh and a quick learner if last night is anything to go by. I'd forgotten just how grateful a sweet little virgin can be when you take the trouble to relieve her of that particular handicap. Tell you what, if you need to take a break in the next couple of weeks and want pleasure without involvement, go for Emily. She needs it and she won't be getting enough from me.'

'You're disgusting.'

'But not frustrated. Back to my place for that swim?'

'No.'

'Angie and Em will be at college. I really do mean a swim.'

'I need to study.'

'We'll do it together. Isn't the first paper on the Metaphysical Poets?' Robin questioned artfully.

'Don't you even know that much?'

'You know me and poets.'

'And metaphysics.' Joe picked up his briefcase. 'A couple of hours, no more. I need to get back in time to talk to Lily.'

'When will you ever learn to take advice?' Robin followed Joe out through the door.

'When will you?'

'When I'm old and have nothing better to do with my time. Will you look at that blonde.' Robin whistled at a girl who was walking along the pavement. 'I'm in love,' he shouted. 'She's turned her head, quick, you get her arms, I'll grab her feet and we'll kidnap her.'

'I think not,' the blonde drawled.

'Theatre, you and me, Saturday night.' Robin beamed.

'Only if I can bring a friend.'

'Will she suit him?' He pointed to Joe.

'We're about to start our examinations . . .'

'So we'll brush up on our knowledge of theatre. Quarter to seven, foyer of the Grand. Don't be late.'

'I don't take orders.'

'I'm an expert girl tamer.' Reaching for her hand, he kissed the back of it. 'You'll be there.'

'Turn up and you'll find out.' She walked away, swishing her skirts, showing a couple of inches of white lace petticoat.

'Did you ever see legs like that?' Robin stood, mesmerised, watching her.

'Yes, and Emily's are better.'

'Alas, they're also no longer a challenge.' He flipped a coin. 'Heads you drive, tails me.'

'I didn't expect you still to be here,' Helen mumbled contritely as she stumbled out of the bathroom to find Jack remaking her bed.

'Mrs Jones has left for the day and your father rang to say he'll be late.'

'I don't need looking after.'

'I know, but I need to feel useful.'

Helen tripped over a rug and fell against him as she made her way to the bed. Her limbs felt heavy and numb, her mouth swollen from the sedative the doctor had given her.

'I was horrible to you earlier.' She could feel tears pricking at the back of her eyes.

Damned tears! Would she never stop crying?

'I noticed.'

'I didn't mean to be. It's just . . .'

Jack lowered her on to the bed and gathered her into his arms. His kindness coupled with the guilt she felt after deliberately hurting him earlier was too much for her to bear. She burst into tears but her sobs were unmarred by the hysteria of the morning. Jack continued to sit and hold her, stroking her hair and murmuring soft words of comfort, until the shadows lengthened and he realised that although her eyes were wet, she slept.

'I said presentable, I didn't expect eye-bogglingly glamorous,' Adam complimented Judy as she emerged from the Ladies cloakroom in a strapless silver taffeta ball gown with matching stole.

'It's my mother's,' she whispered. 'She wore it to last year's Chamber of Commerce Christmas ball. I only hope no one recognises it.'

'As no one here is a member of the Chamber of Commerce I think your secret is safe.' He offered her his arm. 'We're sitting at a table with a few people I work with. How would you like to be introduced?'

'As a friend.' She glanced back at the crowd milling around the cloakroom. She was grateful that her mother had offered to lend her the evening frock, as nothing in her own wardrobe came up to the standard of the gowns most of the other women were wearing.

Adam led her to a large circular table laid for twelve in the middle of the room.

'Wendy.' He smiled at a middle-aged woman who was already sitting down. 'I'd like you to meet a friend of mine, Judy Hunt.'

'That is a lovely dress, Judy,' the woman gushed enthusiastically. 'Wherever did you buy it?'

'I'll get us some drinks, Judy, what would you like?' he asked before Judy had time to reply.

'A Babycham, please.'

Adam went to the bar; it took him a few minutes to push his way through the crush to the front. Leaning forward when it was his turn to be served, he collared the barman. 'A pint of best, please, and a double vodka and Babycham – in the same glass.'

'Em, come here, quick. You won't believe it if you don't see it for yourself.' Angela Watkin Morgan stood at the door of the conservatory and stared at her brother and Joe, stretched out side by side on matching rattan chairs and footstools surrounded by piles of books.

'Go and play somewhere else, Angie, and let the grown-ups study.'

'"Study!" The one word I never thought I'd hear my brother say.' She placed her hand on Robin's forehead. 'Robin, darling, are you ill?'

'No.' Brushing Angela's hand aside, Robin cringed as Emily threw herself on to his lap. 'You're no lightweight, Em, get off.' Despite his protest he made no effort to push her away.

Angela snatched the book Joe was holding and closed it. '*The Metaphysical Poets and John Hall*,' she read slowly.

'We can read the title for ourselves.' Robin came up for air after Emily had pressed him back into the chair and poked her tongue in his mouth.

'Ah, but do you understand it?' Angie perched on the arm of Joe's chair.

'Naturally,' Robin answered.

'Then you two can tell Em and me *all* about it.'

'Robin can.' Joe rose to his feet. Angie didn't move and the chair would have toppled over if he hadn't steadied it. 'I should have left hours ago.'

'Stay the night,' Robin offered. 'We could brainstorm . . .'

'Do,' Angie pleaded, 'Mums and Pops are going to be ever so late. We could play murder.'

'I know your idea of playing murder.'

'No you don't, Joe. You haven't played with me for years and I've grown up in that time.'

'What's the point in growing up if it only makes you even more childish?'

'You're in danger of becoming a bore.' Angela pouted.

'Probably.' Joe reached for his tie and jacket. 'But my sister came out of hospital today and I should spend some time with her.'

'She has her husband.'

'Not for long.'

'Jack is leaving her?' Angie's eyes glittered as she flopped down in the seat he'd vacated and Joe realised she'd been drinking.

'Only to do his National Service.'

'That can take years.'

'Two to be precise.'

'Study tomorrow?' Robin asked, as Joe shrugged on his jacket.

'If we make it my place.'

'OK.'

'Spoilsports.' Angie continued to glare at Joe.

'We can't concentrate when you two are around,' Joe said flatly.

'I'll take that as a compliment.' Emily burrowed under Robin's sweater.

'Want the car?' Robin tossed the keys to Joe, who caught them neatly and threw them back.

'No thanks, I'll walk.'

'Walk!'

'It's only a couple of miles, Angie.' Joe laughed at the stricken expression on her face.

'I can think of better ways of exercising.' Robin slid his hand up the front of Emily's sweater.

'No naughties in front of Angie and Joe,' she squealed, playfully slapping him down.

'Bye.' Realising he'd drifted past tiredness into mental exhaustion, Joe threw his books into his briefcase, opened the door and walked through to the hall.

'I'll see you out.' Angela tottered after him on high heels.

'I'm amazed you can walk on those.' Joe lifted his raincoat from the stand.

'I can't.' She giggled. Turning her ankle, she fell against him, wrapping her arms round his chest to steady herself.

'You're drunk,' he admonished, breathing in brandy fumes.

'Only a teensy weensy ickle bit.' Flinging her arms round his neck she purred, 'If you stay we could be naughty too.'

'I take it you and Em couldn't find anyone at the party to be naughty with.'

'Plenty, but that was at the party. This is now.'

'Try me again when you are sober.'

'Really?' She tried, and failed, to focus on him.

'If you remember.'

'What?' she called after him as he opened the door.

'This conversation.' He closed the door behind him.

'Would you like to come in for coffee?'

'I ought to go home.' The street spun round Judy as she clung unsteadily to Adam's arm.

'Your mother knows the dance isn't over until two.' Adam glanced at his watch. 'It's not even twelve yet.'

'I'm sorry . . .'

'Don't be, I'd had enough too. That room was hot and stuffy.'

As Adam led her down the steps of his parents' basement Judy felt as though her feet were sinking into thick gluey layers of bread dough. 'I can't understand why I feel so ghastly.' She fought the sense of unreality that had settled over her halfway through the evening. 'I've had four Babychams, it's only one more than I have most Saturdays . . .'

'You'll be fine after a cup of coffee.' Opening the door, Adam led her inside, through the kitchen and into the sitting room. 'Make yourself at home.'

Judy looked around as he switched on a sofa lamp. 'Your mother . . .'

'Didn't I tell you? Her and my dad have gone down to my gran's caravan in Trecco Bay for the week. They always do at this time of year.' He looked down at her. 'I'll get that coffee.'

As he left the room, Judy leaned her head against the back of the sofa. She felt befuddled, queasy and tired. She closed her eyes and instantly felt much better. A few minutes' rest, a cup of coffee and she would be ready to go home – and face her mother.

'I wasn't expecting to see you tonight,' Martin grumbled sleepily as Jack switched on their bedroom light.

'Sorry, I didn't realise you were in bed.'

Martin squinted, one-eyed, at the clock. 'Where else would I be at one in the morning?'

'I didn't think.'

'Why aren't you with Helen?'

'Because she's ill and I'd disturb her.' Jack pulled his tie off without undoing the knot and threw it on to the chair.

'You are seeing her tomorrow?' Martin pressed, wondering if they'd quarrelled.

'I promised Mr Griffiths I'd go in before eight. He wants to go into the warehouse and she can't be left on her own.'

'And after Sunday morning?'

'The doctor tried to get me another extension on compassionate grounds but the army wouldn't have it. Mr Griffiths did say something about asking their daily to work a few more hours but he hasn't yet.'

'Everything is all right between you and Helen?'

'Apart from her being ill. Why shouldn't it be?' Jack stepped out of his trousers and folded them along the creases.

'Because you have to catch the ten-o'clock train out of Swansea on Sunday morning and you don't know when you'll be back.'

'You said yourself that everyone gets leave after their training.'

'Yes but . . .'

Jack pulled his pyjamas from under his pillow. 'It's late.'

'That didn't seem to bother you when you came in.'

'Because I didn't know just how late it was. I'm tired, Martin, I have to get up in the morning.'

'And I don't!' Martin exclaimed indignantly.

'It's your half-day.'

'You don't even have to work.'

'I don't want a bloody argument.'

Martin glared at his brother before turning his back and closing his eyes.

Jack switched off the light, climbed into bed and followed Martin's example, but exhausted as he was, sleep eluded him. Crossing his arms beneath his head, he stared up at the ceiling and went over the day. *And they'll be queuing up to hand over a baby to an ex-Borstal boy like you.* Helen's angry, bitter words burned in his mind. He had made her pregnant, it was his fault that she had spent four weeks in hospital and he couldn't even give her the child she longed for through adoption. And now, just when she needed him most, he had to leave her for two years.

What hope was there for them to have any kind of a future together?

Judy shivered as a draught of cold air blew across her breasts. Brian was on top of her, caressing her, murmuring soft words of endearment. A warm tide of weakening relief coursed through her body. Everything was all right between them. It had to be for him to be with her again.

She felt his lips, warm, tantalising, as he kissed her nipples, teasing them to peaks. The boned bodice of her dress was sticking uncomfortably between them but as it was loose, she realised that he must have unzipped it. Folding it back to the waist, she eased herself upwards to allow him to pull the gown from her. It fell to the floor in a swish of starched underskirts brushing against taffeta, as his hand slid up her leg to her stocking top. She was about to stop him when she remembered she had asked him to make love to her.

Knotting her fingers into his hair, she kissed his forehead as he continued to caress her breasts. Her suspenders snapped. Rolling her corset to her waist, his fingers stroked the soft, sensitive skin on the flat of her stomach, as his lips travelled upwards. They pressed down warm on hers as his tongue entered her mouth.

His hand slid into her knickers and pulled them down. It was what she'd told him she wanted but she was suddenly afraid as he rolled on top of her, then, as a strange, new, all-consuming passion began to burn, she didn't want him to stop.

'You awake?' Katie asked Lily as she heard Roy walk up the second flight of stairs to his attic bedroom.

'I wish I weren't.' Lily shifted restlessly in the bed. 'I have to be in the bank all bright-eyed and keen to take dictation at half past eight tomorrow morning.'

'Be grateful you only work every other Saturday.'

'You get every Thursday afternoon off,' Lily reminded her.

'When everything's shut and there's nothing to do,' Katie complained.

'Will you be working the same hours in Lewis Lewis?'

'Every other Saturday off, like you.'

'Great. If we manage to get the same Saturdays off, we can go shopping together . . .'

'If I take the job.' Katie didn't even want to think about leaving the warehouse tomorrow for her new job at Lewis Lewis.

'You're having second thoughts?'

Katie slipped out of bed and reached for her dressing gown. 'Want a cup of cocoa?'

'And a cheese sandwich.'

'A picnic at' — Katie screwed up her eyes as she switched on the light — 'half past one in the morning,' she whispered, when she was finally able to focus on the alarm clock.

'If we're going to be awake we may as well be awake with full stomachs.' Lily felt under the bed with her feet for her slippers. Sliding into them, she lifted her dressing gown from its hook and threw it over her shoulders. Holding her finger to her lips, she eased open their bedroom door.

The largest bedroom had been her Auntie Norah's. Bay-windowed, built over the living room at the front of the house, it had remained untouched since her aunt's death four months before, as neither she nor her Uncle Roy could face sorting through Norah's personal possessions. She and Katie shared the room that had always been hers. Built over the kitchen, it faced the back of the house. Mrs Lannon occupied the third room on the first floor. Set between hers and Norah's, it also faced the back of the house. They tiptoed down the stairs, mindful of the housekeeper, who possessed an uncanny ability to tune in to whatever they were doing, particularly when it was something she could disapprove of, only daring to breathe again when they gained the kitchen.

'You make the sandwiches, I'll make the cocoa.' Katie closed the door quietly behind them.

'Have you told Lewis Lewis you're starting on Monday?'

'They wouldn't have offered me the job if I hadn't.'

'You won't be their favourite person if you back out now.' Lily lifted the bread bin on to the kitchen table.

'I know.' Taking a bottle of milk from the marble slab in the pantry, Katie tipped half a pint into a saucepan and set it on the stove to boil.

'Have you spoken to Mr Griffiths again?'

'Only at work and as Ann is in the office all the time with us I have to be careful what I say. When he came in at the end of today he looked so exhausted, all I wanted to do was make him a cup of tea and tell him to put his feet up. I'm concerned about him. He never complains, but he's not well. His scars ache dreadfully and he's worried about Helen . . .'

It was most peculiar to hear Katie discuss John Griffiths in such an intimate, possessive way. Mr Griffiths had always been a slightly remote figure, as befitted the father of a close friend, but Helen was someone she could talk about. 'We can help by going to see Helen after Jack leaves on Sunday.' Lily cut one cheese sandwich, eased it on to a plate and offered it to Katie.

'That may take some of the burden from John at home but it won't help him in the office.'

'He has taken on a new secretary.'

'Yes, but you should have seen some of the application letters that came in.' Katie stirred the milk as it came to the boil. 'The girls couldn't even spell, let alone type. It was like wading through the examples they used to show us in college on how not to do things. And I'm not sure the girl who got the job is up to it.'

'And that's why you want to stay in the warehouse.'

'That's only part of it,' Katie admitted

'Now the time's actually come, you don't want to leave, even though he more or less told you to go,' Lily guessed.

'He only told me to get out of his life on a private level.'

'Oh, Katie, you were the one who said you couldn't stand working with him the way things are between you.'

'I know, but the thought of not seeing him at all is even worse.' Katie reached for her handkerchief and blew her nose.

'You're disgraceful!' The door burst open and Mrs Lannon stood before them in a knee-length, pink-flowered winceyette nightdress, with metal hair curlers screwed into every inch of her iron-grey hair.

'What's disgraceful, Mrs Lannon?' Katie asked, genuinely mystified.

'You carrying on like this, at this time in the morning, wearing nothing but your nighties.' Storming in, she flung open the pantry door, slamming it angrily when she found no one inside. 'If those boys are outside . . .' She unlocked the back door and stepped on to the metal staircase that led down into the garden.

'There's no one here but us, Mrs Lannon.' Lily made an effort to keep her temper in check after the warning she'd received from her uncle.

'Sorry if we disturbed you, Mrs Lannon, but we couldn't sleep,' Katie explained. 'Would you like a cup of cocoa?'

'I most certainly would not, at this ungodly hour, Katie Clay.' Purple-faced, Mrs Lannon turned to Lily. 'What do you think your uncle would say if he could see you now?'

'He'd probably ask us to apologise for waking you, Mrs Lannon, but we didn't mean to make a noise. That's why we came down here.'

'I've half a mind to wake him.'

'Please don't,' Lily pleaded, 'he's only just gone to bed.'

'So you do have the grace to be afraid . . .'

'I'm afraid for his health. Working afternoons can make him overtired and he only went to bed a short time ago.'

'Then we'll see what he thinks about this in the morning.' She stood, looking at them. 'Well, come on, up you go.'

'Now! But we've just made sandwiches and cocoa,' Katie protested.

'You don't think I'm going to allow you to eat and drink down here with those boys only a floor below.'

'They're probably fast asleep.'

'And two of them are my brothers,' Katie broke in.

'I'm not going to put up with your cheek. Up to bed this minute, both of you. And leave the dishes in your bedroom. I'll clear them tomorrow.'

'We'll eat down here,' Lily snapped, deciding that despite her uncle's pleas she couldn't take any more of Mrs Lannon's carping.

'Well! If that's all the gratitude I'm going to get for everything I've done for you and your uncle, miss, I'm . . .' She stared at Lily. If she was hoping to intimidate her she was disappointed. Lily gazed coolly back. 'I'll speak to your uncle in the morning.' Gathering the remains of her dignity, Mrs Lannon swept out of the kitchen.

Chapter twenty

'JUDY! JUDY!'

As someone shook her roughly by the shoulder, Judy tried opening her eyes but her eyelids were simply too heavy.

'Judy it's two o'clock. Your mother is going to be wondering where you are.'

She sat up stiffly. Every inch of her ached as if she'd been trampled on.

'Your dress is here.' Adam picked it up from the floor and put it in her hands.

She finally opened her eyes to see Adam, his unfamiliar living room, the wedding portrait of his parents taken a quarter of a century before. 'Brian,' she whispered, 'Brian was here . . .'

'He wasn't,' Adam interrupted harshly, turning away from her. He hadn't intended for things to go so far between them but then she had so obviously wanted it to happen – hadn't she?

'I thought you were Brian.' She looked down and saw that she was practically naked and there was dried blood on her thighs.

'There's a bathroom in the lean-to. You'd better clean yourself up before you go home.' His hands shook as he opened a packet of cigarettes.

'You raped me . . .'

'I could accuse you of the same. You were all over me. Even at the dinner dance you couldn't keep your hands off me. And there's plenty of witnesses who'll say just that.'

'You're not even my boyfriend.'

'No, Judy, I'm not.' He tilted his head defiantly. 'But I've put one over on him. The next time you see him you can tell him that I got my own back for that joke he played on me.'

'Joke . . .' She trembled as the full impact of what had happened hit her. 'I don't understand.'

'That perfume and lipstick you gave him. Those kisses Brian painted on my chest – and other places – on Jack's stag night.'

'That wasn't Brian. Katie gave Jack the lipstick and scent. It was Jack . . .'

Sick to the pit of his stomach, unable to face the horror-struck expression in her eyes, Adam turned away. 'You'd better hurry up in the bathroom if you don't want your mother to worry about you.'

Joe hesitated as he reached the junction of Calvert Terrace and Mansel Street. He felt in his pocket. The keys to the basement were on his keyring because he entered the house that way when he borrowed his father's car and parked it in the garage at the back of the house. His father had warned him he would have to walk round the block once Jack and Helen moved into the flat but that hadn't happened and Lily's bedroom was at the back of the house. Not that he thought she'd be up at that time in the morning but . . .

Walking purposefully up Verandah Street, he turned down the back lane. Darkness closed around him and he slowed his pace, giving his eyes time to become accustomed to the gloom. Fixing his attention on the ground, he trod carefully and didn't raise his head until he neared Lily's house.

He stopped, mesmerised by the sight of her perched on the window seat of her kitchen. She was leaning against one side of the bay, her knees drawn up to her chest. He lingered, taking in every inch of her diminutive, slim figure, imprinting it, and the clothes she was wearing, on his memory. From the way the royal-blue candlewick dressing gown that she'd thrown carelessly over turquoise peddle-pusher pyjamas draped round her, to the tiny bows on the ballet-type slippers she was wearing. Her ankles were crossed and she was holding a blue and white striped breakfast cup, resting it on one knee. Her long dark hair fell to her waist, plaited loosely over one shoulder. If he'd been there he would have loosened it, run his fingers through the thick waves . . .

He could almost smell the lemon-scented shampoo she used as it mingled with the delicate perfume of her skin cream and her favoured fragrance, Lily of the Valley. Feel the cool, silky texture of her skin beneath his fingertips . . .

Oblivious to his presence, she continued to gaze out into the night. He caught a glimpse of someone moving in the room behind her but he only had eyes for Lily. Leaning against the garden wall, he fumbled blindly for his cigarettes, pushing one between his lips, too engrossed with her image to look for his lighter. When she finally left the seat and moved too far inside the room for him to see her, he remained staring at the window even after the light was switched off. A flicker of landing light glimmered through a bedroom door on the floor above the kitchen. His heart quickened when a lamp was lit and he realised it was her bedroom. But the curtains were closed.

He imagined her moving around behind them: slipping off the candlewick dressing gown and hanging it on a hook on the back of the door, sitting on the bed and removing her slippers, turning back the bedclothes . . .

The light went out a full five minutes before he visualised her getting into bed. The back of her house plunged into darkness, yet he remained focused on her bedroom window. He imagined her lying between crisp white linen sheets that smelled of lavender and ironing. Her lustrous black plait curled on the pillow beneath her head, her arm resting outside the blankets, her lips slightly parted as she breathed softly through her mouth . . .

The sky paled, the birds began to sing and he forced himself from his reverie. Shivering, he walked the few steps to his garden gate. Some day he wouldn't be exiled to the bottom of her garden, but sharing her bedroom, and neither of them would sleep. They would spend entire nights making love – slowly, tenderly erotically – and they would confide their hopes, dreams and thoughts. There would be no secrets – not between them. Together they would plan their lives and in the morning they would open the curtains to the sun and begin to live out their dreams.

'You and Mrs Lannon had another run-in, Lily?' Roy asked as she ran downstairs.

Lily checked she had everything she needed in her handbag and lifted her jacket from the hall stand. 'She didn't waste any time telling you.'

'She knocked on my door and handed me a letter at six o'clock this morning.'

'I'm sorry, Uncle Roy.'

'So am I.' Tying the belt on his dressing gown, he went into the kitchen. 'Tea and toast?'

'Please. All Katie and I were doing was making cocoa and

sandwiches because we couldn't sleep and she accused us of hiding the boys up here.'

'I don't think she's convinced they weren't here, even now.' He cut two slices of bread and dropped them on to the grill.

'It's absurd.'

'What's absurd is me thinking it was going to work out between you and a woman like that. Norah always used to say she was the most narrow-minded creature in the street.'

'Then why did you ask her to be your housekeeper?'

'Because beggars can't be choosers, love, and I couldn't think of anyone else who'd take the job.' He spooned tea into the pot. 'Unfortunately, now we're back where we started.'

'She's given in her notice?'

'Packed her bags and moved back into her own house at seven o'clock this morning.'

'Because of what I said to her last night?'

'Because of what I said to her this morning when she accused you of . . .'

'Being a tart.' She set two cups, saucers and plates on the table.

'That's not the word she used. She will gossip about you, love.'

'No one who cares about me will listen.' She folded her jacket over the back of a chair. 'Can Katie and I look after the house now?'

'You'll have to until I get someone else. In the meantime Mrs Hunt and Judy are moving in and I'm moving out into Mrs Hunt's.' He turned the toast. 'I telephoned Joy early this morning and she agreed it was the best solution. If you and Katie were to move in with her and Judy it would look as if you'd done something wrong and I was punishing you.'

'I'm sorry . . .'

'So am I but with Mrs Lannon back in her own house next door but one and watching your and Katie's every move, and the boys living downstairs, it's as well to have a respectable woman sleeping in the house.'

'I'm truly sorry. It's not fair on you or Mrs Hunt.'

'No, it's not, but it's only until we can work out a better solution.' He smiled. 'Just don't keep Joy awake tonight with your picnics. You know how hard she works in that hairdresser's on Saturdays.'

'How is Helen?' John stopped the doctor as he walked down the stairs.

'Much better this morning.' The doctor looked at him thoughtfully. 'Can I have a word, John?'

'Of course.' John opened the door to the living room. 'Can I get you something, tea, coffee?'

'Nothing, thank you.' The doctor put his bag on the floor and sat on the sofa. 'I've been thinking about Helen. Have you considered suggesting that she and Jack adopt a child?'

'No.' John sat in the chair opposite him. 'There's so much red tape involved and she and Jack are young . . .'

'She could opt for a private adoption. I could arrange it.'

John looked at the doctor in surprise.

'We – the partners in the practice, that is – have arranged dozens over the years and all of them have worked extremely well.'

'How exactly would they go about it?' John asked cautiously.

'It's very simple. We match childless couples to pregnant women who can't keep their child. I'll be perfectly honest: most of the mothers are young and unmarried – some under sixteen. Terrified of the disgrace of giving birth to an illegitimate child, they don't confide in their families or come to us until they can no longer hide their pregnancy. I have three such patients in my care at the moment. If Jack and Helen are prepared to take any baby, I can match them with a prospective mother right away. If they have a preference for a boy or girl it may take a little longer.'

'You don't want references or checks?'

'How long have we known one another, John?' the doctor asked.

'More years than I care to remember.'

'Quite; enough said. There will be a few expenses. We like to house the mothers in a discreet boarding house rather than a Salvation Army hostel and deliver the babies in a private clinic. It ensures privacy for the girls and better health monitoring for both the mother and the baby. You will also need the services of a solicitor. Either one of my partners or myself will become the legal guardian of the child at birth, we will arrange for it to be fostered by Helen as soon as it can leave the clinic, which will pave the way for formal adoption to take place, usually when the child is a couple of months old. In my experience the bills rarely come to more than a hundred pounds, but then' – he smiled wryly – 'Helen and Jack will be left with the expense of bringing up the child. Naturally, each party will remain completely anonymous to the other.'

'What about an arrangement fee?'

'There is none.' The doctor rose to his feet.

'You do this for nothing?'

'To assuage my conscience. When I was training I spent six months working on a gynaecological ward in Balham. We averaged between ten and twelve deaths a month from backstreet abortions on women desperate enough to risk their health and their lives to rid themselves of a child and that was without all the women who became sterile, or crippled. Twenty years on it's no better. There's four women dying in Swansea Hospital right this minute from septicaemia introduced by knitting needles and Omo douches. And women will continue to die until we change the law.'

'Legalise abortion!' John was shocked by the thought.

'You'd rather women continued to die?' He tipped his hat as he walked to his car. 'Let me know what Helen and Jack decide.'

'You look ill . . .'

'It's probably something I ate at the dinner dance last night,' Judy lied. 'The chicken tasted funny.'

'You shouldn't have eaten it,' Joy lectured.

'I didn't, after the first bite.' Judy picked up her handbag. 'I have to get to the shop.'

'You can't work if you're ill,' Joy admonished.

'The salon's only just opened. How many customers do you think I'll keep if I don't open on a fully booked Saturday?'

'You have to eat something,' Joy shouted as Judy ran down the passage.

'I'll grab something on the way.'

Joy sighed as she poured herself a second cup of tea. She had hoped that Judy's date with Adam would go some way to help her forget Brian, but if anything, Judy looked more miserable than the day he'd left for London.

'No! No! No!'

Terrified that Helen was about to become hysterical again, Jack lifted the breakfast tray he'd brought up for her from the bed and tried to hold her in an attempt to calm her down but she thrust him away.

'I lost my baby!' she screamed at her father. 'Don't you understand, I lost *my* baby a child that would have been *my* son and your grandson. It's not like I lost a purse or a handbag. You can't just go out and buy me a replacement . . .'

'Your father was only trying to help us, sweetheart.' Jack fought to keep his own feelings in check lest he add to Helen's misery.

'Stop it!' Helen glared at him. 'I don't want the two of you trying to make me feel better. I don't want to feel better, I want to . . . I want to . . .' As she dissolved into tears, Jack folded his arms round her, pulling her even closer, while she fought to push him away. Finally she laid her head on his shoulder and shuddered in paroxysms of grief as great rasping sobs tore from her throat.

John looked helplessly at Jack. 'I'm sorry. I only wanted to help . . .'

'I know, Mr Griffiths, and thank you for trying.'

Turning aside, John stole from the room and closed the door softly behind him. The only consolation he could draw from the tragedy that had befallen his daughter was the remarkable strength Jack had found to handle it. He just hoped Helen would be able to cope when she found herself alone.

'Your father meant well, sweetheart.' Jack wiped the tears from Helen's eyes and brushed her hair away from her face.

'I know . . . it's just that . . .' she faltered as she looked up at him.

'I'm going away, you need to get your strength back and although somewhere in the future there'll be the right baby, now is not the perfect time for us to become a family.'

'You really believe that?' she asked seriously.

'That there'll be the right baby for us one day? Yes.' Leaning against the headboard, he cradled her in his arms. 'It wasn't just you who lost the baby, sweetheart, it was us. And I meant what I said in the hospital: much as I wanted the baby, I want and need you more. I couldn't live without you.'

'But you're going to have to and I don't know how I'm going to get through the next two years . . .'

'There'll be leaves and letters. Martin said it goes really quickly.'

'And you believe him.' She snuggled down on his chest.

'Not right now, I don't. But we'll get through it somehow.'

'I do love you,' she said earnestly.

'And I love you. Don't be too hard on your father. He thought he was doing the right thing in talking to the doctor and it's good to know that when I finish in the army we'll be able to adopt a baby if we want to.'

'"If we want to" makes it sound as if you don't,' she murmured hesitantly.

'I want time alone with you first.' He stroked her arm.

'You wouldn't have had that if I hadn't lost the baby.'

'No, I wouldn't have,' he agreed. 'But as you said to your father, we can't replace our baby with another. To us he was very real even though he wasn't born. There may be others but there'll never be the one we talked about.'

She looked up at him. 'Jack, what I said about you being a Borstal boy . . .'

'Was true.'

'I still shouldn't have said it.'

'Forget it, sweetheart.'

'I wish I could. You've been so wonderful and I've been so horrible. And the doctor said we can't even make love and that's so important to a man . . .'

'It's not to a woman?' he interrupted apprehensively.

'Of course it is. It's just that I feel so weak and helpless and . . .'

'Cry it out, sweetheart.' He reached for his handkerchief as her tears soaked his shirt, grateful that this time they were silent. There had to be an end to grief, he only wished it were in sight.

'Lily, how thoughtful! I take it they're for Helen.' Joe opened the front door of his father's house on Saturday afternoon to find her standing on the step holding a bunch of anemones.

'How is she?'

'Better, or so Jack says,' he hedged. He had heard his sister crying early that morning but since then the house had been relatively silent and he had been too much of a coward to go near her, or do more than enquire how she was when Jack came downstairs at intervals to fetch food and drink. He stepped back. 'Do come in.'

'It's time for another coffee.' Robin left the dining room carrying two mugs. 'Hello, gorgeous Lily.' He raised his eyebrows as Lily turned her back to him so Joe could help her off with her jacket.

'Hello, Robin,' she answered, as Joe hung her coat on the hall stand.

'Long time no see.'

'Robin and I are studying,' Joe interrupted, giving Robin a hard look in the hope of warning him off making any more embarrassing comments.

'Don't let me disturb you.' She retrieved the flowers Joe had laid on the stairs.

'We appear to be taking a break.' Robin beamed as he leaned against the passage wall.

'Weren't you making coffee?' Joe reminded him.

Robin looked down at the mugs he was holding. 'So I was. Would you like a cup, Lily?'

'No, thank you, I only called to see Helen.'

'Helen and I thought we heard your voice.' Jack looked down at her from the landing.

'Can I come up?' She smiled at Jack with genuine pleasure and Joe's heartbeat quickened. If only she would smile at him again that way.

'Do. Helen will be pleased to see you. I'm making tea. Would you like a cup?' He ran down the stairs.

'I'd love one, thank you.'

'You'll let Jack make you tea but you won't let me make you coffee,' Robin reproached her.

'You're busy studying.'

As Jack followed Robin into the kitchen, Joe seized his opportunity. 'Are you going to the Pier tonight, Lily?'

'No.'

'How about next week?' he pressed.

'I have no idea what I'll be doing.'

'We could go for another walk . . .'

'Martin and I have made plans for next week, Joe. If you'll excuse me, I can't wait to see Helen.' Turning, she ran up the stairs.

'They're lovely, I'll get Jack to put them in water.' Helen laid the flowers Lily had given her on her pillow.

'I can do it.' Lily picked them up.

'No, stay and talk to me.' Helen grabbed her friend's hand. 'I feel as though I haven't spoken to you or Katie in years. What's the gossip?'

'I'm not sure where to start.' Lily lifted the dressing-table stool close to the bed. Even if she'd been at liberty to do so, she could hardly begin by telling Helen that Katie had fallen in love with her father and was leaving the warehouse, or Judy hadn't heard a word from Brian since he left. 'Uncle Roy and Mrs Hunt have fixed the date for the second Saturday in July,' she began, deciding it was the safest topic.

'Are we all invited to the wedding?'

'I think so. Mrs Hunt's having a small reception in her house afterwards.'

'That will be nice.' Helen thought for a moment. 'Are they going to live in your house?'

'No. Uncle Roy's moving in with Mrs Hunt.'

'So you and Katie are staying in your house with Mrs Lannon.'

'Not exactly.'

Helen raised her eyebrows.

'I quarrelled with her.'

'You quarrelled with Mrs Lannon!'

Jack heard Helen cry out as he carried a tray up the stairs. He hurried forward, then realised it was all right. Helen was actually laughing for the first time since she had left hospital. 'What's funny?' He set down the tray on the dressing table.

'Helen thinks it hilarious that Katie and I annoyed Mrs Lannon so much she moved out of my uncle's house this morning.'

'What did you do to her?' He placed Helen's tea on her bedside cabinet.

'Have a midnight – or rather a two o'clock in the morning – feast.'

'Is that all?' He handed her a cup of tea.

'You expected more?'

'Not from you and Martin.' He grinned cheekily.

'You . . .'

Helen sat up suddenly in bed. 'I've just had a fantastic idea.'

'Whatever it is, I think you should settle down,' Jack frowned.

'Now that Mrs Hunt and Constable Williams are getting married, Judy, Katie and Lily can move into the house in Limeslade to keep me company while you're away.'

'What house?' Lily shifted the stool so Jack could sit on the bed.

'A house I've inherited from my grandmother.' Helen threw back the bedclothes. 'We'll go and look at it right now.'

'We most certainly will not.' Jack rescued the tea from Helen's bedside table before she knocked it over.

'Yes, we will.' She stuck out her tongue at him.

'And how are we going to get there?' he asked.

'Joe can go down to the warehouse and borrow Dad's car. He can drive us there and Lily will help me dress. You will, won't you,' Helen demanded, as Lily looked helplessly from her to Jack.

'I . . .'

'And you'll be able to see it before you leave tomorrow, so you'll know what you're coming back to, Jack,' Helen continued excitedly.

'There'll be plenty of time for me to see it when I get leave, after my training,' Jack protested.

'But I want to see it now,' Helen countered.

'And the flat?' he asked, in an attempt to distract her.

'It's stupid to live in a flat when we own a house.'

'Helen, this is madness.' He steadied her as she staggered out of bed.

'Go down and tell Joe to get the car.'

'He's studying.'

'He won't mind. Go on . . .'

'If I'm going anywhere, I'm telephoning the doctor.'

'Then I'll get a taxi to take me to Limeslade before he gets here.' She glared defiantly.

'You're bloody impossible, you know that?' Conceding, he opened the door. 'You'll look after her, Lily, while I talk to Joe?'

'As much as anyone can when she's in this mood.'

'I'll wear my Aran sweater and green slacks, Lily, that way I don't have to worry about stockings and suspenders.'

It was John, not Joe, who drove Jack, Helen and Lily to Limeslade. Joe volunteered as soon as he heard that Lily was going, but finding the atmosphere of Katie's last day in the warehouse and the endless procession of people who trooped up from the shop floor with small gifts for her more than he could bear, John insisted on driving. Much against his better judgement, as he told Helen when she categorically refused to listen to his and Jack's pleas that she remain in bed.

The weather couldn't have been more idyllic as John turned off the narrow coast road and in through the gates at the side of the house. The sky was a pale, washed blue, there wasn't a cloud in sight and the sun shone down, sprinkling the crests of the waves in the bay below with glittering prisms of reflected light.

Clutching the door key, Helen looked eagerly out of the car window as the house and garden came into view. 'It's beautiful, isn't it?' she asked no one in particular.

'It will be just as beautiful in a week or two,' John agreed drily.

'I can't wait to show it to you, Jack.'

'Why don't you and Jack go inside first,' John suggested tactfully, 'while Lily and I look over the garden.'

'Thanks, Dad.' She opened the door and stepped out before Jack had a chance to walk round the car to help her.

John shook his head and exchanged worried glances with Jack, as Jack offered Helen his arm. 'I wish she weren't so headstrong,' he murmured, as much to himself as Lily.

'With Jack going away, this house may be just what she needs to keep herself from brooding, Mr Griffiths.'

'I hope you're right.' He turned to Lily. 'Right, young lady, would you like a tour of the garden?'

'Yes, please.' Embarrassed, she turned away as he clambered awkwardly out of the car. It wasn't simply his crippled leg and scars. Ever since Katie had confided that she loved him and they'd had an affair, she hadn't been able to stop herself from picturing her friend and John Griffiths together and although she couldn't explain why, it made her feel uneasy – and a little afraid for Katie.

'It's perfect, isn't it, Jack,' Helen enthused. 'I mean, we could move in here right now, this minute . . .'

He sniffed. 'It smells musty.'

'The smell will go as soon as we open the windows.'

'Is the furniture yours as well?' He looked at the solid, old-fashioned pine pieces in the kitchen, and the Victorian mahogany dining set and Rexene-covered sofa and chairs.

'*Ours*, together with two hundred and fifty pounds and some stocks and shares,' she corrected blithely, walking from the kitchen into the dining room, into the living room and back. 'Come on, I want to see upstairs.' She dived into the hall, only to pause before the stairs.

'Grip the banister with one hand and take my arm with the other,' he ordered, seeing her blanch.

Reluctantly, she took the arm he offered. 'Can't you just see us living here?' she gasped, as she climbed the stairs.

'You're in pain.' His forehead furrowed in concern.

'Niggles, not pain.'

'Helen . . .'

'You haven't said anything about the house.'

'It's in a pretty spot.'

'And you can see us living here?'

'I've never imagined living in anything like this.'

'And now you will.' She smiled triumphantly as she reached the landing.

'I'd rather we were moving in together than just you with the girls.'

'But as we can't be together for the next two years, it makes sense. I'll have company and . . .'

'You won't have to face the flat.'

She opened the first door they came to, walked into the room and sank down on the stripped mattress of a double bed. 'You understand.'

He nodded.

'We planned the flat for us and the baby . . .'

He saw a tear welling in the corner of her eye. 'The musty smell is worse in here.'

'Probably because this room has been shut up longer than the downstairs. I dread to think when it was last used.' She pressed down on the cover with the palms of her hands. Jack followed suit.

'It feels damp.'

'And the suite is hideous.' She grimaced as she looked at the shiny maple dressing table, wardrobe and tallboy. 'But it will be all right to start off with. Won't it?'

'Of course, sweetheart.' Wrapping his arm round her shoulders, he pulled her close and they left the room.

'I'm amazed my aunt got a double bed in here,' she commented, as they opened the next door on the landing and looked in on a room that appeared to be bed and nothing else.

'The house was probably built around it. I doubt there's room for a stool, let alone a chair.'

'But there's room to sleep. If Katie, Judy and Lily do move in with me, two of them will have to share the wardrobe in the other room.'

They walked past a third bedroom furnished with a suite identical to the first, then Jack opened the door on a small room that held an enormous roll-top bath, Belfast sink and toilet with high cistern and chain. The walls were banded in white tiles and mahogany dados.

'An indoor bathroom – my first.' Jack smiled.

'The flat had one.'

'Looks like I'll never get to live in it.'

'And a master bedroom. Oh, Jack, just look at that view.' She sank down on the window seat and stared out over the cliff and beach to the sea and beyond it the coast around Port Talbot, and even further out the smudge on the horizon that was Ilfracombe in Devon. 'Can you imagine waking every morning to that?'

'I'd rather wake beside you.' He kissed the back of her neck.

'You're going to have both.'

'I wish.'

'Like you said, two years will soon go.'

He couldn't help contrasting her present attitude with her earlier depression. 'And there'll be leaves.' He fell in with her positive mood.

'I'll have this place all ready for you when you come home after your training, you'll see. All the smells will have gone, it will be shining clean, freshly painted, papered . . .'

He turned her round to face him. 'Don't you dare go overdoing it.'

'I won't.'

'Promise?'

'Promise,' she echoed, looking down into the garden where her father and Lily were examining an overgrown border. 'I wish we could stay here tonight.'

'In your present state you'll catch pneumonia. Come on, sweetheart, it's time to go home.'

'Not home. This is home now, Jack. For both of us.'

Chapter 21

'ALL IT NEEDS is a good clean and clear-out, and Lily, Katie and Judy can help me with that. I'll rope in Martin and Joe to do the heavy work; we'll soon have it looking great. And travelling to work won't be a problem for any of us, a quick run down the hill and we'll be in Mumbles. We'll get the train into town every day. Just think, start the day with a ride along the beach . . .'

'Try stopping for breath between words, Helen.' John parked the car in Carlton Terrace.

'I'm excited.'

'We noticed. Now, back to bed . . .'

'Bed!'

'Bed,' Jack reinforced. 'If only for a rest. Then we can spend the evening together.'

'You coming in, Lily?'

Lily looked from Helen to Jack, not wanting to muscle in on their day together any more than she already had. 'I have to make Uncle Roy's tea.'

'And tell him about the house. You and Katie will move in. And you'll ask Judy . . .'

'I'm sure we will, but we'll talk about it later. Thank you for taking me to see Helen's house, Mr Griffiths.'

'My pleasure, Lily.'

'You will talk to your uncle tonight,' Helen pressed.

'I will.'

'And we'll move in next week . . .'

'Bed, Helen,' her father repeated, seeing her stick out her tongue at Jack.

It would solve a lot of problems, Uncle Roy,' Lily coaxed as she made a pot of tea.

'I can see it would, but Helen has what we call in the force "a chequered history".'

'She is now a respectable married woman. And Katie and I are almost nineteen . . .'

'Not until the end of the summer.'

'And as Helen is married, she is the perfect chaperone.'

'With Jack away for two years, who is going to chaperone her?' he enquired drily.

'We'll chaperone one another. You should see the house. It's beautiful, practically on top of the beach. We'll be able to swim every day in summer.'

'And this house? Have you thought what you'll do with it?' He reached for his pipe and pulled out his tobacco pouch.

'After you marry Mrs Hunt and go to live in her house, Martin and Sam could move up here and we could look into that basement conversion you talked about.' Taking the kettle from the stove, she filled the teapot.

'This is a big place for just Martin and Sam.'

'If we rented out all the bedrooms, we'd soon finance the alterations to the basement and then we could rent that out as well.' Heaping three spoonfuls of sugar into his tea, she added a dash of milk, stirred it and handed it to him.

'There is no "we", love,' he contradicted. 'This house is yours.'

'I'm having trouble thinking of it that way.'

'Not that your idea isn't a good one,' he mused. 'You'd have no trouble renting the rooms with the housing shortage and there are always young coppers looking for good accommodation. But there's also your Auntie Norah's treasures.'

'We could lock off one of the attic bedrooms and store them in there if you don't want them.'

'Norah left them to you, love.'

'There must be some things you'd like to have.'

'I'm not sure.' He looked at her. 'We can't put off going through them much longer.'

'I could make a start tonight.'

'You and Katie aren't going out?' he asked in surprise.

'No.'

'In that case Norah's room can wait until my day off next week. If Helen's well enough, why don't you invite her and the boys round.'

'You mean it?'

'Why not? Mrs Lannon isn't likely to walk in on you and I think I can trust you to have them out by half past ten; not that there's anything you can do with them after half past ten that you can't do before. Joy and I are going to the pictures, but she'll be back by then to sleep over.'

'Thank you, Uncle Roy.'

He looked up at her as he lit his pipe. 'It's going to be strange not seeing you every day.'

'You'll always be my favourite uncle.'

'I'll always be there if you need me.'

'I know that.' She kissed the top of his head. 'I'll go and ask Jack if he wants to come round with Helen.'

He sat back in his chair and watched her leave. It seemed such a short time ago that she'd toddled around in short frocks, with her arms full of picture books, constantly demanding they be read to her. He was happy he was finally marrying Joy, but Lily was very special – the filthy, half-starved toddler he'd found wandering the streets in the blackout who had wormed her way into his affections until he simply couldn't imagine living without her. Limeslade was more than three miles away. What if she got into trouble, had an accident, needed him and he couldn't get to her? He could almost hear Joy laughing at him. 'Children grow up and move away, Roy. It's what they do.'

He looked at Norah's photograph on the mantelpiece as he tried to shake off his mood. 'I'm getting as superstitious as you ever were, girl.' He spoke as if she were in the room with him. 'But then, when it comes to our Lily, we always were over-protective. Weren't we?'

'I'm not happy with the thought of you and Katie moving out to Limeslade.'

'Why not?' Lily asked. She and Martin were alone in the kitchen, making a snack for the others who were playing cards in the living room.

'Because it's miles away and I won't be able to pop upstairs and see you whenever I want.'

'You haven't been able to do that with Mrs Lannon living here anyway.' She handed him a couple of bowls and packets of crisps.

'But now you and Katie have been clever enough to get rid of her . . .'

'We didn't set out to upset her,' she protested.

'You expect me to believe that?' He ducked as she threw a tea towel at him

'You two arguing again?' Katie knocked and pushed open the door.

'Marty thinks we set out to annoy Mrs Lannon and make her leave.'

'Perhaps we should have. Then she would have left sooner. Have you seen the bottle opener? Adam's just arrived with a couple of bottles of beer and some Babychams.'

'It's in the bottom drawer of the dresser.' Lily handed Martin a packet of Cheeselets. 'Make yourself useful; shake those on to a plate.'

'It's also going to be funny living upstairs,' he said, as Katie left with the opener. 'Do you realise, apart from my time in the army, I've lived out my entire life in the basements of this terrace?'

'Below stairs, like a footman.'

'More like a bootboy.' Kicking the door shut, he leaned back against it, pulled her close and kissed her.

'Marty, the others . . .'

'Can't get in while I'm blocking the door. Want to go somewhere tomorrow?'

'Every time we make plans for a Sunday . . .'

'Something happens, I know. But I'm seeing Jack off at ten. He said I could borrow his bike, so I thought we'd jump on it and escape for the day. That way if the world does cave in, we won't know about it until we get back. And I intend to be late. Very late.' He held her gaze for a moment before moving his lips downwards and nuzzling the nape of her neck.

'Katie, Judy and I promised Jack we'd stay with Helen tomorrow.'

'If I persuade Katie to sit with her, can you spare me a couple of hours from, say, half past ten on?'

'Only if Katie and Helen don't mind.'

'That's a date. I've always been able to bribe Katie.' Slipping his hands round her back, he squeezed her tight and kissed her a second time. She clung to him as his tongue moved into her mouth and his fingers slid upwards to caress her nylon-clad breasts.

'Marty . . . we need to talk,' she gasped when he finally stopped kissing her.

'I'm going too far?' he questioned seriously.

'What do you think?'

'Possibly, for the time and place.'

'I'd say definitely.'

'Tomorrow we'll be in a different place.' He touched his lips to hers again, lightly, so lightly they tickled tantalisingly over hers. Gripping the back of his head, she wove her fingers into his hair and kissed him back with a passion that bruised his mouth.

'But we'll still talk,' she warned, as the living room door opened and he released her.

'Whatever you want,' he whispered, feeling he would do anything she asked of him, just as long as she carried on looking at him the way she was looking at him at that moment.

Outside in the back lane, Joe leaned against the garden wall, inhaled his cigarette and watched Lily's kitchen window intently. His breath caught sharply when Martin lifted her sweater and moved his hands beneath it. A red haze blurred the scene as his imagination took hold and he visualised himself in Martin's place. He felt the perfumed warmth of Lily's body under his fingertips, listened as her breath whispered past his ear, tasted the sweetness of her lipstick on his mouth. Ran his hands over the smooth, padded contours of her breasts – slipped his fingers beneath her bra straps . . .

Without warning they broke free and Martin opened the door behind him. Someone joined them in the room. He tossed away his cigarette but didn't open the garage door until both Lily and Martin had left the kitchen and switched off the light. Only then did he remember the excuse he'd used to leave the house.

'I said half an hour and we've been here two.'

'And I'll be glad when you've gone and can't bully me any more,' Helen bit back at Jack.

'That will be soon enough.' Jack rose to his feet and held out his hand to help her up from the sofa.

'I didn't mean . . .'

'I know.' He watched her as she walked past him to hug Judy, Lily and Katie. 'See you downstairs in a few minutes, Martin.'

'Just as soon as I've helped Lily clear up here.'

'Thanks for the beer, Adam. See you around.' He shook his hand. 'Sam.'

'Take care of yourself, mate.' Sam shook Jack's hand warmly.

'You'll call tomorrow,' Helen asked Lily, Judy and Katie, as they walked with her and Jack to the door.

'We'll be round in the morning and Lily will join us in the

afternoon,' Katie answered brightly. Martin had cornered her in the kitchen earlier and told her about his and Lily's plans.

'Thanks, I really appreciate it. See you then.'

'You'll be up to say goodbye in the morning, Jack.' Katie's voice trembled. She was close to both her brothers and knew exactly what effect Jack's absence was going to have on her. She had missed Martin dreadfully during the two years it had taken him to complete his National Service. And every day he had been far from her she had imagined him shot in Cyprus, or hurt in an accident, leaving her hundreds of miles away, unable to do a thing to help.

'I will, sis. Goodnight, everyone.' Taking Helen's arm, he steered her gently out of the house.

'If you don't mind, I'll be going too, Lily.' Judy followed Jack and Helen out through the door.

'But you . . .'

'I'll see you tomorrow.' She walked up the street. It had been purgatory to sit in the same room as Adam all evening and pretend nothing had gone on between them. But the shame of what had happened the night before weighed too heavily for her to confide in her friends – or confront Adam again.

'Dad, Joe, I'm back,' Helen called as she opened the door.

'In the dining room, love.' John glanced up from a pile of papers as she and Jack walked into the room. 'Joe left some books at Robin's. He's driven up to get them.'

'Not whisky.'

'Perhaps that as well. He told me to tell you that even if he stays over, he'll be back in time to say goodbye to you tomorrow, Jack. You all packed and ready to go?'

'As much as I'll ever be.'

'I think I'll have an early night,' Helen announced.

'That's the first good idea you've had since you came home, Helen.' John glanced at his watch.

'I know I stayed a lot later than I said I would, but . . .'

'You and the girls couldn't stop talking.' Jack gave his father-in-law an apologetic look.

'*You* wouldn't be able to stop talking if you'd been locked up in a hospital with a load of schoolmarms for nurses, who shout "quiet there" every time someone as much as sneezes.'

'You were going to bed, Helen,' John reminded gently.

'Goodnight, Dad.' She kissed his cheek and turned to Jack. 'Help me upstairs.'

He offered her his arm, noticing that she put more weight on it than she had done when they had walked around the house in Limeslade.

'All of a sudden I feel shattered,' she confessed.

'I'm not surprised.' He switched on the light and helped her to the chair.

She glanced round at the single bed, shelves full of books and bric-a-brac, some of it childish. It was the room she had slept in all her life and somehow Jack, big, burly and masculine, didn't belong in its pink-and-white prettiness, even though he was her husband. 'Some marriage this is turning out to be.'

'It's going to be a great marriage as soon as you're well.' He closed the curtains.

'And you're out of the army.'

'Can you manage from here?'

'I don't need bathing and putting to bed like a baby, if that's what you mean.' If he had suggested he stay and share her single bed and just simply hold her through the night she would have kissed him and hugged him with all the strength she possessed, but he went to the door.

'I'll be round as soon as I'm packed and dressed in the morning. About nine suit you?'

'I'm not promising I'll be out of bed.'

'I hope you won't. You need to rest. Goodnight, sweetheart.' He kissed her gently on the lips, then left.

She continued to sit on the chair while he ran down the stairs. She heard him talking briefly to her father, then the front door opened and closed. As she struggled to her feet a pain shot across her operation scar. Tears came to her eyes.

Furious with her own weakness, she brushed them away with her hand, smudging mascara across her face. She looked a wreck – she *was* a wreck. If she were Jack, she'd want to get as far away from her as possible.

She thought of all the stories she'd heard about National Service and the girls who hung round army camps. Jack would have free time, he'd be able to go down to the pub, meet and talk to other girls. They'd flock round a boy with his looks. What if he fell in love with one of them? A pretty, healthy, girl who never cried and who could give him all the babies he wanted.

The lilting strains of a string quartet drifted out as Robin opened his front door.

'I'm sorry, I don't want to intrude . . .'

'You're not.' Robin pulled Joe into the hall.

'But you're having a party.'

'Mums and Pops have some Arts Society thing on, complete with real musicians. It's boring as hell. Angie, Em and I have holed up in the billiard room.' He opened the door just as Emily took a shot and skidded a cue across the baize.

'You want Pops to kill me, Em?' Robin shouted.

'Let's face it, Robbie, I'm just bloody hopeless.' She smiled inanely.

'Only at some things. Whisky?' Robin waved his father's decanter under Joe's nose.

'I came to get my book.'

'Book!'

'I left my John Donne here. Have you seen it?'

'I haven't looked at a book since our brainstorming session. The housekeeper dumped what she called "your rubbish, Mr Robin" in the corner over there.'

Kneeling beside the pile of odds and ends, Joe extracted his textbook.

'You're not going.' Angie waylaid him as he went to the door.

'I have a lot more studying to do.'

'We've just persuaded Robin to take us away from this mausoleum to a party.'

'Who's having a party this close to the exams?' Joe asked.

'Our art class. A midnight swim on the beach in Oxwich.'

'We picked the wrong subject, Joe, we should have studied art,' Robin observed cryptically.

'You can't draw,' Emily protested.

'Neither can you.'

Instead of being furious at Robin's observation, Emily giggled.

'It's almost time to go.' Angie lifted her skirt above her knees as she sat on a stool. 'Why don't you come with us, Joe? It's going to be fun.'

'Puritanical Joe doesn't understand the concept of fun.' Robin took the cue from Emily and replaced it on the rack.

Joe hesitated for the barest fraction of a second. 'I haven't a costume.'

'Borrow a pair of my trunks,' Robin offered.

'Thanks.'

'That's settled, then.' Angie smiled.

'It'll be a good night,' Robin confided as they went upstairs to his bedroom to fetch swimming costumes. 'The last one of these Jeremy went to, all the girls stripped off and went skinny-dipping.'

'And the boys?'

'Enjoyed the view.'

'You'll keep an eye on her for me?' Unbuckling the belt on his jeans, Jack sat on a chair and struggled to peel a fourteen-inch jean leg over his foot.

'That goes without saying.' Martin sat on the bed and waited for his brother to undress. There wasn't room for both of them to move around at the same time. 'And the girls will be in Helen's house every five minutes, even before they move out to Limeslade. You know what they're like.'

'They will all be working during the day.'

'Did Mr Griffiths ask Mrs Jones . . .'

'To work a couple of extra hours and keep an eye on her? Yes. But she's no real company for Helen,' Jack observed. 'She's an interfering old bat like Mrs Lannon.'

'From the way Helen was talking earlier, she's going to be too busy to be lonely. All those plans she has for moving out to Limeslade and redecorating the house.'

'I don't want her doing too much.' Jack dropped his shirt and underwear into their laundry bag. 'She'll make herself ill and land herself back in hospital.'

'There'll be enough people round her to make sure she doesn't.'

Jack pulled on his pyjama trousers and stepped past Martin towards the bed. Pausing for a moment, he extricated his wallet from his jeans pocket and opened it. 'Present for you.' He handed Martin a small, thin packet wrapped in brown paper.

Martin turned it over suspiciously. 'What's this?'

'Something I should have used and didn't until it was too late and won't have a use for again.'

Martin unwrapped the brown paper. 'French letters.'

'As you recognise them I won't embarrass you by telling you how to put them on,' Jack teased.

'I saw enough of them in the army.'

'And used them.' Martin's silence told Jack what he wanted to know. 'I got a couple . . . after – talk about locking the stable door after the horse had bolted. One of my mates said the best place to get them is in the barber's in the Uplands. Unlike the chemist, there's only blokes serving in there.'

Embarrassed, Martin pushed them into his underwear drawer.

'I thought with the way things are between you and Lily . . .'

'She's a decent girl.'

'And Helen isn't.'

'Of course she is. It's just that . . .'

Jack started to laugh.

'What's funny?'

'You, me, this conversation. Little brother giving big brother tips on how not to get his girlfriend pregnant. "Don't do as I did, do as I tell you." It sounds like one of those father-son conversations from a sentimental film, where the kid gets it all wrong because the father's too strict. And about you and Lily . . .'

'Some things I don't talk about,' Martin broke in curtly.

'I don't want to know. But just in case you're too thick to work it out for yourself I saw the way she looked at you tonight. And if you've any sense you'll use those' – he nodded to the drawer – 'before someone else moves in on her. She's a good-looking girl and what's more important, nice, and for some peculiar reason she likes you.' Turning back the bedclothes, he climbed into bed.

'I love her,' Martin confessed.

'I noticed when you were six years old. But it's got a lot worse in the last ten years or so.'

'I'll never be able to give her the life she deserves on a mechanic's wages.'

'So you're going to hand her to some rich guy because you're poor?' Jack asked.

'No, but . . .'

'Go forward one step at a time, Marty.'

'And getting her into bed is one step?' Martin questioned seriously.

'Yes.'

'A girl like that wants marriage.' Martin sat on the chair and unfastened his shoelaces.

'Eventually.'

'Before she gets into bed with a man.'

'Not necessarily.'

'It was all so easy for you, wasn't it,' Kicking off his shoes, Martin pushed them under the bed. 'You got Helen pregnant and there you were, new job, flat, wedding . . .'

'And no baby and a sick wife.'

'Helen will get well, there'll be other babies.'

'There won't.'

Martin whirled round and stared at his brother, wondering if he'd heard him correctly.

'Helen can't have any more children.'

'Are you sure . . . there's other doctors . . .'

'It's definite.'

'Oh God, Jack . . . I'm so sorry.' Martin felt the words were totally inadequate.

'What are you going to do?'

'My National Service.'

'When you're ready, you could adopt . . .'

'Perhaps.' Jack didn't want to discuss John's offer to arrange a private adoption for him and Helen because, despite all the assurances he'd given Helen about 'the right baby for them', he wasn't at all sure how he felt about taking on someone else's child. 'But that's one of the reasons it's important to me that you and Lily work out. I won't make a father but I might make an uncle when the time comes. And there's Katie, if she ever gets round to noticing boys.'

The misery etched on Jack's face convinced Martin it wasn't the right time to break the bombshell about their sister and John Griffiths.

'You won't tell anyone about Helen,' Jack urged. 'Not even Lily.'

Martin shook his head. Sometimes it felt as though his life was nothing but secrets and always other people's.

Joe stood on the beach, staring at the moon as it painted a shimmering silver path across the sea towards the horizon. Oblivious to the squeals of Angela's and Emily's classmates as they ran in and out of the waves in half-hearted attempts to evade the boys chasing them, he concentrated on conjuring Lily's image. Her eyes shining with reflected light as they danced in the Pier ballroom – the sad smile on her face when he had asked her to marry him in the churchyard at Oxwich – she and Martin in her kitchen, mouths glued together, Martin's hand fumbling beneath her sweater . . .

'You should go in, Joe. The water's fabulous. It's always warmer at night than during the day.' Shaking out a towel, Angela threw it round her shoulders as she stood beside him.

'I may do, later.'

'Thinking of your examinations' she probed.

'Yes,' he lied.

'Robin says you're bound to get a first.'

He glanced at her. She was wearing a gold two-piece swimsuit, splattered with tiny white flowers that glowed silver in the moonlight, the waist cut snugly into her slim figure, highlighting her slenderness, and the top plunged low, revealing the valley between her well-rounded breasts.

'Like what you see?'

'I only have to look down there to see a whole lot more.'

Following his line of vision, she saw Robin running after a nude Emily, brandishing her one-piece swimsuit. 'That girl strips at the drop of a hat.'

'Only Robin's hat that I can see.'

She gazed coolly at him. 'Robin's right, you are a Puritan when it comes to sex.'

'If by that you mean I think it should be special between just two people who keep their bodies for one another, I'll agree with you.'

'You're only young once.'

'Angie, save me.' Emily ran up behind her. Unhooking Angela's top, she tossed it to a boy behind Robin.

'Rules of engagement. Lose your top, you lose your bottoms.'

'Help, Joe.' Angela flung a towel round herself and ran ahead of him up the beach.

He followed, conscious of a couple of boys running behind them but when they reached the dunes they were alone.

'I'm freezing. Dry my back for me.' Stripping the towel from her shoulders, she tossed it to him before turning round.

'You are cold.' He touched her shoulders.

'I said I was. Ow, not so hard. I'd like to be warm *and* keep my skin if possible.' Turning back, she faced him. 'It's too dark for me to see your blushes.'

'Or me you.'

'But you can feel.' Taking his hands, she opened his fingers and clamped them over her exposed breasts. 'Still coy, Joe? You can call it heat treatment if you like.' When he didn't remove his hands, she kissed him and as her cold, damp body pressed against his, he first caressed, then pinched her nipples, all the while wondering if that was what Martin had been doing to Lily under cover of her sweater.

'So you're not a Puritan after all,' she murmured, moving her head away from his.

'We should be getting back.'

'We should. There is nothing quite as uncomfortable as making love in sand. It gets in all the wrong places.' Wrapping the towel round herself once more she took his hand and led him back towards the sea.

'You're catching the ten-o'clock train?' Helen knew the answer to her question but she felt she had to say something to fill the silence that had fallen between her and Jack.

'That's the time on the warrant.' Jack paced to the window and looked out over the vista of gardens, backyards and the backs of the houses fronting Mansel Street.

'You'll write?'

'As soon as I have an address.' He turned to face her. 'You?'

'I'll start a letter tonight and send it the minute I get your address.'

He sat on the bed beside her. 'Six weeks' training will soon pass . . .'

'It already feels like a lifetime.'

He hugged her. 'You knew I hadn't done my National Service when we married, sweetheart.'

'To be honest, I didn't even think about it. There was . . . were', she corrected herself, 'so many other things to think about.'

'I might not be stationed too far away.'

'And you could be sent abroad.' She shivered at the thought of being separated from him by hundreds of miles.

'If I'm not, it might be possible for you to come and rent somewhere close by where I'm stationed.'

'Really?' She tried to smile at him.

'I'll look into it. And in the meantime you have to concentrate on getting well. If you're up to it we'll have a second honeymoon after my training. According to Marty I'll get a couple of days, maybe even a week. But for now' – he glanced at his watch – 'I have to go.'

She lifted her face to his and kissed him fervently.

'Take care of yourself.' Gently he unwound her arms from round his neck.

She nodded as she looked down at her hands, not trusting herself to answer him. She hadn't cried that day – yet – but she sensed it was only a matter of time.

'I'll write as soon as I get there and telephone if I can. Promise me you won't overdo it moving into the house in Limeslade before I come back on leave.'

She nodded again.

'I love you, Helen, don't ever forget it.' He went to the door and hesitated. On impulse he turned back and, sitting beside her on the bed, wrapped his arms round her. When he released her she buried her head in the pillow. She knew he was looking at her; then she heard the door opening and closing softly, and he was gone.

Chapter 22

HANDING OVER A penny for a platform ticket, Martin took Jack's case and led the way along the platform to the third-class carriages. Opening a door, he waited until Jack stepped in, then handed him his case. 'Don't worry about Helen. We'll all make sure she's fine. Think of yourself for a change. You're not going on a picnic. All that square-bashing takes it out of you.'

'I'm fitter than you ever were,' Jack retorted.

'I guarantee you won't be feeling fit a week from now,' Martin warned. 'And resist the temptation to answer the sergeants back, it's not worth it.'

'The voice of experience speaks.'

'All you'll get is punishment and cancellation of leave. And how will you explain that to your wife?' The guard blew the whistle. Martin stepped back and closed the door. Jack opened the window and leaned out. 'Do yourself a favour.'

'What?' Martin called out as the train began to move up the platform.

'Hold on to Lily. You two were made for one another.' He shouted something else, but it was lost in the noise of the train rattling over the tracks. Martin waited until the last carriage rounded the curve before walking back down the platform to Lily.

Martin rode Jack's motorbike up the gentle slope that led from the town centre, through the Uplands shopping centre, along Sketty Road to the suburb of Sketty and on to Gower Road.

He was aware of Lily's arms round his waist and her head resting on his shoulder as they left the villages of Killay and Upper Killay behind them and reached Fairwood Common. The wind caught his hair, blowing it back from his face as they swept past grazing Gower ponies, sheep and cattle. The road ahead was straight and clear. Turning his head, he smiled at Lily, before rounding the curve of the high stone wall that closed off the gardens of Kilvrough Manor and headed down into the wooded valley of Parkmill.

Turning right, he drove up a narrow lane that led through the woods to Giant's Grave, a favourite picnic spot for school outings. He recalled sitting cross-legged on the grass, while his elderly teacher droned on about ancient burial practices. Slowing to walking pace, he stopped the bike alongside a fence that enclosed the flat-bottomed grassed valley that held the chambered stone tomb. He stepped off and held out his hand to Lily. 'You all right?'

'I survived.' She pushed her hair back behind her ears.

'You didn't like it.'

'Better than I thought I would,' she answered ambiguously. 'Helen and Judy told me they were both terrified the first time they rode on the back of Jack's and Brian's bikes.'

'I tried to go steady.'

'I'm not used to sailing through the air at thirty miles an hour with nothing but a jacket between me and disaster.'

'You thought we'd crash.'

'Once or twice.'

'I'll go more slowly on the way back.' Unbuckling the pannier, he took out the picnic she had packed for them. 'What kind of sandwiches have you made?'

'Wait until lunchtime and you'll find out.'

'And where are we going to have this picnic?'

'The perfect spot, which is about six miles that way.' She pointed up the valley.

'You've got to be kidding.'

'Follow me and see.'

'It is good of you and Judy to spend the day with Helen.' John watched Katie preparing a tray in the kitchen.

'She is my sister-in-law, Mr Griffiths, and a very good friend to both Judy and me,' she replied.

'All the same, this is your one day off a week, you must have things to do.' The conversation was outwardly innocuous – the look he gave her anything but.

'Helen, Judy and I have a lot of catching up to do.' She looked away from him as Joe entered the room, unwashed, unshaved, with his hair on end.

'You look like something the cat dragged in,' John said. 'Was it rough picking up those books?'

Joe instinctively checked the flies on his pyjamas were closed and his dressing gown wasn't open when he saw Katie. 'I didn't realise we had company.'

'You haven't, Joe.' Katie picked up the tray. 'Helen has. Excuse me, Mr Griffiths.'

'Allow me.' John opened the door for her.

'Was it something I said?' Joe asked, as John closed the door behind her.

'What?'

'Didn't she seem spiky to you?'

'Spiky?'

'Spiky – hostile – frosty –'

'Not so I noticed.'

'I forgot, she's your secretary. You're probably used to her.'

'I suppose I am.' John was careful to keep any inflection that could be misinterpreted from his voice.

'Last night – I really did need those books.'

'I didn't say you didn't, Joe.'

'It's just that . . .'

'You're entitled to let your hair down once in a while. You have been working very hard. Just don't let it down too close to the exams.'

'I won't.' Joe looked after John as he wandered into the dining room, cup of tea in hand. He seemed to be behaving oddly, but on reflection no more oddly than him. And last night had been rough. If he hadn't known better he would have called Angie a tease. She knew just how to get a man going and then switch off. Had it been as she said – the sand – or was it something more? Something wrong with him that turned all girls off when he allowed them to get close. Lily – and now Angie, who he didn't give a tuppenny damn for.

'I refuse to walk one more step.' Martin pulled off the leather jacket he had borrowed from Jack along with his bike, spread it on the grass and sat down, leaving enough space for Lily to sit next to him.

Lily breathed in deeply. They were in a grassy copse, enclosed and sheltered by silver birch, their branches a luxuriant green that hadn't yet quite reached the full leafy splendour of summer. Above them the sky was a deep cerulean blue, marred by a few wisps of cloud. It was a beautiful and peaceful scene until a bird called to its mate in a raucous cry that was more like the screech of a saw than birdsong.

'I can't believe we've finally made it,' Martin said as she sat beside him. 'We're on the Gower, miles from anywhere and completely alone.'

'I feel guilty just being here.' She leaned back on her hands.

'Why? You know Katie and Judy will take care of Helen.'

'You didn't see her yesterday when she insisted on visiting her house in Limeslade.' She shook her head. 'I've seen Helen wound up before, but it was as though she was possessed.'

'Mr Griffiths and Joe are at home, so it's not as if Katie and Judy are alone with her.'

'That doesn't make me feel any the less guilty – or selfish.' She opened the food bag. 'Are you hungry?'

'No, but I could murder a lemonade.'

'It's going to be warm,' she warned.

'Are you telling me you can't make everything perfect?'

'A perfect world might be a boring one.'

'I could handle boring' – he stared into her eyes – 'provided you were there.'

She gave him one of the enamel mugs she'd packed and the bottle of lemonade. Setting them aside, he cupped her face in his hands and kissed her gently and lovingly. As she responded, he pulled her down on the grass, moving his body alongside hers.

'I'm not comfortable,' she complained as her elbow hit a rock.

'Remind me to pack a mattress on the back of the bike the next time we manage to get away.'

'A double.' Sitting up, she slipped off her short jacket and cardigan, rolled them into a makeshift pillow and pushed it under his head.

'I have to admit that is better.' He wrapped his arm round her shoulders as she rested her head on his chest. 'But it's doing nothing for my thirst. Mark the spot I was lying on, so we can get back to it.' Reaching for the lemonade, he opened it. 'If you don't want me to tip this over you you'll have to move.'

'Spoilsport.' She took the mug he handed her. 'It is horribly warm.'

'But wet.' He levered the top back on the bottle. 'Now, where were we?'

'Lying nice and peacefully until you decided you had to have a drink.' She waited until he stacked the mugs and lemonade behind them before moving back on to his chest.

'Last night you said we had to talk.'

She fingered one of the buttons on his shirt, absently opening and closing it. 'We do.' Lifting her face to his, she stole another kiss.

'That is the kind of talking I understand.'

'But not the kind I had in mind.'

'You want to know if I'm serious about you.'

'No.'

'All girls want to get married . . .'

'Not this girl,' she interrupted.

'Not ever?' He was unaccountably alarmed at the thought.

'I wanted to fall in love, Marty, I have. It's better than I dreamed it could be and for now it's all I want.'

'How long is "for now"?' he ventured.

'I'm enjoying the present, especially this present, too much' – she hugged his chest – 'to want to look too far forward.'

'You must have some plans for the future.'

'Beyond making you drive more slowly on the way back into town, not many,' she joked.

'Tell me about them.'

'There's my uncle's wedding. I'm looking forward to seeing him and Mrs Hunt getting married at last. And then there's moving into Helen's house in Limeslade and swimming every day it's warm enough without having to take a bus out to one of the bays.'

'And you and me?'

'I'm here with you now, Marty.' She left the button unfastened and started playing with the one below it.

'And tomorrow?' He suddenly found it difficult to breathe.

'I'll get up early, eat breakfast, walk to the bank, and spend the day taking dictation from Mr Collins and watching my step with Miss Oliver who's in charge of all us girls and . . . Bother, it's bad enough having to work in the week without thinking about it on the weekend. Why did you make me do that?'

'I didn't and I thought you liked your job.'

'I do, but I like this better.' She snuggled closer to him. 'What about you, do you like your job?'

'When I'm working on an engine with a fault that I can put right.'

'What about the ones you can't put right?'

'They remind me how much I still have to learn.' The blood coursed headily round his veins as she unfastened a third and fourth button on his shirt and slipped her hand between it and his vest.

319

'You don't mind the grease and the dirt?'

'All boys like playing in dirt and the job's not bad. I only wish the pay was better so I could save some real money.'

'To open your own garage.'

'You remember me telling you that?' he questioned in surprise.

'I remember everything you tell me.'

'I'd like to work for myself, but it would cost a bomb to set up. Even if I managed to rent the right premises, I'd have to buy all the tools and spares and if the customers didn't start rolling in right away I'd be in serious trouble. Lily . . .' He grabbed her hand as she tugged at his vest, freeing it from his jeans. 'You know I love you.'

'Yes.'

'And you know I'd ask you to marry me if I had enough money to support you.'

'That I didn't know.'

'I thought I'd made it obvious . . .'

'Only that you love me and there's a world of difference between love and marriage. As you said yourself about Jack and Helen, it's a lot of responsibility; if anything, more so for a boy than a girl. A wife and possibly children to support, your whole life mapped out for you . . .'

'You do remember everything I say.' He sat up and looked at her.

'You'd prefer me not to?'

'Sometimes. I behaved like an idiot that night. It's just that I want you to know if I could support you I'd ask you to marry me tomorrow and if you're worried about anything . . .'

'What should I be worried about?'

'Ending up in Helen's predicament,' he blurted out, conscious of the blood flowing into his cheeks.

Hugging her knees to her chest, she faced him head on. 'And I won't end up pregnant and unmarried like Helen because you don't want to make love to me, or because you'll take precautions?'

'What!'

'There's no need to look outraged. I know all about birth control, or at least as much as Auntie Norah knew.'

'She talked to you about it?' He couldn't have looked more stunned if she'd told him she could speak Swahili.

'And sex,' she added. 'Auntie Norah told me that she made love to her husband before they were married, but she made sure he used a French letter so she wouldn't get pregnant.'

'She told you that!'

'Why so surprised? You knew we were close.'

'Yes, but parents don't talk to their kids about things like that.'

'They do if they don't want them to get into trouble. Auntie Norah's husband was ten years younger than her and as she was over forty and, according to her, pretty inexperienced when they met, she wanted to be sure she could cope with every aspect of married life. So she decided to have the honeymoon before the wedding. It must have worked because Uncle Roy told me they were very happy before her husband was killed in the war.'

'I never thought I'd hear a girl talking like this.' He reached for his cigarettes so he could conceal his embarrassment in the ritual of lighting one.

'You think two people in love shouldn't discuss sex?'

'No – yes . . . I . . .'

'You'd prefer to just do it.'

'It might prove less embarrassing,' he replied honestly, regaining his composure.

'I'm not embarrassed to be discussing it and you shouldn't be after what you tried to do last night with our friends in the next room.'

'Perhaps I did what I did because I knew with everyone around it couldn't go too far.'

'And now?' She looked around at the deserted countryside.

'I haven't tried anything on,' he remonstrated.

'Yet.'

'Is that an invitation?' His voice was strangely hoarse.

'What you said about me getting pregnant, I would hate it, Marty. It would hurt my uncle who deserves the very best from me, as well as be disastrous for us. If we make love – and that is an "if" – I'd want you to use a French letter and be very, very careful because Auntie Norah told me they are not infallible.'

His hands began to shake and he tossed his cigarettes aside. 'Do you want us to make love?'

'When the time is right, don't you?'

'I'd be lying if I said I didn't.'

'Have you wondered what it will be like – for us?' she added, lacking the courage to ask him if there had been a girl in his past.

'It keeps me awake at night and stops me from concentrating during the day, but I never dreamed that you thought about it too.'

'Even after I told you I loved you?'

'Boys talk about nothing else but girls . . .'

'Are sugar and spice and everything nice.' She smiled. 'Don't you believe it.'

'I have some French letters,' he confessed.

'You bought them for us? Or was there . . .'

'Jack gave them to me,' he interrupted, avoiding her questions. 'Along with a father-son lecture.'

'Jack lectured you!' She burst into peals of laughter at the picture he conjured up, breaking the restraint that had fallen between them since she had brought up the subject of sex. 'I'm amazed he found the nerve.'

'The kid may only be eighteen but no one can accuse Jack of lacking nerve, not learning by his mistakes or passing on the lessons he's learned. So what happens now, Lily?'

'We take things slowly. One moment at a time.' Fingering the buttons on her blouse, she slowly slipped each one from its loop. When she'd finished she slid it off, revealing a pink silk slip and matching pink bra. Setting her blouse aside, she moved towards him. As he kissed her, she pulled his shirt free from his jeans.

'You're beautiful.' He caressed her shoulders, sliding his hands down the length of her naked arms.

'And you're a handsome man, Martin Clay.'

Running his hands through her hair, he tugged at the band holding her ponytail. She reached up, unclipped it and her hair tumbled to her shoulders.

'I love you, Lily Sullivan, and I'm glad we're taking it slowly.'

'So am I.' Pushing him down on to the grass, she rested her head on his chest, then lifted her head and kissed him again.

Richard Thomas faced Esme across the dining-room table in her mother's house. His wife, who had suffered from acute hypochondria for the last twenty of their forty-five years of marriage, had taken to her bed after the lunch their housekeeper had prepared, a habit that had resulted in him looking increasingly to his club and friends for the comforts usually associated with home. He had few illusions about his life. Neither his fellow club members, nor his friends, would look kindly on a scandal precipitated by Esme's allegations if she made them public, as she had threatened to do after the will reading. That was why he had taken time out on a fine Sunday afternoon to visit her, instead of falling asleep over the newspapers in a deckchair in his garden. 'I didn't have to come here, Esme,' he said abruptly. 'I could have waited until tomorrow and sent this last communication from John's solicitors by messenger.'

'Why didn't you?'

'Because I'm concerned about you.' For the first time since he had known her, Esme hadn't bothered with her looks. Devoid of make-up, her face was pasty and heavily lined, making her look older than her thirty-nine years. Her hair, lank, greasy and in need of retouching at the roots, was clipped back from her forehead. She was dressed in a white cotton blouse and tailored black skirt, both well cut and expensive, but there were unmistakable make-up stains on the shirt collar and the hem of her skirt had dropped, the fraying cloth sending threads clinging like spider's legs to her snagged stockings.

'You couldn't give a damn about me.' She emptied her brandy glass.

'You're wrong, Esme. I do care, very much indeed.'

'Why, because of your long-standing friendship with my family?' she sneered.

'Partly.'

'Let's not forget you are my godfather,' she mocked, 'even if you did take my knickers down when I was only sixteen.'

'You're so drunk you're delusional.'

'You'd like to pretend it never happened, wouldn't you.'

'You wanted . . .'

'Wanted!' She refilled her brandy glass with an unsteady hand. 'I was so bloody innocent I didn't have a clue what you were doing. You were the great Uncle Richard I'd been taught to please from the day I was born.'

'Esme . . . Esme . . .' He repeated her name until she quietened. 'How long have you been drinking like this?' When she didn't answer him he left his chair, went to the sideboard and opened the left-hand cupboard. A full bottle of sherry stood next to one of brandy. 'There were a dozen bottles of brandy here the day your mother died and I doubt the mourners went through one. Let's be generous and say they did, that still means you've drunk ten in less than a week.'

'How do you know how many bottles there were?'

'I checked the inventory I asked your mother's housekeeper to make.'

'You want me to pay for my mother's brandy . . .'

'Esme,' he repeated softly as if he were speaking to a recalcitrant child. 'Look at yourself in the mirror and see what you're doing to yourself.'

'Whatever I've become is the result of what you, John and Joseph have done to me!'

'There's no need for hysteria.'

'My own son won't let me near him,' she cried, 'and now you come here to tell me that John is threatening to leave me penniless . . .'

'Only because you're blocking the divorce he wants.'

'He wants! You want! Joseph wants! What about what I want?'

The more she raised her voice, the softer his became. 'What *do* you want, Esme?'

'What every woman wants. Financial independence . . .'

'John's offering it to you,' he said shortly.

'In a poky tradesman's flat.'

'If you sell it and the shop he's prepared to give you, you'll have enough money to buy a cottage.'

'A cottage, when my mother left this.' She emptied her glass and hurled it across the table. 'I'll show him . . . I'll burn down his bloody warehouse with him in it. I'll . . .'

'That wouldn't be very sensible, Esme.' Retrieving her glass, he slid it back towards her. 'That warehouse isn't only John's income, it's yours. Burn it down and it could take him years to build his trade back up again, and that's supposing he's prepared to put in the work. What would you both live on in the meantime?'

'He'd have the insurance.'

'Capital soon dwindles when people try to live off it and legally he wouldn't have to give you any of it. He could even go bankrupt and then you really would be penniless.'

'Think you have all the answers, don't you.' She stared at him. 'How many other girls did you seduce besides me?' She reached for the brandy bottle again. 'I've heard stories that would create a scandal that would rock this town. Make things so hot for you that you wouldn't be able to live here, let alone practise law.' She leaned towards him. 'I'll get back at you. The lot of you . . .'

'Esme,' he reached for her hand.

She snatched it away with such force that she sent her chair rocking.

'John has offered you a very reasonable settlement,' he persisted. 'As your solicitor I'm advising you to take it. Sell the shop and the flat if you want, buy whatever kind of place you like. You could live very comfortably on the annuity John's prepared to give you. You'd be financially secure . . .'

'I'd have no social life, nothing . . .'

'If you lived quietly – and soberly,' he added pointedly, 'given time . . .'

'I'll be dead in time.'

'Esme, you're not making it easy for anyone to help you,' he said forcefully.

She looked at him through brandy-glazed eyes.' You're afraid of me, aren't you?'

'I pity what you've become.'

'You're terrified of me, of what I'll say. Well, so you should be. I told Joseph . . .'

Realising she was about to say too much, just as she had done with her son, she fell silent.

'What? Esme, what did you tell him?' When she refused to answer, he gripped her wrist and squeezed it hard. 'What did you tell him?'

'That you're his father. He had a right to know,' she added defiantly as he released her.

'I've given you my professional advice, Esme. If you choose to ignore it there is nothing further I can do for you.'

'I won't take John's offer. I'll . . . I'll . . .'

'Believe me, there is nothing you can do without making yourself look even more foolish and degraded than you already are.' Opening the french window, he walked out on to the veranda, stepped out of sight and lit a cigar. Puffing on it, he looked out over the bay. A few intrepid children were braving the waves, squealing as they jumped in and out of the surf. He turned back and caught sight of Esme through a small side window. She was still sitting at the table, her glass full, the empty brandy bottle at her elbow. As he watched, she lifted the glass and drank it down in a single swallow. Staggering, she left her chair and went to the sideboard, overturning a small side table as she crashed into it. At the third attempt she managed to wrench open the door to the drinks cabinet. She leaned forward and lifted out the last bottle of brandy. Holding it carefully with two hands as if it were a precious artefact, she returned to her seat.

He didn't wait to see any more. Throwing his cigar into the shrubbery, he walked purposefully back to his Bentley.

John tossed the letters his new secretary had typed for him into his in-tray. They all bore spelling mistakes and none could possibly be sent out as they were, but he couldn't face calling the girl in to correct them. He glanced at the clock; it was only half past twelve but after a morning when she had made just about every error that could be made it felt more like early evening. He couldn't recall Katie making any mistakes during her first few days in the office but perhaps that was because he didn't want to. Was he being hard on this girl just because she'd taken Katie's place?

Ann knocked on the door. 'I'm going down to the canteen, Mr Griffiths. Would you like me to get you something?'

He shook his head. 'No thank you.' He left his chair, limped to the window and looked down into the yard. Half the stockroom staff and a fair proportion of the floor assistants were sitting on a low wall, eating sandwiches and enjoying the summer sunshine. As he pulled the blinds he had a sudden urge to walk to Lewis Lewis, wait until Katie left for her lunch break – and then? He imagined the conversation they would have if he tried to plead with her.

Please come back.

As your secretary.

That's all I'm free to offer.

I can't.

He lifted his suit jacket from the back of his chair. 'If anyone wants me, Ann, I'll be in the dining room of the Mackworth.'

'Yes, Mr Griffiths.'

Taking his stick from the umbrella stand, he opened the door and headed outside. The weather was more like late than early summer and the pavement broiled beneath his feet as he made his way up High Street. As it was early, the dining room was comparatively empty. Taking the unobtrusive corner table he preferred whenever he ate alone, he ordered soup, an omelette and, after a short debate in which indulgence won over abstinence, a glass of white wine.

'Your secretary said I'd find you here.' Richard Thomas clicked his fingers at the waiter as he slid into the chair opposite John's. 'I'll have a beefsteak, rare, with new potatoes, salad and a gin and tonic. And I'll have the drink right away.'

'Yes, Mr Thomas.' The waiter scribbled Richard's order on his pad.

'Did you know that Esme's been drinking heavily?' Richard asked as the man left them.

'I saw her with a glass of brandy at the funeral.'

'By heavily I mean a bottle, not a glass, a day.'

'I didn't realise.' John fell silent as the waiter arrived with his wine and Richard's gin and tonic.

Richard waited until he was out of earshot before continuing, 'I called to see her yesterday afternoon to discuss your ultimatum. I found her drunk, abusive and in no condition to confer about anything. As I left, she started on the last bottle of brandy in the house, so I decided to wait until today before attempting to contact her again. Then, last night I had a call from her cousin, Dorothy Green.'

'I know Dot.'

'Apparently she had several telephone calls yesterday evening. She could hear breathing but no one spoke at the other end. Then she thought she recognised Esme's voice but it sounded distant. She telephoned a neighbour of Esme's mother. He went to the house, looked through the window and saw Esme lying on the floor. He called me and, given the state I'd found her in earlier, I sent for a doctor I know. He arranged for Esme to be admitted to a private nursing home.'

'You should have telephoned me.' Guilt pricked John's conscience. Had the letter he'd asked Mark to send triggered Esme's drinking?

'To watch her having her stomach pumped?' Richard derided as he picked up his gin. 'I saw no point in disturbing you while she was unconscious. There was nothing you could do and the doctor assured me she was in no immediate danger. However, the drink was only part of it. When we broke in, she was clutching an empty bottle of sleeping pills that had been prescribed for her mother.'

'She had taken them?' John went cold at the thought.

'The doctor thought so but there weren't enough of them to do any serious damage.'

John closed his eyes for a moment, unable to bear the thought that he had made Esme wretched enough to attempt suicide.

'Only Esme knows whether she meant to kill herself or not and when I saw her this morning she wasn't saying anything, one way or another.'

'My solicitor's letter . . .'

'Frankly, John, it couldn't have helped.'

'You said she was in no condition to discuss anything.'

'I believed she was too drunk to take in much of what I said yesterday afternoon, but it is possible that she understood more than I gave her credit for.'

The waiter disturbed them with John's soup. Appetite gone, he pushed the consommé aside. 'I'll go and see her.'

'Before you do, we should consider some ways of keeping this quiet. I take it you do want to avoid a scandal, if only for the children's sake.'

'Yes.'

'The nursing home isn't cheap. Last night I gave my personal guarantee that the bills would be paid.'

'I'll settle them,' John assured him.

'If you're not going to eat your soup, could you please signal the waiter? My steak should be ready. I'd hate it to get cold while he waits for you to finish your starter.' As John called the waiter over, Richard continued, 'Arrangements will have to be made for Esme's future. After this, she can't live alone.'

'No.'

'A reconciliation . . .'

'I'll talk it over with my solicitor – and Esme,' John interrupted, his heart sinking at the prospect of having to live with her again. But if it was that or her life . . .

'I wouldn't concern myself too much about consulting Esme if I were you, John. She's in no fit state. She made some preposterous allegations yesterday. I realise she was drunk but should she ever repeat them in public I would have no option but to sue her for slander.'

'What allegations?'

Richard looked around to make sure they couldn't be overheard, then lowered his voice. 'That I am Joseph's father.'

Chapter 23

THE NURSING HOME was set high on a hill on Gower Road. John had no problem finding it. Leaving his car, he walked to the door and rang the bell. A pretty young girl in a dark costume opened the door.

'I'm here to see Mrs Esme Griffiths.'

'Mr Griffiths?' she asked.

'Yes.'

'Mr Thomas telephoned to say you were on your way. Please come in.' She ushered him through a tiled hall into a waiting room furnished with leather chairs and sofas. 'Would you like tea or coffee, Mr Griffiths?'

'Neither, thank you.' He didn't know whom he was more irritated with, Richard Thomas for taking control of Esme's life, or Esme for putting herself in a position where Richard had been able to do so.

A middle-aged woman joined them. 'Mr Griffiths, I assume.'

'Yes, matron.' The receptionist closed the door behind her, leaving him alone with the woman, who looked friendlier and more approachable than the staff who had nursed Helen in Swansea General.

'How is my wife?' he asked.

'Recovering well. Provided she has someone to take care of her, she may leave tomorrow.'

'She needs nursing care?'

'No, but . . .' The matron cleared her throat. 'When a patient is found in a situation where alcohol and pills are involved it is as well to keep a close eye. I understand she has been living alone.'

'Yes.'

'You will need to make other arrangements before we discharge her. Would you like to see her?'

He didn't want to be alone with Esme but he could hardly refuse to see her when he was in the same building. 'Is she well enough to receive visitors?' he hedged.

'Yes, her cousin, Mrs Green, is with her now. I'll ask her to leave.'

'No, please don't. I know Mrs Green and given the situation between myself and my wife . . .'

'Mr Thomas told us you were separated.' She gave John a look he interpreted as reproachful. 'If you'll follow me.'

John walked behind the matron up the stairs and into a comfortable room that overlooked manicured lawns bordered by well-tended flowerbeds. Esme and her cousin Dorothy sat in chairs positioned to enjoy the view. Esme didn't even look up as they entered, but Dorothy left her seat and kissed his cheek.

'It is good to see you looking so well, John.'

'Would you like me to send something up? Tea perhaps.' The matron looked from John to Esme.

'Tea would be nice, thank you,' Dorothy replied for them. 'Won't you take my chair, John?'

'I can stand.'

'There's no need.' She pulled another chair into the semicircle before the window.

'How did you know I was here?' Esme sounded husky as if her throat were sore, and John recalled Richard Thomas mentioning that she'd had her stomach pumped.

'Richard Thomas came to see me. How are you feeling?'

'As you see.'

'The matron told me you can leave tomorrow.'

'We've just been talking about that,' Dorothy broke in brightly. 'I would like Esme to come and live with me.'

'In your flat above the hat shop?' John remembered Esme's hostile reaction to the shop and flat he had offered her as part of the divorce settlement.

'Only temporarily. I'm putting my shop on the market. It's high time I did something with my life besides sell hats.'

John looked from Dorothy to Esme, not sure what was coming next.

'If you give me cash instead of the shop and flat in Mumbles I'll buy a place in Bath,' Esme said flatly.

'You want to move to Bath!'

'I want to get out of Swansea and Dot has friends there. But I'll need the annuity as well as the cash.'

'And if I pay you both, you will go ahead with the divorce?' John could scarcely believe what he was hearing.

'On one condition.' Esme turned to him and looked him coldly in the eye. 'You make sure Katie Clay stays away from Joseph.'

Dumbfounded, it was as much as he could do to meet her angry stare.

'Don't look as though you have no idea what I'm talking about. I told you I saw the way she looked at Joseph at Helen's wedding. It's bad enough that Helen is married to a Clay without Joseph getting entangled with another.'

'You don't have to worry about Joe and Katie Clay,' he muttered, finally finding his voice.

'If you're saying that to get your precious divorce . . .'

'Joe is spending a lot of time at the Watkin Morgans'. He went to a beach party with Angela yesterday.'

Esme smiled, a sad little smile of pathetic triumph that reminded John just how seldom he had seen her happy.

When he left the nursing home Dot walked John to his car. As he turned to her to say goodbye, she kissed his cheek. 'I'll be honest with you, John, there is no way I would be able to afford to move to Bath if you weren't buying a place for Esme. My flat and the shop are heavily mortgaged. When I cash in all my assets and add them to what I inherited from Esme's mother, I'll have barely enough to buy myself into a new business venture I'm trusting to provide me with a living.'

'And if it doesn't work out?' he asked, sincerely concerned for her.

'I'll be in trouble. But' — she smiled wryly — 'don't worry, I won't come running to you to bail me out. My business partner has more than enough capital to keep us afloat until the profits start coming in.'

'Are you sure, Dot? I'm fond of you and not just because of what you're doing for Esme,' he said awkwardly. 'You've always been kind to me and Helen and Joe. I'd hate to see you get hurt.'

'I won't — financially, that is,' she qualified. 'Emotionally is another matter. You've probably guessed my partner isn't just my business partner.'

'I'm in no position to judge anyone.'

'He also has a wife he has no intention of leaving.' She paused, waiting for him to say something and, when he didn't, added, 'No one can accuse me of going into this venture wearing rose-coloured glasses.'

'I've never been able to understand why a kind, caring,

331

compassionate, beautiful woman like you isn't happily married with a dozen children.'

'The answer to that is simple. I made the mistake of marrying the wrong man and then the even bigger mistake of divorcing him before my twenty-fifth birthday. People in Swansea don't forget a divorce, or forgive a divorcee. I count myself lucky that I was able to sell hats to them for as long as I did.'

'You could have married again,' he suggested.

'I might have, if anyone had asked me,' she said briskly. 'Esme has one thing right. Decent people don't socialise with divorcees and decent men don't marry them. They make passes at us, because they assume that every woman who's lost her man to the courts has to be panting for attention of the bedroom kind. But no matter how much they may protest they like a woman in private, if she has a broken marriage they take care never to be seen in public with her.'

'I'm sorry.'

'You're not to blame for the faults of Swansea society, and Bath is far away enough for Esme and me to make a fresh start. We'll tell everyone we've lost our husbands to the graveyard, rather than the divorce courts. That will make us marginally more respectable. Then we can embark on new careers as hard-working merry widow businesswomen.' She smiled optimistically.

'I can't see Esme working, let alone hard. And certainly not at the kind of thing that brings in money.'

'You never know, but then, with what you're paying her, she doesn't need to. And I have heard there is a very good amateur dramatic company in Bath.'

'You've done your homework.'

'I thought I should, as I intend to live there a long time.'

'Have you gone as far as picking out a house?' He opened the car door and leaned on it.

'Apartment. On the ground floor of a Georgian town house with a well-proportioned, high-ceilinged drawing room, two large bedrooms and bathroom. The kitchen is small, dark and poky but then as neither Esme nor I is a cordon bleu chef, we'll make do with cold meat, salads and sandwiches on the days we can't afford to eat out.'

'How much is it?' Leaning forward, he slotted his keys into the dashboard.

'Less than you would get for the shop and flat in Mumbles if you put it on the market. I'll ask my solicitor to send you details.'

'Richard Thomas?'

'My business is too insignificant to warrant his attention.' She stood back as he stepped into the car. 'Do you want an actual figure?'

'If it's too much I'll let you know.'

'I won't rook you.'

'I never thought you would.' He held out his hand. 'I wish you – and Esme – well, Dot.'

'Esme was a fool.' She held on to his hand after she shook it. 'If she'd had any sense she would have taken good care of you and your marriage after the way you came to her rescue.'

'I wasn't aware that I was rescuing her at the time. If I had been, I probably wouldn't have married her.'

'She told me you never once reproached her.'

'That's not to say I didn't want to.'

'Really?' she murmured in surprise. 'You never gave me the impression of being bitter.'

'I wasn't about Joe. The anger and the bitterness came later after Helen was born and we stopped sharing our lives and a bedroom.'

'I'm surprised you've waited this long to divorce Esme.'

'Perhaps it's taken me this long to realise that a marriage doesn't necessarily have to be for life.'

'I hope you find happiness, John,' she said earnestly. 'You deserve it, although I can't begin to imagine the woman who would be good enough for you. Do you know that if I'd got to you before Esme she wouldn't have stood a chance?'

'Now you tell me.'

'Take some advice from a woman who really messed up her marriage. Try to concentrate on the good things. You've done a wonderful job of bringing up Joe and Helen.'

'Thank you.'

'Give them my love and tell them they're welcome to visit their mother in my place any time they want to before we leave for Bath – and afterwards. I'll make sure there's a bed settee in the drawing room.'

'I will.' He gunned the ignition.

'Just one more thing.' She leaned in through the car window. 'Tell Joe to be careful around Richard Thomas.'

'Then he is . . .'

'I spoke to Richard earlier. He told me what Esme said. He took the precaution of warning the staff in the nursing home about her accusations in case she made them again. He threatened to sue anyone who repeats them. If you or Joe mention it he might do worse than sue.'

'He asked you to warn me.'

'He didn't have to. I know Richard just as well as, if not better than, Esme and in exactly the same way. Now do you understand why I'm so eager to leave Swansea?'

John drove towards the gates of the nursing home and stopped the car. If he turned left he could be in the warehouse in fifteen minutes. He glanced at his watch. It was three o'clock, plenty of time to take his new secretary in hand and show her how to use a dictionary but to his right the road snaked over Fairwood Common and down the Gower. Cliffs – sea – beaches – rolling hills and countryside – green farmlands bordered by woods . . . He had to do some serious thinking and the office was no place for that. He turned right.

He didn't stop until he reached the end of the peninsula. Parking the car above the steep cliffs of Rhossilli Bay, he limped down the path that led towards the causeway and the promontory of Worm's Head. Although the sun shone from a clear sky, the wind that blew in from the sea was cold and cutting. He stopped and looked around, breathing in what felt like the first real air he'd inhaled in months.

Sheep grazed everywhere, finding footholds on precarious narrow ledges. Gorse bloomed yellow against the pale, coarse coastal grass. Below, to his right, gulls circled, crying above the skeletal timbers of the wreck of the *Helvetia* that thrust upwards through the sand, reminding him of the ribcages of the dinosaurs he'd seen in the Natural History Museum when he'd taken Joe and Helen on a trip there over ten years ago.

He had always loved Rhossilli. It was one of the most inaccessible beaches and consequently the least frequented. His disfigurement had led him to seek out solitude until first Esme, then the children had come into his life. And Katie . . .

He walked on, gradually sinking deeper into his thoughts until he became impervious to both the wind and the beauty around him. In a few months he would, if Esme kept her word, be free. She had promised to contact Richard Thomas that afternoon, sign the divorce papers and grant him his freedom. The decree could be finalised in a month or two. And then?

It was what he wanted, but where did that leave him with Katie?

He came up with all the reasons why he shouldn't be optimistic. Esme had proved fickle before; she might prove so again despite all her assurances. And Katie had come to terms with the way things were between them. It hadn't been easy for her, but she was forging a fresh life for herself. She'd begun a new job, she'd be meeting new people, perhaps even someone nearer her own age, who could offer her more than he could. Someone younger, without health problems who wouldn't need nursing through a decrepit old age when she was still a young woman.

It would be best not to tell her what had happened with Esme. To leave things as they were, rather than run the risk of disappointing her a second time. If and when his divorce was final he would see her again. That shouldn't prove too difficult as she was moving in with Helen. Then he would find out if she had built herself another life. One in which there was no part for him to play.

'Where do you want this, Helen?' Martin shouted as he and Sam manhandled an enormous trunk into the house.

'Upstairs, in the front bedroom,' she called back from the depths of the cupboard under the stairs.

'What you got in here, dead bodies?' Sam stopped and propped the end of the trunk on his knees so Martin could negotiate me first few stairs.

'Six. All boys I killed for not working hard enough.'

'The way you're driving us, I believe it,' he retorted acidly.

'I could make it seven.' Helen adjusted the scarf she'd tied corner-wise over her hair with a bow on top, as she emerged from the cupboard with her aunt's ancient carpet sweeper.

'Just as well we borrowed the largest van your father has, Helen. You girls don't half accumulate some stuff.' Adam walked into the living room with a suitcase. 'This is the third one I've taken up for Lily. 'When Martin and I were in the army we were allowed one kitbag . . .'

'You also wore the same clothes all the time.' Lily emerged from the kitchen with a tray of tea and biscuits.

'You make it sound as if we never changed them.' Making a valiant effort, Martin bent his knees, straightened his back and heaved the trunk upwards, high over the banisters.

'When you did, it was only for exactly the same outfit, so there was no point in you carting around a dozen when three would do. Who wants chocolate biscuits?' she asked.

'That's not fair; we're in no position to grab our share,' Sam complained, as he and Martin finally hauled the trunk on to the landing.

'Tell me how many you want and I'll keep them for you.' Lily sugared Martin's tea and stirred it.

'I'll have half a packet and Martin will have the other half,' Sam gasped as he took the full weight of the trunk for a moment.

'Just as well I bought two, then, isn't it?'

'You little darling.'

'Hands off my girl, Sam,' Martin warned, not entirely humorously.

'It's beginning to look like home. Don't you think?' Helen asked, seeking reassurance.

'If by that you mean it looks chaotic and lived in, I'll agree with you.' Lily opened the door to the dining room and shouted to Katie and Judy. 'Tea up.'

Helen burst out laughing as they walked in.

'What's funny?' Katie pulled a face as she brushed a cobweb from her nose.

'You two couldn't be blacker if you'd been down a pit.'

'I *feel* as if I've been down a pit. That china pantry of your aunt's is unbelievably filthy.' Judy wiped her hands on her overall before reaching for one of the mugs.

'China cupboard of ours,' Helen corrected. 'The china is all right, though, isn't it? When I checked it, I didn't find any chipped or cracked pieces.'

'It's fine, or rather it will be when it's been washed,' Judy agreed. 'The peculiar thing is, it didn't look that dirty until we lifted it out.'

'We should have spent a few more evenings cleaning this place before we moved in.' Lily handed Martin his tea as he walked down the stairs.

'Everything was clean and tidy last night,' Helen protested.

'It was,' Lily granted. 'But it would have been clean in all the hidden places if some bright spark hadn't suggested that we leave the downstairs cupboards until we moved in.'

'We wouldn't have moved in for another week if we had. What with the hours those two work . . .'

'I'd like to see you set up a new hairdressing salon.' Judy checked the state of her hand before taking a biscuit. 'Between old age pensioners coming in with the cut-price perm vouchers my mother had printed to drum up trade and the crache checking whether I can do the latest Shirley Eaton style, I don't know whether I'm coming or going.'

'And you can imagine the impression I'd make in Lewis Lewis if I tried to skip off early after I've only been there a month.'

'There's a world of difference between early and putting in an hour's unpaid overtime every night,' Helen lectured Katie. 'I still don't see why you had to leave the warehouse. My father doesn't say much, long-suffering soul that he is, but everyone I spoke to the last time I was in there said the new girl isn't a patch on you.'

'You had me to order around, Helen.' Lily gave Katie a sympathetic look of commiseration as she handed round the biscuits.

'Only when you weren't spooning with Martin.'

'We do not spoon.' Slipping his arm round Lily's waist, Martin reached for a biscuit. 'But if you don't think we've been pulling our weight, I'll give Lily a hand to scrub out the kitchen cupboards as soon as we've brought in the last load from the van.'

'Oh no, you don't pull that one. You can help Sam clean the windows while I work with Lily in the kitchen.'

'What do you have in mind for me, sergeant major?' Adam ignored Judy, who moved pointedly away from him as he returned from upstairs, and smiled at Helen, giving her a look that set Martin's teeth on edge; Adam was getting far too familiar with his sister-in-law for his liking.

'You can scrub out the food pantry,' she ordered.

'He's allowed in the kitchen and I'm not!' Martin exclaimed.

'The food pantry's not the kitchen, Martin. Come on, another hour and we'll have it finished.'

'Have you thought of a career in the police force, Helen?' Sam griped. 'The sergeant down the station is only half as pushy as you. He'd probably welcome some pointers.'

'I thought we were never going to finish.' Martin grabbed Lily's hand as they crossed the road and ran down the path to the beach.

'Only because you wanted a swim.'

'I wanted some alone time with you,' he said seriously. 'I didn't think it was a good idea for you to move out here before Helen's house started eating up every minute of your spare time. It seems months since I've really seen you.'

337

'Try last night.'

'I don't call a quick kiss outside your uncle's front door after we finished cleaning Helen's living room seeing you.'

'It's all finished now.' She smiled. 'So you can do as much of "really seeing me" as you like from now on.'

'You mean it?' He looked sceptical.

'What's this? "Poor, hard-done-by Marty week"?'

'You don't feel in the least sorry for me, do you.'

She laughed at his attempt at a soulful expression. 'No.'

'Why did I have to pick such a hard-hearted girlfriend? Ah.' He smiled. 'I remember.'

'What?'

'She buys two packets of chocolate biscuits at a time. Hey . . . that hurt,' he protested, as she hit out with her plastic beach bag.

Dropping the bag that held her own and Martin's towel on to a rock above the tideline, she stripped off the old cotton dress she'd worn to clean the kitchen.

'Good God, Lily!'

'Do you like it?' Desperate to appear unconcerned, she checked that the straps on the brassiere top of her scarlet two-piece swimsuit were straight.

'I've never seen so much of you.' He glowered at a couple of boys who turned their heads in her direction.

'I saw it in Lewis Lewis's window when I went there to meet Katie one night from work last week. She dared me to get it and I told her I would if she would.'

'Katie's bought a two-piece like that?'

'Not like this, hers is blue.'

'I'm amazed they put it in the window. If Mrs Lannon had seen it, she'd sue Lewis Lewis for indecency, not to mention what she'd do to you for wearing it.'

'It's not that revealing, is it?' she asked, perturbed by the way he was looking at her.

'The honest truth is yes.'

'You don't like it.'

'If we were alone I'd love it. But we're not alone,' he qualified, as more boys turned their heads in Lily's direction.

As she followed his line of vision a wolf whistle rent the air. 'Last one in the sea is a wimp.' She ran down the central sandy strip of beach into the water.

'Wait!' Almost falling over his jeans as they entangled themselves round his ankles, he charged after her, pushing a couple of boys who'd followed her aside as he plunged into the water.

'That was cold.' She glared at him, debating whether to splash him back after he had splashed her and risk getting even colder, or retreat out of reach.

'Can you swim?' he asked.

'Of course. You?'

'Regimental champion.' Catching her hand, he pulled her out into deeper water, kicking his feet up when it reached his waist.

'I might be able to swim but I'm not a fish,' she gasped as the water came up to her chin.

'Now who's a wimp?'

'Me. I hate the cold.'

'Then come here.' He opened his arms and she swam into them. 'You're a heat leech,' he complained.

She looked into his eyes and realised the same thought was in both their minds. They had never been so close wearing quite so little before, not even on their weekend trips down to the Gower woods.

'I could stay here all night treading water as long as you were in my arms,' he murmured.

'We'd freeze into two blocks of ice.'

'If we remained this close, there'd only be one.' Bending his head to hers, he kissed her.

'People can see us from the beach.'

'Let them.'

She looked over his shoulder. 'Sam and Adam have just come into the water, and Katie and Judy are changing on the beach.'

'Then I suppose I'd better leave this for another time.'

'You working on Saturday, Marty?' She tried to sound casual but her heart was thundering so loudly she was amazed he couldn't hear it.

'I told you, it's the first day of my holidays. You?'

'I'm free, but Helen's going into the warehouse to help with a fashion show and she'll be there all day. Katie's working and Judy will be at the salon.'

He slipped his hands round her back and pulled her even closer. 'If you have plans I hope they include me.'

'If you come round early, we could swim before I make us breakfast.'

339

'How early?' He suddenly felt as if his heart had travelled to his mouth.

'The others will have left by nine.'

'I'll be knocking on your door at five past.'

'How did it go?' Robin pounced on Joe as soon as he left the hall where they'd sat their final examination.

'Not too bad.'

'Hear that?' Robin yelled as candidates continued to spill out of the building. 'Griffiths here says it wasn't too bad.'

'It was tragic,' Thompson declaimed mournfully. 'I may as well drown myself now. Save my father a job when he sees my results.'

'Use my pool,' Robin offered, 'or if you prefer, Pops's whisky.'

'Is that an invitation to a pool party?' Thompson's misery evaporated as his face split into an enormous grin. 'Hey, everyone, back to Robin's for a pool party.'

'Are your parents up for this?' Joe asked, as he and Robin were swept along by the tide that surged towards the car park.

'I overhead Pops tell Mums last night that he was expecting some sort of breakdown after all the studying I've been doing.'

'You can't be serious?' Joe questioned.

'One of the perks of having a doctor for a father. You can pinch his medical books, read up on symptoms and drop them casually over the dinner table. Headaches, inability to concentrate, insomnia, loss of appetite . . .'

'You ate three meals at lunchtime,' Joe contradicted.

'Only because my loss of appetite won't allow me to eat at home. How about –' Robin stood back and watched Thompson pile into a car with half a dozen others including his redheaded girlfriend – 'we drive home via the art college, and get Em and Angie to round up some girls.'

'You've dropped Thompson's redhead?' Joe pulled out his cigarettes.

'Freda – good Lord, no.'

'Her name's Freda?'

'Not exactly stunningly romantic, is it.' Robin helped himself to one of Joe's cigarettes. 'She confided that her parents have no taste for the exotic.'

'Unlike you.'

'Ever wondered what a threesome is like?' Robin lifted his eyebrows suggestively.

'No!' Joe was taken aback by the question.

'Sorry, forgot there for a moment that I was talking to Puritan Joe.'

'You've a mind like a sewer,' Joe pronounced acidly, 'and I'm fed-up with you trying to shock me.'

'I'm not. I've been reading this book . . .'

'Pornographic book.'

'That depends on your definition. I prefer erotic and I thought that with Em and Freda at the same party . . .'

'And Thompson,' Joe reminded him.

'He has no head for whisky and I'll make sure he has plenty.'

'Do the girls know what you have in mind?'

Robin winked. 'That would spoil the surprise.'

'Sometimes I wonder how much of what you spout you actually believe.'

'All of it, dear boy, all of it.' He slapped Joe's shoulders as he turned back to the others. 'Tell the housekeeper to let you in. Joe and I are off to hunt up a few more girls in case the ones we have wear out.'

'Make sure they're pretty,' Thompson cackled.

'I'll bear you in mind when I pick them out.' Robin turned back to Joe. 'I've just had another thought. We could go past your place and invite your sister and the gorgeous Lily.'

'My sister's moved to Limeslade,' Joe said flatly.

'Better still, it's just up the road.'

'She's married.'

'I'm broad-minded.'

'She's also ill.'

'Still! I thought she only lost a baby,' Robin dismissed casually.

'It's a bit more complicated than that.'

'Excuses . . . excuses.' Robin's smile became a leer. 'There's still the gorgeous Lily.'

'Who works all day in a bank.'

'What boring people you know. We can always put notes through their doors.'

'I think not.'

'Party pooper.'

'The last place I'd take my sister or Lily is one of your parties.'

'I suppose you think I should count myself lucky that you're coming.' Robin tossed Joe his keys as he jumped into the passenger seat of his car.

'You don't want to drive?'

'Stop at the first off-licence. I intend to get a head start on the rest of you.'

Chapter 24

HELEN STOOD IN front of her bedroom mirror and studied the scar that ran from the centre of her breasts to three inches below her navel. Red, inflamed, it marred her white skin, puckering it into unsightly bumps. Jack had told her he adored the way her skin looked and felt, smooth – like silk. He had loved caressing her, running his hands over her . . .

She closed her eyes and stroked her stomach, trying to imagine it was Jack who was touching her. The scar even felt ugly. It was thick, horrible and lumpy beneath her fingertips and, as if that weren't enough, either side of it were pockmarked dents where metal clips had been inserted to strengthen the stitches.

It was so unfair. She'd lost her looks, she'd never have a baby and she wasn't even nineteen years old. Jack was so handsome he'd have no trouble finding someone else but she –

She opened her eyes and forced herself to look into the mirror again. Her face, her hair, her breasts, her arms, her legs paled into insignificance when set against the hideous, repulsive mark that dominated her body. She thought enviously of the two-piece swimsuits Katie and Lily had bought, and how she would never be able to wear a two-piece again. And suddenly the import of what had happened hit her full force and she sank down, naked, on to the bed.

She hadn't cried once while she had been organising the move into the house. There had been no time between making what felt like a million and one lists of things to do, people to contact, colour schemes to be picked out for her kitchen and bathroom, and finding a decorator who wouldn't cost the earth. Looking back, she realised that she had deliberately filled every waking moment with practical considerations, barely leaving herself time to write to Jack at the end of each exhausting day because she hadn't wanted to think. And now all of sudden that was all she had left to do.

All the pleasure she had felt yesterday at having a house in a perfect spot overlooking a beautiful beach dissipated. What was the point in having a house when Jack wasn't there to share it with her – and there would never be any children to run down to the beach and play in the sand and the sea?

As she rose from the bed she allowed her tears to fall for the first time since she had moved in. Walking quickly, restlessly, she went into the bathroom and opened the cabinet. Moving aside plasters, face creams and witch hazel, she found what she was looking for, an almost full bottle of aspirin.

'We'll only be next door . . .'

'We've had hundreds of parties without you, Mums,' Angela Watkin Morgan reassured her mother. 'No one's going to wreck the place.'

'It's not the house we're worried about.' Her father surveyed the crowd of boys jumping in and out of the pool. 'Your brother and his friends have been under a lot of pressure. They're entitled to let off steam but if any of them gets dangerously drunk . . .'

'We'll call you right away,' Angela promised.

'You don't want someone choking . . .'

'No one will, Pops.' Robin adopted what Angela called his 'responsible look' which, all his friends knew and his parents had apparently never discovered, only went expression deep. 'Don't worry, Joe and I will keep an eye on things.'

'That's a bit unfair on Joseph who's as entitled to let his hair down as the rest of you.' Dr Watkin Morgan winked at Joe as he opened the door for his wife and escorted her out of the house.

Robin unbuttoned his shirt. 'I'm for the pool.'

'Is that wise, Robin, after what you've drunk?' Joe counselled.

'There's so many bodies in it there's no room to drown.' Angela dribbled a thin line of chlorinated water as she unwrapped an enormous towel from herself to reveal a white and gold two-piece swimsuit. 'If you're playing barman, Joe, mine's a . . .'

'Brandy, I know.' He pushed his way into the crowded dining room and reached for the bottle.

'Make it a Sherry. And' – she gave him a warm smile – 'a small one.'

'Turning over a new leaf, Angie.' Emily giggled as Robin twanged the strap of her bra top.

'Something tells me I will need to be in full possession of my faculties for what's going to happen later.' She lifted her eyebrows as she took the glass Joe handed her.

'Forfeits,' Thompson shouted from the den. 'First to get the top of a two-piece is king.'

Before Emily had a chance to defend herself, Robin unclipped the back of hers and pulled it off her.

'You beast!' Emily covered her breasts with her hands as every eye in the room focused on her.

'Come on, sweetheart, you know you like being looked at.' Robin pulled her hands away, holding them high above her head as he slowly rotated her in front of the boys.

'When you've finished with that one, pass her over, Robin,' Thompson slurred.

'I hate you, Robin.'

'No, you don't, darling.' Dropping Emily's arms, he kissed her. 'And as king, I say the first one to get a bottom gets to stay king for the night.'

Picking Emily up, Robin carried her through the conservatory to the pool, held her over the water and waited for the swimmers to clear a space, before dropping her in. Diving after her, he floated to the surface seconds later, brandishing the bottom of her swimsuit.

'I'd better stop Robin before things get out of hand.'

'What out of hand, Joe?' Angie purred, grabbing his arm. 'A party wouldn't be a party without Emily stripping.'

He jerked back as she closed her hand on the front of his trousers and unfastened his fly. 'Angie . . .'

'If it would help things along, I could follow Emily's example.'

Aware that the whisky he'd drunk had gone to his head, he tried to sound casual, but his 'Thank you, but no', pitched to be heard above the shrieks from the pool, came out more prudish than blasé.

'There's something you should know about me, Joe. I strip only in private and as a preliminary. Aren't you going to ask to what?'

Acutely conscious of her fingers exploring his underwear, he swallowed hard before shaking his head.

'Tell me, Joe, what does it take to get you into bed?'

'Some feeling between me and the girl,' he murmured thickly.

'I'll show you feeling.' She pulled him back into her father's study and closed the door. Locking it behind her, she dropped the key down her top. 'You want out of here you have to come and get it.'

Before he realised what was happening her tongue was in his mouth and she'd pushed him on to the sofa. Her two-piece and his shirt landed on the floor at the same instant, seconds later his trousers joined them. One thought flashed through his mind as he entered her. This was practice for when he married Lily.

Suddenly it all made sense. Everything he had ever read suggested that the man should be experienced. The woman submitted and the man showed her a good time. It was the way of the world and how could he show Lily a good time without finding out what a woman liked first?

'Helen.'

Helen heard someone call her name, but she continued to sit on the bed, staring at the pills she'd tipped out. There had to be a hundred of them. Would they be enough, and even if they were, could she swallow that many . . .

'Helen!' This time the cry was followed by a knock at the door, so she knew she hadn't imagined it. She looked at the clock. Last night she had told Lily and Katie she would spend the morning in the garden, sunbathing and tidying the overgrown flowerbeds and it was already past two o'clock.

She went to the window and shouted 'coming', before she realised she didn't have any clothes on. Grabbing her old one-piece bathing suit she pulled it on and threw her towelling beach robe on top. Checking her reflection in the mirror, she washed her tear-stained face and ran a comb through her hair before running down the stairs and opening the door. 'Adam, what on earth are you doing here?'

'I had the afternoon off, so I thought I'd have a swim, and where better to swim than Limeslade Bay? And, after my swim, I thought I'd visit my old friend Helen and take her lunch.' He held up a couple of paper bags. 'Pasties, crisps and apples, no expense spared, the absolute best the corner shop had to offer. It's glorious out here. If you dig up an old blanket we could eat on your lawn – after I flatten it a bit.'

'I was thinking of catching a bus into the warehouse,' she lied, feeling ill at ease alone with him.

'You'll still have to eat. And although I've brought food I have no drink. Don't suppose you feel like making a pot of tea? I'm parched,' he added, sensing her reluctance.

She hesitated; then, deciding that as anyone could look over her garden wall it was public enough, she capitulated. 'All right, but you stay here. I'll bring a blanket out in a moment.' She went into the kitchen and put the kettle on before running upstairs to the airing cupboard. She had given most of her aunt's clothes and bedding to the Red Cross but she had kept back a couple of blankets for the beach. Fishing one out, she opened the bedroom window and dropped it on Adam's head. By the time she had made the tea and carried it and a tray of crockery outside, he had spread the blanket, taken off his shirt and was stretched out, sunbathing.

'This is the life.' He sighed contentedly. 'You don't know how lucky you are not having to work in weather like this.'

'I start in the warehouse on Monday.'

'I don't know why you're in such a hurry.'

'Because it's boring staying at home all day with nothing to do and because the doctor says I'm fit enough.' The doctor had also told her she'd be fit for something else and Jack had written to say he would be getting a full week's leave at the end of his training, he just wasn't sure how soon it would be, which was why she'd been examining herself in the mirror. And if Adam hadn't interrupted her . . .

'Good pasties,' he commented, breaking in on her thoughts.

'Yes.'

'How would you know? You haven't taken a bite out of yours.'

She picked it up from her plate and nibbled a corner. 'Adam, I don't want you to take this the wrong way but I am a married woman.'

'I was at your wedding,' he reminded her drily.

'I don't think you should come round here when I'm alone. It's different when the girls are here or when you come with Sam and Martin . . .'

'It's Thursday.'

'Yes,' she concurred, mystified by his train of thought.

'I thought Katie had a half-day in Lewis Lewis.'

Helen smiled in relief. 'The shop has, but the office doesn't close and they're particularly busy at the moment buying in the autumn range.'

'I didn't know.' He tried to look innocent. He had overheard Katie telling Lily that she had to work that day.

'You're still keen on her, then,' Helen probed.

'Do you have any gardening tools?'

'Pardon?'

'Gardening tools. You've some fine plants here. They'd look even better if they weren't choked by weeds and if you've a mower or a pair of garden shears this lawn could do with cutting.'

'I didn't mean to pry,' she apologised.

'And I didn't mean to make you feel awkward by coming here when you're alone.' Turning on to his stomach, he looked up at her. 'If you can put up with me for a bit longer, I'll take a look in the shed after we've finished eating and make a start.'

'You don't look like the type to know anything about gardening.'

'I've been helping my father with his allotment since I was a nipper.'

'You amaze me.'

'That's me, wonder boy,' he murmured deprecatingly, smiling at her as he held out his cup. 'Do you think that tea's brewed by now?'

'Hey, lady, if you're not too proud to get on the back of a bike, I'll give you a lift home.'

Lily whirled round as she left the bank to see Martin, sitting on Jack's bike, waiting at the kerb. 'Marty, this is a surprise.' Dressed in a clean white shirt and jeans, he looked as though he'd just shaved and stepped out of a bath. Holding her handbag she climbed on the bike and caught a whiff of Old Spice aftershave, which he only wore when he went out. 'Haven't you been to work today?'

'I had a chat with the boss yesterday and suggested that if I went in an hour early he could let me leave an hour early.'

'That's great.'

'It wasn't great at half past five this morning. The only thing that got me out of bed was the thought that I'd have time to go home, bath and change before I met you.' He gave her a quick, conscious smile. 'I enjoyed that swim we had and there's no point in you living in Limeslade if you don't take advantage of it.'

'Absolutely.'

'And . . . the good news is, I'll be able to do it every other day. Unfortunately so many of the other mechanics thought it was a good idea too the boss has split us into two shifts.'

'You had tea?' She linked her hands round his waist.

'No.'

'What would you like?' she asked.

'I get fed as well? This gets better and better.'

'As it's my turn to cook I picked up pork chops for Helen, Katie and Judy and me at lunchtime. If you stop at the butcher's I'll get an extra one for you unless you prefer something else.'

'Pork chop is fine.' Turning his head, he gave her a chaste kiss on the cheek before starting the engine.

Joe rolled off Angie and the sofa on to the floor. Despite all the poems he had written on love, requited and otherwise, he hadn't quite known what to expect of his first physical experience with a woman. Passion spent, he was conscious of a faint feeling of disgust and revulsion for the animal-like act he and Angela had performed. Concerned only for his own physical needs, he had given no thought to the spiritual.

When he finally made love to Lily – as he was certain he would do – he knew that it would be an almost religious experience for both of them, involving their hearts, minds and souls as much as, if not more than, their bodies.

'You all right, Joe?'

He felt Angela fumbling for his hand and pulled it away. 'Yes.' Refusing to look at her, he reached for his underpants and pulled them and his trousers on before tossing her the towel.

'You're in a hurry to get dressed.'

'Everyone will be wondering where we are.'

'They are all too drunk to spare a thought for us.' Turning on her side, she looked him in the eye without making any attempt to cover herself. 'Joe . . .'

'Yes,' he snapped irritably.

'It's no big deal,' she murmured coolly.

'How can you say that?' Leaning against the wall, he stared straight ahead at the bookshelves, looking anywhere but at her.

'Because people have been doing it since the beginning of time. If they hadn't, we wouldn't be here.'

'Is that all lovemaking means to you?' he questioned savagely. '"Something people do"?'

'Not entirely, because people do it with varying degrees of satisfaction and success.'

Although he knew he was going to regret asking, he dared, 'And us?'

'It's such a shame that one of the most pleasurable of all human experiences can be marred by a misplaced sense of guilt. I understand, now, why Robin calls you Puritan Joe.'

349

'How you can lie there like that, knowing I don't love you . . .'

'You think I should be ashamed of my body?' she questioned coolly.

'I think you should keep it for someone who loves you,' he countered angrily.

'What is love?'

'Now you want a philosophical discussion on the meaning of the word.' He paced to the door, before remembering she had secreted the key in her two-piece. He looked down at the scraps of gold nylon lying on the floor and decided against fumbling through them to find it.

'I think you're confusing some childish ideal of what grown-up emotion is like with sex.' She turned on to her back and stretched out as if she were deliberately trying to embarrass him.

'And we just had sex.'

'Give the man full marks.' She rose to her feet. 'And unlike Robin, I don't do it with everyone.'

'But you've done it before,' he rebuked.

'Didn't your mother tell you a gentleman never asks a lady about her past?' she chided. 'And don't try telling me you haven't. You were engaged to that girl . . .'

'Almost,' he corrected.

'Then you didn't . . .' She broke into peals of laughter. 'Oh Joe, don't tell me you bought the ring before you got her to rock and roll with you. That is absolutely priceless and so like you.' Fishing the key from the folds of the towel lying next to her, she flung it at him. As he caught it, she kissed his cheek. 'When you've grown up, darling – and not before – you can come back for more.'

'As soon as I've put the chops in the meat safe and changed into my costume I'll be with you for that swim.' Lily climbed off the bike.

'I'll see if any of the others are around and want to join us.' Propping the bike against the garden wall, Martin looked down at the beach. Although it was early evening the sun was still warm and the sea sparkled as invitingly as he remembered from his childhood – only now he had far better memories to associate with swimming. He could recall every curve of Lily's body as she had nestled close to him under cover of the water, and that remembrance, more than any other thought, had spurred him out of bed that morning before the larks had even opened their eyes.

Lily glanced at her watch. 'Judy and Katie won't be in until the six-thirty Mumbles train comes in but Helen should be home.' Unlocking the front door, she went into the house.

Hearing voices in the side garden, Martin wandered round the front of the house. He froze, watching Helen and Adam who were stretched out, side by side face down on a blanket, sunbathing in swimsuits. Oblivious to his presence they were eating cherries from a bowl and seeing who could spit the stones the furthest. Rolling on to his back, but no further from Helen, Adam idly tickled her between her shoulder blades. As she squirmed, he moved his hand downwards.

'That's far enough, Adam.'

Adam glanced up and smiled, an expression Martin interpreted as triumph. 'Hey, Martin, I thought I heard the bike. Want a cherry?' Adam offered the bowl as if he, not Helen, owned the place.

'No.'

'What's far enough, Marty?' Helen propped herself up on one elbow.

'Adam knows,' he answered darkly.

'Why so glum? You and Lily haven't quarrelled again, have you?' she asked idly.

'No, we were going for a swim and I came to ask if you'd like to come with us, but I see you're otherwise occupied.'

Forgetting her earlier reservations about spending the afternoon alone with Adam, and without stopping to consider that she was only wearing her swimsuit and Adam had changed into his trunks after clearing one of her flowerbeds, Helen bristled with indignation. 'We're just sunbathing.'

'I'm sorry I disturbed you.' Martin turned on his heel.

'You didn't. Martin . . .'

'Lily will be waiting.'

Rising, Helen ran after him, stepping in front of him just as he was about to enter the house. 'That was rude . . .'

'And you're married to my brother.'

'You think I've forgotten?'

'Have you?' He confronted her.

'You're being ridiculous. Adam is a friend . . .'

'Close friend.'

'How dare you!' Furious at his insinuation, she slapped him soundly across the face.

'What on earth's going on?' Lily ran down the stairs in a cotton dress, carrying her beach bag.

'Your boyfriend thinks I'm behaving like a tart.'

'You said it, Helen, not me.' Crossing his arms, Martin stood his ground.

'All I was doing was sunbathing in the garden with Adam.' Helen appealed to Lily. 'And Adam hasn't even been in the house, just the garden. He's cleared a flowerbed of weeds, which is more than you've done . . .'

'This is your house, Helen, not mine,' Martin reminded her.

'Exactly, and I can invite anyone I choose to into it.'

'I'll see you on the beach, Lily.' Turning his back on Helen, Martin crossed the road.

Lily stepped on to the path.

'Don't tell me you're taking Martin's side,' Helen demanded indignantly. 'Just because he's your boyfriend . . .'

'I'm not taking any side . . .' Lily faltered as Adam strolled round the side of the house in the briefest of red bathing trunks, his chest and legs covered with tightly curled blond hair a shade lighter than his head.

'Problems, Helen?' He wrapped his arm round her waist and gave her a big smile.

'No.' Helen removed his hand.

'Then why the big freeze?'

Lily could see why Martin was angry. Before Adam had appeared on the scene she might have been prepared to put his reaction to Helen sunbathing with Adam down to his overprotective attitude towards his younger brother. But the sight of Helen and Adam wearing so little in the intimacy of Helen's garden, coupled with Adam's familiarity towards Helen, shocked her, making her feel as old-fashioned, narrow-minded and disapproving as Mrs Lannon. And at that moment she was livid with Helen for putting her in a position where she felt that way.

'Martin called me a tart.'

'You called yourself a tart, Helen.' Lily slung her bag over her shoulder. 'There's pork chops for your tea in the kitchen.'

'It's your turn to cook,' Helen shouted after her as she ran down the path.

'I'll do it another night. Martin and I will be eating out.'

'Lily . . .' When Lily didn't acknowledge her, Helen glared at Adam. 'Put your clothes on and get out.'

'Helen . . .'

'Just do it.' She went inside and slammed the door.

'I was about to ask if I could use your bathroom,' he called through the letter box.

'There's a bush behind the house.' She charged up the stairs to her bedroom and pulled the curtains.

'She said he'd cleared a flowerbed so he must have been there for the best part of the afternoon if not the day.' Martin sat on the beach after he'd stripped off his clothes.

'There's no use dwelling on it, Marty,' Lily said firmly.

'Admit it, you're as angry with Helen and Adam as I am.'

Stripping off her dress, she laid her towel on the sand and sat beside him. 'You know Helen; she's always been headstrong. If you try to warn her about something she takes it the wrong way and does things she would never dream of doing if she gave herself time to think. Look at her and Jack . . .'

'And the way they got married,' he interrupted.

'Before then,' she said quietly. 'Mrs Griffiths was always warning Helen to "stay away from wild Jack Clay" when your sister wasn't around.'

'"Just wild Jack Clay" or those "savage uncivilised Clay boys"?' When she didn't answer he added, 'You don't have to tell me that half the women in the street disapproved of us as a family.'

'You're being oversensitive again.'

'No I'm not . . .'

'We were talking about Helen and your brother.' She steered the conversation back on track. 'She loves him.'

'I wish I could be as sure as you.'

'I am,' she said emphatically, negating any further protest. 'But I am also sure that what attracted Helen to Jack in the first place was the warnings her mother gave her to stay away. Mrs Griffiths's disapproval made Jack irresistible. As Joe always used to say, telling Helen not to do something was a one hundred per cent certain way of getting her to do it.'

'And Joe knows her – and you – so well,' he snapped, annoyed with her for bringing up his name.

'Joe knows Helen as well as you know Katie,' she responded evenly. 'And it won't help matters if you try quarrelling with me as well.'

'I'm sorry,' he murmured contritely, 'I shouldn't have had a go at you, but the last thing Jack said to me, was "look after Helen" and I feel responsible for what she does.'

'You can't stop her from inviting Adam to her house,' she sympathised.

'What do you suggest I do? Write to Jack . . .'

'No. First you swim out beyond our depth with me so I can heat leech. Then we'll swim back, dry off, change and drive down to the fish and chip shop for tea.'

'And the pork chops?'

'Helen can eat the two spare ones if she can face them,' she said decisively. 'If we leave her alone for now, I might be able to talk her round to seeing things from a sensible point of view later.'

'And if you don't?'

'Then we'll talk again about you writing to Jack.'

'Isn't it Lily's turn to cook?' Judy hobbled into the house after a ten-hour stint in her mother's new salon.

'It is.' Helen crashed the frying pan on to the stove and unwrapped the newspaper from round the pork chops. She had been incensed to see two parcels in the meat safe, one containing a solitary chop, which presumably meant that Lily had picked it up after she had bought the others so Martin could eat with them.

'If it's Lily's turn, how come you're doing it?'

'Because she's not here and I am.' Helen had watched Martin and Lily swim from her bedroom window, all the while wishing she had the courage to join them. After they had emerged from the sea, they had changed under cover of their towels on the beach. She had run down to the kitchen when they had begun to walk up, expecting them to come into the house, but instead, she had heard Martin's bike start up and realised they had left. Then Katie had arrived so exhausted from work that she had gone to sleep on the sofa after exchanging less than half a dozen words with her.

'You could wait for her to come back. I'm sure she won't be long; it's not like Lily to forget her turn.' Judy kicked off her shoes and wriggled her toes blissfully on the cool linoleum. 'I think I'll buy a high stool for the salon. This standing on my feet all day is killing me.'

'She won't be back.' Helen cut a knob of lard from a block and threw it into the pan. 'She's buggered off with Martin.'

'Language!'

'And who elected you "Miss Prim and Proper"? A couple of weeks ago you were swearing like a trooper.'

'I've learned the error of my ways.' Judy sank down on a kitchen chair. 'If Lily really has gone, I'll help in any way I can as long as I can do it from here.'

'You can peel the potatoes.' Helen lifted an enamel bowl half full of water and potatoes from the sink and slopped it on the table in front of her.

'Be an angel, pass me the peeler and a saucepan of clean water,' Judy begged.

'By the time I've finished running around for you I may as well do it myself,' Helen griped.

'And who's upset you today?' Judy took the knife Helen handed her and set to work.

'If you must know, Martin.'

'Marty!'

'Yes, bloody "Mr butter won't melt in my mouth" Marty.' Helen broke the head off a match as she tried to light it.

'You going to tell me what your brother-in-law did, or just fume about it?'

'He may be my brother-in-law, but that doesn't give him the right to tell me who I can and can't invite into *my* house.'

'I didn't say it did.' Exhausted after spending the entire day listening to an endless stream of middle-aged customers' opinions on everything from the new rock and roll music that was corrupting the younger generation to how ridiculous Teddy boys looked in their luminous socks and Edwardian jackets, and how their presence made it too dangerous to venture out on the streets after dark in case one of them was carrying the dreaded flick knife – that everyone had heard they armed themselves with – but had never actually seen – the last thing Judy felt like was a quarrel with Helen.

'He must have picked Lily up from work on Jack's bike . . .'

'Lucky Lily,' Judy broke in.

'Are you going to listen to me or not?'

Judy held up her hands, a potato in one, knife in the other. 'I'm listening.'

'He saw Adam and me in the garden and blew his stack. Called me a tart . . .'

'Who called you a tart?' Katie stood, disorientated, in the doorway, rubbing her eyes.

'Your brother.'

'I don't believe you.' Katie spoke quietly, yet so forcefully that Helen had the grace to back off.

'He didn't disagree with me when I called myself a tart,' she protested defensively.

'What was Adam doing here?' Judy asked quietly.

'If you must know, he came looking for Katie.'

'I may be missing the point but I'm only a simple secretary. Why did you call yourself a tart?' Katie asked.

'Because I could see what Martin thought of me when he saw me sunbathing with Adam.'

'He came looking for Katie but you ended up sunbathing with him.' Judy had tried to come to terms with what had happened between her and Adam the night he had taken her to the dinner dance but it hadn't helped when he had continued to join in everything they did, behaving as if she meant no more – or less – to him than Katie, Lily or Helen.

'He sorted one of the flowerbeds for me. I made us tea, then Martin arrived. You should have heard the way he carried on. He behaved worse than any outraged father.'

'You were just sunbathing?' Judy pressed. 'He didn't try anything on . . .'

'Now you're starting on me.' Helen turned on Judy. 'Yes, I am sure that we were just sunbathing.'

'And you had your clothes on.'

'Our costumes and the garden is a public place.'

'Not that public, Helen, it might have been better if the two of you had gone down the beach.' Katie took a knife from the drawer, pulled out a chair and picked a potato out of the bowl.

'Why should I when I can sunbathe in my own garden?' Helen finally lit a match at the fourth attempt and turned on the gas.

'Because people talk and that's probably what Marty was thinking about,' Katie defended. 'Jack's hot-tempered. If he heard rumours . . .'

'About me and Adam!'

'Katie's right,' Judy broke in swiftly, 'and you won't be the only one writing to him, Helen.'

'You two and Marty would write and tell him that I was sunbathing with Adam Jordan . . .' Helen began hotly.

'Don't be silly,' Katie interrupted. 'And it's not just us. All the boys have Jack's address. He has a lot of friends on the building sites and in the warehouse; some of them are bound to come up here to swim. It's one of the easiest beaches to get to and you can't walk down to it without passing this house. You know what terrible gossips Swansea people are. Marty's probably worried that someone might say something and Jack will get the wrong end of the stick.'

Helen washed three pork chops under the tap, set them on a plate, scooped a second knob of dripping out of the jar when the first had melted and placed it together with the chops in the frying pan. 'That's ridiculous.'

'Is it?' Katie took over the conversation again. 'You only have to look at Martin with your brother.'

Helen looked at Katie carefully. 'I didn't know Martin was jealous of Joe.'

'It's not something Lily would talk about to you. After all, you are Joe's sister. But I think Marty finds it difficult to forget Lily was almost engaged to him.'

'But there's nothing going between them now.'

'I think Lily's finally managed to convince him,' Katie said carefully, 'but it's been hard for him to accept and he still watches her every time he sees her talking to Joe.'

'I didn't know.' Helen turned the gas under the frying pan down low. 'You're close to Martin and Jack.'

'Very,' Katie said fiercely. 'We've always had to look out for one another.'

'Which is why Martin lost his temper with me tonight.'

'If he did, I'm sure he was only thinking of Jack – and you,' Katie added tactfully.

'You believe that?'

White-faced with strain, Judy rose from the table. 'I don't think you should let Adam come round here again, Helen, whether he's looking for Katie or you . . .'

'He's one of the crowd,' Helen interrupted. 'I can't just tell him to stay away.'

Judy looked at Katie and Helen. There was no way she could explain to either of them why they should stay away from Adam Jordan without telling them what had happened and she simply couldn't face losing their friendship. It was hard enough living with the disgust she felt for herself after that night, without losing their respect as well. 'I'm sorry, I'm not hungry, Helen. I'm going to bed. Please don't disturb me.'

357

Chapter 25

'BEEN CELEBRATING?' JOHN asked, as Joe walked unsteadily into the living room. He smelled the whisky and noticed the glazed expression in Joe's eyes but refrained from making further comment.

'Robin had a pool party.' Joe fell unsteadily into a chair.

'It broke up early.'

'Most of the boys were too drunk to stand, let alone party any more.' Joe attempted to prop his legs on the coffee table. Missing the edge by two inches, his heels crashed to the floor.

'You're all entitled to let your hair down after the way you've been working.' John smiled.

Joe nodded, as a tide of sour, whisky-tainted bile rose in his mouth.

'Summer ball tomorrow.'

Joe nodded again.

'I have to talk to you about something.'

'That sounds serious.'

'It can wait.'

'I'm not very drunk.' Making a supreme effort, Joe managed to focus on John. 'Tell me now.'

'You won't remember a word I've said tomorrow.'

'I might,' Joe enunciated carefully. 'If not, you can bring it up again.'

John looked at his whisky glass. It was almost empty but he decided against refilling it because he'd feel obliged to offer Joe one and he'd had more than enough. 'Your mother's been taken ill.'

'You expect me to be sorry after the way she's treated us?'

'She's going to be all right . . .'

'Bully for her,' Joe bit back truculently.

'It's not just that, Joe. It's something your Aunt Dot said.' He looked Joe in the eye until he was sure he had his full attention. 'She wanted to warn you off saying anything to Richard Thomas.'

'Such as?'

'Apparently your mother said something to him when she was . . . taken ill. He threatened to sue the nursing home staff who overheard her if they dared to repeat her allegation.'

'And this something she said was about him being my father.'

Forgetting his earlier resolve, John reached for the whisky bottle. 'You know he's your father?'

'She told me after grandmother's funeral.'

'You didn't say anything.'

'I didn't want to upset you.' Jack slumped back in his chair. 'Is he my father?'

John shook his head as he refilled his glass. 'I honestly don't know, Joe.'

'How many men did the bitch sleep with?'

'I won't allow you to talk about your mother that way . . .'

'Why not?' Joe questioned caustically. 'You can't stand her . . .'

'Whatever else, she is your mother,' John reminded him forcefully, 'and just because I no longer want to remain married to her doesn't mean I'll stand by and let you call her names.'

'Women of her class are all the same. All they think about is sex and money. They strip off and open their legs for any man with a big enough bank account . . .'

'What happened tonight, Joe?' Disturbed by Joe's ramblings John realised he was drunker than he'd originally thought and wished he'd never brought up the subject of Richard Thomas.

'Nothing,' Joe slurred. 'Absolutely bloody nothing.' He began to laugh.

'You're overwrought; you've been working too hard . . .'

Joe stopped laughing as suddenly as he'd begun. 'You're right, Dad — or is it John? I'm going to bed.'

'Want a hand?'

Joe shook his head again and regretted it as the room began to spin alarmingly around him.

'Want some black coffee before you go up?'

'I'll be all right.' Staggering to his feet Joe lurched through the door. John watched him leave, then listened intently as he stumbled up the stairs and into the bathroom. He waited for the water to stop running before walking up behind him. Joe was lying face down on his bed. He moved his head to a more comfortable position, removed his shoes and, taking a blanket from Helen's room, covered him.

He stood back and watched him for a few minutes. The boy he had

359

regarded as his son from the day he'd been born was young, bright, clever, tipped to get a good degree, had an excellent job waiting for him at the end of the summer, had inherited more money than he could possibly want in one lifetime and had a girl like Angela Watkin Morgan throwing herself at him. To all intents he was set to lead a charmed life. What he couldn't understand was why he felt so worried for him when all Joe had done was drink too much on the day he finished his examinations.

Helen wrenched open her front door the minute she heard the bike engine. 'Sorry.' She stepped back, embarrassed at interrupting Martin as he was about to kiss Lily.

'You wanted something?' Martin questioned coldly.

'I was hoping to talk to you.' She had the grace to look shamefaced.

'Me or Lily?'

'Both of you. I know it's late but . . .'

'We'll be inside in a minute.' He turned back to Lily unwilling to forgo his goodnight kiss.

'Remember tomorrow,' Lily reminded him as the minutes ticked by.

'We're having an entire day together.' Locking his hands behind her back, he pulled her close.

'Starting early, which is why we should find out what Helen wants.'

'I'm greedy, I want tonight as well as tomorrow.'

'Marty . . .'

'All right, give me a minute.' He propped the bike against the wall as she walked into the house.

Lily opened the door to the living room to see Helen sitting alone. 'Where are the others?'

'Judy went to bed almost as soon as she came in and Katie went up half an hour ago.'

'Are they all right?' Taking off her coat, Lily hung it on a hook on the back of the door.

'Katie said she's just tired but Judy didn't look well.'

'Have you checked on her?'

'She said she didn't want to be disturbed but the last time I looked in on her, she was sleeping.' Helen went into the kitchen and returned with a tray. 'I prepared some coffee. I thought you and Martin might like some.'

'That was thoughtful.' Given Helen's unpredictability, Lily hadn't been sure what to expect.

'Coffee?' Helen asked Martin as he walked in.

'Please.'

'Won't you sit down?' Helen poured hot water on to the instant granules she'd spooned into the cups as Martin sat beside Lily on the sofa. 'I wanted to tell you that you got the wrong impression earlier about Adam. He had the afternoon off, so he decided to go for a swim. Afterwards he called in here on the off chance as a friend.'

'Friend,' Martin repeated sceptically.

'If you must know, he was hoping to see Katie,' she revealed, feeling as though she were being disloyal to Katie.

'In the afternoon when she works,' Martin said flatly.

'On a Thursday afternoon when she works in a department store.' Helen handed him his coffee. 'It is half day in Swansea.'

'Office staff don't have half days.' Martin helped himself to sugar and milk.

'Adam didn't know that.'

'Katie has told him she's not interested in him.' He placed his cup on the table.

'That obviously hasn't stopped Adam from hoping she'll change her mind.' Helen was close to exasperation.

'Then perhaps I should have a word with him and tell him that when my sister says no, she means it.' Martin's temper rose along with his voice.

'Katie has handled the situation with Adam perfectly well by herself until now, Marty. I'd let her carry on, unless she asks for your help.' Lily took the coffee Helen gave her and sat back next to him.

'I just wanted you to know that there's nothing going on between me and Adam, there won't be and I'd appreciate it if you didn't write to Jack . . .'

'You thought I'd write to Jack about this!' he exclaimed, conveniently forgetting that he'd talked to Lily about doing just that.

'You won't?'

'The last thing Jack needs when he's finishing his basic training and on the point of being sent to God knows what forsaken corner of the world is a letter from me or anyone else telling him that his wife is . . .'

'A tart.' Helen looked him in the eye.

361

'I wasn't going to say that.'

'Then what were you going to say, Martin?'

'If I were going to say anything to Jack – and I wouldn't consider it unless I thought someone else was about to tell him what you were up to – it would be along the lines of "entertaining Adam in her house in the afternoon when everyone else is at work".'

'I suppose I deserve that,' she conceded.

'And even then, I would only say something, because I know he would never forgive me for holding back anything important about you. He's my brother, Helen, I owe him . . .'

'I've had the family talking-to from Katie, thank you. I may not have realised before, but I do know now, just how close you three are.'

'Katie knows about this?'

'I talked to her and Judy about it.'

'What did they say?' Taking Martin's hand, Lily leaned against his shoulder.

'More or less the same as you two.'

'That what you and Adam were doing could give rise to gossip,' Martin suggested.

'Yes,' Helen agreed. 'But that's not to say the four of you aren't hopelessly old-fashioned fuddy-duddie. But OK, there could have been gossip and it might have upset Jack if he'd heard about it. All I can say in my defence is that I didn't think and since I've come out of hospital I've been lonely when you three have been out at work all day. But from tomorrow it's going to be different. I have a fashion show to organise and I'll be in the warehouse more or less every day from now on, so' – she forced herself to look directly at Martin – 'there'll be no time for me to entertain Adam, or anyone else for that matter, when Lily, Katie and Judy are at work.'

'I know it's not easy for you with Jack away . . .'

'But you still think I should shut myself into a cupboard until he comes back, or at least go into mourning.'

'I think you should carry on going out with Lily, Judy Katie, the boys and me,' Martin said. 'As one of a crowd.'

'Starting tomorrow down the Pier.' Lily smiled, relieved that the situation between Helen and Martin was resolved.

'Dancing,' Helen murmured doubtfully.

'Why not?' Martin questioned. 'What can anyone possibly say if half the crowd consists of girls and your brother-in-law is there as well?'

'The Mrs Lannons of this world would find plenty.'

'Jack would never listen to the Mrs Lannons of this world.'

'I'll see how tired I am after working.' She left her chair. 'And speaking of which, I should go to bed.'

'Sleep well, and don't bother about the cups. I'll clear them,' Lily offered.

'You spending tomorrow here, Lily?'

Lily gripped Martin's hand. 'We planned to.'

'There's three pork chops in the meat safe,' Helen reminded her. 'You could have them for your dinner.'

'I'll buy something in the village for tea and cook for all of us.'

'That would be nice. 'Night, Lily. Goodnight, Martin.' Helen held out her hand.

'Goodnight, Helen.' Martin shook her hand and kissed her cheek. 'What you said earlier about Katie, Jack and me being close, that goes for you too. You're one of us now. A Clay, and don't you forget it.'

'That was a nice thing you said to Helen.' Lily held on to Martin's arm as she walked him to his bike.

'It's true, she is a Clay. I only hope Jack won't live to regret making her one.'

'He won't.'

'That's my Lily, ever the optimist.' He gazed across the bay. 'Every time I look at the sea, I understand why you wanted to move here.'

'The sea's only part of it, Helen's house gives all four of us independence.'

'Until Jack comes back.'

'Two years is a long time.'

'It seems endless at the beginning of National Service but it goes by in a flash. No sooner was I in the army than I was out of it.'

'I'm glad you won't be going away again.'

'So am I.' He kissed her. 'See you in the morning.'

'Bright and early with your swimsuit.'

'Until then.'

She closed the gate as he wheeled the bike out. Leaning on it, she watched him start the engine and drive off down the road. Tomorrow was going to be a day she would remember for the rest of her life. She just knew it.

* * *

'I wasn't expecting to see you this early. Tea?' John held up the pot as Joe joined him in the kitchen.

'Is there any coffee?'

'Is that your way of asking if I'll make it?'

'Yes.' Joe opened the cupboard door and rummaged among the bottles of pills and patent medicines. 'Are there any Alka Seltzer?'

'Bottom left-hand shelf last time I looked,' John directed.

'Was I very incoherent last night?'

'How much do you remember?'

'Getting home . . .'

'I hope you didn't drive Robin's car.'

'I shared a taxi with a couple of girls.'

'Do you remember talking about Richard Thomas?'

Joe looked at John blankly for a moment, then a hazy memory unfolded. 'You said something about Aunt Dot telling you he wasn't my father.'

'Not quite. I said if he is, he's denying it.'

'And you don't want me to talk to him about it,' Joe said slowly, fumbling through his fudged recollection of their conversation.

'Dot warned me that he doesn't want to talk to you or anyone about it.'

'He can't expect me just to ignore what my mother told me.' Joe found the Alka Seltzer, tore a couple free from their paper wrappings and dropped them into a glass.

'I don't know what he expects. But I do think you should take Dot's advice. He's not a man anyone would want to cross.'

'Good morning, dear father, dear brother, isn't it a lovely day.' Anxious to appear fully recovered and cheerful, Helen breezed in from the front door.

'God, that's all I need, a chirpy sister.'

'Poor, Joe.' Helen slipped her arm round Joe's neck and watched the Alka Seltzer fizzing in the glass. 'Did he drink too much last night, then?'

'I'd say so.' John reached for another cup and saucer. 'But it's best to take no notice, love. Tea?'

'Please, and toast. I'm starving.'

'Didn't you have breakfast before you left home?'

'Sort of, but I'm still ravenous.'

'How can you "sort of" have breakfast?' Joe growled.

'It was "sort of" on the hop. Katie's alarm didn't go off and, as she's usually first up, we were all late and I had to fight for the bathroom . . .'

'Four women in a house with only one bathroom.' Joe almost smiled. 'There is justice after all.'

'For what?' She pushed a couple of pieces of bread under the grill.

'All the times you've locked me out of ours.'

'There were only three of us this morning. Lily has the day off. Katie, Judy and I had to run down the hill and even then Katie and I only just made the train, so breakfast was apples and bananas eaten on the way.'

'Judy and Katie work Saturdays?' Joe checked.

'Katie works every other, but when did you see a hairdresser closed on a Saturday?'

'I've never thought about it.'

'You're in the real world now, Joe, it's time to start thinking.'

'Run that by me again.'

'It's a well-known fact that students don't work.' Helen was too concerned with turning the toast to pick up the nuances in Joe's questions. 'So what do you have lined up for me today, Dad?'

'Planning meeting for the fashion show starts at eleven. The date's fixed and the invitations have gone out but we need to organise the refreshments, choose the models and decide which outfits from our autumn collection should be modelled and which should be placed on mannequins around the store.'

'And before that?'

'There's a couple of catalogues I'd like you to look at.'

Helen took the toast from under the grill, handed one piece to her father and spread hers thickly with butter and strawberry jam before holding it up to Joe. 'Want some?'

'Absolutely not.' He almost retched at the sight.

'Grumps.' Turning to John, she continued their conversation, leaving Joe to his hangover – and thoughts.

As Katie, Judy and Helen were going to be out all day, the chances were he'd find Lily alone, if not in the house then on the beach, and tonight was the summer ball. Informal, nowhere near as grand as the graduate ball, it was still a social event to be reckoned with. If he could persuade her to accompany him to that . . .

He might have to drive her down to the warehouse so she could buy a new frock and from there he'd take her to Judy or Judy's mother. They would definitely fit in an appointment for Lily, if she asked them to.

'Can I borrow the car, Dad?'

'For how long?'

Joe glanced at his watch. 'About an hour from now, until mid-afternoon.'

'You'll have to walk down to the warehouse to fetch it and make sure you get it back to me by half past five at the latest.'

'Will do.' Joe tweaked Helen's ear.

'Why the big grin?'

'I've just remembered that I can go upstairs, run a bath and soak in it for hours – and hours – and hours – without anyone banging on the door and telling me to hurry up. While you, poor old thing, have to make do with whatever time the girls leave you.'

Helen stuck out her tongue at him. 'It's worth coming back from the warehouse in ten minutes to hammer on the door for old times' sake.'

'You'll find it locked,' he gloated.

Martin shaded his eyes as he parked his bike next to the house. A short, dark-haired girl wearing a crimson two-piece swimsuit was waving to him from the beach and there couldn't be two girls with that figure or swimsuit . . . Five minutes later he was standing beside her. 'You couldn't wait for me,' he reproached.

'I cleared up after the others, did their washing as well as my own, hung it out, cleaned the house, laid the breakfast table and as there didn't seem to be anything else to do and I couldn't sit still, I came down here to see what the water's like.'

'And what is it like?' He wrapped her towel high round her shoulders as she shivered.

'Freezing.' She picked at the buttons on his shirt. 'I need you to keep me warm.'

'Give me two minutes to change and I'll be with you.'

'I'll go in the sea. It's cold but warmer than standing out here.' Lily had spent most of the previous night tossing and turning, unable to close her eyes for thinking of what the morning would bring. Now it had actually arrived she felt oddly shy and embarrassed, both peculiar emotions when she considered how close she had grown to Martin during the past few months.

'No splashing,' he warned, as he joined her in the water.

'You're actually admitting you're cold.'

'You're the one who said it was freezing. One quick swim out to the rocks and back.'

'Do we have to go all the way?' she asked, as they reached the halfway point.

'Chicken.'

'It'll be warmer this afternoon and in the meantime we could go up to the house. Have you eaten?'

'You told me to come before breakfast.'

'I'll make you bacon and eggs.'

'I'd prefer toast and cereal.'

'Really prefer,' she asked earnestly, 'or you've become used to them because they're easier to make?'

'It probably started out that way, but now I really would prefer them.'

'Just as well we have a box of Grape Nuts and a pot of strawberry jam, then.'

'I hate Grape Nuts.'

'There may be some Puffed Wheat.'

'No cornflakes or marmalade?'

'No cornflakes, no marmalade,' she confirmed.

'I can see I am going to have to teach you how to eat.'

'Or I'll teach you.' As soon as she was in her depth she waded up the beach to the shallows. Wrapping her towel round her bust, she tucked in the top so it would stay up and slipped her feet into her rubber beach shoes. 'Let's change in the house. If I use the bathroom first, I'll make the food while you change.'

'And there's so much to make for toast and cereal.'

'I have to cut the bread.'

'And that's such hard work,' he teased.

'You're asking for it.'

'This?' Pulling her close, he kissed her.

'Not this, trouble,' she threatened, as he released her.

'I love trouble when it comes in a package your shape.'

Martin was standing on the landing when Lily left the bathroom, carrying her two-piece and wearing only a bath towel. She looked into his eyes and he held the look for a moment, before following her into her bedroom and closing the door. Taking her into his arms he kissed her again, and she allowed the damp towel and swimsuit to fall to the floor. His breath caught in his throat as he saw her naked for the first time. Lowering his head, he kissed each of her breasts in turn. Stepping back from him, she turned down the bed and slid between the sheets, watching as he stripped off his towel and bathing suit.

She drew her breath in sharply as the full length of his naked body came into contact with her own.

'If you're not sure about this . . .'

'I've never been more sure of anything in my life, Marty.' She moved even closer, revelling in the feel of his bare legs against hers. She hadn't known quite what to expect, but this intense, sensuous intimacy was wholly new and overwhelming, engendering emotions she hadn't dreamed she possessed. 'I love you and whatever happens between us afterwards, I want my first time to be with you.'

Lowering his head to hers, he kissed her gently on the lips, and suddenly there was no need for any more words.

Joe parked his father's car in his sister's drive and stepped out. It was a fine, clear day but the wind was keen, bringing a coolness to the air that belied the sunshine. He looked down over the beach. A mother sat on a deckchair, three small children playing with pebbles and sand at her feet. An elderly couple walked arm in arm down to the sea, preceded by a Pekinese dog. A line of young boys were climbing the cliff path but there was no sign of Lily, which meant she'd be in the house – unless she had gone into town.

Trembling with barely suppressed excitement, he tried the front door. To his delight he found it unlocked. He stepped lightly into the hall, walking on the balls of his feet, hoping to surprise her, but the living and dining rooms were empty. He went into the kitchen. The table was laid for two. Could she possibly be expecting him?

Running as quietly as he could up the stairs, he called her name and opened the door of the bedroom Helen had proudly shown him after it had been decorated, telling him it was to be Lily's.

'Mr Davies to see you, Mr Griffiths. Shall I put him in your office?'

'You can show him into my office, Miss Richards,' John corrected his new secretary, who never failed to irritate, simply because she wasn't Katie. He turned to Helen and the buyer. 'I shouldn't be long.'

'Take as long as you like, Mr Griffiths, Helen and I are doing just fine.' The senior Ladies Wear buyer nodded in approval as Helen picked out a nylon dress overall that the manufacturers were using Anne Shelton to advertise.

'In other words, you two will do better without me.'

'Not at all, Dad.' Helen smiled. To her surprise, she didn't even have to force the smile. Choosing clothes for a fashion show was even more fun than she had hoped it would be and a task she would never have classed as work. As far removed from the drudgery of a junior's life in Richard Thomas's office as a formal ball in the Mackworth was from a church youth club hop.

'Coffee for two, please, Miss Richards,' John prompted, as he passed her desk in the outer office.

'Yes, Mr Griffiths,' she answered, sensing she had earned herself yet another black mark for not offering.

'John.' Mark Davies rose from a chair and held out his hand as John walked in.

'This is a pleasant surprise. Since when do solicitors work Saturdays?'

'When they spend all Friday in court and don't have time to read important documents until the following day. I thought you'd like to know that we've had everything back from Esme via Richard Thomas. The decree nisi should be made absolute at the end of next month.'

'You're serious?'

'You knew all along that the bulk of the work had been done. The delay was only down to Esme being difficult.'

'The end of next month,' John repeated slowly.

'You could buy me lunch to celebrate.'

'Anywhere you want.'

'The Mackworth.'

'Fine,' John murmured absently.

'You look shell-shocked. What's the matter? You can't believe you'll be a free man in six weeks unless, that is, you can't wait for someone else to bolt the shackles on to you,' he joked.

'If she'll still have me.'

Mark stared at John, uncertain he'd heard him correctly, as John's secretary knocked on the door.

'Coffee, Mr Griffiths.'

'Forget it, Miss Richards.' John beamed, as the significance of Mark's news finally sank in. 'Mr Davies and I are going out to celebrate. Tell the senior buyer and my daughter to go ahead with whatever decisions they want to make. I won't be in again until late this afternoon.'

Martin and Lily looked up from the rumpled sheets as the bedroom door opened and swung back on its hinges. Joe stood, pale-faced and wild-eyed, in the doorway.

Martin was the first to recover from the shock. 'Get out, Joe.'

'Lily, you love me . . . why . . .' Joe continued to stand, fixed and immobile, staring at her.

'Please go, Joe . . .'

'You love me,' he repeated dully, as if he hadn't heard her. Then suddenly, without warning, he dived towards the bed. 'I love you . . .' Grabbing Lily's hair, he locked his fingers into the roots and tried to drag her from the bed.

Lily screamed as the pain grew unbearable. All she could think of was the conversation she'd had with Martin after he'd fought with Adam.

I'll never hit anyone again.

Even if they're trying to hit you?

Especially if they're trying to hit me.

Martin leaped out of bed. Clenching his hand tightly round Joe's wrist he squeezed, using all the strength he could muster until he forced him to relinquish his grip on Lily's hair. 'Don't you dare touch her ever again,' he cried, forgetting he was naked as he stepped between Lily, who fell back sobbing on to the bed, and Joe.

Raising his fists, Joe lashed out. Martin ducked, head butting Joe in the stomach, he took him unawares. As Joe staggered back, Martin punched him on the jaw, following it up with one to his eye, and pushed him out of the room. He slammed the door and leaned on it, locking him out. 'Are you all right, Lily?'

'I think so.' She touched her head, her scalp was tingling so much she was surprised to feel her hair. She was convinced that Joe had pulled it out by the roots.

Still leaning on the door, Martin stooped and picked up his towel from the floor; tying it around his waist he listened, before opening it gingerly and looking out. As far as he could see the stairs and hall were empty.

'Don't leave me, Marty.'

'I have to make sure he's out of the house.' He checked the bathroom and other bedrooms, and ran down the stairs in time to see

Joe drive off along the road. Locking and bolting the front and back doors, he closed all the downstairs windows before returning upstairs.

He sat on the bed beside Lily and gently smoothed her hair from her face. 'I'm sorry, darling. Did I hurt you?' he asked as she winced at his touch.

'Joe did. I'm glad you hit him, Marty. I didn't think you were going to . . . if you hadn't . . .'

'Ssh.' Cradling her against his chest, he stroked the side of her face. 'I won't ever let him hurt you again.' He kicked his feet on to the bed and slid between the sheets next to her.

'He must have been watching me to know I was here . . . he must have thought I'd be alone . . .'

'He could tell people we were in bed. Your uncle . . .'

'Uncle Roy would understand and I don't care about anyone else.' She clung to him fiercely.

He folded his arms round her. 'I love you, Lily Sullivan, and I've just discovered how much.'

'And I love you, and nothing else matters. Does it?' She lifted a defiant face to his.

'No, it doesn't.' All of a sudden he realised he meant it.

'I see you've decorated your face for the summer ball,' Robin quipped, as Joe walked through the Watkin Morgan house and out on to the poolside patio where Robin, Angela and Emily were sunbathing.

'You look as though you've gone a couple of rounds with a professional boxer.' Angela left her steamer chair and ran her fingers lightly from the bruise on Joe's jaw to his swollen eye. 'I'll ask Pops to take look at you.'

'Don't bother.' Joe sat on the nearest chair.

'It's no bother, he's only in his study.'

'Drop it, Angie, it's nothing.'

'How did you do it?' Emily nosed.

'Fed up with him chasing her, the gorgeous Lily lashed out.' Robin sipped the whisky punch Emily had mixed for him. 'I was joking.' He shrank back as Joe loomed over him.

'Joseph, how lovely to see you; have you come to discuss tonight's arrangements?'

'Tonight, Mrs Watkin Morgan?' Joe repeated in confusion.

'The summer ball, you ass. Take no notice of Joe, Mums, he's had an accident with a door.'

'So I see. Perhaps my husband should look at you . . .'

'It's fine, Mrs Watkin Morgan,' Joe snapped, obviously on edge.

'Angie, get Joe a drink, there's a darling, it's absolutely baking out here.'

'Whisky punch, Joe?' Angie rose from her seat.

'If that's what everyone else is drinking.'

'Goes with the weather.' Robin emptied his glass. 'Another for me while you're at it, sis. So, not that you're unwelcome, but why did you come?'

Joe watched Angie as she mixed the drinks. Her gold nylon two-piece swimsuit left very little of her slim, firm body to the imagination. And after what had happened between them the day before, he didn't even have to use that, just his memory. 'To ask Angie if she'll go to the summer ball with me.'

'And the gorgeous Lily?'

'Is dead and forgotten.'

'Hear that, sis?' Robin called. 'Joe's come to invite you to the summer ball if you can stand the sight of his bruises.'

Eyes sparkling, her mouth split into a smile designed to showcase her perfect teeth. 'I'd love to go with you, Joe.'

'I'll pick you up at seven.'

'No, we'll pick you up.' Robin swung his legs down from the steamer chair he'd sprawled out on. 'Swim?'

'I have a few errands to run before tonight.'

'Sure I – or Angie – can't persuade you?'

'Sure.' Joe took the drink Angela handed him and finished it in two long draughts.

'You were thirsty,' she flirted, conscious of her mother in the den behind them.

'Yes.'

'See you at seven, Joe.' Angie kissed his bruised cheek.

'I'll be waiting.' Setting down his glass, he walked back through the house.

Chapter 26

'WAS JOE EVER like that with you before?' Martin lay stretched out next to Lily on the same blanket that Helen and Adam had used to sunbathe on in Helen's garden.

'Violent, you mean?' Lily understood him at once. 'Never. There's something else I want you to know about Joe and me . . .'

'I don't want to know anything about you and Joe,' he cut her short.

'Please, Marty. I don't want any secrets between us. I need to say this and it's nothing I'm ashamed of, or anything that will make you more upset with Joe than you already are.' She sat up besides him. 'You know Joe was the first boy to ask me out. He even came round to ask Auntie Norah's permission to take me to the pictures. It felt odd to begin with because I'd only ever thought of him as Helen's older brother, but I grew to like him and I knew Auntie Norah and Uncle Roy approved of my going out with him. And after some of the stories I'd heard from other girls about having to fight off boys, I was relieved that he always behaved like a perfect gentleman. The most we ever did was kiss and nine times out of ten it was a peck on the cheek.'

He held her look. 'Then he never touched you . . .'

'Not in the way you have – and did after a couple of dates.'

Ashamed of the jealousy that had almost finished their relationship before it had even begun, he sat up next to her. 'That puts me in my place.'

'You only did what I wanted you to.' She smiled mischievously, before becoming serious again. 'I should have known we could never be friends in the way I thought we were after I gave him back his engagement ring, because every time we accidentally met, he hinted he wanted more. But it was never more than a hint and I brushed off his invitations to dinner and balls, because they always seemed to be half-hearted – almost like a joke between us. Shortly after I began to go out with you, I told him that if I'd ever had any feelings for him they'd long gone, so when he bumped into me after work one day and suggested we become friends, there didn't seem to be any reason not to be. I thought he'd soon find himself another girl . . .'

'Can't you see those were no accidental meetings, Lily?' Martin interrupted. 'And now, he broke in on us, he attacked you . . .'

'And I should have seen it coming,' she insisted, taking a share of the blame. 'When we were together Joe spent most of his time either making up fairy stories, that with hindsight I think he half believed, or planning out the perfect future for us. Now, I think that he lived more in that story-book world than reality.'

'Did he still talk about your future together after you gave him back his ring?' He leaned against the wall of the house.

'He occasionally mentioned his plans but it was always in a "remember this" kind of way and I never thought for one minute that he was waiting for it to happen. When we were about to get engaged, he said he would buy a cottage for us near Llandaff where he was going to work. It was going to have a big garden, roses round the door, leaded-glass windows, something like a cross between Goldilocks and the Three Bears' cottage and Little Red Riding Hood's, and to me just as fanciful. Inside it was going to be furnished like a palace. He talked about blue and silver, and gold and green colour schemes. He even planned a honeymoon in France.' Shading her eyes against the sun, she tried to read the expression on Martin's face. 'Looking back, even in the beginning when he showed me the engagement ring he'd bought, I think I sensed that something was wrong but I had nothing to compare Joe and me with except your brother and Helen, and I knew from something Helen had let slip that she had made love to Jack. Judy joked about Brian pulling off her bra every time they were alone and all Joe wanted to do was kiss me goodnight and hold hands.'

'And that wasn't enough for you.' His eyes were dark, enigmatic and she wished she could read his thoughts.

'It was enough for me with Joe. But I didn't look or think further than our engagement and that never really happened.'

'So even when you were almost engaged to Joe you thought that some day there'd be someone else for you.'

'It wasn't as definite as that. I was living day to day. I'd just lost Auntie Norah, Joe was safe, steady, undemanding, a bit like an older brother, I suppose, although I've never had one so I don't know what that's like. When my mother turned up at the party and Joe walked away from me I was upset, but looking back, only because of my mother. I think even then I was relieved that it was over between us because he wasn't the right one for me.'

'And I am?'

She knelt in front of him. 'I need you to know that you're not only the first man I've made love to, but the first man I've really loved.'

He kissed her. 'Perhaps I should talk to your uncle about what happened.'

She threw her arms round his waist. 'With Joe or what Joe saw us doing?'

'Better we tell your uncle everything than he find out from Joe.'

'Uncle Roy has enough to worry about, planning his wedding. Besides, I don't think Joe will tell anyone what happened because he'd have to admit he's a Peeping Tom. Creeping in on us . . .'

'I was a fool not to lock the front door.'

'Helen may have given him a key, so it wouldn't have made any difference.'

'We might have heard it turning in the lock.'

'And we might not have,' she countered. 'It happened, Marty. All we can do now is try to forget it.'

'I can't forget that he hurt you.'

'Thanks to you, not for long.' She looked into his eyes. 'And as for what happened before Joe walked in, I never want to forget that as long as I live.' She reached for his hand. 'The girls won't be in for another couple of hours.'

'And?'

'The sun's getting too hot to lie out here any longer.'

'I love you, Lily Sullivan.'

'I know,' she whispered as she pulled him to his feet.

Joe walked out to meet Richard Thomas as he parked his car in the drive of the house in Langland.

'You said it was urgent.' Richard climbed out of the driver's seat.

'It is.'

'I assume it's something to do with the house.'

'No.'

'I don't work on Saturdays.'

'You of all people, Mr Thomas, should know that I have sufficient money to pay your fees.'

'No amount of money buys my services on a Saturday, Joseph.' Richard opened his car door.

'I only need five minutes.'

Richard glanced at his watch. 'And that is all you have. I'm on my way to a golf match.'

'Are you my father?' Joe held Richard's glare for what seemed like hours, although it could only have been a minute or two, and he was the first to turn his head away.

'If you ever ask me that question again, I will sue you to the point where you won't be able to afford the services of a shoeshine boy, let alone a solicitor.'

'Then you deny it.' Forgetting his resolve to stay calm, Joe allowed his anger to surface.

'Publicly, for both our sakes, I most emphatically do.'

Joe lowered his voice. 'And privately?'

Richard hesitated for a moment before answering. 'If you are ever in trouble I will do whatever I can to help you.'

'Because I am your son.'

'Because your grandfather was my closest friend.'

'Did you put any of your own money into the trust fund my great-aunt set up for me?' Joe questioned harshly.

'No.'

'And my grandmother's will?'

'Was written exactly the way she dictated it. You can check with her doctor and vicar if you don't believe me.'

'You seduced my mother . . .'

'Your mother is a fantasist, Joseph.'

'You never slept with her?' Joe challenged.

Richard Thomas leaned against his car. 'Your grandmother told me that she caught your mother sneaking boys into her bedroom before her sixteenth birthday and never the same one twice. Any boy in her set could have fathered you.'

'And you? Is it possible . . .'

'The only thing I can tell you for certain, Joseph, is that John Griffiths is not your father. And I'd appreciate it if you never mention this subject again, to me or to anyone else.'

'You give me your word about my trust fund and grandmother's will?' Joe pressed, realising he'd get no more from Richard Thomas than he already had.

'I give you my word.' Richard looked Joe straight in the eye. He almost convinced himself as well as the boy, but then he'd had a lifetime's experience of lying.

'No.'

'Please, Katie, we can't leave you alone, not on a Saturday night,' Lily pleaded.

'I have a headache. The last thing I want to do is to go down the Pier. I want a quiet walk on the beach.'

'I'll go with you,' Judy offered eagerly, anxious to avoid Adam Jordan.

Katie refused Judy's offer. 'I'd rather be by myself and Martin's expecting you, Lily.'

Lily looked at Judy and Helen in exasperation. 'All right.' She pulled on her gloves. 'We'll go down the Pier but we'll be back early.'

'Please don't, not on my account.' Katie lifted her jacket from the hook on the back of the door and checked that her front-door key was in the pocket.

'We did what we could,' Helen said as they followed her out of the door.

'I just wish . . .' Lily bit her lip.

'What?' Judy asked.

'That I could help her,' Lily answered, as she slammed the door behind her.

'Will you stop looking at the door every five minutes,' Sam griped to Martin. 'The girls said they'd be here and they will.'

Martin paid the barmaid for the beer he'd bought for himself, Sam and Adam, and followed Sam to a table on the edge of the dance floor. He had spent the entire day with Lily, refusing to leave her until Katie, Helen and Judy had returned. But concerned that even then Joe might come back, he had found it difficult to tear himself away.

It had been an almost perfect day for him and, he hoped, Lily – almost, because although Lily had insisted she had recovered from Joe's attack, his presence hung like a black cloud over the remainder of the time they had spent together. In the afternoon they had walked on the beach, but even there he had caught himself looking over his shoulder every time a car drove along the coast road to see if Joe was in it.

'You and Lily have a good day?' Adam sat down and sipped his pint.

'The water was a bit cold, but the sun was warm.'

'I didn't ask about the sea.'

'I know you didn't.'

'Lover boy doesn't want to talk about his girl,' Adam mocked.

'No.' Martin gave Adam a warning look.

'Nice house Helen has there,' Sam broke the tension. 'And, believe it or not, the sergeant took pity on this poor rookie when he drew up the last roster and I have a whole Sunday off tomorrow. Do you fancy spending it at the beach?'

'Limeslade beach?' Adam asked.

'Are there any others?'

'Thirty or so on the Gower, more if you count Swansea Bay and head out Porthcawl way.' Adam offered round his cigarettes.

'We can ask the girls what they think,' Martin suggested cautiously, not wanting Helen – or Lily – to feel they were imposing. Beyond tonight, he and Lily hadn't made any definite plans. He would like nothing better than to spend tomorrow with her – even if the others were around – but what if she wanted to spend it with the girls and only agreed out of politeness?

'It is a public beach.' Adam lit their cigarettes before his own.

'But it would be nice if we could use the house to change and make the odd cup of tea,' Sam commented. 'So how about it?'

'Fine by me,' Martin agreed.

'Good, you'll ask Helen, then?'

'Why me?' Martin questioned.

'She's your sister-in-law.'

'And here are the lovely ladies.' Rising to his feet, Adam pulled three chairs out from under their table. 'Where's Katie?'

'We couldn't persuade her to come.' Judy took the chair furthest from Adam, leaving Helen no option but to sit next to him.

Martin winked at Lily who was wearing a white, off-the-shoulder, gypsy-style frock that showed off her tan.

'You look smart,' Sam complimented Judy who was wearing a dress similar to Lily's in bottle-green. 'What would you all like to drink – Babycham?'

'I'll have an orange juice, please.' Helen, who had dressed soberly for the Pier for the first time in her life, was wearing a navy-blue shirtwaister, trimmed with white braid round the collar, edge of the short sleeves and pockets. More suitable for the office than a dance, she had chosen it in the hope of impressing on Martin that she had no intention of flirting with anyone.

'You're late,' Martin complained to Lily as Adam went to the bar to help Sam with the drinks. 'There's nothing wrong, is there?'

'Only Katie point-blank refusing to come with us. She said she's tired but she's been using that excuse for weeks now.'

'If we leave early, I'll walk you home and try talking to her.'

'It might be better left until tomorrow.' She smiled at Sam as he handed her a Babycham and a glass.

'You want to see me tomorrow?'

'Not if you don't want to,' she teased.

'Carry on like this, Lily Sullivan, and you'll have to throw stones to keep me from your door.'

As Sam and Adam sat down with their drinks, Martin surprised Judy by asking her to dance. She looked at Lily, but Lily only laughed.

'Go ahead. I'm not his keeper.'

'To what do I owe the honour?' Judy murmured guardedly as Martin led her out on to the almost deserted floor.

'When I returned to the flat this afternoon there was a letter waiting for me from Brian.'

'Did he say anything in particular?'

'He asked me to tell you that he's missing you, thinking about you and he'd like to write to you.'

'He has my address,' she said shortly.

'Shall I tell him that in my next letter?'

'That's up to you.'

'Then I will.'

'Is that all he said?' she asked tentatively, after a few minutes' silence.

'About you.'

'Is he all right?'

'He complained that he's worn out with doing double shifts, there's more work than he can cope with and London is a big, hot, noisy, impersonal city, especially in summer.'

'You've just reminded me of a few of the reasons why I left.'

'Then you won't be going back there?' Martin asked.

'No.'

'That sounds very definite.'

'It is, Martin,' she said brusquely, 'so don't try to talk me out of it.'

'I wasn't, and remember I'm only the messenger.'

The music stopped and they stood back to applaud the band. 'Thanks for being a friend to both of us, Marty, but I'd appreciate it if you wouldn't mention Brian again.'

'Even if he asks me to give you a message?'

'Just tell him what I told you. If he wants to contact me, he has my address.'

'Just as you have his.'

'Pardon?'

'If both of you sit back waiting for the other to make the first move, you could be in for a long wait,' he advised as he walked her back to their table.

John slipped the letter he'd written into his pocket as he went to his car. It had taken him over an hour to write a couple of lines and he wasn't happy with the result.

Dear Katie,

Perhaps you could call into the office one day on your way home from work. There is something that I would like to discuss with you.

Yours sincerely,

John Griffiths

It gave no indication of what he felt – or his hopes. But then he didn't know if there was someone new in her life. And if there was – he tried to consider all the implications objectively as he drove through Mumbles but as he passed the turn to the Pier he imagined Katie sitting there with Helen and the girls, the boys around them . . . Sam and Adam – he realised that he had no right even to try to contact her again after bringing her so much unhappiness. If the road hadn't been too narrow to accommodate a three-point turn he might have been tempted to drive back.

Parking at the side of Helen's house he walked to the front door and knocked. When no one answered he removed the letter from his pocket and looked at it for a moment.

Finally deciding that things were best left as they were, he returned to his car, stopping when he caught sight of a solitary figure walking on the beach. He opened the door and reached for his walking stick.

* * *

'You haven't asked why I danced with Judy,' Martin murmured in Lily's ear, as they danced to a smooch version of 'Harbour Lights'.

'If you want me to know, you'll tell me.'

'I thought all girls were curious.'

'Not this one.'

'Brian wrote and asked me to tell her that he was missing her.'

'Really?' She moved her head from his shoulder and looked at him.

'Do you know what really happened between them after Jack's wedding?'

'I haven't a clue,' she answered quickly – too quickly.

'You're a terrible liar, Lily Sullivan.'

'Just as well.' She smiled. 'You'll always know when I'm not telling you the truth.'

'Do you think it's serious between Lily and Martin?' Judy asked Helen as they watched them dance.

'I hope so. It would be nice if one of us were happy.'

'How about making me happy and having this dance with me, Judy.' Sam held out his hand as the band played the last chords of 'Harbour Lights' and went into another slow dance, this time 'The Magic Touch'.

'Helen.'

She hesitated as Adam stood before her.

'I was hoping you'd give me a chance to make up for the way we parted the other day. It was stupid. After all, we are friends. Jack and me and you,' he added persuasively.

She took his hand. 'As long as you remember that I'm married and don't hold me too close.'

'Hello, Katie.'

Katie looked up, instinctively checking the beach was deserted before using John's Christian name. 'Hello, John.'

'All alone.'

'The others have gone down the Pier.'

He fell into step beside her. 'Why didn't you go with them?'

She shrugged her thin shoulders.

His heart went out to her. 'Oh, Katie . . .'

'I don't want your pity,' she snapped. 'You don't want me . . .'

'I want you to be happy. I thought that if you found someone younger . . .'

'I told you I couldn't be happy without you.' Moving away from him, she sat on a rock, clasped her hands round her knees and stared at the sea.

He stood beside her. 'I came to give you a letter.' Taking it from his pocket, he handed it to her.

'What does it say?' The wind caught her dark hair, whipping it across her face as she looked up at him.

'That I'd like to talk to you.' He took a deep breath as he tried to decipher her features in the gathering twilight. 'My divorce will be final in six weeks. If you're still prepared to put up with the gossips, the pointed fingers and the people who will call both of us names and not very pleasant ones, we could get married.'

She stared at him as if she couldn't believe what he'd said.

'The last few months have been the most miserable of my life.'

'You want me,' she whispered.

He met her gaze. 'Oh yes, Katie. I want you.'

When Sam left Judy to go to the bar, she returned to their table to find it empty. As she sat down a freckle-faced, ginger-haired boy approached her. 'Hi. You're Judy, right?'

'Do I know you?' Judy eyed him doubtfully.

'Alun Jones. Don't you remember, Brian Powell introduced us. I worked with him before he went to London.'

'You're a policemen.'

'Guilty as charged.'

She wondered if she was doomed to be surrounded by police officers for the rest of her life. There were so many other professions. Why didn't she ever meet a lorry driver or shop assistant?

'Dance?'

'Thank you.' She forced a smile and took the hand he offered.

'What did you think of the game?' he asked as they reached the dance floor.

'What game?'

'Football, Swans played Cardiff today.'

'I didn't know.'

'You don't follow football.' He stared at her as if she were a Martian.

'No.'

'Ah, then you're a cricket fan.'

'I can't stand it.'

'I've never met a girl who couldn't stand cricket before.'

'Some girls lie.'

'About liking cricket?'

'It has been known,' she assured him solemnly. Looking over his shoulder, she smiled broadly as she saw Jack in the doorway. Breaking free from her bewildered partner she waved to him. Jack waved back, then his face darkened. She turned, just in time to realise that Adam had seen Jack as well and was kissing Helen full on the lips.

Joe led the way to a table placed well away from the dance floor. He intended to dance as little as possible that evening, even if it meant quarrelling with Angela.

'Waiter.' Robin clicked his fingers. 'Two whiskies and two brandies. No, on second thoughts make it four of each. Start the night as you mean to go on,' he said to Joe, as the waiter left.

'Too drunk to stand.'

'I'm not supposed to tell you but Angie made quite an effort for you tonight. That gold lamé dress of hers cost Pops an absolute fortune. It's a genuine Balmain, whatever that means.'

'I'm flattered.'

'No need to be so bloody sarcastic.'

'I wasn't,' Joe protested a little too vehemently.

'So what changed your mind about the gorgeous Lily?'

'For Christ's sake stop calling her that.'

'I won't say another word. And here are the two most beautiful women in the world.' Robin rose unsteadily from his chair and greeted Emily with a kiss. 'I've ordered you two brandies. Each.'

'That's my boy.' Emily sat beside Robin and leaned forward in her low-cut dress, a silver version of Angela's that displayed her cleavage.

'I always go weak at the knees whenever I see men in evening dress.' Angela laid her hand over Joe's.

'Where are those drinks,' Robin muttered impatiently.

'Here, sir.' The waiter laid eight coasters on the table.

'Same again,' Joe ordered recklessly, after following Robin's example and downing one of his whiskies in a single swallow.

'Shouldn't you two slow down? It's going to be a long evening.'

'Why, Angie, this is a celebration, we've just finished our exams.'

'There are other things in life besides alcohol.'

'But few worth having.' Robin laughed at his own joke as he tossed a ten-pound note on the waiter's tray to cover the cost of the drinks.

Martin and Lily were so wrapped up in one another that the dance hall was in uproar before they realised anything was amiss. It was only when Helen screamed and Adam reeled across the room after Jack had punched him that they saw what was happening. Martin ran after Jack as he followed Adam. Sam was already between them, but so were two doormen. One grabbed Jack and pulled his hands high behind his back, while the other helped Adam to his feet.

'We've had trouble with you before,' the manager barked, staring at Jack.

'I'm a police officer . . .' Sam began.

'Off duty, aren't you, son.' The manager gave Sam a patronising look.

'Yes, but . . .'

'We won't need you. I've already telephoned the station.'

'Please, can I talk to my husband?' Helen was pale, but her voice was remarkably steady.

'One of these is your husband?' The manager was clearly unconvinced.

'Yes.' She looked at Jack, who turned away.

'Ask the police when they come. Get the two of them into my office, stay with them until the police come and no visitors,' he ordered the doormen.

'Just so you and the missus know.' Adam pushed his face as close to Jack's as the doorman holding him would allow. 'I've got my own back for that trick you pulled on your stag night. And frankly, mate, I don't know what you see in her.'

'I didn't want to kiss him. He forced me,' Helen cried, as the doorman dragged Jack, who was still trying to lash out at Adam, away.

'I'll go down the police station and see if I can sort something out, Helen,' Martin consoled clumsily. He caught Sam's eye and Sam shook his head doubtfully.

'Jack saw me kissing Adam. I didn't want to . . . but you saw Jack, he doesn't believe me . . . I should never have danced with Adam . . .'

Martin drew Lily aside. 'Get Helen and Judy home, love.'

'And Jack?'

'Sam will come with me down the station and if your uncle is on duty he may be able to help us. If we manage to get Jack out tonight, I'll send him to Helen on his bike.'

384

She looked at Helen, white-faced, shaking as the shock of what had happened began to sink in. 'Promise.'

'I promise.'

'Go, Joe! Go, Robin! Go, Joe! Go, Robin! Go, Joe . . .'

The chants of their fellow students resounded in Robin's and Joe's ears like medieval battle-cries as they stood opposite one another on high stools and downed mixed pints of whisky, beer and whatever else the boys had poured into the mugs.

Finishing his drink before Robin, Joe swayed precariously, then felt Angela's hands steadying his legs.

'And Joe is the winner.' Thompson lifted him down just as he was about to fall. 'For Joe's a jolly good fellow . . .'

'You all right?' Angela asked, as he propped himself up on the bar.

'Wonderful. You?'

'Stupid question after what you've drunk. Joe, you know I adore you and I'd do anything for you. Will you please do one tiny thing for me?'

'I'll consider it.'

'Stop drinking now,' she begged. 'We've both had enough. I'll ask someone here to get us a taxi; we can go home to bed. Mums and Pops won't mind you sleeping in mine. They adore you as much as I do . . .'

'See you in a minute.' Straightening his suit jacket, Joe brushed a couple of flecks of whisky from his lapel and walked out of the door. He knew he was drunk but he'd never been clearer in his mind in his life. The Watkin Morgans wanted him for a son-in-law and Angela wanted him for a husband because he had a substantial trust fund, a house in Langland, his grandmother's money and good prospects. If Martin Clay had come knocking on their door after Angela, he would have been given the boot, yet Martin had the one girl in the world whom he loved – 'had' in every sense of the word.

To put it in Robin's crude terms, Martin had taken Lily's knickers down. The pure, virginal bride he had dreamed of marrying for over a year was soiled – damaged beyond repair. He had offered Lily everything he owned and she had thrown it back in his face for a common mechanic who lived in a rented basement.

And there was his father. He smiled grimly – both fathers; kind, generous John Griffiths who had never quite understood him and the bastard who was prepared to call his mother a whore to get out of the responsibility of having to own him. And his mother who very probably was a whore . . . *I'll ask someone here to get us a taxi; we can go home to bed. Mums and Pops won't mind you sleeping in mine. They adore you as much as I do* . . . Was that his future – marriage to a girl as shallow, social-climbing and money-grubbing as his mother, with morals to match?

He walked out of the front door of the hotel and looked up and down High Street. A double-decker bus was coming towards him. He read the name on the front: *Morriston*. Only when he was certain the driver had no chance to stop did he step out in front of it.

Chapter 27

'WE CAN REALLY get married in six weeks?' Katie took John's arm as they walked slowly along the beach.

'We have a lot of plans to make.'

'And people to tell,' she said thoughtfully, thinking of Jack and Helen and Joe.

He stopped and looked at her. 'You're absolutely sure?'

'Positive.'

'I don't even mind you working in Lewis Lewis as long as I can come home to you every night,' he joked.

'I could come back to the warehouse.'

'We have more important decisions to make, like where you want to go on honeymoon and where we're going to live . . .'

'You love the house in Carlton Terrace.'

'I loved the house in Carlton Terrace,' he said seriously. 'I was happy there with my grandparents and miserable with Esme. Perhaps it's time for a new start.'

'Where?'

'Anywhere you want provided it's in easy travelling distance of Swansea. We could go further down the Gower or to Mumbles . . .'

'I'd be happy to live in a shack as long as it's with you.'

'I believe you would.' He stopped at the foot of the cliff path. 'We could go on a luxury cruise for our honeymoon, to America or the Mediterranean.'

'Is that what you want?'

'I want whatever will make you happy.'

'I don't want to go anywhere where there'll be other people.'

'You want to be alone?'

'With you,' she qualified. 'We could rent a cottage. Oh John.' Her eyes gleamed in the darkness. 'We could go to Cornwall. My mother went there once when she was a girl. She said it was beautiful. I know it's a long way but . . .'

'You'd prefer to go to Cornwall rather than America or the Mediterranean?' He laughed.

'Yes please.' She hesitated, 'But only if you want to.'

'We'll go to Cornwall, my love.' He scarcely dared to believe that someone so beautiful and unspoilt was going to be his wife. He offered her his hand as they began to walk up the path. 'There's so much we don't know about one another. I don't even know how you feel about children.'

'You want them?'

'If you do.'

'But you have Joe and Helen.'

'And if I had my way I would have had a lot more. But we have all the time in the world to think about it.'

'I don't have to. I'd love to have your children. They'll be wonderful, just like you.'

'Hopefully with their mother's looks.' Taking her into his arms, he gazed at her. 'I'm going to find it very difficult to believe that someone as young, beautiful and adorable as you can love a man like me, Katie Clay.'

'Then I'll have to spend the rest of my life convincing you.' Closing her eyes, she kissed him.

'So that's why Katie wouldn't come to the Pier with us.' Helen stared into the darkness as she, Lily and Judy opened her garden gate and walked up the path to her house. Katie's silhouette, outlined in the light that spilled out of the hall through the open front door was unmistakable, but the man she was kissing had his back towards them. As they broke free, he turned.

'You . . .' Lost for words, Helen glared contemptuously at her father before storming into the kitchen. Lily followed her and closed the door. 'Did you see that?' Helen demanded. 'My father and Katie . . .'

'Keep your voice down, Helen,' Lily pleaded. 'Can't you see that they love one another?'

Helen whirled round. 'You knew about this?'

'Only since Katie took the job in Lewis Lewis.'

'I'm his daughter and you didn't think to say a word!'

'Katie asked me not to.'

'I bet she did,' Helen retorted viciously. 'Pretending to be my

388

friend so she can move in on my father . . . no wonder she threw over Adam Jordan. He hasn't anything like the money . . .'

'It's not like that between them, Helen,' Lily interposed swiftly. 'She told me she fell in love with your father and he with her, just after she started working for him and that's why she left the warehouse. Your father felt that because he was still married to your mother he couldn't offer her anything and she couldn't bear to see him every day . . .'

'How many other people know about this?' Helen asked coldly. 'My brother, Martin . . .'

'Martin knows.'

'You told him.'

'No, and he doesn't know Katie's confided in me. Katie mentioned that your father told Martin some time ago, but he wasn't happy about it.'

'I bet he isn't. It's disgusting. He's nothing but a dirty old man and she's looking no further than what she can get . . .'

'I'm sorry you feel that way, Helen.' John pushed open the door and walked in, holding hands with Katie.

'How do you expect me to feel!' Helen shouted. 'You divorce my mother so you can go off with my friend . . .'

'Your mother and me divorcing had nothing to do with Katie.'

'So that came later, when Katie realised you'd be free and she could move in and be set up for life.'

'Remember telling us that you knew Jack was the right one for you and that it was your time?' Katie's calm, clear voice silenced Helen where John and Lily had failed. 'Well, it was like that for me with John. He's the kindest, gentlest, most generous man I know and I don't mean about money. I would love him if he had nothing. In fact I'd prefer it because then no one could accuse me of wanting anything from him except his love. And he does love me, Helen, yet he was prepared to give me up because he was afraid of what the gossip would do to you and your brother.'

'You disgust me. Both of you. Get out of my house . . .'

'My divorce will be finalised in six weeks. The day after I intend to marry Katie,' John said quietly. 'I'm sorry you feel the way you do about us. If you change your mind, you'll be welcome at our wedding. And no matter what, I want you to know that I'll always be there if ever you need me.'

'I never want to see or speak to either of you again.'

'If putting my own happiness first has caused you pain, Helen, I apologise.' He turned to Katie. 'Are you coming?'

'To where?' Helen snapped.

'Does it matter, Helen?' he asked. 'You've made it impossible for her to stay here.'

'Is he . . .' Trembling and more sober than anyone had a right to be after what he'd drunk, Robin turned a terrified face to his father.

'Hardly a scratch on him.'

'Honestly?' Angela broke in fearfully, too afraid to look at Joe who was stretched out on the pavement behind them. 'You're not just saying that, Pops?'

'No.' Dr Watkin Morgan looked sternly at his children. 'But he deliberately walked in front of that bus. It was pure luck he went down between the wheels. There's no doubt that he tried to kill himself.'

'That's ridiculous. I saw him fall.' Hilary Llewellyn who'd been kneeling beside Joe rose to her feet and walked towards them. 'It was an accident.'

'It didn't look like it from where I was sitting,' the driver contradicted, as he huddled under a blanket in the gutter, sipping the hot sweet tea someone had given him for shock.

'He'd just taken part in a stupid drinking competition.' Hilary turned to the doctor as an ambulance arrived. 'Surely he doesn't need to go to hospital if, as you just said, there's hardly a scratch on him.'

'He needs psychiatric evaluation. I've arranged admittance to Cefn Coed.'

'Joe needs to sober up at home not in a psychiatric hospital.' Hilary returned to Joe as the ambulance driver leaped from his cab.

Dr Watkin Morgan confronted her. 'I won't take responsibility.'

'Then I will. My car's parked round the corner. I'll take him home.'

'You know where he lives?'

'Yes.' She turned to the ambulance driver and his mate. 'Will you give me a hand to get him into my car, please.'

Angela and Robin stood back and watched while Hilary took charge and loaded Joe into her car.

As she drove away, their father drew them aside. 'Hilary Llewellyn is a capable woman but I suspect that this time she has bitten off a great deal more than she can chew.'

'Pops, you don't really think Joe tried to top himself,' Robin muttered nervously.

Dr Watkin Morgan looked over to where the bus driver was still arguing with the police. 'Until this thing is settled one way or another, I strongly advise – no, insist, absolutely insist – that you both stay away from Joseph Griffiths.'

'But he's tipped for a first. He has a brilliant future . . .'

'Perhaps not any more,' the doctor broke in harshly. 'How did he behave before he went outside?'

'No different from any of the rest of us, we were having a good time.' Robin was having difficulty in blocking the image of Joe, bent double, a red blanket draped over his shoulders being helped into the back of Hilary's car, from his mind.

'And that is exactly what you'll tell the police if they question you. I suppose he was sitting at your table.'

'He was escorting me.'

'That's something you need to play down; better still, don't mention it, Angela. From now on Joseph Griffiths was never more than a boy on the edge of your crowd. You really didn't know him that well at all. Understand?'

Robin was the first to recover. 'Yes, Pops.'

'Now go back in there and carry on as if nothing's happened.'

Setting her face into the wide-mouthed smile she had practised so often in front of the mirror, Angela followed her brother inside.

'Jack and Adam are lucky.' Roy sat beside Martin and Sam in the waiting room. 'The manager of the Pier is content with a warning and a ban, which will affect Adam more than Jack, seeing as how Jack will be away for the next couple of years. The sergeant won't give the go-ahead for a prosecution as the manager is content to let all charges drop in the hope of avoiding adverse publicity, and as Adam isn't seriously hurt, I've succeeded in talking him out of pressing charges against Jack.'

'He tried?' Martin questioned indignantly.

'He did, but I pointed out that there is such a thing as provocation,' Roy said grimly.

'What happens now?' Martin rose to his feet.

'Both of them are free to go. The only question is which one do we release first.' Roy looked from Sam to Martin.

'Might be as well to let Jack go first,' Sam suggested. 'After the way Adam behaved, and the things he said about Helen, Martin and I might be tempted to pick up where Jack left off.'

'I swear to you, Jack, nothing has happened between Helen and Adam . . .'

'And you've been with her every minute of every day since I left.' A leaner, fitter Jack, with extremely short hair that gave him the appearance of a hard man, crossed his arms over his chest, propped himself against the dresser in the basement kitchen and glared at Martin.

'Of course I haven't, but I spend as much time as I can with Lily and Helen hardly ever leaves her house.'

'Adam says he's been up there. He even knew the colour of the bedroom curtains and bedspreads . . .'

'He would, seeing as how he helped us to move the girls in there,' Sam interrupted, attempting to support Martin.

'And he's been sunbathing there alone with Helen.'

Wishing the police had kept Jack and Adam apart, Martin continued, 'Lily and I walked in on them. Helen hadn't even allowed him in the house because she was afraid there might be gossip.'

'She was dancing with him, she kissed him . . .'

'Not because she wanted to. He forced himself on her.'

'How do you know?'

'Because I know Helen and she said so,' Martin snapped, coming the closest he ever had to losing his temper with his brother.

'I don't believe her.'

'Look, you're home . . .'

'For a week.'

'You have your orders.' Sam set the kettle on to boil. The last thing he wanted was tea, but he had do something.

'For Cyprus, minimum eighteen-month term.'

'I'm sorry, Jack, but as I was saying, you're home, you're sober, here's the keys to the garage and your bike, and by the way, thank you for lending it to me. You've been to Helen's house?'

'Yes.'

'Then you know where it is. Ride out there, talk to her. If you only have a week . . .'

Jack glanced at the clock as he hung the keys back on to the board. 'Anyone want a game of cards?'

'Jack . . .'

'I don't want to talk about Helen, Martin. I've a bottle of rum in my pack; you, Sam and I can either sit down and have a boys' night in, or I can leave right now.'

'To go where?' Martin asked in exasperation.

'Back to camp.'

'You have leave.'

'So do all the boys but not all of them had somewhere to go, so I'll have plenty of company.'

'You stubborn . . .'

'No matter what, I am leaving on the first train out of here in the morning.' Jack picked up his pack. 'Do we have this last night together or not?'

Martin looked at Sam; he knew what he was thinking. If they went along with Jack's night in, there was a chance that they might talk him into staying and possibly even seeing Helen. What Sam didn't know was that once Jack made up his mind to do something he did it, no matter what it cost him, because he was afraid of being considered weak if he didn't.

'I promised Lily I'd tell her if they let you go tonight,' Martin demurred.

'Have they a telephone in the house?'

'No.'

'Then it will have to wait until morning, won't it?' Jack pulled the bottle of rum from his pack and took three glasses from the cupboard. 'You can go to Limeslade after you've seen me off.'

Hilary put a cup of strong black coffee in front of Joe as he sat slumped over the kitchen table in John's house. 'Want to talk about it?'

Joe shook his head.

'I lied for you tonight, Joe. You do realise that if I hadn't, you'd be in a psychiatric ward right now.'

'Yes,' he whispered hoarsely.

'Suicides don't have brilliant futures,' she said callously.

'I know,' he mumbled, 'and I'm grateful . . .'

'Keep your gratitude. I don't want it and I warn you now, I've no intention of letting you get off lightly.' She lit two cigarettes as she sat opposite him and passed him one. 'Is it money, or a girl?'

He lifted his head and looked at her. 'No girl and too much money.'

'I'm listening.'

Somehow it all came out, his love for Lily, her betrayal, his bastard status, his mother's marriage to John Griffiths, Richard Thomas, his disgust at Robin's and Angie's morals . . . and all the while he spoke she listened quietly, only leaving the table to make more coffee or empty the ashtray that stood between them.

When he finally finished she sat back and studied him as she handed him yet another cigarette.

'You think I'm pathetic, don't you.' He braced himself for her condemnation.

'I think you've behaved like an immature idiot, but you're hardly pathetic. Have you thought what you're going to do with yourself now?'

'Not walk under any more buses,' he replied flippantly.

'You've a whole summer ahead of you. You could put it to some use.'

'And do what?'

She looked him in the eye. 'I may have just the job for you.'

'Job?'

'Don't look so horrified at the prospect of doing some real work, Joe. You never know, it might prove the making of you.'

'Joy, I'm sorry for waking you . . .'

Joy rubbed the sleep from her eyes and turned on the hall light. 'Have you any idea of the time, John?'

'Yes, and I wouldn't have disturbed you unless I had to. I've Katie in the car.'

'The girls, Judy . . .' She began anxiously.

'They're fine.'

'Then why is Katie here?'

'Because I've had an argument with Helen. I was hoping you could put her up.'

'An argument . . .'

'I want to marry Katie, Joy. And I won't be able to until my divorce is final in six weeks. Tonight I told Helen about us, and she – let's just say she wasn't sympathetic. In the meantime Katie has to stay somewhere and I was hoping . . .'

Joy looked past him to his car. Katie was sitting in the front seat, staring down at her hands. 'Bring her in.'

'You'll take her . . .'

'For tonight. Now is not the time for a deep discussion. We'll talk again in the morning.'

'Miss Llewellyn.' John barely recognised Joe's tutor in her evening dress as he opened his front door. 'Is Joe all right?'

'He's just gone up to bed. I'm glad I caught you. I'd like to have a chat.'

'Please go in.' He opened the door to his living room. 'Can I get you a drink?'

'After the example your son has just set, I shouldn't, but I'll have a small brandy if you have it.'

'Joe was drunk?' He poured her a drink and handed it to her.

'Very. He . . . fell under a bus.' She repeated the version of events she had given Dr Watkin Morgan. 'But don't worry, he was extremely lucky. Apart from a couple of scratches he's fine.'

'Really?' John looked keenly at her.

'You don't believe me.'

'I've been worried about him for some time,' John acknowledged, as he poured himself a drink and sat opposite her.

'He's been working hard for his degree. Young people today see pressure everywhere, even where there isn't any. But none of it is your fault; you've done a superb job of bringing him up, Mr Griffiths. And Joe admires and respects you. In fact, he told me a lot about you tonight.'

'He did?' John murmured warily.

'We had a long talk. I thought, and Joe agrees with me, that it might be an idea for him to get away this summer. I'm driving down to France tomorrow. I run a summer school there for children who've lost one or both parents in the war. I can always do with an extra pair of hands. Joe's the right age to get on with most of the children. He's agreed to go with me.'

'It's good of you . . .'

'Not at all. I'll be here about ten o'clock to pick him up.'

'Thank you.' John offered her his hand as he walked her to the front door.

'Don't worry, Mr Griffiths,' she said, as he helped her on with her stole. 'I'll look after him.'

Unable to bear the silence that had fallen between her, Lily and Judy since her father and Katie had left the house, Helen left her chair and paced restlessly to the window. Pulling back the curtains she stared at the empty road.

'This is all my fault,' Judy murmured wretchedly.

Helen turned round. 'Don't be ridiculous,' she snapped tensely.

'I knew something about Adam, I should have said and I didn't . . .'

'Should have said what?' Helen demanded.

'Adam's still angry about that trick the boys played on him on Jack's stag night. He wanted to get his own back on them – on all of us. He succeeded with me and Brian, and now he's succeeded with you and Jack. I should have said something and I didn't . . .'

'Slow down, Judy, you're not making much sense,' Lily warned.

Judy sat forward on the edge of her chair and stared down at her hands. 'Remember the night Adam asked me to go to the dinner dance with him?'

'Yes.' Lily nodded, conscious of Helen listening intently behind her.

Slowly, hesitantly, Judy began to tell them what had happened between her and Adam. How she'd almost fainted halfway through the evening, how he'd offered her coffee and she'd gone with him into his home expecting to find his parents there, how she fell asleep and woke believing Adam was Brian. How cheap, dirty and degraded she felt when she found herself lying almost naked on his sofa.

'Adam must have got you drunk,' Lily declared flatly. 'The boys said he put vodka in Jack's beer on his stag night; it sounds to me as if he put it in your Babycham the night of the dinner dance.'

'I've never felt so awful,' Judy concurred.

'Everyone gets drunk at least once in their life,' Helen said, in an attempt to make Judy feel better.

'Not everyone wakes up practically naked next to a man who isn't even her boyfriend.'

'Had he . . .' Helen looked intently at Judy.

'Yes.'

'You're sure?' Helen pressed.

'Yes,' Judy whispered miserably, 'Do you want me to go into the sordid details?'

'Don't!' Helen felt sick at the thought.

'Are you pregnant?' Lily asked.

Judy shook her head. 'I was worried for a couple of weeks, but I couldn't tell anyone, not you, not Katie, not my mother. I was so ashamed I couldn't bear the thought of anyone else knowing what I'd done. But if I had said something, you wouldn't have danced with Adam tonight, Helen, and Jack . . .'

'You do realise Adam raped you,' Lily interrupted, seeing the incident as she knew her Uncle Roy would.

'I tried telling him afterwards that I was a virgin, that I hadn't wanted to sleep with him and I hadn't known what I was doing, but he said I hadn't given him that impression. He pointed out that he hadn't had to force me, or even undress me because I'd done that myself. And it's true, I did help him to undress me because I thought he was Brian and you can imagine how that would look if I told the police.'

'Lily's right, that's still rape,' Helen said forcefully. 'You have to go to the police right away, tell them . . .'

'Don't you understand, Helen, it would be my word against Adam's and he said everyone at the dance saw him trying to peel me off him after I'd had a few drinks. Besides, even if I did go to the police and they believed me, not Adam, everyone would know about it. I'd be pointed out as the girl who was raped . . .'

'Oh, Judy.' Lily hugged her.

'My life is ruined. No boy will ever look at me again once they know about this.'

Helen tried desperately to think of something she could say that would help Judy.

'It could have happened to any girl, any one of us . . .'

'Neither of you would have gone to the dinner dance with Adam, let alone allowed him to get you drunk,' Judy contradicted

'I might not have got drunk with Adam but I did once with Jack,' Helen revealed.

'With Jack, when you were alone with him?' Judy asked.

'Yes.'

'That's the difference, you love Jack, he loves you and you trust one another. He would never have taken advantage of you the way Adam did me.'

'If you won't go to the police, then you have to forget it ever happened,' Helen advised.

'How can I?' Judy's eyes were dry but anguished as if her pain went too deep even for tears. 'I thought – hoped – that Brian and I would get married some day. And now I feel like one of those women who go to bed with men for money. I loved Brian, he's left me and no one is going to want me ever again . . .'

'You've done nothing,' Lily insisted adamantly.

'No man wants a girl who's slept with someone else. I'm dirty . . . damaged . . .'

'You can't believe that about yourself,' Lily persisted.

'You're the same person you always were.' Helen reached for her hand.

'No, I'm not. Adam made me feel like a slut. As if I make a habit of getting drunk and going to bed with men I hardly know. I wanted my first time to be with Brian, to be special. Something we'd both remember.'

Helen recalled her first time with Jack, how much it had meant to both of them and she burned with anger when she thought of how Judy had been robbed of that by a man who had used and abused her.

But far worse was the thought that Judy really believed that there was no one else in the world for her except Brian, and how she'd probably never see him again. She knew just how Judy felt. It had been that way between her and Jack – and Jack had seen her kissing Adam but, unlike Brian, he would come back to her. She just had to believe it.

They all started at a knock on the door. The letter box opened. 'It's Roy Williams. One of the patrols said they saw a light on here. Are you girls all right?'

Lily pulled back the bolts, opened the door and gave him a hug.

He walked into the living room. 'It's after one. Why aren't you in bed?'

'We're worried about Jack.'

'Jack and Adam were both released without charges hours ago.' He saw the forlorn expression on Helen's face and added, 'Jack was so exhausted from travelling down here he almost fell asleep at the station. Martin and Sam took him home. I've no doubt he's sleeping now and will be out to see you first thing in the morning, Helen. Not that he'll find a bright and sparkling wife as she's still up at this time of night.' Seeing the girls were exhausted, he stepped back into the hall. 'As I'm on duty I'd better be off.'

'Thanks for stopping by and telling us, Uncle Roy.' Lily followed him to the door.

'Pull the bolts behind me, love.' As he opened the door he said, 'I'm on mornings on Monday. Do you fancy calling in after work?'

'I'll make you tea.'

'Good, I miss your cooking. Helen looks upset.'

'We'll look after her.'

'Look after yourself, love. You should have been in bed hours ago.'

'Katie . . .' She fell silent as she tried to think how to tell him about Katie and John Griffiths.

'Yes,' Roy prompted.

'She had an argument with Helen. She left with Mr Griffiths earlier tonight.' One look at his face told her he already knew about Katie and John Griffiths.

'You don't have to worry about Katie, love. John will see she's all right. In fact, knowing John she's probably asleep at Joy's right now. You won't forget to bolt the door behind me.'

Chapter 28

HELEN GLANCED AT her watch as she stood in front of the boys'
basement door. It was only just after nine o'clock. Worried sick about
Jack, angry at what Adam had tried to do to her and Jack, and
succeeded in doing to Judy – furious about her father and Katie – she
hadn't closed her eyes all night. Tired, irritable, she had a foul
headache, but rejecting Lily's and Judy's advice that she might miss
Jack who could be travelling in the opposite direction towards
Limeslade, she had insisted on catching the first train out of Mumbles
into town. But now she was terrified. What if Jack shouted at her for
dancing with Adam – or, even worse, refused to speak to her at all?
Steeling herself, she knocked on the door. It opened almost
immediately.

'Come in, Helen.' It was as though Martin was expecting her.

'I've come to see Jack.'

'He left on the seven-o'clock train.'

'I don't understand.' She looked around the kitchen in bewilderment, half expecting Jack to walk through the door.

'He's returned to camp, Helen,' Sam explained.

'When is he coming back?'

'He's not.' Martin's hand shook as he pulled out a chair for her.
'This was his embarkation leave before leaving for Cyprus. He's been
posted there for at least eighteen months.'

'No, he can't . . .'

'I'm sorry, Helen. Won't you sit down?'

'No!' Without thinking what she was doing, Helen fled from the
basement and ran to her father's door, hammering on it until he
opened it, still dressed in his pyjamas and dressing gown. Wrapping
his arm round her shoulders, he closed the door and led her into the
living room.

'Jack's gone,' she blurted between sobs. 'He was here yesterday and he saw me kiss Adam Jordan, and now he's gone back to camp . . .'

'You kissed Adam Jordan?'

'Yes . . . no . . . I danced with him and he kissed me. It was to get his own back on Jack for some stupid prank. I didn't want to kiss him; he only did it because Jack walked into the Pier . . .'

'Sit down and calm down,' he ordered. 'I'll make us a pot of tea.' He couldn't help thinking as he went to the kitchen how like Helen this was. Last night she had told him she was disgusted with him and she never wanted to see him again, and here she was, first thing in the morning, all thoughts of him and Katie driven from her mind by a misunderstanding – if that was the right word – that had sent Jack back to army camp when he should have been spending his leave with her.

'You're not shocked?' Katie asked Joy as they sat over a pot of tea at the breakfast table.

'No. And if you'd heard half the things I have from my customers over the years, you'd be unshockable as well. John Griffiths may be twenty years older than you but I watched you grow up. You had the knowing look in your pretty face of a forty-year-old when you were five years old, which is hardly surprising considering some of the things that went on in your house. John's kind, gentle, if he has a temper I've never seen any sign of it, which is remarkable when you consider how long he was married to Esme. Her antics would have been enough to try the patience of a saint. But then, perhaps John is one.'

'I love him and I know I can make him happy, Mrs Hunt,' Katie said simply.

'I wish you all the best, love. It's not going to be easy for either you or John. People can be cruel – and envious – and it's my guess Helen isn't going to be the only one to say what she thinks.'

'I know she's not.' Katie stared down at the crumbs on her plate.

'You're not sure you can face them?' Joy questioned, wondering if she should point out some of the other problems that could lie ahead, if Katie did marry a man twice her age.

'I've never cared what people say about me, Mrs Hunt, but I'm worried for John.' Joy was oddly shocked at Katie's casual use of John Griffiths's Christian name, but schooled by years of experience in her salon she kept her composure. 'John's not like me, he's so sensitive . . .'

'Katie.' Joy shook her head fondly at her. 'You're going to make him a wonderful wife. And twenty years isn't that big an age gap. I've known lots of marriages – very successful ones – where the husband has been that much older than the wife – and more.'

'Really! You're not just saying that?'

'No.' The only successful marriages Joy had personal knowledge of where the husband had been twice the age of the wife were the kind where the wife had been given a blank chequebook and a lot of expensive jewellery, but somehow Katie didn't seem to fall into that category.

'Thank you, that means a lot to me.' Katie's eyes shone, like a child who'd just been shown a glimpse of Christmas.

'We ought to talk about practical things. You can stay here until you're married . . .'

'Thank you, Mrs Hunt. I'd really appreciate that.'

'And I could help you to organise your wedding, if you want me to.'

'I haven't spoken to John about it, but I know neither of us will want a fuss. Just the two of us in the Register Office.'

'You'll need witnesses and I think I can speak for Roy when I say we'd be honoured.'

'What are you going to do?' John asked Helen, as she was halfway through her second cup of tea.

'I don't know. I love Jack and now I won't see him for years. That's if he ever comes back . . .'

'The way I see it, you have two choices,' he interrupted, before another flood of tears materialised. 'You can either stay in Swansea and cry, or buy a train ticket and go after him.'

'To an army camp?'

'He's on leave and if I know soldiers he won't be spending much time in the camp. He'll be in the nearest pub drinking with his mates.'

'And if he won't talk to me?'

'At least you will have tried.'

'Thanks, Dad.'

'What are you going to do?' he asked as she left the sofa.

'Find out when the next train leaves and if I have time, go home and pack before I catch it.'

'I'll telephone the station while you finish your tea. Then, if we've time, I'll drive you home so you can get some clothes. Best take a few, you could be gone a couple of nights.'

'You're with your father?' Lily looked in astonishment from Helen to her father's car parked in the drive.

'Jack's gone back to camp. I'm going after him and I only have an hour to pack and get to the station to catch the next train.'

'We'll give you a hand.' Judy ran up the stairs ahead of them.

'Have you seen Katie?' Lily asked, as they followed.

'No.'

'She isn't with your father?'

'She wasn't in the house with him this morning that I saw. God! I said some awful things to them last night.'

'Yes, you did.'

'I'll say sorry.'

'Only if you mean it, Helen,' Lily warned.

'It will take some getting used to, Katie and my father.'

'Yes, it will, but she's still the same Katie you've always known. And your father is a special man. Just look where he is now, waiting outside for you, after you told him he disgusted you and ordered him and Katie out of the house.'

'I'll talk to him.' Lifting a suitcase down from the top of her wardrobe, Helen started throwing things into it, the whole of her underwear drawer, six nighties. Five minutes later Lily fetched her toilet bag from the bathroom and laid it on top of everything before closing and locking the case.

'If you're missing something you'll just have to buy it,' Judy said practically.

'Buy . . . I've only fifteen shillings in my purse.'

'I can lend you some.' Lily delved into her handbag. 'I have two pounds and some change.'

'I'll pay you back as soon as I can.'

'Take it off the rent.'

'I can manage one pound ten shillings.'

'Thank you.' Helen hugged them in turn. 'Wish me luck.'

'Good luck,' they shouted down the stairs at the back of the door as she rushed out.

'Fifty pounds.'

'Dad . . .'

'You'll need money. Go into the Ladies and hide it well. I borrowed it from yesterday's takings in the warehouse and I paid for your ticket with a cheque.' He handed it to her. 'Look after it.'

'I will.' She ran into the Ladies, locked herself into a cubicle and pushed the roll of notes her father had given her into her bra. She didn't dare hope, but if Jack did talk to her perhaps . . . she forced herself to think about something else, lest she jinx what little chance she had of saving what was left of their marriage.

'Train's in, you'll have to run,' John shouted, as she emerged on to the platform.

Throwing her arms around his neck, she kissed him. 'Thank you, I don't deserve a father like you, and tell Katie I'll try to understand. I really will.' She dived on to the train just before the porter closed the door. Pushing down the window, she added, 'She's a very lucky girl,' just as the train started pulling out.

'We weren't sure whether you boys would come today, or not.' Judy looked up from the deckchair she was sitting in, as Martin and Sam walked through the gate into the garden.

'We didn't bring Adam,' Sam joked caustically.

'After last night I don't think any of us wants to see him again.'

'You know Helen's left?' Lily asked Martin as he sat on the grass beside her.

'Mr Griffiths called in after he took her to the station. He also told me what happened here last night with Katie.'

'Have you seen Katie?' Judy adjusted the straps on her swimsuit, pulling it higher.

'Yes. She's staying with Mrs Hunt until she gets married. Mr Griffiths also said he talked to Helen on the way to the station and he thinks she's coming to terms with the idea of him marrying Katie.' Martin reached for Lily's hand.

'I'm not sure I'll ever be able to think of Katie as Mrs Griffiths,' Judy said slowly.

'She'll always be our Katie.' Lily smiled at Martin.

'Come for a walk?' he asked.

'Do you mind, Judy?'

'I don't.' Sam grinned.

'I'm glad you said that, Sam.' Judy smiled maliciously. 'The grass needs cutting and there's a pair of shears in the shed. You may need to sharpen them first but there's a stone next to the back door that's ideal . . .'

'I'm no gardener.'

'Practice makes perfect.' She looked up at Lily and Martin. 'What are you two waiting for? Go.'

'Do you have a room, please?'

The manageress of the hotel looked Helen up and down, and made it obvious that she didn't like what she saw. 'Yes, but it will be twenty-five shillings a night. In advance.'

'Does that include breakfast?' Helen asked, incensed by the woman's attitude.

'Full English breakfast.'

'If it is a double room, I'll take it,' she said decisively.

'I see, you're one of those.'

'One of what?' Helen questioned, mystified.

'This is an army town . . .'

'And I'm an army wife.' Helen drew off her gloves and waved her engagement and wedding ring at the woman.

'And I'm Princess Margaret.'

'My husband has leave. I'm hoping he'll join me here.'

'And I don't believe a slip of a girl like you has a husband.'

Helen opened her handbag and rummaged through the contents. She'd pushed a letter from Jack into it so she would have his full address. 'There.' She slammed the envelope down on the desk. 'Mrs Jack Clay.'

'And who's to say that you are Mrs Jack Clay?'

'Me.'

Helen turned to see Jack standing behind her.

'You're her husband?'

'Yes.'

'Are you staying here too?'

'And if I am?' Jack answered, avoiding the question.

'It will be another ten shillings a night – in advance.'

'Including breakfast,' Helen pushed.

'Including full English breakfast. Both of you have to sign the register.' The woman handed Helen a pen. After she wrote down the Limeslade address, she handed it to Jack. As their fingers touched, he turned away and her heart pounded erratically. So much depended on what was going to happen in the next few minutes. 'Room twenty.'

The woman waited until Helen handed over two pound notes, before pushing a key and five shillings change towards her. 'The bathroom is at the end of the corridor on the right. Breakfast will be served from seven o'clock until half past eight tomorrow morning. If you are only staying the one night you will have to vacate the room by ten or pay for another full day's occupancy.'

Helen took the key. There was a lump in her throat that prevented her from speaking, but even if it hadn't been there, she doubted she would have been able to thank the woman.

'Don't bother to call a porter, I'll carry my wife's case.' Taking it, Jack led the way up the stairs.

'How did you know I was here?' Helen asked, struggling with the key.

'Martin telephoned the camp from Mr Williams's house. He left a message that you were following on a later train. I would have met you at the station if I'd got it earlier, but it went round three barracks before it found me.'

'But you didn't know about the hotel . . .'

'It's the only decent place, or rather the only place a decent woman would go into for miles.'

'That's what the taxi driver said. But that woman was horrible.'

'She's used to tarts trying to book in.'

'Tarts?'

'Pros who want to make a few quid entertaining blokes in their room.'

'How do you know about them?'

'Barrack room talk.' He looked coolly at her. 'I haven't scraped that low down the barrel in the six weeks we've been separated.'

Blushing, she opened the door, holding it so he could carry her bag in. 'Thank you for coming to find me.'

'This town is no place for a woman alone.' He sat on the only chair in the room.

'Be honest, if you had received the message in time to meet me at the station, would you have sent me back?'

'That would have been difficult; there isn't another train that reaches Swansea today. You're a fool . . .'

'I had to see you to let you know there's nothing between me and Adam.'

'I think that got sorted when he shouted he'd got his own back on me for what I did to him on my stag night.'

'Then why did you run off this morning?'

'Because when I saw you dancing with him, I realised there was no way I could hold you to a marriage when I was leaving the country for a year and a half. It wouldn't be fair to ask you to stay in night after night and I couldn't bear the thought of you going out with other men. So I decided it would be easier to end it.'

'I was with Martin and Lily . . .'

'So Martin said.'

'You could have at least tried to talk to me, told me how you felt.'

'I didn't think there was much point.'

'I love you, Jack. I know I was horrible to you when I was in hospital and I wasn't much better after I came home. And now I'll never be able to have the children you want . . .' Without warning she began to cry. 'I hate doing this, it's not fair . . . but every time I try to talk to you about the baby, I . . .'

Opening his arms, he held her tight.

'Can we at least stay together for your leave?' she begged.

'That will take care of the next week but what about the next two years?'

'I don't know, Jack.' She lifted her face to his. 'I honestly don't. But what I do know is that I love you and I'm prepared to fight for our marriage. If that means staying in every night until you come back . . .'

'I have no right to ask you to do that.'

'But I'd do it, and willingly. I have a job I like now, working for my father in the warehouse so it's not as if I'd never go out or see anyone, so . . .' She faltered as she remembered her father and Katie. Her father had warned her that Jack didn't know about them and now, when she was fighting to save what was left of their relationship, was no time to drop that bombshell.

'What, Helen?'

'How can I prove to you how much I love you?'

He looked down at the bed. 'I can think of one way.'

'You haven't seen my scar, it's horrible, ugly . . .'

'No part of you could possibly be ugly.' He unbuttoned her dress. When she was naked, he lifted her on to the bed and kissed the jagged line that marred her skin. And after that, nothing else seemed to matter to either of them – for a while.

'You look serious,' Lily said to Martin as they walked hand in hand down the beach. The sun was setting, casting crimson and gold light over the horizon and on to the surface of the sea. 'Is it Katie or Jack?'

'Neither. I've come to the conclusion that a big brother can only do so much. They have to find their own way.'

'Katie will be happy with Mr Griffiths.'

'That's my Lily. Always wanting to believe the best of everyone. And what's your forecast for Jack and Helen?'

'They have to sort themselves out.'

'I think those are the harshest words I've ever heard you say about anyone.' He stopped at the edge of the sea and looked at the waves crashing almost to their feet. 'What about us, Lily?'

'I love you.'

'And I love you.'

'Then we're fine.'

'No we're not.'

'I told you that's enough for me . . .'

'But not for me.' Catching both her hands, he looked deep into her eyes. 'I've discovered I want more. Much much more.'

'Like what?'

'An engagement to start with, marriage as soon as I've heard that I've passed my exams, which will be any day now. And who knows after that, children . . .'

'Marty, you said you'd never be able to support a wife.'

'I know and I won't, not in the way I'd like to support you. But plenty of couples get by on what I'll be paid when I qualify. But I warn you, Lily, the best we can hope for to begin with is to rent a basement in Carlton Terrace. Your uncle's if he'll let us. We could put our name down for a council house but there's an enormous waiting list and there's no guarantee that we'd get one, even if we waited years and years.'

'Now that's a romantic proposal a girl can't refuse.'

'It gets worse. I pinched your signet ring and pressed it in soap to get your ring size when you weren't looking, but then I remembered you have better taste than me, so you should really choose your own. But in the meantime I bought you this in the gift shop in the amusement arcade.' He handed her a silver-coloured ring set with a bright-red glass stone.

'Marty, it's perfect.' She kissed him.

'That's enough joking. It cost one and six . . .'

'And I wouldn't swap it for all the diamonds in Africa. Please, put it on.' She held out her left hand.

'You can't be serious. I have some money saved. I'll buy you . . .'

'I don't want another ring.'

'You are serious, aren't you?' he whispered huskily.

'Deadly.'

'I don't mean about the ring. You'll marry me, basement flat and all?'

'Marty, I've something to tell you, but before I do you have to promise me you won't be angry.'

'How can I promise you that, if I don't know what it is?'

'It's not really bad.'

'If it's something you've done, Lily, whatever it is, it won't make any difference to the way I feel about you.'

'It's not something I've done, Marty.' She hooked her arm into his. 'More like something I own. Now, you promise you'll remember I love you.'

'Tea for the workers.' Judy carried a tray out into the garden for Sam.

'About time too.' Dropping the shears, he sat in one of the deckchairs.

'You expect me to serve you?'

'Yes. Judy.' He looked at her as she poured out the tea. 'You still going out with Brian?'

'Obviously not as he's in London and I'm here.'

'You know what I mean.'

'Yes and the answer's still no.' She handed him the mug and the sugar bowl.

'You know I was stuck on Katie.'

'That was pretty obvious.'

'I thought that perhaps you and I could go out together one night,' he suggested diffidently. 'See a film . . .'

She shook her head.

'Because of the stunt Adam pulled on you?'

She almost dropped her cup. 'You know.'

'He said some things down the station last night about you as well as Helen. I told him that if he ever repeated them I'd ram his teeth down his throat.'

'Thank you.'

'So.' He smiled. 'Do you want to see a cowboy or a musical?'

'Neither,' she retorted angrily. 'If you think that because I was stupid enough to allow Adam Jordan to take advantage of me I'm desperate enough to repeat the same mistake with you . . .'

'I never thought any such thing.' His colour heightened as he looked at her.

'So it would be just a film?'

'Most definitely.'

'And we'd go Dutch and as friends?'

'Yes.'

'Then I'll think about it.'

'Fine.' He leaned back in the deckchair. 'This is the life.'

'Not for long. You still have half a lawn to cut.'

Helen snuggled under the blankets and laid her head on Jack's shoulder. 'My father gave me some money.'

'Why? You're my wife and responsibility now.'

'We can pay him back. It's enough for us to take our first holiday together.'

'In Weston-super-Mare.' He turned to her and spread her hair out on the pillow above her head. 'We'll go there tomorrow.'

'Why Weston-super-Mare?'

'Because Adam Jordan's parents always used to take him there for their summer holidays and I was jealous as hell.' He kissed her. 'And now I've got the girl, I want the place as well.'